VENICE NOIR

VENICE NOIR

EDITED BY MAXIM JAKUBOWSKI

This collection is comprised of works of fiction. All names, characters, places, and incidents are the product of the authors' imaginations. Any resemblance to real events or persons, living or dead, is entirely coincidental.

Published by Akashic Books
©2012 Akashic Books

Series concept by Tim McLoughlin and Johnny Temple
Venice map by Aaron Petrovich
"Venus Aphrodisiac" Copyright ©2012 Peter James

ISBN-13: 978-1-61775-073-1
Library of Congress Control Number: 2011960951

Akashic Books
PO Box 1456
New York, NY 10009
info@akashicbooks.com
www.akashicbooks.com

MESTRE

LAGUNA VENETA

CAVALCAVIA

PONTE DELLA LIBERTÀ

PORTO MARGHERA

VENICE

LIDO

LAGUNA VENETA

GULF OF VENICE

CANNAREGIO

GHETTO VECCHIO

RIALTO BRIDGE

SANTA MARIA FORMOSA

(See Below)

SANTO STEFANO

PIAZZA SAN MARCO

PONTE DEI SOSPIRI

PALAZZO DUCALE

CALLE LARGA XXII MARZO

CANAL GRANDE

TABLE OF CONTENTS

INTRODUCTION
Slowly Sinking

I t's one of the most famous cities in the world.
Immortalized by writers throughout the years, frozen in
amber by film and photography, the picturesque survivor
of a wild history whose centuries encompass splendor, decay,
pestilence, beauty, and never-ending wonders. A city built on
water, whose geographical position once almost saw it rule
the world and form a vital crossing point between West and
East. A city of merchants, artists, glamour, abject poverty,
philosophers, corrupt nobles, refugees, courtesans, and unforgettable lovers, buffeted by the tides of wars, a unique
place whose architecture is a subtle palette reflecting the suc-
cessive waves of settlers, invaders, religions, and short-term
rulers.

Venice is ever present in the popular imagination, and
there is no denying its incomparable visual beauty. The flow
of the Grand Canal and its cortege of palazzi, the famous
bridges, the thousand and one churches, Piazza San Marco
and its pigeons (and annual floods), the glassblowers of Murano, the Doge's Palace, the calm waters of its lagoon, the
117 neighboring islands so full of dark history and legend, the
gondolas, carnival time, the markets overflowing with food,
fish, jewellery, and trinkets—all images that evoke the beauty
and strangeness of Venice in everyone's mind, whether you
have been there or not.

They call her La Serenissima, La Dominante, the Queen

of the Adriatic, the City of Water, the Floating City, and the City of Canals.

Venice has always been a magnet for writers, and the pilgrimage there has become a necessary rite of passage. An endless list would include, in no particular order of importance or chronological order (somehow chronology is of no importance when it comes to Venice; it is a city to a certain extent frozen in time, poised on a knife edge between the past and the future, where decay is an integral part of the surrounding atmosphere): Thomas Mann, Lord Byron, Daphne du Maurier, D.H. Lawrence, Jan Morris, Patricia Highsmith, Kazuo Ishiguro, Henry James, Goethe, George Sand, Robert Browning, Goldoni, Ruskin, Evelyn Waugh, Mark Twain, Shakespeare, John Berendt, Donna Leon, Tiziano Scarpa, Marcel Proust, Michael Dibdin, Dickens, Joseph Brodsky, Hemingway, Philippe Sollers, Sarah Dunant, Ezra Pound, and possibly the best-known Venetian author of them all, Giacomo Casanova, the great seductor and the epitome of Venice's edgy blend of sensuality and morbidity. And don't get me started on all the filmmakers who've attempted to catch the true essence of Venice on celluloid, while dodging the clichés and the tourist throngs . . .

Whether they have lived there at some time or not, all these authors have written about Venice and its fascinating atmosphere, its smells and colors, its people and visitors, in a myriad of different ways. So why yet another book about Venice? As Erica Jong puts it, "Was it Henry James or Mary McCarthy who said, 'There is nothing new to say about Venice'?"

Unlike any other place, the new Venice is also the old Venice, and change in this most curious of cities is something almost imperceptible and invisible to the naked eye. Walking just a few minutes away from the Rialto Bridge, for instance, and losing yourself in backstreets, where the canals and small connecting bridges leave just enough space to pass along the buildings without falling into the water, it's as if you are stepping into a past century altogether, with no indication whatsoever of modernity. You wade through a labyrinth of stone, water, and wrought-iron bridges, and after dark feel part of another world where electricity isn't yet invented, a most unsettling feeling nothing can prepare you for.

In a city overcome by tourists, that would not be able to make a living without them, the ambiguous relationship between visitors and residents becomes a source of tension and studied hesitancy. Venice today is indeed a city in decline, slowly sinking with no real plans yet settled upon to avert the inevitable further decay, where the population is shrinking year after year, its youth abandoning its shores for lack of opportunities outside of service industries or actual criminality. At its center are the architectural splendors, on its margins the industrial port and factory zones and all their attendant murkiness. A complex but perfect background for the seductions of "noir," and despite the contrast between a rich historical past and the evolving present, as was the case in the volume dedicated to Rome in this same Noir Series, which I edited with Chiara Stangalino, a fresh canvas for writers to conjugate new waltzes in darkness, balancing the old, the new, and the in-between, the undeniable beauty of the surrounding landscape and the rotten core on the inside that of course never features on all the picture postcards of Venice most of us blissfully ignore to our peril.

I've always felt that Venice belongs to the world, attracting us from all over in its spiderweb of beauty, crumbling stones, and water, so this time around I didn't just invite Italian writers to let their imaginations loose on the city, and summoned the mischievous and noir imaginations of writers hailing from the UK, the USA, Canada, France, and Australia too. The portrait they draw in *Venice Noir* is compelling, as hapless visitors and troubled locals wander the canals, bridges, and waters of La Serenissima, with a heartful of darkness and wonder, evoking all the secrets, sounds, sights, and smells of the city. And there's not even a gondola in every story! Which goes to show that in any noir city, you should expect the unexpected.

Maxim Jakubowski
February 2012

PART I

AMONGST THE VENETIANS

CLOUDY WATER

BY MATTEO RIGHETTO

Cannaregio

Translated from Italian by Judith Forshaw

T he sun had set a couple of hours ago and, like every
evening, a light mist started to rise slowly from the
water, blanketing the whole city.

Alvise was sitting in the stern of his small boat—an old patanella with a half-scraped hull. He was moving quietly along
Rio della Misericordia, trying not to think about anything but
Tania, who he would soon be seeing. She knew exactly how to
make him relax.

They had met by chance a few months before, friends of
friends, which is nearly always how it happens in a city where
people's social lives mainly take place in the local bars. They'd
chatted as they had a few drinks, and they liked each other;
they started seeing each other a few days later.

Tania was twenty-five and worked in a small shop sell-
ing kitsch souvenirs in Rio Terà San Leonardo, not far from
the rented flat where she lived. Alvise was ten years older
than she was and didn't have a proper job. Or rather, he didn't
have one anymore, since he'd been fired by the petrochemical
company in Porto Marghera where he had worked for almost
fifteen years. With no wages coming in, he had begun work
as a porter, toting tourists' luggage from Piazzale Roma to the
nearby hotels, an exhausting and badly paying job. However,

he had given this up almost immediately, when Dario, an old school friend, had met him one day in his local bar and, between glasses of white wine and chitchat, mentioned an interesting job that they could do together—"A job that will solve all your problems," Dario had told him that day. And, in fact, his proposal sounded so interesting that Alvise said yes without thinking twice.

He was still about ten minutes away from Tania's house when he realized that the packet in his jacket pocket had only two cigarettes left in it and that his fuel tank was almost empty.

He did a quick calculation and worked out that he would have enough gas to get to her house and then back home, but the fags were a different matter: with just two left he could survive for no more than an hour, and he well knew that he wouldn't find a single tobacconist in that part of the city. Like a Pavlovian response, he looked round anyway, vainly searching for a sign with a white T, then he spat into the water, pulled the second-to-last cigarette out of the pack, and lit it. Although he was dosed up with painkillers, his shoulder hurt more than ever, and the humidity that ruled over Venice like a tyrant certainly didn't help him get any relief. He had an insane urge to see Tania, and the nearer he got to his destination, the more his desire to touch her grew inside him, to hug her and enjoy her warm body, even if deep down he felt worried and restless in a way he had not felt recently. He breathed out a cloud of smoke that blurred into the mist. He smoked the cigarette down to the filter, then tossed it into the canal that cuts through the heart of Cannaregio, one of the most working-class and rundown neighborhoods of the city, and finally he looked at his watch. It was quarter past nine, and he noticed that there wasn't a soul on the stark Fondamenta degli Ormesini, except for a couple of tourists—probably American—who looked like they were lost among the alleys and squares and were trying to get their bearings, consulting a guidebook. Alvise thought that the tourists were all the same; they managed to see only the surface of Venice, just like when you look at the surface of the sea and think you've seen it all.

No one else around, neither to the right nor the left. No one.

After a few minutes his old patanella finally reached its destination. He slowed down, turned off the engine, and glided under the bridge that leads to the Jewish quarter, then gently drew up by the bank and moored the boat. He looked around and, careful not to strain his aching shoulder, jumped down to the ground. He checked the time again: twenty past nine. He went over the wrought-iron bridge and down into Campo del Ghetto Nuovo, striding confidently.

Tania lived very close by. She lived on her own in a small apartment on the fourth floor of one of the tallest buildings in the city. On the ground floor there was a yeshiva where Hasidic Jews from all over the world used to come to study and pray day and night like they were possessed.

Alvise crossed the large square and headed toward the main wooden door of the building. He rang the bell and, while he was waiting for Tania to answer, peeked through the windows of the orthodox school, where he saw dozens of young men praying and reading the Talmud out loud, swaying like grandfather clocks, apparently in the throes of a collective ecstasy. Every time he saw them there he had a strange feeling that was somewhere between rapture and a deep compassion, a mixture of admiration and pity that not even he was able to understand clearly.

"Who is it?" asked Tania over the intercom.

He didn't answer, and for a moment he stood looking at the pale young men, all the same, dressed in black, with ringlets that sprang out from under their hats and white shirts drenched in sweat from the movement of their prayers.

He watched them fascinated, careful not to be seen, and it was as if their prayers were so powerful he could imagine them leaving the building and rising up into the sky like steam.

When he climbed the stairs and crossed the threshold of the tiny flat, he was immediately assailed by the strong smell of incense floating throughout the house.

"Indian samskruti. I got it today. Do you like it?" she said to him as she welcomed him and took off his jacket.

"A bit strong . . ."

"It's for meditating. I really like it, but if you want I'll put it out."

Alvise shook his head, touched his shoulder, and settled down on the green sofa that stood in the small kitchen-cum-living-space.

"Does it still hurt?" the girl asked, gazing at him adoringly.

"It'll pass."

Tania had clearly only just come out of the shower: she was wrapped in a silk dressing gown and her long dark hair, still slightly wet, fell over her shoulders and onto her chest.

"It's because of the carousel, isn't it?" she said.

"What?"

"The pain in your shoulder . . ."

"Right."

Alvise was on edge; he couldn't speak and he felt strange, as if something were hovering around him without ever completely revealing itself.

Tania noticed straight away the veil of anxiety over his face and realized that it would not be easy to get him to relax that evening, unlike other times. Of course, she knew perfectly well that it wasn't the first time that his work awaited him; Alvise had never taken it lightly, but that evening she saw that he was more nervous than ever. To put him at ease, she lit some perfumed candles that she had dotted around the flat and turned off the lights, creating a much more intimate and warmer atmosphere. Then she went into the kitchen, opened the fridge, and returned with a bottle of Raboso and two glasses.

"Shall we have a drop?" she suggested, moving close to him.

"Good idea."

She smiled and sat astride him, letting her silky dressing gown open to reveal most of her body. Tania poured out the wine for both of them and clinked her glass against Alvise's.

"To us!" she said, moving her lips toward his.

"To us, Tania!" he replied, finally loosening up and kissing her.

They drank their glasses of wine and then poured another round as they began to caress each other.

Tania headed over to the hi-fi, put on an Erykah Badu CD, picked the track "Didn't Cha Know," and then went back to him. She slipped off his sweater and shirt and unfastened his pants; she took off her dressing gown and, with desire in her eyes, slowly sank down to his feet. He closed his eyes and put his head back against the sofa as he felt her breath on his stomach and then moving lower, grasping his cock and sliding it into the enveloping heat of her mouth.

After a few seconds Tania stood up, kissed him passionately, and softly asked him to lie down on the sofa, mounting him and slowly slipping him between her thighs.

Despite the pleasure of the sex, Alvise couldn't help thinking about what he would have to do a few hours later; a thousand confused thoughts were bouncing around his head and he couldn't drive them out. He tried to concentrate on screwing, but the Jews came to mind; several feet below they were swaying and rippling with the same motion as Tania. He looked at her wonderful body moving backward and forward above him and the black waves of the lagoon that were waiting for him out there flowed through his mind, together with images of planes landing and taking off. Just like that, without any reason.

A few moments after they had both come, she climbed off his body, all breathless and sweating. They stayed there in silence for a while, then she put her dressing gown back on and poured another two glasses of Raboso, while Alvise lay with his gaze fixed on the moldy ceiling where a thick blanket of incense had settled.

"What are you thinking about?" Tania asked, emptying her glass.

"Nothing."

An ocean of silence passed.

"What the fuck's up with you tonight, Alvise?"

He remained silent for another moment, then said, "I think tonight will be the last time, Tania."

She picked up a jar of arnica cream and said to him: "Let's have that shoulder."

He gave in to her willingly, and while Tania was massaging his shoulder, he lit the last cigarette in the pack.

"If you lose, all the worse for you," she said, reading aloud the motto Alvise had had tattooed on his back as if he were a playing card.

When the girl had finished, she went over to a cupboard and brought out a box that contained some grass and cigarette papers.

"So, if I've understood right, tonight's going to be the last carousel?" she said, starting to roll herself a joint.

"I think so. It's too risky. I just have to stop playing."

"But up till now you've earned good money, haven't you?"

"I *have* put quite a bit of money aside."

She licked the paper and lit the joint, taking a couple of long drags.

There was complete silence for a few minutes, then Alvise finally said: "Why don't you come away with me, Tania? We'll get out of Venice and start a new life somewhere else!"

She laughed then fell silent again.

Alvise glanced at his watch. It said quarter to eleven; the minutes had flown by and it was time to go.

"Can I have another glass?" he asked her.

She took hold of the bottle and poured him some more wine, which he drank in one gulp, as if he wanted to draw their evening together to a close with the gesture. Then he put out the stub of his cigarette in the ashtray, stood up, and got dressed.

"Please be careful!" she told him. She gave him a kiss, and before walking him to the door, added with a smile, "If you lose, all the worse for you," and winked at him.

"Don't worry. See you tomorrow," he said, starting to leave. "Oh, Tania . . ." he remembered, "I don't suppose you've got an extra cigarette I could have? I've finished mine."

Tania quickly went back into her tiny living room, retrieved one of her extra-light cigarettes, and handed it to him.

Alvise left, crossed the Campo del Ghetto Nuovo without meeting a living soul, walked up and down the iron bridge again, and in a few seconds he was back on board his patanella. He switched on the engine, turned around, and retraced his route along Rio della Misericordia, thinking about the work that was awaiting him.

By now it was eleven, the mist on the canal neither lighter nor more dense than before, and he met only a few small boats on the way. He lit Tania's extra-light cigarette and after just three puffs he threw it into the water, disgusted, asking himself how anyone could smoke such muck. He passed by the snow-white, gleaming Miracoli church and made a quick sign of the cross, more as a habit to ward off bad luck than out of belief, then he pulled up to get a packet of his cigarettes, at last, from the vending machine near the majestic, imposing façade of San Zanipolo, the largest church in Venice, and finally he resumed his journey home. His shoulder still ached—less than before, but it still ached.

Dario would be coming around to pick him up at midnight in his boat, and together they would head out into the lagoon, to the island of Santa Maria della Grazia. There, Giorgio would be waiting for them, and they would go take part in the carousel, hoping that everything went according to plan and that no one discovered them: not the extremely fast, slim-line boats of the carabinieri and customs and excise, nor—which would be worse—the "Barracudas," the name given to the terrifying gang of illegal clam fishermen. These were men capable of anything, with supercharged boats, powerful radar, and lookouts everywhere, with their Albanian deckhands who flew down the canals at forty or fifty knots.

He lit a cigarette, resumed his journey toward Castello, and, finally, after having passed under twenty-four bridges, arrived in Calle del Lion, where he lived in an old damp flat. It was half past eleven; he moored the patanella and went into the house to get ready. His father had gone to bed awhile ago and the only noise in the flat came from the large clock that stood on the cupboard in the living room, its pendulum incessantly swinging from side to side. It was something that was incredibly important to the old man, a memento of his wife who had died a few years before, but Alvise could not look at it, and definitely did not want to hear it. One of these days he would get rid of it, that damned pendulum, perhaps by throwing it into the lagoon, so that it would be silent forever.

He went into his bedroom, unlocked an old bedside table eaten by woodworm, and pulled out rolls of large-denomination bank notes held together with yellow elastic bands. He wanted to check that it was all there: more than sixty thousand euros. So much money. A huge amount. Not even by working for years and years like a slave at the petrochemical company would he have been able to save all that money, much less by working as a porter in Piazzale Roma. What was crazy was that he had scraped together that amount in just a few months, working a dozen times or so, for a few hours a night. And if everything went well, that night he would make another five, or perhaps even ten thousand more.

He put everything back where it had been, covered up the rolls of money, and locked the drawer. Quarter to midnight.

He dressed warmly in dark oilskin overalls that made him look like a diver, and put on thick waterproof boots; then he picked up his heavy fishing gloves, his cigarettes, and a lighter.

Ten minutes to midnight. Outside he heard the rumble of Dario's boat.

Alvise took a deep breath, lit a cigarette, and went out.

The two men greeted each other and set off very slowly, motoring along Rio della Pietà in silence, deep in their own thoughts.

The farther they traveled, the hazier the yellow lights of the streetlamps in the alleys and along the canals on either side of them became, and the more they were softened by the mist that lay over everything like a gentle shroud. The humidity was so infuriating; it percolated through the bones and made the air feel heavy and a thousand years old.

In the west, a pale full moon, blurred by the haze, seemed to drowsily watch over the lagoon that lay beneath.

After a few minutes the two men came out into the San Marco basin, then crossed the San Giorgio Maggiore canal, careful not to hit a couple of vaporetti. Passing alongside the floodlit basilica, they headed for the small island of Santa Maria della Grazia, known as the Cavanella. Once they reached it, Dario switched off the engine and tied the rope to a mooring.

Compared to Alvise, Dario was a skinny guy, and his past was full of rather disreputable incidents, such as fraud, theft, and mugging. He had been in prison on various occasions—he'd never managed to get away with much—and once he was out, he would always start hanging out again in the roughest neighborhoods of Castello.

"What time is it?" he asked Alvise.

"Twenty past twelve."

"Ten minutes to go. Giorgio should be here any minute now."

They got off the boat and each lit a cigarette.

Dario breathed his first drags deeply, and then said: "Let's make the most of it. Once we're over there we won't be able to smoke, otherwise they'll be able to see us from a distance."

"Right," said Alvise.

Dario rubbed his beard and pulled a Luger P08 out of his jacket, checking that it was loaded and stroking the barrel. At that moment they heard the chugging sound of a boat coming toward them from the Giudecca. When it was about fifty yards from the mooring, it flashed three times like beams from a lighthouse. It was the prearranged signal. It was Giorgio.

Dario then picked up a flashlight from his boat and responded in the same way. By then, it was a few minutes past twelve thirty.

Giorgio was about forty, most of those years spent either in his local bar on the Giudecca or at the Rialto fish market, where every morning he was paid to unload crates of the fish that God provided in the lagoon. He had long hair tied back in a ponytail; he was huge, and he never laughed. Never. His nickname was "Musoduro," or Hardnose, and he always went around armed with a nine-millimeter Beretta M9 Parabellum.

His boat looked like a spaceship: it was a large drift boat with a 150-horsepower engine, a big echo-sounder on board, and those enormous rigs that suck up the whole of the sea, innumerable cages, vibrating dredges, rotating rakes, turbo-blowers, and a gigantic hydraulic pump. Plus various ropes as thick as a man's wrist, heavy nets, two mini flashlights to be used only if necessary, and a small tender where additional loads could be taken aboard if the catch had been good.

"Let's go. The clams are waiting for us!" he said in the lumbering voice of someone who utters only a few words every three or four hours.

They all boarded the drift boat, which was called *Doge*, and headed out with the engine purring quietly. They left the Cavanella landing and after a few minutes entered the dark lagoon blanketed by a layer of mist that rippled over the surface of the water like the oppressive incense Tania had lit.

Alvise's heart was beating fast, he could feel his hands and feet starting to sweat, and thoughts began to run through his head: they moved quickly, appearing in an instant, racing around, and then disappearing. Just like moths in the bulb of a streetlamp. He was aware that the risk they were running was high; he understood that going to scour the lagoon bed in the prohibited area was a very dangerous business; he knew that if the Barracudas were to find them, he and his two accomplices would be in serious trouble.

It was because of this that he was sweating and because of this that he had a strange sense of foreboding, and he had already decided in his heart that this would be the last time. The last. Of course, you could earn well—very well—chiseling a bit from those men: poisonous "megaclams" fished from the dead, toxic water opposite the petrochemical company, near the industrial waste pipes.

A business that made a good deal of money, as the Barracudas well knew; they ran an out-and-out criminal operation to catch the largest and most contaminated clams: thousands of tons sold on the mainland, but also in Rome, Milan, Naples. An illegal turnover of hundreds of millions of euros that then disappeared in the casinos of Slovenia or Montenegro, in luxury hotels and spas in the Dolomites, in holiday villages in Thailand.

The three men on board the *Doge* headed toward Fusina; they entered the Scoasse canal and were absorbed by the darkness of the night. Dario had his eyes closed and looked like he was praying, Giorgio was scanning the lights of the petrochemical plant on the horizon, and Alvise kept scratching his neck and rubbing his aching shoulder: he couldn't clear his mind of those disturbing premonitions, and even if he tried to focus on the tackle that lay at his feet, a series of hideous figures crowded into his thoughts in a flurry of grotesque and frightening images. The lingering smell of the incense drifted into his mind, along with the annoying pendulum of the clock in the living room and the nodding heads of the Jews in the yeshiva. For an instant he even seemed to feel seasick, something that was impossible, he thought.

At a certain point, Giorgio veered to the right and took the Fasiol canal. Quarter to one. They looked like a small militia ready to swoop, ready for a precise military assault.

If things went well, as they had the previous times, in less than ten minutes they would have fished about forty kilograms of clams. After two hours they would have picked up almost a ton. All toxic, full of dioxins, oils used for cooling power transformers, and pesticides. After a couple of days someone would have bought them in their fishmonger's or eaten them in some restaurant or trattoria, with a certificate of provenance, transport papers, and a clean bill of health, all false and deftly provided by Giorgio thanks to substantial bribes. If everything went smoothly, in one night they could earn perhaps forty thousand euros in the teeth of the Barracudas, the real professionals in a racket that generated as much money as drugs, if not more. Millions and millions of euros. Cash.

It was the dirty war of the lagoon, a kind of wild west.

In the meantime, their boat proceeded toward the center of the lagoon with the engine chugging steadily, passing the wooden poles dotted here and there to mark out the navigation channels. These would emerge unexpectedly in front of the boat; often, on the tops of the poles there were seagulls perching that appeared suddenly like specters among the thinning banks of mist. Around them there was a strong smell of decay and putrid water, a disgusting stench of dead fish and rotten seaweed; they saw nylon bags, floating pieces of wood, and plastic bottles drifting at the mercy of the tides, rising and falling, never floating away, as if that vast pool of semistagnant water were a huge lake of gasoline, dense and frighteningly flat.

Once they arrived in the middle of the open water, Alvise raised his head and looked around: at that moment the mist was less opaque, and behind him Venice was clearly visible, lit up in the night with the bell tower of San Marco looming over the red rooftops of the city.

They were finally on the last stretch; Giorgio turned into the Canale Vecchio in Fusina and advanced toward point X, located exactly in the middle of the lagoon, between Venice and Marghera. It was as if the place were suspended between the most beautiful city in the world and the ugliest: on one side the magical lights shining on the history, the eternal beauty, the architectural and artistic elegance of the bride of the sea; on the other, the cold halogen beams of the floodlights illuminating one of the largest centers of Europe's chemical industry as if it were daytime. As if you found yourself between an aesthetic paradise and a visual hell.

Giorgio headed confidently toward the shallows; he glanced at the readings on the echo-sounder and then switched off the engine. As the drift boat glided forward another twenty yards, everything fell into a deep and unsettling silence.

"We're here!" he said.

Dario stood up, grabbed the rope, and dropped the anchor right in front of the channel where the chemical plants dumped their waste. Alvise tipped the boat's engine back and submerged it almost completely in the cloudy water, then took a large iron pole, fastened it to the engine, and rammed it into the bottom of the lagoon bed with all the strength he had. He felt an agonizing pain in his shoulder that suddenly spread into the whole of his chest like a powerful electric shock, but despite everything he stood fast and got ready for the most important part of the operation.

Silence.

A few minutes past one. Around them the lapping of the

small black waves that broke against the hull. A sense of uneasiness permeated the entire area. A black sensation, as black as the deep night that enveloped them. Black like the water beneath their feet. Black like the feeling Alvise experienced as he maneuvered the iron pole and fitted it to the engine.

"All done?" Giorgio asked him in a whisper.

"Done!"

Dario signaled his okay to Giorgio, grabbed hold of a large cage, and lowered it off the stern, alongside the engine.

"Let's go!" he said.

Giorgio turned the key in the electrical control panel and switched on the *Doge's* powerful engine; at that point the double propellers began to spin dizzyingly, eating into the sand and ripping at the lagoon bed. Alvise held tightly onto the iron pole, while Giorgio accelerated and Dario dropped the cage under the water and prepared another. Without saying a word, the three men each focused on his own task and continued like that for a few minutes, until, at long last, their actions achieved their predetermined goal and the boat started to turn like a carousel. Sure enough, the keel of the *Doge* began to move and spin around, at first slowly but then faster and faster, in a kind of whirling loop-the-loop. At that moment, the propellers on the outboard motor began to stir up a vast quantity of frothy sludge. Giorgio was hardly able to pull up the first cage: it was already full of clams, thick, fat, and bloated with hot and horribly polluted water.

Five, nine, sixteen turns of the carousel.

One, two, three cages packed with clams.

In the distance, from two sides, the lights of Venice and Porto Marghera. Around them, nothing. Under them, the filthy water that moved as if it were retching and spewing up kilos—tons—of toxic clams together with the foaming water and the seabed that came to the surface with all its smell of decay and death. Above them, the flashing lights of the umpteenth airliner ready to land at Marco Polo.

Dario activated another extractor and began to tip dozens of kilos of mollusks directly onto the boat: they came out of the lagoon like coins from a broken slot machine.

Twenty-five past one. The *Doge* was filling up.

Alvise gritted his teeth and looked up at the sky, toward a plane. He didn't know how much longer he would be able to stand it; his shoulder felt shattered, as if someone had injected into it a cocktail of glass shards, needles, and hot chilli pepper.

Half past one. The *Doge* was already teeming with seafood and Alvise felt that the veins on his neck and forehead were about to explode.

One thirty-one. Dario spotted a light in the distance. He watched it suspiciously for a moment and halted the operation. He could now see that it was coming closer, at an incredible speed.

"Stop everything!" he yelled at Alvise, and then, turning to Giorgio: "Someone's coming! Go! Go!"

Giorgio and Alvise looked toward the south and saw what was happening.

Giorgio switched off the engine for a moment and, when the boat stopped turning, became aware that the beam of light did not belong to the floodlights that were standard issue on the customs and excise boats. Which was probably even worse. He swore bluntly and barked an order to the other two: "The Barracudas! Come on! Fuck! Come on! Pull everything up and lie flat, cause we're really gonna move!"

Dario pulled the last cage on board, full of mollusks, and helped Alvise unfasten the iron pole from the engine. By then, the beam of light had almost reached them and they could hear the rumbling of the engine of the boat that was cruising straight toward them.

"Go! Go!" Alvise shouted, lying down on the deck and making a rapid sign of the cross. Meanwhile, Dario started swearing nonstop and resolutely pulled out his gun.

Giorgio switched on the engine and set off at full throttle in the opposite direction, toward the Ponte della Libertà, which ought to lie somewhere far in front of them, but wasn't yet visible to them.

Although the *Doge* was speeding like a rocket across the surface of the water, the beam of light behind them grew closer and closer, and suddenly, instead of one light there were three.

"How many fuckers are there?" yelled Giorgio, his ponytail flying in the wind as he raced along at nearly fifty knots.

"Faster! Faster!" Dario roared, gripping his Luger.

Alvise lay among the stinking clams and gazed at the faint image of the moon that leaped across his field of vision with the jolting of the hull. He knew that if it were the Barracudas, he and his partners should be prepared for the worst. And deep down he knew perfectly well that the people behind them *had* to be the Barracudas; he was certain of it when they began firing submachine-gun rounds and pistol shots. Then, as if by magic, the pain in his shoulder became just a distant memory.

Giorgio and Dario started to return fire as best they could; they were like two sardines trying to escape a shark hungry for flesh. The other boats were getting closer and closer. Always closer.

The chase became desperate, with Giorgio zigzagging in a frenetic race toward the darkness, trying to avoid wooden poles, shallows, sand banks, and bullets that buzzed like bees a few inches from their ears.

Shooting, shooting, shooting. From one side and from

the other. Shooting and yet more shooting, until, just as they were skirting the island of San Giorgio in Alga, a bullet hit the *Doge's* pilot in the head; he let go of the controls and fell into the water like a sack of potatoes. The engine of the drift boat died suddenly and in an instant they slowed to a stop, allowing their pursuers to reach them almost immediately. All the while, they continued to fire like men possessed and roar like ferocious animals.

Alvise was also hit; a bullet had grazed his thigh and blood was seeping from his oilskin trousers. With immense effort he got up and plunged into the water like a fish, hoping that no one had seen him. He descended to the seabed and tried to swim toward the old deserted island.

He accidentally drank some of the cloudy water: its fetid smell and its acidic, brackish taste reminded him of rotten fish. There was a burning pain in his leg and he could feel himself getting weaker, when he bumped into something large above him. He quickly realized it was Giorgio's body that was floating helplessly with its head split open. A feeling of panic seized him, but an instinctive spirit of survival made him persevere, and so he swam forward another few yards until he managed to land on the island. He struggled out of the water and gasped for breath that seemed would never come, then he looked toward the *Doge*, lit softly by the mocking moon. He was aware of men shouting at someone and then shooting. Soon he heard the splash of a dead weight falling into the water and realized that they had executed Dario. Then the beam of a flashlight struck him like the midday sun.

"There's the third one! He's on the island!" shouted a hoarse voice.

A boat moved and pointed its prow toward the abandoned quay.

In his attempt to escape, Alvise fell several times, but in the end he entered the thick, impervious undergrowth, dragging himself with difficulty and repeatedly catching on pieces of glass, old sacks of garbage, debris, syringes, used condoms, and every other type of human detritus. He could hear the boat landing at the quay and the hurried steps of the men who had come to do to him what they had just done to his companions. Alvise reached the ruins of the old monastery that stood on the island and, feeling that his heart would burst at any minute, pushed himself further forward and hid inside the walls of the ancient, crumbling crypt, where a flock of bats fluttered away like a fading cloud. Meanwhile, the light of his tormentors' flashlights became stronger as they advanced after him. Alvise peered at the woodland surrounding him and a flurry of meaningless images flashed through his brain.

If you lose, all the worse for you, he thought.

"He's over here! He's over here!" one of the men shouted, shining his flashlight on Alvise, blinding him.

"You dirty bastard. The clams are ours!" a second voice cried out.

Alvise heard a gun being loaded.

"After tonight you'll never steal again," the first man said. "Shoot him in the head, Alkan!"

"No, please!" Alvise begged, his voice trembling.

In that split second he seemed to smell the perfume of Tania's body, feel her breasts, her lips, and an instant later he had the worst sensation of his life: the certainty that everything would end now, and then there would be nothing more.

"Come on, Alkan. What are you waiting for?"

"Don't kill me," Alvise spluttered again. "I'll do whatever you want, but don't kill me."

A shot. A second shot. The echoes swept through the

woods and then out over the lagoon all around them.

A few seconds later, several feral cats hidden among the brambles let out an eerie lament and the men who had ventured onto the island returned to the quay where their associates were waiting for them.

With his fading eyes staring upward, Alvise made out the blurry image of an enormous airliner slowly crossing the sky. He tried to raise a hand to catch hold of it, hang onto it, fly away from the city forever, while his final breath escaped his mouth. Then nothing.

And on the black lagoon the familiar deep silence returned.

THE COMEDY IS OVER

BY Francesco Ferracin

Calcavia

Translated from Italian by Judith Forshaw

First of all, let me say that I'm someone who has always voted for the left.

By conviction rather than because of social background, given that mine is a family of solid upper-middle-class conservatives.

On countless afternoons in Campo Santa Margherita, between one wine-and-campari "spritz" and the next, I have always stood up for a multiethnic, atheist, and social-democratic Italy, the population made up not only of those who were born here but also those who have been compelled to come here.

I'm telling you this just so you don't think I'm a member of the Lega Nord or that I'm one of those priggish old dears who fill up the hairdressers of the northeast. And I want to make it clear from the start that I had my faults too.

I don't think I need to tell you my name, or provide you with details about my background—which you can work out to some extent from the way I talk.

All you need to know is that I was born in Venice (the lagoon), I'm a thirty-four-year-old woman, I'm five foot four, and I weigh 115 pounds.

On the evening of December 16, 2007, I went out for a pizza with friends.

It's something that we didn't get to do often enough, because what with work, boyfriends, and various other things, it's not as if we have much time left over to have fun.

But once a month, on a Friday, Chiara, Giulia, Caterina, Zaira, and I used to go out and let our hair down. Usually a pizza, or Chinese—although we didn't feel like risking it after the time Cate got ill. We chatted about this and that, but had a rule that work and politics were left at home. Then, after the coffee, we'd jump in the car and go somewhere to dance.

That evening we decided to go to the Molo Cinque, one of the few places on the Venetian mainland where you could have a particular kind of evening. No, wait—don't imagine that I'm the sort of girl who likes the pretty boys who go there just to show off their new clothes, or the nerds who use fake IDs to get in and then pretend they've forgotten they're with a lady when it's time to pay the bill.

It's not a place where I go to pick someone up. The type of men I like are completely different. They shouldn't be too good looking (there's always a risk of dormant homosexuality), nor too tall (we'd look ridiculous), nor too poor (that would just be embarrassing). They have to have a beard (maybe) and a degree in an arts subject.

My ideal man?

A philosophy professor (with at least an associate professorship, obviously).

I've had affairs with professional men as well, but I found them as dull as my brother, and they perhaps found me a bit too demanding. It was clear that none of them ever thought my keen intelligence was as important as a nice firm ass, something that at the time I was very far from having.

But I digress.

Returning to the subject at hand: once we'd paid for the pizza, Caterina wanted to go home to her husband, as she always did; he sulks whenever she comes home after eleven.

Meanwhile, Chiara had a baby with a temperature.

So Giulia, Zaira, and I were left.

I ought to mention here that of the three of us, Giulia is the real looker.

Tall. Blond. Looks great for thirty. Truly blue eyes. She's an assistant in a dentist's office and has never had any luck with men. (God knows why I thought it worth mentioning that.) Unlike the vast majority of our crowd, which is about twenty people all told, Giulia has never been interested in politics. She says she's a believer, and I suppose she really is, seeing as she comes from somewhere near Treviso.

Zaira is originally from the Middle East but she came to Italy when she was a baby. Her father is a journalist for *Il Gazzettino* and her mother teaches in a school that specializes in sciences. So she doesn't fit the profile of a typical immigrant.

Not that it would have made any difference to us—quite the opposite. Several times Andrea and Filippo, the frontal and temporal lobes of our group, have tried to introduce people from other ethnic backgrounds into our ranks, but for one reason or another it never worked out.

I can say that that was hardly surprising, though I didn't know then everything I know now.

But let's start at the beginning.

The Molo Cinque was packed. What with a recession on the doorstep and everything else, people seemed to feel an overwhelming need to enjoy themselves. Maybe they wouldn't buy themselves a new pair of shoes, or they'd purchase their clothes at Oviesse instead of Macelleria (where the "right people" do their shopping). Perhaps they'd keep their old car and update their iPhone instead. I still had the first model, but who cares—I'm hardly one of those bourgeois types.

There were loads of people and they were having a great time. They were dancing, drinking, laughing, and flirting. Two fit young men buttonhole us. They offer to buy us drinks. They ask us to dance. Each of us in turn, although it's obvious that both of them are trying to hook up with Giulia. By the third vodka and lemon, the better looking of the two makes his move. Giulia doesn't go for it. He leans in to kiss her. She slaps him. Insults fly—*whore* is the only one I feel I can repeat here, just to give you an idea of the level they descended to.

The bouncers arrive and do what they're paid to do.

All three of us are a bit shaken up by what happened. And, it has to be said, a bit drunk. We therefore decide to go home.

Because she was worried about finding somewhere to park, Giulia came in my car, which I left on one of the side streets off Via dell'Elettricità, right in middle of the Porto Marghera industrial area.

Not one of the better areas, according to right-wing residents of Mestre.

Those of us on the left, however, say it's the beating heart of Mestre. Or of Venice.

A little way from the Molo there's the glorious community center—Rivolta—that I went to when I was a girl, when I used to smoke pot and listen to the Neapolitan hip-hop/reggae group 99 Posse.

The Marghera that was once working class and is now a social laboratory, as Filippo always says, that doesn't miss a single ethnic festival.

A social laboratory . . .

Frankenstein's monster was born in a laboratory too.

We say goodbye to Zaira, who, with her usual luck, had

found a space a few yards from the door of the club, and we set off in silence.

We walk as far as the crossroads at Via della Pila and carry on till we're almost under the Mestre flyover, the one that links the bypass to the Ponte della Libertà, and to Venice.

For those who aren't familiar with the area: on the left, Mestre, the station, and Via Piave, or rather the scrapheap; on the right, Marghera and the commercial port with the Fincantieri warehouses.

My Polo is parked on the right-hand side of the street, between an old BMW and one of those Chryslers that looks like it's out of a Batman comic. The sort of man I would have most liked to run into that evening.

Giulia and I were walking along side by side. The air was cold. The night silent. So silent it almost hurt.

The sound of our heels on the frosty pavement echoed like metal between the empty buildings, the offices of high-tech service-sector firms and businesses.

Behind us, suddenly, the voices of two men. A foreign accent. Probably Arab. But it could also have been Slav or Albanian for all I knew.

Voices that sounded cheerful.

Probably they were boys who had just left the Molo, like us, and were still on a bit of a high. As we all were, if you get what I mean.

I turn around, instinctively, and see them walking a dozen yards behind us.

I can see only their silhouettes, enveloped by the darkness. But from the way they shamble along, they seem young.

This should reassure me, but instead a shiver runs down my spine. I look at Giulia—she's a bit nervous too—and I smile at my customary prejudices.

We're near the car now.

I press the button on the key and the sidelights flash their friendly greeting.

Another lovely evening with friends was nearly at an end.

A weekend of Christmas shopping awaited me.

How could anything bad happen? In Marghera?

I didn't have time to finish the thought before I found myself lying flat on the ground.

The last thing I remember seeing were Giulia's eyes wide open in an expression of terror.

Only the empty eye sockets of the buildings lining the street saw the rest.

I come to.

I don't realize right away what has happened.

Frankly, I don't think I really realize for weeks.

I struggle to keep my eyes open.

I touch my face, which seems damp, not knowing that it's my blood oozing from above my right eye and from my broken nose.

At first I think I must have slipped on the icy pavement. Then I remember the two men.

My head's spinning, but I can't feel anything. Not pain. Nor cold. Nothing.

I feel nothing.

It's as if the world around me has started to move more slowly.

I touch my head. My hair is sticky. It too is soaked with blood, from another deep cut, above the nape of my neck.

I try to get up but can't.

In that instant I become aware of two things. No, three.

First: Batman doesn't exist.

Second: I still have all my clothes on.

Third: there's no sign of Giulia.

I ought to imagine the worst. To shout. But I don't have the strength to do anything.

I try to get up, but my legs won't support me. I feel ridiculous. And a bit embarrassed. I hope no one sees me like this.

My father. I need to call my father, I think to myself.

I look for my phone but can't find it. Obviously.

My handbag's not here either, nor the car keys I had in my hand until a few seconds before.

Seconds. Yes, because I don't think more than a few seconds could have passed since the moment I fell. If I hadn't seen the two men behind us, if I hadn't seen Giulia's expression, I could easily have kept thinking I'd slipped on the icy pavement.

In reality I was unconscious for at least fifteen minutes, one of the doctors would explain to me later.

They stole everything. Including the car.

But they didn't rape me.

Don't say anything.

I can't tell you what time it was. Even my Swatch is gone. Nor can I tell you how it was possible that no one noticed me crawling along the fun-filled streets, so close to incredibly busy nightclubs. Someone must have seen me.

Probably people were so used to seeing strange things around there that they weren't curious enough to ask what a girl with her face covered in blood was doing crawling around on her hands and knees in the middle of the night.

They would have thought I was a prostitute.

And maybe they would have thought that I went looking for it.

I manage to get to Via Fratelli Bandiera, God knows how. On the other side of the street the lights of the clubs are still lit. The sound of guitars and drumbeats escapes from the Vapore.

I think I can hear confused shouting.

But not even a glimpse of any other people.

I drag myself across the road; I pass between the cars parked under the flyover and spot the red Guardia di Finanza building. I would never have thought that one day I would be happy to see it.

It takes so little to change your opinions.

In fact, I made a lot of discoveries that night:

1. *Venice isn't a safe place.*
2. *People have no problem leaving you to die in the street.*
3. *People do it because they're afraid.*
4. *This fear is caused by the fact that the world isn't the place we'd like it to be.*

The most important thing of all, however, I only discovered many days later, when I left the intensive care unit:

The world is the way it is mainly because there are people who think the same way I used to think.

Now, you'll probably say that the head injury is making me talk crap.

A psychologist called it post-traumatic stress disorder. *Disorder* . . . psychologists have a great talent for euphemisms. After the third euphemism I told mine to fuck off. He told me it's normal for a patient to tell him to fuck off. I ask him if it's normal for them not to pay his bill. He smiles benevolently. I throw the first object that comes to hand (a metal pen holder). I miss him by a whisker, unfortunately. He is totally gobsmacked and I have him cowering in his chair like an asshole.

My father paid the bill anyway.

The world is what it is mainly because there are people who think the same way I used to think.

Not just people with left-wing views, you understand. There are also people who aren't left-wing who believe that most immigrants are the victims, not the criminals. That poor people are fundamentally good whereas the rich are bad. And that we, the moralists, are the executioners (because the more radical you are, the more you think it's other people who are moralists—even those who, although they think like you, don't think *enough* like you).

The most cynical among you will say—and you won't mince your words—that I'm a hypocritical whore. You'll object that one can't pass judgment based solely on personal experiences, however dramatic they may be.

An intelligent person, as I claim to be (and on this point, you're right—I've claimed to be one for years), should strive to maintain his or her objectivity.

Otherwise you end up with the same old prejudices.

I have just one reply to your objection: kiss my ass.

And, furthermore, do you know where you can stick your objectivity?

But I don't want to be any cruder that I have to, so I'll leave it to you to draw your own conclusions.

On that hospital bed, between my mother's tear-jerking performance and the indignant tirades of my lawyer brother, a series of new thoughts began to take shape in my brain.

Thoughts that didn't resemble even vaguely the politically correct ideas I had held since my university years.

Racist thoughts.

Thoughts dripping with a furious anger.

And the more I thought about what I would have liked to do to those two animals, the better I felt.

My father was the one who took it worst. From the day when I was admitted to hospital, he had become a permanent visitor at the police station on Via Colombo, where he had several friends in positions of power.

I was forgetting: my father is a lawyer too.

"Those sons of bitches will rot in jail," he swore.

I don't know why, but this possibility made me even more angry instead of reassuring me.

"Jail? They deserve hanging!" my brother snapped.

Well . . . this is just talk, I thought, although even hanging seemed to me to be letting them off lightly.

And I didn't yet know that Giulia and I had made the front page of all the local and national papers.

Or rather, it was Giulia, not me, who made the front pages, the dead one of the two of us.

Her body had been found a few days after the crime, in a canal somewhere near Fusina.

And no one thought they needed to tell me.

Poor thing. She's already suffering from shock, they would have thought as soon as they heard the news.

They even went to the funeral, while I was stuck in my bed at the Angelo hospital dosed up on painkillers.

I don't know what expressions were worn by my circle of friends and acquaintances. And who knows if even they talked about me. Probably they were offended, seeing as I hadn't wanted any visitors except for my relatives. They were bound to resent it. And deep down they surely thought I'd only survived because I wasn't as hot as Giulia.

Maybe Zaira, Chiara, Caterina, and the others thought it was partly my fault because I'd parked under the flyover when everyone knows that girls shouldn't wander around on their own at night in the "social laboratory."

I'm sure that, even if they didn't say it, they thought the wrong woman had died. Giulia was nice, good, beautiful, never started an argument. She never forced her opinions on anyone (because, let's face it, she didn't have any).

That big mouth with the rich daddy survived. The big-assed fanatic with her red Marxist views and evergreen hope. The one who doesn't practice what she preaches.

I decided I didn't want anything more to do with any of them.

Along with Giulia, all my friends died too.

I don't hold anything against my family for keeping me in the dark. I would have done the same in their place, and if I had seen my blue, purple, and red face, my head half shaved, if I had read my medical records, I would probably have alerted the nearest mental institution.

Broken nose, fractured skull, brain hemorrhage, various broken bones (ribs, humerus, tibia, to list just the most important). A couple of cracked vertebrae, because I had the good fortune that the two men's combat boots weren't steel-capped, unlike the chain with which one of them delivered the first and final blows.

"It's a miracle you're still alive and haven't suffered any permanent damage," that southern idiot of a commissario (and friend of my father) had said to me.

"Pure Venetian," my father had replied; he was proud of his pedigree. "We're hard-headed."

"It's lucky for you that those two Moroccans thought they'd killed her."

Two Moroccans? How did they know they were two Moroccans? I asked myself.

Yet again, no one had thought there was any need to tell

the victim that the murder suspects had been arrested the day before Giulia's naked body was regurgitated by one of those canals full of industrial waste.

A body that was pretty well decomposed, I imagined.

"We wanted to protect you," my mother had said.

And then my brother, elated: "The evidence they've gathered is convincing, to say the least."

How could I bear a grudge?

They had always warned me and I'd said they were paranoid. My brother always objected to my more exotic acquaintances, and I'd called him a fascist.

I mostly paid for my studies myself. They gave me about a thousand euros a month, but I said their money was dirty, made from the sweat and exploitation of people like those who nearly killed me.

My body took nearly a year to heal completely.

There were still scars, but by then I didn't care about my appearance anymore.

The one positive note was that everything that had happened had got me down to my ideal weight for the first time in my life. And it had given me a nice ass. In fact, the rehabilitation program had made me develop a taste for the gym. I had become acquainted with my abdominals and with the muscles in my arms.

My tits had turned into pecs and my buttocks into a gluteus maximus.

Not much in the way of consolation, I hear you say.

Well . . . I'd say it was, and you'll soon see why.

First, however, I have to tell you about Abdullah Boukhari (nineteen) and R.H. (sixteen).

Abdullah was born in a little village near Agadir on the south-

ern Atlantic coast of Morocco. Shitty childhood in a shan-
tytown. Dealer in cannabis and whoring for the occasional
elderly Englishman ever since he learned to put his dick to
work. Before leaving Morocco on a boat he'd even spent a
couple of months in jail. A tough jail where he had the opportunity to enjoy new sexual experiences.

R.H. came from Casablanca. He used to visit Italy regularly, staying with an uncle who worked in a textile factory
somewhere near Vicenza. His childhood wasn't great either,
but nowhere near as bad as his accomplice's. He could have
just stood around catching flies at home, if his father hadn't
died and his uncle hadn't had the bright idea of bringing him
to Eldorado.

The two meet in Jesolo, where they push drugs together
outside the discos. However, they're a bit too young to work
freelance and so they end up being used by some of their fellow Moroccans.

This situation doesn't particularly suit them so before long
they decide to clear out and come to our happy town.

They don't manage to make a living for themselves here,
however, so they seek help from social services. They're put
up in a hostel. They're given food and clothes.

R.H. would have liked to go back to his uncle and try
earning an honest living, but Abdullah persuades him not to.

Two weeks later they start scouring the areas with the
liveliest nightlife, on the lookout for easy money.

A month after that they see us coming out of the Molo.

Giulia's blond hair dazzles them; they can't think clearly,
what with the alcohol and drugs.

They follow us. They attack us.

Abdullah is the worst. He has brought a chain with him,
complete with padlock. He is the one who splits my head

open. "That bitch is still alive then?" he allegedly said before the police took turns letting him have some of what he gave me.

Their plan was to rob us. Then, when they saw what Giulia looked like, they improvised. They bundled her into the car and drove her to Fusina where they raped her.

It was Abdullah who killed her, hitting her repeatedly with the chain.

Conclusion: Abdullah is in prison, paid for by the taxpayer, and will likely stay there for a while, though there's always a chance that good behavior or some pardon will let him out. And even if he does the full thirty years, when he gets out—with a clean slate, transformed and rehabilitated—he'll still have at least a third of his life to enjoy.

R.H., on the other hand, ended up in a rehabilitation center because lawyers, social workers, psychologists, and astrologers showed that he was a victim of both his older accomplice and circumstance. However, he shoved his dick in my friend too.

He kicked me too.

But he did it because of French colonialism and society.

It took me awhile to find him.

And it wasn't particularly easy to kill him.

It was my first murder. Well, what did you expect? That it would be a walk in the park?

The idea came to me while watching *Kill Bill* on DVD. For months my best friend had been Amazon.co.uk., where I bought the classics of the American action genre. My favorites were films about revenge and those where ordinary people get really pissed off and wreak bloody havoc in the style of Sam Peckinpah.

I had always loved Tarantino, despite never having seen any of his films. I had read loads of reviews and knew he was a master of the pulp genre. Senseless violence, but with a lot of irony and a voguish stylistic flavor. There was deep irreverence and extensive quoting from the great filmmakers, so cinema buffs like us were bound to like him.

I absolutely loved *Kill Bill*. I watched it dozens of times and in my head I pictured myself wandering around Mestre in a yellow tracksuit, armed with a sword, searching for those two shits.

However pissed off you might think I am, I never thought—not even for a second—that what I saw could ever happen in real life.

Not until I met Rado at the gym.

Rado deserves a whole chapter to himself, but I don't want to bore you with pointless details.

Rado was thirty-seven. He was a Serb. Not bad looking either—tall, slim, muscular. He had fought in the war—or rather, wars. He had fought in Croatia, Bosnia, and Kosovo.

Rado had been a Chetnik.

Then things had all gotten a bit fucked up over there, so he shaved off his beard and came to Italy to seek his fortune in the import-export business.

Rado was my "man of providence."

We became friends. He appreciated my new body and couldn't care less about the scar that had made my right eyebrow too high.

He fucked like a god. I doubt my ex-friends had ever experienced anything like it. And how else could someone fuck if he had killed dozens of men. Some in cold blood, but mostly not.

We went out together. We became lovers. We rented an apartment in Via Cappuccina.

And when I introduced him to my family, it caused quite a scene.

Rado taught me everything I know.

He taught me to make friends with guns. To take them apart, to clean them, to tell one from another. To appreciate the differences in caliber and weight. To test the recoil.

He taught me to shoot, and for my thirty-fourth birthday he gave me a beautiful .22 caliber Sig Sauer with a silencer.

It was Rado who put me in touch with the Balkan underworld. And it was he and his friend Pavel who discovered where R.H. was hiding—real name Reduan Hamoud.

Both of them had offered to sort him out for me, but I was opposed to the idea as a matter of principle.

I had to look him in the eye before killing him.

Reduan seemed to have started a new life. That's what you say, isn't it, when someone fucks up then—who knows how—realizes what they've done and tries to behave as if it never happened?

He was working in Venice as a waiter in a little restaurant for tourists behind the Zattere.

By now he was nineteen and the state had decided that he had paid his debts to society.

I'm sure that even if he sees me he won't recognize me.

I sit down at an outside table with a view of San Sebastiano, and I wait for someone to bring me a menu. As luck would have it, it's Reduan who attends to me, just like three years before.

He looks at me and says hello with an ivory smile. Clearly he doesn't recognize me. And how could he? My body is thin now, almost mannish. I have short hair and there isn't a trace of make-up on my face. My nose isn't aquiline anymore, just a bit flat.

If they'd seen me that evening, in jeans and a military jacket, not even my old friends would have recognized me.

"I'd like a diavolo pizza," I tell him. "And a beer."

"Small?"

"Are you kidding?"

Reduan smiles. A nice smile.

We look each other in the eye. His eyes aren't evil. Large. Round. Dark. Framed with eyelashes that look drawn on.

A good-looking boy, it has to be said.

He's bound to be thinking that the old lady is flirting.

I eat the pizza. I drink the beer. I order a coffee and pass time reading Il Gazzettino.

It gets to midnight and there are only a few of us left in the restaurant. I pay the bill and head out before I start attracting too much attention. A few yards away there's a bar that serves my purpose. Full of people getting drunk.

I order another beer and start drinking it outside, mingling with the summer crowds.

From my position I have a great view.

I have time for another couple of beers before the owner of the restaurant next door turns off the lights and Reduan comes out with two of his coworkers.

I have already paid for the beers.

I wait for the three men to head down an alley, then I start following them at a safe distance.

I begin to worry that they're going to stick with him all the way home.

Instead, they separate at Piazzale Roma.

Reduan gets on the 7 bus with me behind him. He looks tired.

Half an hour later we cross the Dell'Amelia flyover and get off just after the bypass. The same bypass that witnessed the attack on me.

Reduan crosses Via Miranese and heads quickly toward Via Ancona.

I keep following him, thinking it would have been better if I hadn't drunk four beers. It's not that my head is spinning, but I have the feeling of being surrounded by shadows.

I'm wearing a baseball cap and sunglasses.

There are two boys sitting on scooters in front of a gate leading to a block of flats. They glance at us then go back to smoking their joint.

Reduan walks along, unsuspecting, not even a dozen yards ahead of me. It's still too far. I lengthen my stride and pull out the .22, the silencer ready for the occasion. Via Ancona is bathed in darkness. Just one streetlamp works out of every three and the sky is covered with clouds.

Suddenly, as if warned by a sixth sense, Reduan turns around.

He notices the gun.

An expression flickers across his face that I've seen somewhere before. He opens his mouth to say something, perhaps to shout out, but I second-guess him and plant a bullet in his arm.

Fuck, I think to myself, since I had aimed for his heart. Fuck those beers.

Now the Moroccan really does start screaming. A high-pitched scream, almost like a woman.

He starts to run off, holding his arm and shouting, *Help, Mommy!* or fuck knows what in the language of where he's from.

I follow him and when I'm a couple of steps away I shoot

him three more times. Two shots miss their target and hit a parked car, one hits him in the back.

I stand over him. I smile when I see he's crying.

"I'll tell Abdullah you're waiting for him," I say, then I empty the magazine into his chest.

His screams and the Renault's car alarm have brought a few people to their windows, but the darkness and my disguise are enough to guarantee me a degree of anonymity.

Once I get back to Via Miranese I call Rado and tell him to come pick me up in front of the Cadoro supermarket.

I felt a strange euphoria. I felt a lightness. I would have liked to sing. There wasn't a single trace of remorse in me, nor any regrets.

It's true that the actual moment was very different from how I had imagined it. And that the words I'd dreamed about saying for months and months had come out a bit wrong. As if the voice that spoke them still belonged to the girl I had been before that evening in Marghera.

I had killed a man.

And nothing happened.

It was like New Year's Day or the day after your birthday when you're young. You think you ought to feel different, but in the end it's just another day gone by.

The nights that followed I slept like a log. No dreams. No nightmares.

They wrote about the murder in the papers. About the man in the cap. About the brutality with which that poor boy (with a criminal record) had been killed. In a neighborhood where people don't usually get killed. Where criminals go to live, not to commit crimes. It's not like it's Naples.

I was sure the police were groping around in the dark. I

had been careful not to leave any clues. And the gun, despite its sentimental value, was now lying at the bottom of the Salso canal.

Of course, there was the possibility that during their inquiries the police would come up with the idea of questioning me.

If they did, I would be ready.

"I'm sorry," I said to the police officer, sounding rather contrite. "In spite of what he did to me, I would never have wished him dead."

It was clear that the policeman didn't believe me, but that didn't matter. Despite my new look, I am still the daughter of a well-known Venetian lawyer. I have a first-class degree, and the evening of the murder I was at the cinema with my fiancé, who at that moment was in Milan on business.

"What did you say your boyfriend's name is?"

I hadn't said. "Radovan Petrovi," I stated, realizing that it wasn't quite the same as saying Giacomo Baldan.

The officer made a note.

"Should I call my father?"

He looked up from his notebook. "Not at all. These are just formalities. You can go home and forget the whole thing."

I went home and poured myself a double.

Rado had gone to Milan to find out if it were possible to get the other Moroccan out of jail early. In a body bag, obviously.

I phoned him and told him about the questioning. It was probable they would want to talk to him as well.

Although my revenge wasn't yet complete, I started to think about what I would do afterward.

Going back to the museum wasn't even an option. I had shut down my old life, as I've already explained.

However, in Mestre you can't be out of work without being noticed. Especially if your boyfriend is a professional criminal.

I spent a couple of hours in front of the mirror and came to the conclusion that I should dress in a way that is more in keeping with my social position.

Then, in the following order, I would have to: a) get back in touch with my family; b) ask my father and brother to give me a shitty job in their law firm; c) arrange for Abdullah to join his friend as soon as possible; and d) say goodbye to Rado.

The last would be the most difficult, because my little Rado isn't the type to appreciate being dumped.

And it wouldn't be easy to find someone who fucks like him, but at my age sex isn't everything. Right?

I sorted out points a) and b) in the days that followed.

"Good grief, you look like a lesbian," said my brother; we hadn't seen each other for almost a year. Still, it was better than the words with which he said goodbye to me: "If I'd known you were going to end up with a Slav, I would have made sure you stayed a communist."

My father and my mother were nicer. They believed in the parable of the prodigal son, and I really missed my mother's roast pork.

"We understand how hard it's been for you. But don't think it's been all that easy for us either. You don't know how worried we've been."

Meanwhile, I was stuffing myself like someone at the end of Ramadan. Speaking of Ramadan, I'll tell you now that—point c)—he would hang himself in his cell three months after I started work as a PA in the family firm. Just so you don't think my return to the fold was peppered with good intentions.

Quite the opposite.

The first dinner with my family ended in hugs and kisses. My brother walked me to the Accademia Vaporetto stop, his arm protectively draped around my shoulders.

"Have you ever thought of taking a self-defense class?" he said to me as we walked along. "It could make you safer."

I responded with a smile, remembering that before resolving point d) I would have to scrounge a couple of guns from him.

As expected, Rado didn't take it very well. He started yelling. He threatened to kick my ass, but then he got the picture.

He said that I wasn't the only woman he was fucking anyway. But that, despite everything, he would miss all our little games. He made it clear that he was always around if I should ever want to start them up again.

We stayed friends.

The day I moved into the penthouse with a view of the Salute, bought for me by my parents, he gave me a new .22 (this time an elegant Walther P22) and told me that now that I had an interesting job, we could also do a bit of business together.

I took possession of a walnut desk in the Rialto office and a Mercedes SLK parked in Piazzale Roma.

Awhile later I head back to the Molo. Not to go on the prowl, because I still don't like provincial pretty boys, and now if I want to fuck properly I know where to go.

While some say the recession is passing and Italy is about to enter a new era, people always behave the same way. They dance, they drink, they dance, they flirt, they drink, they go to the bathroom to snort a bit of the good stuff they get from Rado's friends, they dance. In short, they enjoy themselves.

I watch them for a while, then I get bored and leave.

I park a long way from the entrance, under the flyover, near the Fincantieri warehouses. Quite a way on foot.

For the occasion, I'm wearing a tiny miniskirt that emphasizes my nice firm ass.

I walk. It's cold. A nice cold like the cold I feel inside.

The night is quiet. There isn't a soul around.

They say a woman shouldn't wander the streets of Marghera on her own anymore.

Behind me footsteps echo between the walls of the empty buildings. It looks like even the high-tech service sector has decided to go elsewhere.

A man's voice. The accent is Italian.

Perhaps.

There's the smell of rape in the air.

I pull out my gun from under my Cavalli jacket, and before I turn around I think that, after tonight, Batman can go fuck himself.

COMMISSARIO CLELIA VINCI

BY BARBARA BARALDI

Mestre

Translated from Italian by Judith Forshaw

I

Night had fallen like a heavy blanket over the city of Mestre. Clelia looked out of the window. The Bora, the northeast wind with its erratic, ill-mannered gusts, was tormenting the tops of the maritime pines. As a little girl, her father would light a fire during the long winter nights. They would all sit together around the fireplace, and he would tell her that the wind could steal the souls of careless passersby. "When the Bora blows, you have to stay at home, safe. Anyone who braves the wind risks losing their soul, as well as their hat," he would say to her in his deep voice. And the little Clelia would open her eyes wide and beg him to tell her the story of Grandpa Domenico, who had rescued Isabella's hat one windy night and had made her fall in love with him. In the glass, Clelia could see the reflection of her round face with its soft features framed by short black hair; her large brown eyes stood out clearly. The roofs of the houses reflected the leaden light of the streetlamps. Smoke escaped from a few chimney pots, suggesting a domestic warmth that hadn't been felt in her own home for a while. Clelia thought how nice it would be to go back to her childhood and hear once again that incredible, romantic story, narrated in her father's voice.

But he had been dead a long time, and she wasn't a little girl anymore. She could stay at home to escape the wind, but she couldn't escape her anxieties. Not since Giovanni had left her, to start a new life with another woman. "It's too hard living with a policewoman," he had said to her, not looking her in the eye. They had been having problems for some time, and the love they shared for their daughter Laura wasn't enough to keep them together. In the last two years Clelia had struggled to ensure that her daughter didn't suffer because of the absence of a man in the house, trying to create a cozy home environment and attempting to limit her overtime as much as possible. Sometimes, after supper, she even found the energy to take a look at her daughter's homework. The most difficult moments were the weekends that Laura spent with Giovanni's new family. Laura would come home thrilled; she would chatter about the two little twins, the children Giovanni had had with Giorgia, his new partner. She was so beautiful, as well as being such a good cook—a full-time housewife. For Clelia, Giorgia was the template of the perfect woman: a nice, straightforward mother and wife. The partner that Giovanni would have liked her to become. But he had never succeeded with her. Clelia loved her work too much. When, at just twenty-three, she had passed the exams to go into the police force (before she had even finished her law studies), she had known that it would be a difficult environment, especially for a woman. And male competition had made itself felt right from the start. Giovanni, who was then her fiancé, had raised the first objections. "Couldn't you do a normal job?" he had asked her one evening. They had just made love. They were still in each other's arms, their skin burning and their hands clasping their bodies tightly together.

"What do you mean, *normal*?" she had asked with a smile.

"I don't know . . . working in an office, or a shop in town. I could even see you as a lawyer. But being a policewoman is dangerous. You'll be walking around armed. You might see people die. And I'd be worried all the time knowing you were out there."

"But I'd be out there to protect honest people. People like you, darling." Clelia had run her finger over his nose and then his lips. An affectionate gesture that had been lost during the first years of marriage, after too many fights and after reconciliations that became less and less satisfying.

"Mommy?" Laura's small voice called her back to reality. The little girl, from under the covers, was waiting for her usual goodnight kiss and chat before going to sleep.

Clelia sat on the edge of the bed and stroked her hair.

"I don't like the wind," Laura confided, looking in the direction of the window.

"But the wind brings stories from all over the world, sweetheart. If you learn how to listen to it, you'll never feel alone," said Clelia, continuing to stroke her hair.

"Will you tell me a story?"

"I'm very tired, but I promise that if you're good and close your eyes the wind will bring you a lovely story. It's traveled a long way, the Bora, to get here to us. It's come through woods and forests. Through its eyes you can see fabulous animals . . ."

"And maybe a fairy?" asked Laura.

Clelia was lost in thought again. That weekend her daughter was due to go ice-skating with Giovanni and Giorgia. For weeks she had talked of nothing else. Giorgia had been the local skating champion, but then, according to Giovanni, she realized that she had to give up an adolescent passion in order to focus on real life. That was the truth of the situation:

for him, Clelia's desire to pursue a career in the police was a childish dream. A way of following in the footsteps of her father, her hero, killed in an ambush while working as a bodyguard for Judge Di Gennaro.

"Mommy, why don't you come skating with us too?" asked Laura in an attempt to reclaim her mother's attention. "I know you're sad when you stay at home on your own."

Clelia forced a smile. "I can't skate. I'd end up breaking my leg," she replied, her voice tinged with a note of melancholy.

"But the twins can't skate either! They're too little. They'll just stand and watch us and Daddy and Giorgia will take turns skating with me."

"Thank you for the lovely thought. I'm sure you'll be really good, a real ice princess. I'll come another time, I promise."

Laura's eyes darkened. She knew that kind of promise. It was a way of softening a no.

The ringing of the phone shattered the moment of intimacy between mother and daughter. At that time of night it couldn't mean anything good.

"Sorry," Clelia muttered. She had no choice but to run into the corridor and rummage for her phone in her bag. "Where did I put the damn thing? Ah . . . here we are!"

The voice at the other end sounded frantic. "Clelia, it's Franco. I wouldn't have disturbed you this late if it wasn't something really urgent."

"What is it?"

"Just over an hour ago someone called HQ to report a noise that sounded like a shot. Officers found a body—it's Luciano Restivo, the owner of an ad agency on the Lido. You must've heard of him—he made a name for himself with those campaigns for the Venice Film Festival."

"Yes, I know the name. Is it murder?"

"That's the thing. Everything suggests suicide, but my sixth sense says it isn't. You know when my alarm bell goes off?"

"I know it well, your alarm bell. It usually means trouble."

"Judge Carmine Mezzogiorno is here already. I'd feel better if you'd come over here and share your opinion."

"Give me the address. I just need time to find a babysitter and then I'll be there."

Clelia arrived at the Ad Work agency with an ominous feeling in her bones. The street was crowded with police vehicles. An ambulance was parked in front of the gate, surrounded by a small crowd of onlookers. Inspector Franco Armati came toward her with one of his crooked smiles. He was a good-looking man, Armati, and he knew it. Chestnut-brown hair, always tousled, aquiline nose, untidy beard, and blue eyes ringed with laughter lines that only added charm to his seemingly disheveled appearance.

"I have to say that you're even more attractive than usual this evening, Clelia."

"Spare me the sweet talk, Franco—you sound like a geriatric Latin lover. Where's the body?"

"Always in a hurry, eh? It's one of the things I like about you most."

Clelia gave a snort, but she couldn't help letting a smile play on her lips. In the beginning Franco's one-liners had annoyed her. As the commissario, she was still his boss. Besides, she didn't put up with sexist remarks. She was an officer in the police force, and the fact that she was a woman was irrelevant. Then, as time went on, she had discovered that Franco was the best colleague she could wish for, vigilant and thorough in investigations: he didn't leave any stone unturned and his razor-sharp instinct helped him to solve complicated cases. In addition, he was the only person who ever noticed—with just one glance—if something was wrong in Clelia's private life. "Everything okay, boss?" he would ask. "Sometimes a coffee's all you need to feel better." He always managed to get a smile out of her.

"This way." Franco led her along a narrow corridor lined with doors, all closed, to the office of the agency's chief executive, Luciano Restivo. As she went in, she was struck by the sharp smell of blood. The body was sitting at the desk, its head bent backward. The wall behind was awash with blood and splattered with bits of brain. One hand was still resting on the desk, next to a piece of paper with writing on it. The other hung down near the floor, a few centimeters from an automatic pistol.

"The gun?" Clelia asked her colleague.

"It belonged to Restivo. It's licensed."

Clelia moved toward the body to examine it close-up. It was a horrendous sight: the man had shot himself in the mouth. She managed to stifle a feeling of revulsion. From her jacket pocket she pulled out a pair of latex gloves, slipped them on, then picked up the sheet of paper; it looked like a goodbye note. She read it carefully.

"Notice anything strange?" Franco asked her.

"Yes, actually. Some letters are more pronounced than others."

"I knew you'd notice. And have a look at what they spell out if you put them together."

Clelia took a Post-it and a pen from the desk, and set to work on the highlighted letters. The first was an *m*, followed by a *u*. After a while, her eyes widened. "It says *murder*," she whispered.

"Perhaps Restivo was forced to write the note, and he

tried to leave a final, desperate message. I'm sure it's not suicide, even if someone wants to make us think it is," concluded
Inspector Armati.

II

Judge Carmine Mezzogiorno's office was big and bright. The
white marble floor reflected the light that filtered through
the large windows. By the side of the desk were two luxuriant
ferns, and, on the walls, framed photographs of the highest
state appointees.

"I'm willing to consider opening a murder file. The highlighted letters in the suicide note can't be just coincidence."

"That's what I think too," said Commissario Clelia Vinci.
"Inspector Armati sends his regards," she added. "He couldn't
come with me because he's questioning a witness."

"Give him my regards. Naturally, I ask you to keep me
informed about any developments in the inquiry."

"Of course." Clelia bid him goodbye with a strong hand-
shake and marched out of his office. She quickly ran down the
stairs of the Tribunale della Repubblica and left the building.
She paused for a moment to admire the vast expanse of Piazza
San Marco, the only true piazza in Venice. She glanced up
at the gray sky, streaked with clouds. A sustained rumbling
announced the first drops of rain, which gradually became
heavier. The tourists who crowded the piazza took refuge inside the basilica or under the arched colonnades of the Procu-
ratie, so-called because the building once housed the offices
of the Procurators of St. Mark.

Clelia decided to permit herself a coffee in the eighteenth-
century Caffé Florian. She strode in and ordered an espresso.
History had unfolded in front of the full-length windows of
the most celebrated Venetian coffee shop. It had played host

to, among others, Charles Dickens, Lord Byron, Ugo Foscolo, Silvio Pellico, Modigliani, D'Annunzio, Eleonora Duse—and, as Florian's was the only café of the time that women were allowed to enter, it was said that Casanova used to stalk his romantic prey here. But Clelia held onto an important personal memory linked to the café: in the Oriental Salon, painted by Pascuti, its walls adorned with exotic women dressed in skimpy outfits and pairs of lovers, her husband had proposed to her. His eyes had never once left hers as he had asked her. "You're stubborn and not very likely to change your point of view if you think you're right. You're proud and touchy. And you've chosen to take up a career I don't like, but I love you. Clelia Vinci, will you marry me?" he had said to her without pausing for breath. She had looked at him, her eyes teary with emotion, and had uttered a single word: "Yes." Clelia fought against the urge to go into the Oriental Salon. She hadn't set foot in their since she and her husband had split up, even if every now and then she went back to the old Caffè Florian—despite the fact that she would then be in a bad mood for the rest of the day. She drank her bitter, still scalding espresso in one gulp.

A few minutes later she was at the quay where the police motorboat was moored; she waved to the uniformed officer who was waiting for her. The journey toward the Santa Croce district, the oldest part of Venice and home to the Questura, proved to be more difficult than expected because of the Bora, which was still blowing, forming ripples on the surface of the canals. Clelia, despite having been born in the city on the lagoon, had always suffered from seasickness.

Half an hour later, pale and slightly the worse for wear, she joined Inspector Armati in his office. She found him deep in conversation with Rossana Piva, Restivo's charming personal assistant. The young woman's eyes were red from crying and she sobbed as she talked.

"He had no reason to do something like this . . . I think Luciano had a meeting yesterday evening."

"What makes you think that?" asked Armati.

"He didn't tell me exactly, but there are five of us at Ad Work and it's rare for all the work to be finished by six, so we often stay late. But yesterday evening it seemed like Luciano couldn't wait to be left on his own."

"The fact that Mr. Restivo wanted to be on his own, couldn't that suggest he was planning to commit suicide?"

Rossana jumped to her feet. "No!" she cried, clenching her fists. "Luciano would never have done that . . ."

After she left, Franco looked at Clelia. "What did you think?"

The commissario replied, "Her reaction was a bit over the top."

"I thought so too. Maybe there was something more than a working relationship between Restivo and his secretary. She's a very attractive girl, and a colleague of hers just told me she was the last person to be hired, but has risen very quickly in her career."

"What do you mean?"

"Besides being the boss's PA, it just so happens she has been personally handling negotiations with some of the most important clients."

Clelia gazed out of the window. It was raining heavily and the sky looked like a sheet of steel.

"You're miserable today," Franco said to her.

"Sometimes I wonder how come you know me so well. Do you know that my ex always said I don't show my feelings enough?"

"After lunch I'm meeting Restivo's widow. Do you want to

grab a bite with me and then we can go there together?"

"Okay. Laura's with her father for a few days anyway, and the more time I spend at work the better I'll feel."

Neither Clelia nor Franco had armed themselves with an umbrella, so they ran through the rain to the nearby bar. Clelia's hair was dripping wet. Franco brushed a strand from her face and smiled at her. She shivered, but not because of the cold. They ordered two sandwiches and sat at a table in the corner.

"I called Enrico Lettieri, Restivo's lawyer, and he seemed pretty shaken up as well," said Franco.

"Do you think he'll be able to tell us anything useful?"

"I think so. I found out that Lettieri was a good friend of Restivo, someone he really trusted. He's out of town at the moment, but he'll drop by the station on Monday."

III

The Restivo villa, with its art nouveau design and huge garden, stood in the area near the Lungomare d'Annunzio on the Lido. Mariasole Vincenzi Restivo had been a very beautiful woman: you could tell from the shape of her face and the light that occasionally lit up her eyes, green like precious stones. But time had superimposed on her features a certain harshness. Clelia imagined that she must have suffered greatly in her life. A woman understands these things. The thought contrasted with the ostentatious splendor of the house's decor.

Restivo's widow led them into a classically styled sitting room and offered them a seat on a sofa upholstered in golden velvet, with exquisite inlaid wooden arms.

"Is that an original?" asked Franco, pointing at one of the paintings.

"Yes. It's a Canaletto, painted in 1730. My father was an

art dealer. The other paintings are originals too—they're part of the family collection. As an only child, I inherited them together with this villa."

"It's truly amazing," Clelia said, looking up at the ceiling frescoed with flowers.

"Sometimes I think it's too big. Especially for a woman on her own." There was a note of sadness in her voice.

"I'm sorry for your loss. It must be awful," Franco mumbled quickly.

During their brief chat, the woman proved to be happy to talk at length about the nineteenth-century copy of the *Nike of Samothrace* that dominated the hall, of the virtues of her Filipina maid, and of her gardeners' poor work ethic. On the other hand, she was reluctant to talk about her husband. It appeared that their relationship had cooled after their daughter, Annalisa, had been admitted to a psychiatric hospital in Marghera.

"Signora Restivo, I'm sure it's difficult for you to talk about this, especially now. But can I ask why your daughter's in the hospital?"

For a long while Mariasole simply gazed around the room. Clelia thought that perhaps she hadn't heard the question. She was about to repeat it when the woman cleared her throat. She caught Clelia's eye, peered straight at her, and replied: "The only thing wrong with my daughter is that she was born a girl."

Inspector Armati leaned forward. "Why do you say that?"

"Because girls are good at falling in love with the wrong man. Now excuse me, but I'm rather tired and I'd like to rest."

As they left, the two police officers noticed a silver station wagon parked under a canopy in the villa's courtyard. Clelia guessed that it belonged to Mariasole, given that she was currently alone in the house. She wondered what made so many women choose such huge cars.

It was dusk when Commissario Vinci and Inspector Armati left the villa. The sky above the Lido was stained with orange streaks that faded toward the horizon. The rain had finally stopped, but the weather forecast said that high tides would be back again soon.

"When I see sunsets like this, I feel nothing's impossible. Perhaps two people—like you and me—could even fall in love again . . ." said Franco, his eyes fixed on the road ahead.

Clelia didn't respond. At the commissariato, Armati had a reputation as a bit of a charmer. Six years ago he had lost his wife in a horrific car accident, and since then he had not been seriously involved with anyone. At first he had fallen into a deep depression, but then he had begun going out more often with women he described as "friends." People all have their own ways of dealing with their pain, thought Clelia. But Franco was different with her. When he talked to her, his voice became gentler. He was attentive in a way that went beyond the relationship between an inspector and his superior officer. He couldn't help worrying if she was looking anxious. Franco Armati would never have admitted it—not even to himself—but what he felt toward Clelia was very close to love. Clelia was definitely not indifferent to the charms of her colleague, but the only man in her life, Giovanni, had always tried to change her. He had never accepted her work, and he had ended up using their daughter Laura to blackmail her. How many times had Clelia been made to feel that she wasn't a good mother, that she left her daughter on her own too often, or that she brought her most difficult cases home with her? Love—for Clelia Vinci—was a complication and, at this particular moment in her life, there wasn't room for another complication. So she didn't respond.

Once she got home, Clelia heated up a cup of milk and forced herself to eat a few biscuits. She felt on edge and she couldn't help imagining Laura with Giovanni's new family. Who knew if during the weekend Laura would think about her at all.

Clelia read the pathologist's autopsy report: there was no trace of gunpowder on Restivo's index finger, so it was impossible for him to have pulled the trigger of the gun. Someone had made him write a fake suicide note.

IV

"Hi, Annalisa. This is Commissario Vinci and Inspector Armati. They're here to ask you some questions. Is that okay?" the psychologist asked the girl sitting opposite her.

Annalisa had her mother's green eyes, but her stare was vacant. The blankness was that of a child who had grown up too quickly. Blond hair framed her pinched face; her thin lips turned down at the corners and were edged with fine frown lines. She simply nodded, and continued playing with the ring she wore on the ring finger of her left hand.

"Can you tell us about your father, Annalisa?" Clelia began.

"My father is a very bad man."

The commissario glanced at Armati in surprise. Then she asked: "Why is he a bad man?"

"He thinks he can make me forget what he did, with all these pills. The pills keep me quiet, but I'll never forget." She stressed the word *never* as if it were a promise, or a curse.

The psychologist pushed a lock of hair behind her ear and said: "Annalisa, please. Your father loved you. And he's no longer with us. I explained it all to you yesterday, do you remember?"

"He's dead." Annalisa burst out laughing. "He won't be able to hurt anyone anymore." Then she became serious again and turned her head toward Franco. "Roberto had blue eyes, just like yours. He gave me this engagement ring after we'd been together for just a month," she said, stroking the ring that sparkled on her finger. "Are you engaged, inspector?"

Franco swallowed loudly. "Err . . . no," he replied, embarrassed.

"My father killed Roberto. Because he couldn't stand another man touching his baby girl."

"Annalisa, your father didn't kill anyone. You shouldn't talk about him like that." The psychologist's disapproval was visible in her face.

"They asked me to talk about my father, and that's what I'm doing. Do you know what my Roberto always used to say?" She paused for a moment, then pressed her lips together in a faint smile and said: "*Convictions are more dangerous enemies of truth than lies.* It's something Nietzsche said. My father's convictions killed Roberto and imprisoned me here. And now more people will die . . ." She bit her bottom lip and sought Clelia's eyes. "Look for the truth, commissario. Don't be fooled by appearances."

The psychologist frowned at Annalisa. "You're getting upset. You can talk to them when you have more control of yourself." Then, turning to the two police officers, she said: "I'm sorry, but my patient is in no condition to continue with this questioning at the moment. Let's go back to my office."

Clelia saw that there was no point in challenging the woman; it was an ultimatum, not an invitation.

Doctor Sofia Ghelfi had been looking after Annalisa Restivo for a couple of years; her care had begun when the girl returned alone from a trip to Tunisia—her fiancé, Roberto

Milan, had been arrested in Monastir and had then disappeared without a trace. Once they were in her office, the psychologist let out a long sigh. She looked down at the floor, then toward Clelia. "It seems that Roberto was found in possession of drugs at the airport, while Annalisa, thanks to the intervention of the family's lawyer, Lettieri, was brought back home without a criminal record. Since then, Annalisa has blamed her father for the loss of her one great love."

"Love. It's always love that's to blame," Armati muttered.

The psychologist pretended not to have heard. She continued: "Annalisa developed an acute depressive syndrome with a persecution complex, and shortly after her return she was admitted here, where I follow her progress personally. Recently she seemed to have regained an equilibrium, but in the last few days that has vanished."

"In your opinion, what's caused this relapse?"

"Annalisa had a visitor, about a week ago. We don't allow patients to receive phone calls from outside, but the visitor, disobeying our rules, handed her a cell phone. By the time I arrived, Annalisa was in tears and kept shouting Roberto's name."

Clelia's face lit up with a flash of intuition. "I'll need to know the name of the visitor."

"I'll check the records right now." Sofia reviewed a folder and moments later announced: "Francesco Bonifazi."

V

Francesco Bonifazi lived in a small apartment on the edge of Mestre with two other architecture students. He was surprised to find two police officers at the door. He glared at them, full of hostility. "Do you have a warrant?"

"Of course not," Armati replied, annoyed. "We're here unofficially. But, if you prefer, I can call the judge and have you summoned to appear in court for questioning. I can promise you that will be a lot less pleasant."

The boy, dreadlocks hanging down to his shoulders and a stud in his nose, seemed to think about it for a few seconds, then said: "Come in. I was just making coffee."

They entered a kitchenette in which chaos reigned. Unwashed plates were piled up in the sink. On every surface there was a jumble of cans, glasses, and cutlery.

"Let's get straight to the point. Luciano Restivo was killed on Thursday night. I've heard that you visited his daughter Annalisa at the hospital a few days before."

"So what? Can't a person visit an old friend?"

Clelia moved toward Francesco. "Don't take us for idiots. You don't have the time and neither do we. That was the first time in two years you've visited Annalisa. I know you let her take a phone call that upset her. You're in touch with her ex-fiancé—isn't that true?" Although Annalisa maintained that Roberto was dead—and that her father was to blame—Clelia had sensed that this wasn't the case.

Francesco put the coffee pot on the stove. "I've always thought there's no point in talking to the cops. You decide for yourselves what the truth is, and most of the time it's the innocent who are the losers."

"Like Roberto Milan?"

"Exactly. Roberto and Annalisa were crazy about each other, but her dad couldn't accept that a boy with his background, who loved having a good time, could get engaged to his daughter. Tunisia was supposed to be their first holiday, an unforgettable trip." He stopped talking for a moment, then peered directly at Clelia and said: "And in a way, it was. Roberto was framed. Someone hid the drugs in his jacket pocket. The airport police were waiting for him. He was banged up and Annalisa was brought back to Italy by Restivo's bulldog, his lawyer. I think his name is Lettieri."

"You're making some very serious accusations."

"The truth is difficult to hear. And to think that for a second I thought I saw the glimmer of justice in your eyes, commissario."

Clelia Vinci reflected on the fact that in just a couple of days two different people had pointedly asked her to search out the truth. She looked across at her colleague. She had to play her cards right. "We know Roberto Milan came back to Italy." She didn't have any proof, but she decided to follow her instincts. Annalisa's ex-fiancé had a perfect motive for killing Restivo: revenge. She added: "If you know where he is, you have to tell me. We can help him, before he makes any more mistakes."

"So you're accusing him of murder? Don't you think he's already paid enough? And for a crime he didn't even commit."

At that moment the sound of running caught their attention. They heard the click of the front door opening and then it slammed shut.

"Clelia, quick! It's Roberto Milan!" shouted Franco, rushing out into the hall. Without waiting for his colleague, he dived down the steps, holding on tightly to the banister. From the stairwell he managed to glimpse the figure of a boy with long hair and a long beard, wearing an army-green parka. "Stop!" he shouted.

The boy took no notice and ran out of the block of apartments. Franco, ignoring the fact that he was already out of breath, kept running without a pause, until he caught up with him. He flattened the boy against the wall of an old building and, holding him still with one arm against his throat, searched him. He was clean.

"I had nothing to do with it!" Roberto cried out.

"You can tell that to the judge." Franco tightened the handcuffs around his wrists.

VI

"Roberto Milan's still maintaining he's innocent," said Clelia, as if she were thinking aloud.

"He's spent the last few years in prison in Tunisia—do you think he wants to be sent away again?" Franco retorted.

"Still, those aren't the eyes of a murderer. There's regret, like when a love affair ends."

"I didn't think you could be so romantic, Clelia. But come on—we need to stick to the facts. Everything points at Roberto Milan being guilty of murder. Restivo ruined his life, so once he was back in Italy, he faked the man's suicide. Don't forget that he'd spoken with his ex-fiancée just a few days before. Perhaps he hoped he and Annalisa could get back together again, once he'd gotten rid of her father."

"Have you heard anything from Lettieri?"

Franco glanced at his watch. "No. We had an appointment half an hour ago in my office, but he didn't show up. I tried calling his cell, but it's switched off."

"And the office?"

"No one's answering."

"That's odd. At this time of day his law firm should be open. Shall we go and pay him a visit? If I'm not mistaken, the office is in the San Polo district, not far from here."

They boarded the police motorboat and Inspector Armati moved to the controls. The surface of the Grand Canal reflected the palazzi and the moving clouds like a mirror. It struck Clelia that she would never get tired of the magic of Venice. Certain views still took her breath away even though she had marveled at them thousands of times. It happened as they passed under the Ponte degli Scalzi, with its single Istrian stone arch. Franco went slowly, and every now and then he stole a glance at her. Neither of them talked during the journey.

In twenty minutes or so they arrived at Lettieri's offices. The front door was ajar.

"Anybody there?" called out Inspector Armati.

Papers were scattered over the floor of the entrance hall. The phone had been thrown to the ground. A woman's leg was sticking out from behind a desk. Commissario Vinci approached the body and checked the pulse. "She's still alive," she whispered. "Someone must've hit her over the head."

Inspector Armati took out his Beretta and walked slowly toward Lettieri's office, while Clelia, service gun in hand, covered his back, crouching next to the desk.

"It's a mess in here. Come and look," Armati said. The commissario joined him. Enrico Lettieri had been murdered. His body, which was lying faceup on the floor, was covered in stab wounds. There was blood everywhere.

Instinctively, Clelia covered her mouth with her hand.

"The killer went at the victim in a fit of rage," said Franco. "Lettieri tried to defend himself as best he could. See? Multiple cuts on the hands and arms. Then he was struck in the chest and stomach, but the fatal wound was presumably the one to the throat."

"You contact the station, and I'll call an ambulance."

Just before the ambulance arrived, Lettieri's secretary regained consciousness. "They buzzed the intercom," she spluttered. "They said they had to deliver a package and I opened the door. I had my back turned—I was putting a file away—when someone hit me. I felt an excruciating pain in my head. I must've passed out . . ."

"Can you tell us anything about the voice?"

"All I can tell you is that it was a woman's. I can't believe that Signor Lettieri was killed while I was here . . . It's awful," she said, unable to hold back the tears.

"Try to stay calm. You're safe now," Commissario Vinci reassured her, clasping her hand in a motherly way. Then she stood up and looked at Franco. "Roberto Milan is innocent."

"You were right, Clelia. I was wrong about him being the murderer."

"But we weren't wrong about the motive: it's revenge. A revenge someone's thought about for years." Commissario Clelia Vinci pushed a lock of her dark hair behind her ear and frowned.

"What do you mean?" At that instant Inspector Armati's cell phone rang. "It's Rossana, Restivo's secretary," he said, surprised, before answering.

The girl sounded frightened: "Inspector, please! Come here now. I'm scared—"

"Calm down, miss. The important thing is not to open the door to anyone."

"I got a phone call, a threat. They said all the traitors will die and that Lettieri was murdered. It can't be true!"

"I'm afraid it is. We're at his office now—we're still searching it."

"It's not possible! It shouldn't end like this!" she sobbed.

"Rossana, try to stay calm. Tell me exactly what happened."

The girl's agitated breathing could be heard on the other end of the line. After a few seconds of silence, Rossana began talking again: "Me and Luciano were in love. It's not what you think . . . I wasn't with him just because he was someone important. I really loved him, and he loved me too! So much that he'd made up his mind to run away with me."

"What?!" exclaimed Franco. "And why didn't you tell us this before?"

"I was afraid." Rossana explained that no one knew that Restivo's ad agency was going through a difficult time. Before long, Ad Work would have had to declare bankruptcy. So Restivo had falsified the accounts and, with embezzled funds hidden away in a tax haven, he was getting ready to leave Italy with Rossana.

Franco pressed her further: "Who knew about your getaway plans?"

The girl replied: "Only Lettieri."

"Where are you now?"

"I couldn't stay in my apartment in Mestre. I didn't feel safe. I'm at 140/B Calle de la Madonna, near the Rialto Bridge. Luciano bought this penthouse for us to meet. It was our love nest."

"Are you sure that no one else knows about your *nest*?"

"Only Lettieri knew. He told me to keep quiet and not to talk to anyone, but then I got that threatening call. I got scared and I decided to call you."

"You did the right thing. Nothing bad is going to happen to you."

"But it will! They've killed Luciano, Lettieri, and now they're coming after me! They said they know where I am and they'll kill me." She stopped talking suddenly. "Someone's here!" she screamed.

"Rossana, stay calm. Who said they'd kill you? Stay with me, we're on our way!" But the phone had already gone dead. "Let's go!" the inspector barked at Clelia.

On the way to Calle de la Madonna, Franco explained to her what Rossana had said on the phone.

"There's no doubt now—it's clear who's behind these

deaths," the commissario said. "I just hope we're there in time."

"I've told them at the Questura. They said they'll get there as quickly as they can, but there aren't many motorboats available, and we're closest."

As soon as they were near the Rialto Bridge, Franco moored the boat. The famous bridge, with its arcades and white stone, was packed with tourists taking their souvenir photos. Franco held out his hand, helping Clelia to step ashore. They started to run, cutting through the chaotic crowd of passersby. When they reached Calle de la Madonna, they noticed that the front door of 140/B was open. Franco doubled over to catch his breath and Clelia sank back against the wall, gasping.

"Wait here," said Franco after a moment, looking her straight in the eye.

"No. I'm coming with you. It might be dangerous."

"I'd prefer that you stay here and watch my back, in case the killer tries to find a way out."

"I'll be able to watch your back better if I'm just behind you."

"You're so stubborn. Okay then."

With their guns drawn, they headed up the steps. The building seemed deserted. Presumably it was made up of luxury apartments, currently vacant. The elevator wasn't working, or perhaps someone had deliberately tampered with it.

By the time they were outside the apartment, they were both short of breath again. Clelia's hands were sweaty and she had a tightness at the back of her throat. There was a key in the lock. "That must be Luciano Restivo's key," she whispered. "The killer must still be inside."

"Be careful," Franco said quietly to her before sidling into the entrance hall. Perhaps it was in that very instant that Clelia realized how much she cared about him.

As they cautiously approached the living room, a muffled groaning caught their attention. The noise was coming from the room at the end of the hall. Armati burst in, followed by Clelia a step behind. What greeted them was a sight that froze their blood: Mariasole Vincenzi Restivo was on her knees on the bed, her hands fastened tight around Rossana's neck. The girl's eyes were staring, her face turning blue, her tongue protruding.

"Let her go! Now!" shouted Clelia, pointing her gun at Mariasole.

The woman looked up, loosening her grip. Rossana started coughing.

"Move away from the bed with your hands up."

Mariasole seemed to come out of a trance. She glanced around her, as if she didn't understand where she was, and she let go. Slowly, she slid across the covers until she reached the window. "We women are so good at choosing the wrong man," she murmured. She grabbed the handle of the window frame and opened the shutters.

"Don't do anything stupid," said Commissario Vinci in a firm but gentle tone of voice.

"I gave Luciano everything. My youth, my beauty. A daughter. He was no one, but with my money he was able to make his way in society." Mariasole's face was a mask of pain. "And now he wanted to leave me. He was bankrupt. He would've run off to the tropics to enjoy life with that slut of a secretary, while I would have been left here. They would have taken everything from me to pay his debts. Even the house that my father built and loved so much. But I discovered everything, and I wouldn't let him hurt us again."

"No one's going to hurt you anymore. We're here now, to help you."

"No one can help me. It's too late. My husband was a bad man. He made my daughter ill—did you know that? He took away the love of her life, but even then I was able to forgive him. Not this time. This time he's paid, and all the others had to pay as well."

Clelia realized that Mariasole was about to do something rash. She started to advance slowly toward her, moving around the bed. "Just take it easy," she said, but her words were lost in a gust of cold air. Mariasole looked at her helplessly. Clelia saw the glimmer of green in her eyes that must have made her so beautiful when she was young. Mariasole threw herself out of the open window.

Clelia rushed forward, trying to grab hold of her, but it was useless.

A thud, then silence.

VII

The sunset blazed in scarlet streaks against the leaden sky behind the psychiatric hospital in Marghera. The Bora had returned, and the howling of the wind echoed through the branches of the trees. Clelia, breathless, got out of the police car and started to run toward the entrance. Behind her, Franco struggled to keep up.

Roberto Milan was sitting on the steps, staring down at the ground. In front of him passed two nurses with a stretcher carrying a body covered by a white sheet. They loaded the stretcher into the back of an ambulance where a small group of hospital employees had gathered. Clelia made her way through the crowd to where Dr. Sofia Ghelfi was standing.

"What's happened?"

The psychologist studied her for a long while before replying. Then she murmured: "I don't know how it could have happened. Annalisa . . . she found a newspaper . . . There was something about Roberto Milan being arrested—"

"She must have thought history was repeating itself," Clelia interrupted. "That people like them don't get a second chance at happiness."

"She cut her wrists sometime before dawn. She used a bread knife; it's possible she took it from the kitchen."

"She couldn't have known that her boyfriend was being released this morning."

"She was such a sweet girl. I can't believe it . . ." Dr. Ghelfi couldn't hold back a sob. "Excuse me," she cried out, hurriedly retreating toward the doors of the hospital.

Franco shook his head. "Mother and daughter, both of them ended up the same way."

Clelia moved closer to Roberto Milan. She bent down, trying to look him in the eye. He didn't return her gaze. He just said: "For two years all I've done is dream about the moment when I'd hold Annalisa in my arms again. But I couldn't protect her from the world. Or from herself." Clelia laid a hand on his shoulder. Roberto shrank from her touch. "Is this the kind of justice you joined the police for? Your law should have protected Annalisa. And instead it's killed her." The boy's voice trembled with rage.

Clelia noticed that he was wearing a silver ring, identical to the one Annalisa had worn. She remembered what the girl had said: Roberto had given her the ring only a month after they had gotten together. Clelia couldn't help thinking that the ring—representing the promise they had made to each other—had become the symbol of a shattered love affair. "I'm sorry," she murmured.

Franco came closer and took her arm for a moment. "We should go," he said. Indeed, there was no reason for them to stay. They went back to the car and headed full speed in silence toward the Ponte della Libertà. Commissario Clelia Vinci stared stubbornly at the landscape beyond the car window. It wasn't just an innocent girl who had died that day, but also the hope she had clung to that—despite all the suffering and death—something good could be salvaged.

When they arrived at the Questura, Franco invited her into his office. He closed the door behind her and began to speak: "Sometimes things don't turn out the way we want. You've got nothing to blame yourself for, Clelia."

"Thanks for saying that, but it's not true," she replied. She paused, then: "Certain people come into the world like shooting stars. You look up at the sky and all that's left is a shining trail. Sometimes I wonder why I chose this job."

"You chose it so you could keep your father's dream alive. Your dream, Clelia."

"My dream's becoming a nightmare. Or perhaps it's just all this wind; bit by bit it's taking my soul."

Franco took a step toward her, but Clelia stopped him. "Sorry. My daughter's waiting for me at home. I think I've already neglected her far too much recently. And for what?"

Franco stood motionless, watching the silhouette of his boss disappearing down the corridor.

A few days later, Clelia took her daughter to Murano. The days were getting longer and the air brought with it the first signs of a biting spring that seemed intent on sweeping away the ghosts of the winter.

The church of Santi Maria e Donato rose up in front of them in all its grandeur. Light glinted off the red bricks and the white marble columns. Clelia sat down on a bench and helped Laura put on her rollerblades. Then she pulled a package out of her coat pocket. She unwrapped it to reveal the small crystal unicorn they had bought a few minutes before in one of the glassblowers' workshops. She gazed at the blue shimmer of its coat, its outstretched wings, and the mane that seemed to be tousled by a never-ending breeze.

Laura started skating backward and forward in the large square, waving her arms and shouting to attract her mother's attention. Her voice sounded muffled by the time it reached Clelia.

Clelia looked at her and forced a smile.

LITTLE SISTER

BY FRANCESCA MAZZUCATO

Ghetto Vecchio

Translated from Italian by Judith Forshaw

The Old Ghetto. That's the name of the area where she lives, but if anyone asks she says she lives near Cannaregio. She doesn't like saying the word *ghetto*. Some words are too blunt, too aggressive, and because of their meaning they are left unspoken. She knows that ghettos exist but she doesn't want to use that name. And she knows that we create them, we invent them, and there are lots of people who choose to live in them out of fear. In fact, she is always on her own, she has an unvarying routine that she follows every day, and she inhabits what she calls in her head her personal ghetto, a ghetto constructed with painstaking care. It's about having a boundary. She walks along it and never attempts to cross it. She has lived like this for so many years and it works for her. Or rather, she has made it work for her. It is a fundamental issue.

She lives in a tiny house that gives off lots of different smells; they change depending on the day, her mood, the weather, the amount of work she has to do. She has always been hypersensitive to smells. Smells and flavors are subjective, they have no independent reality. She didn't know that before she discovered the kaleidoscope of different sensations and different reactions that produce all the various smells that emanate from people, from the boats loaded with fish, and even from the streets, bridges, and squares of the city. She has always wanted to live here, in this particular area of Venice. She could have chosen many other places and she could still change her mind. There's nothing keeping her here. She can't go back, that's for certain, but she can, if she wants, move somewhere else. Relocate, if she wants. With so many different cities to choose from, sometimes the idea pops into her head, but the next second it vanishes: she can't. She feels complete here, even in her solitude. In the voluntary prison she's lived in for years.

My neighbors must have been cooking vegetables, revolting vegetables, there's a disgusting smell on the landing, damn them, their complete lack of respect makes me shudder, I'm going to be sick, I'm running to the bathroom.

She works most of the day and often at night as well; she doesn't mind working hard or that she doesn't do specific things at specific times. Sometimes she loses track of the time and isn't sure if it is afternoon or evening, or which day it is. She forgets to eat. Apart from working, she puts load after load of washing in the machine because she likes watching it going around, the motion hypnotizes her; she reads romances, imagining lives that are outside her own experience and seem heavy with exotic, exaggerated emotion. Or else she lights scented candles. Only certain types. Perfumes she can tolerate and that make her feel good. She has carried out various experiments over the years. When those experiments have failed she has suffered the consequences. Now she knows perfectly the fragrances she doesn't merely tolerate but that have a positive effect on her mood. She fills the house with them, as well as with incense sticks. She loves incense. She knows she is surrounded by a very strong protective force. It can be a ghetto, but it can also be a shrine. She shapes it herself.

I can still see myself as a little girl with Plasticine and clay, I liked making things, I liked molding lots of different shapes, and I liked the smell of the clay, I've never come across such a lovely smell, other smells can be so insignificant, a void, even unpleasant or overwhelming, mortuary smells.

All she needs is a computer, a stack of paper, and plenty of Biro pens that she arranges methodically next to her keyboard. On the left are two pencils and a sharpener. She works on the Internet; she writes content for blogs and other people's websites and manages various social networks for businesses. Her psychologist advised her to take a break and sharpen a pencil when work gets too stressful. She wasn't expecting advice like that. She didn't know what she was expecting, but it wasn't that. It has to be said that the psychologist doesn't know very much about her, though he spoke with enviable confidence.

"Do it slowly, as if it's the most important thing in the world, and do it consciously."

She thought about it a bit then bought two pencils, and every now and then she follows the psychologist's advice. She stops and sharpens. When he suggested it, making it sound almost like a matter of life and death, she had to stop herself from laughing—it seemed banal, ridiculous, pointless, childish; how on earth could she fight stress by sharpening pencils? And yet it's vital. It works. With time she has come to realize that.

There are lots of different websites for which she writes copy. Agritourism, hunting and fishing. She populates the pages of *Venezia per voi*, a local online magazine that pays really badly, but is just about enough to get her budget to balance; yet it's totally unrewarding work, so when she finishes a job for them, she stops, takes a deep breath, and then sharpens a pencil. She has to. She thinks they're crazy. Writing about Venice is absurd. Venice is something you live, you don't write about it, or even photograph it; Venice is an idea, a hologram, a refraction.

Venice is a transgression, fate. She knows that. She knows it was *her* fate, and she is resigned to it.

They think they're so trendy and so up-to-date, but this site is crap, I chose Venice because I was desperate but I was drawn in by its spell, and the mysterious gloom of the lagoon that resembles my thoughts so closely, one day I'll write an article with the headline "We're Crap," I'll put it online then I'll disappear off the radar, changing all the passwords first. I should do it as soon as possible, I know, but the money they pay me comes in handy. (Smells of kosher cooking from the restaurant below again, I understand why, of course I do, but how come they have to conspire? Don't they know that their smells CONSPIRE against my well-being? They must realize that, damn them.)

She follows the advice of her psychologist and very slowly sharpens the yellow and black pencils; the points often break when she underlines something in one of the books taken from the towering pile on the floor. The volumes are next to a black bookcase, plain and hard-worn, that has stayed with her through so many moves, including this final one to Venice. The pile is balanced precariously, and sometimes she knocks the books to the ground deliberately.

The bookcase itself is perfectly organized, almost obsessively so, with books divided by subject and in alphabetical order. There's a reason behind this: every day she refers to the books stacked up on the floor, picking out ideas for websites and other matters—it's not that she copies things, she just needs inspiration and then she uses her imagination and her creativity. They come in handy; the content of the blogs she puts online is very straightforward, they don't need much: sometimes she makes things up without any help, but sometimes she draws a total blank and gets stuck, so she looks for inspiration. It's legitimate, after all; she changes a couple of words and, hey presto, the tone changes in a tweet, or LinkedIn, or the Facebook profile of a company or a publishing group.

She chooses the appropriate words with care. Words like *transgression, live the message, chimera, corroded, snagged, dilemma.* Words that lend themselves to so many different interpretations. She selects them. When she has filled in the profile, when she has tweeted on behalf of the publisher of books on Jewish history, when she has populated a site or a blog with content, she looks at what she has done and is pleased with the result. *Chimera* is a wild-card word she uses for various business types. *Trend* is another.

Dilemma also has its uses, which is only natural. There can't be anyone who has never faced a dilemma.

Words smell good, words hide infinite meanings, words are Rubik's Cubes, Christmas snow globes—snow falls if you turn them upside down—words are perfect, you can use them to improve reality, they aren't like acrid body odors that flood your nose and brain: if you could simply live among words, inside them, life would be a wonderful dream, now I'll sharpen pencils, I know it's the right time, first I'll find another two words, balance *and* run-up, *I'll dust them off and there they are, perfect for slipping into various* contexts. Flexible, benign, and sterile. Just words. Nothing more. Why do I even have to live in the real world?

She asks herself this as she types furiously on the keyboard, her fingertips—especially at night—feel worn out, they become sore and cracked, they sometimes bleed. Sometimes she cuts herself and makes her fingers bleed on purpose; it's her way of feeling like a martyr. Blood. It drips copiously from a wound on her big toe and she looks at it. It's not good. It makes her have strange thoughts. So she goes out. She goes outside and walks along the Strada Nova to the Santi Apostoli church to admire the Tiepolo. She used to be able to gaze at it for hours, she didn't need to sharpen pencils, she wasn't so sensitive to smells, and she didn't feel like she lived in a ghetto. Now she stays for two minutes at most. Even in the church there are smells she doesn't like, and often there are people who reek. She doesn't understand how people can go and look at the Tiepolo while giving off such a disgusting stink.

I can't help it, it's one of those moments, I touch myself, I trawl special websites with animated GIFs where I watch all sorts of sexual acts repeated on an endless loop, it's the one sexual activity I'm allowed here, in my personal ghetto, in this virtual world where I often pretend to be something other than what I really am. I stay at my desk as if I am working, I watch those mindless, monotonous penetrations, and I let my hand drop down between my legs, inside my clothes. By this stage it doesn't take much. I linger over details, I examine them minutely, I concentrate on a huge, erect member, on a breast, on a mouth, and before long I reach an orgasm, solitary and all mine. Solitary and with no smells or tastes. It's perfect. Simply perfect, even if afterward, every time, I furiously sharpen both pencils. I need to buy two more for backup so I always have them ready.

* * *

It's been years since she has had a boyfriend but she doesn't feel any need for one. She couldn't bear having to get used to a man's smell again. Sometimes she goes to visit her one female friend. A Chinese girl who works in a restaurant on the edge of Cannaregio. She calls her Anna; she doesn't know how to pronounce her Chinese name, nor does she care. She knows that all—or almost all—Italians call her Anna. The only Italians who use her Chinese name are the ones who want to pretend they're not racist.

She became her friend to rescue her. In the girl's parents' restaurant she has inhaled some of the most disgusting smells she has ever known and has felt them seeping into her skin. Uniquely revolting. Something indescribable.

The first time when—without thinking—she ate there, she ran out and threw up in the street. That slimy food, for sad people with no sense of taste or smell, made her feel humiliated. It often happens to her, all it takes is one little thing and she becomes aware of a burning sense of humiliation that she struggles to control.

Anna has to work there but she would like to study and she loves music. At 2040 Cannaregio in Campiello Vendramin stands Palazzo Vendramin Calergi. Because of its perfect symmetry the palazzo is considered the greatest expression of the Renaissance in Venice. The design of the palazzo was entrusted to Mauro Codussi in the sixteenth century and, during the two hundred years that followed, it became a template for other grand Venetian houses. The great composer Richard Wagner stayed in the palazzo, and died there on February 13, 1883. She always takes Anna there: "Let's go and see Richard," she says. And she feels she's doing a good deed.

However, Anna stinks of restaurant smells when they get

to the palazzo. It isn't her fault, poor thing, but she can't help noticing. She's more tolerant with Anna than she is with any other human being, though Anna doesn't ask for tolerance, nor does she feel the need to talk too much. She knows she's a bit strange and often sullen. Anna likes her because she gives her an excuse to have a break from work, but there is something that puzzles her about her friend's behavior: she never eats with them, not even when her mother makes Peking duck, one of her most delicious recipes that their regular customers adore. She doesn't even think about it; she refuses without looking anyone in the eye, shrugs her shoulders, and says: "I'm going back to the ghetto."

A bloody fucking shower, next time I'll make her understand that if she doesn't get into the habit of taking a bloody fucking shower before she comes out for a walk with me, and there's one next to that disgusting bathroom in the restaurant, I'll stop coming around to take her out and save her, she MUST know that I'm saving her, she doesn't seem to understand anything, perhaps because she's Chinese, but she's the only human being I have any real contact with, I'm not asking for much, just a bloody shower before she nods that perverse baby face and agrees to meet up again.

Venice, interior, night. She is at her desk, as usual, and her head's spinning.

She has to get up and stretch. She's been at her desk for hours and she's done nothing but type in order to meet a deadline. She looks out of the window at the gasoline-blue night that has enveloped the ghetto and makes the city look like the lagoon and the lagoon look like the city.

She has just built a fan page on Facebook for a third-rate singer who performs in sleazy clubs.

She listened to a couple of songs. She thought they were insulting. You can't spoil the grandeur of Venice with that type of pointless music; she immediately stopped the CD. Regardless, she accepts every piece of work, more than ever before. Absolutely everything. She doesn't choose. She used to, and she has a flashback to that time. To those moments when she felt clear-headed and present and not alone.

I take the pills I have to take in the morning and the world stops seeming so hostile, I take the pills, I line them up, some are small and white and others are so big that I have to break them into pieces to swallow them, but they were very clear, without these pills my obsession with smells will return. At first they'll be generic smells, they could be disgusting or delicious and they could carry on for years, but sooner or later I'll go back to suddenly smelling the mortuary smell, and then it's all over. They've told me that. We have to keep you far away from that smell, you know that. Yes, I know. That smell will destroy you. You saw your sister in the mortuary and it was a real smell. At least it seemed real to you, but mortuaries have no smell. That one had a smell, it got into me and it lives inside me. And then I read up on it: mortuaries reek of formaldehyde, of decay and rotting flowers. Especially flowers. The doctor lied to me. Don't worry about that smell, with the medication we'll make it go away. Of course we will; it's okay. You have an olfactory hypersensitivity. It's not a good thing. Well, sometimes it is, but don't worry about it. Your sister. What are you trying to tell me? Your sister . . . there was an incident, that man attacked her and stabbed her, it shouldn't have happened. I agree. It shouldn't have happened, it really shouldn't have. It's a terrible tragedy for a young girl like you, but you'll see that time can be an excellent healer. But what were they talking about, healer and time? It didn't turn out like that.

* * *

With the medication, at one time, the ghetto around her used to fade, and sometimes she was even able to accept the fact that the terrible attack had happened to her sister, who was only twenty years old. Her beloved, extraordinary sister, cheerful and living life to the fullest, funny and intelligent. Well, she didn't totally accept it, to be honest; she always used to think that destiny, fate, or the god she had stopped believing in had been dreadfully unfair. That life had sunk its teeth into her, with exceptional cruelty. That she had been wounded irreparably. All the more so because the only person she had was her sister, and a boyfriend she dumped immediately after the tragedy. They had lost their parents very young. Someone in the city where they lived, and whose name she didn't want to remember, used to call them "the little orphans" but they would shrug it off and they only needed each other. That was certainly true. And it was nice to need just each other. When her sister was around she had never felt all alone like she does now. She had never needed to sharpen pencils, or stop when she was supposed to be entering the updated resume of a manager looking for work on LinkedIn.

That bitch on the floor below has overdone the perfume again, she's drenched in it, it's making me retch, it wasn't enough to arrange for her cat to disappear, and make her so crazy that she's still looking for it, pathetic, putting up posters on the lampposts, looking for Lulu, yes, you've got your work cut out trying to find her, I throttled Lulu and threw her in the lagoon where no one will ever find her. She was a stupid stinking cat, just like her owner, but since that wasn't enough for her, I'll have to think of something else, we'll see.

Venice, interior, night, she is sharpening pencils furiously but it doesn't help, she feels like she's a nonreturnable bottle, a free sample with no commercial value. She's afraid. She's afraid that THAT smell will come back. She doesn't want it to, but she knows she can't do anything about it. If she takes the medication that stops her from being aware of it, it's like she's being unfaithful to the memory of her sister, like forgetting about her; if the smell has to come back, it will. She is fatalistic in that sense. *Fatalistic* is a good word, very ambiguous. It refers to fate. And fate has treated her very badly, so much so that she has had to take it out on Lulu, and on the old caretaker of the building where she and her sister used to live. "Poor little orphan, life must be tough now that you're on your own, eh?"

Of course life's tough, you old fuck, I'll show you what I mean, I'm coming into your house, a house that reeks of old flesh, rotten teeth, and death, I'm coming in and asking for a bit of sugar, putting on the adorable expression of a poor little orphan, and you'll ask me if I want some of your disgusting cordial and while you go and get it for me I'll do what I have to do, taking you by the throat because you stink of decay and I can smell it, and anyway I'm leaving for Venice tomorrow and no one will be able to connect me to you and your death, I'm going too far away.

She sharpens and sharpens, she has just finished masturbating as she watched a really short video; this time there was a woman being treated like a slave who was eating from a bowl like a dog, an exceptionally violent S&M video, and she got so aroused that she cried out as she came, something she never does, but the violence of what she saw lit up hundreds of tiny imaginary lightbulbs around her, as if there were a swarm of fireflies in the room.

And every lightbulb had a smell, including just a hint of THAT smell.

You will never have to smell it again, don't ever forget to take your medication, of course, doctor, thank you very much, and remember that it's your imagination that creates the smell, there is no mortuary smell and you really can't smell it (still the same lie).

Of course, doctor, but doesn't that mean I'll stop feeling that my sister's with me? No, of course not, you'll remember her in your heart.

My heart. How stupid people are, spouting nonsense about the heart. She updates the content of a website for soulmates and uploads an article on a portal that recommends alternative tourist routes *for anyone planning their Valentine's Day.* It's a weird evening, she can feel it. It's an evening charged with a different fate. She's finding it hard to get a grip, she's aware that even her movements are clumsier than usual. She falls, she gets up again. Her head aches and her bones are sore. And that's not all. She's hungry. She knows that this late in Venice there isn't much choice. And the smell is getting stronger. Venice isn't a metropolis, she doesn't want to go too far, she could pop into Anna's Chinese restaurant. Yes, that's the only solution. She could have some plain rice, or simply pick up Anna and they could head off to some old osteria that would have something nicer. Will Anna have taken a shower? While she's thinking about that she opens the drawer where she keeps her kitchen utensils and strokes them one by one; they're beautiful. She has a collection of knives that she ordered from a TV ad. ("Poor little orphan, you're right to think about defending yourself," they said to her in that other city, the one whose name—and everything else—she has erased from her mind.) They were delivered to her after just a few days, surprisingly few. Straight away she thought they were beautiful. Wonderful knives with wooden handles and blades just how she wanted them. Exactly like the ones she'd seen so many times in her nightmares. She takes one and puts it in her bag. It's incredibly sharp. Perfect. She's hungry. Will it be enough to stop at the Chinese place? Will she be able to control herself? Plain rice perhaps? She doubts it. She cleans her teeth twice and rinses three times with mouthwash, her usual ritual. She goes out and the ghetto embraces her with its remote beauty, but she doesn't want to be embraced. Nocturnal Venice would embrace her too, cities are able to do that, but she feels the embrace would distance her from the smell and she doesn't want to drive it away. She brushes off the embrace of the city like someone would brush off an annoying fly. She sways slightly. Her fingertips are still sore, she imagines a trail of blood following her.

The Chinese restaurant is still open. With her left hand she caresses the knife in her bag, and she feels her cell phone and purse to make sure she's got them with her, a habitual check she almost always does. She could wait. Perhaps she should. She could go on working and go on sharpening pencils whenever she feels uneasy. Stay in her personal ghetto. Instead she does it. She touches her nose with her right hand. Then she lets it fall with an abrupt movement. She doesn't say hello to Lulu's owner who is still putting up posters: *If anyone has seen this cat, please phone xxx. Reward offered.*

You were only twenty, you were restless, fickle, and beautiful, you were my family and they want me to stop feeling you near me but I can't let them do that, you will always be with me; you do know that, my darling? I'm nothing if you're not near me, my life is noth-

ing, I miss you and I missed feeling you close as I do now, there's the smell, your very last perfume, yes, it's really there, I can smell it, it's only right that this is how it is, none of the doctors I met understood anything, they wanted to control me, control my sense of smell, my mind, my emotions, but they didn't succeed, you'd be proud of me, little sister.

She goes into the Chinese restaurant and waves at Anna's mother. Anna walks toward her.

"I'm hungry. Do you want to come to the osteria near the bridge?"

"Don't you want something here?"

"No, you know I don't really like Chinese food."

"Okay, wait a minute while I get my bag."

Anna had walked close by her, very close, and she had definitely been aware of something: she hadn't taken a shower.

Don't worry about me, little sister, everything's all right, you're still near me.

PART II

SHADOWS OF THE PAST

PART II

LIDO WINTER

BY MAXIM JAKUBOWSKI

Lido

T he vaporetto turns the bend.

You've seen it in countless paintings by Canaletto, Turner, and others, a thousand and one photographs and movies and TV documentaries, but still the eternal view unfolds like a slow-motion epiphany.

The Grand Canal in all its majesty. Canal Grande.

Moving past the Ponte degli Scalzi, the choppy waters flowing all the way downstream toward the Rialto Bridge that looms in the gray distance, the crumbling stone outposts on either shore like parallel rows of zombie guests at a wedding waiting for the bride and groom to troop past and be assaulted by clouds of confetti, the domes of churches in the hinterlands, the procession of palazzi straight from the pages of history and guidebooks: Gritti, Dona Balbi, Zen, Marcello Toderini, Calbo Crotta, Flangini, Giovanelli, and on and on, like a litany of open-mouthed operatic celebrations of decay and grandeur, the sound of water lapping in the wake of the vaporetto's passage, the unique smells of La Serenissima, gulls above observing your steady journey toward the open spaces of the lagoon, past the markets, and finally the Ponte dell'Accademia and onward beyond Piazza San Marco and the Doge's Palace and into the murky emptiness that separates the principal part of the city from the nearby islands.

It's not the first time you've made this journey, but it always takes your breath away as the façades unrolling on both sides of your field of vision steadily unveil centuries and more of history, of stories imagined and read about. Of classic movies. Of books. Stories that stick in your throat and in your mind like rough diamonds full of fury.

The hiccuping engine of the vaporetto guides you into open waters past the final promontory of the Giudecca, beyond the tip of San Giorgio Maggiore, and cuts through a cluster of lingering mist, heading for the fast-approaching line of land of the Lido.

He wraps the black cashmere scarf tighter around his open collar as the marine breeze makes its coldness felt. Looks around. Since the San Marco stop, there is just a handful of passengers left on the vaporetto. Mostly locals with bulging shopping bags, a couple of teenagers busy texting on pink cell phones, hopefully not to each other, a well-dressed businessman of some sort whose hairpiece is an uncomfortable match for his russet moustache.

And sitting right at the back, lost in distant dreams of an unfathomable nature, the young woman. He'd distractedly noticed her boarding the vaporetto at the Santa Lucia train station, running down the stone steps toward the embarcation point, holding her bag in one hand, her golden hair flowing behind her. It was just about to leave and she'd only caught it with a few seconds to spare.

Her green mac is now unbuttoned, displaying the violent fire of a red sweatshirt over skinny black jeans. Even though, like him, she is obviously a tourist, she appears different. As if she belongs here somehow amongst the cold breeze of the lagoon.

And come to think of it, how does Jonathan appear to onlookers? Just a tourist with no luggage. A man with wild gray hair curling out of control, his stocky frame bulked up within a heavy brown leather coat. Middle-aged, unremarkable.

The vaporetto shudders to a slow halt in front of the pier, and the passengers disembark. Jonathan is in no hurry and allows the locals to stream past him before he even rises from his wooden seat. As he steps off onto the island, he gives a final look back at the vaporetto. The young woman is no longer sitting in the rear, although he had somehow not noticed her overtaking him. Strange. He looks ahead at the small tree-lined piazza, which hosts the vaporetto station. The other passengers are dispersing in two or three separate directions but there is no sign of her. He sighs and mentally speculates how tall she had actually been. Her posture had reminded him of Kathleen. Who'd been five feet eleven. And lithe and clumsy and surprisingly submissive between the sheets. Jonathan sighs again as memories come streaming back in a torrent before he deliberately cuts them off. Now is not the time.

He looks ahead. The piazza is empty, like a set for a ghost town in a movie. Shuttered cafés on both corners of the main road which, he remembers, leads a few miles farther down to the beaches. And the big hotels and casinos.

But somehow it now appears so different, as if his memory is playing tricks on him and he hadn't actually been here all those years back.

A car crosses the piazza in front of him at a low speed and it's something of a shock, a disconnect. You just don't expect cars in Venice. But he reminds himself this is the Lido and not Venice itself. A random thought occurs to him: Do they ship the cars in from somewhere? How?

Jonathan then recalls the forgotten fact that Giulietta had come here by car once. At film festival time. There is some ferry that comes in from somewhere on the mainland, but he can't precisely remember where from.

That was when they'd met.

She'd conducted a brief interview with him in London. She hadn't made too much of an impression on him at the time. But during the course of the following months, they had begun corresponding. About one thing or another. Gradually the tone of the exchange had become personal and soon they had tacitly agreed that they would meet again in Venice at the film festival and both knew they would become lovers.

His initial surprise was that she was so much taller than she had been in his memory. And uncannily beautiful too.

She'd driven there in her father's camper with a girlfriend who had managed to get them a press pass through an uncle who worked for RAI. Had found an isolated area near Mala-mocco to park at night toward the southern tip of the island. Not that Giulietta ever slept there at night, being in his bed until the early hours of each morning when the screenings began, some of which they would attend together, sometimes holding hands in the darkness.

Behind him the vaporetto leaves, cutting through the wa-ters, returning to Venice. Jonathan glances around. A long road disappears ahead, in all likelihood leading toward the Lungomare, he remembers. All roads south on the Lido in-variably reach the Lungomare, the Adriatic.

He sets off. Was it the second or third turn to the left? He tries both and is soon lost. Every small turn off the main road looks alike. Unable to find the small hotel where they had first fucked. Is it because in winter everything here seems different? He stumbles his way back to the main road. There is no one around he can ask for directions and he can't get a connection on his iPhone and search Google Maps.

The cold breeze is insidiously finding its way through his heavy leather coat. He shivers as every bone in his body protests.

"You took a wrong turn."

Jonathan swivels around.

It's the young woman from the vaporetto. Out of nowhere.

He looks her straight in the eye. She holds his stare, her painted Mona Lisa lips fixed in a semblance of irony.

"How would you know?" he queries.

"I know," she says.

"You've been here before? Do you live here?"

"I just know," she says.

From the moment he first heard her voice, he has been glued to the spot. He feels an ache in his right hip. Her eyes are ice green, deep wells of certainty.

"Okay," he says.

"Follow me." The young woman's voice is transatlantic, impossible to pinpoint. She could as easily be British or American, or even from elsewhere, the words carefully modulated, the product of expensive elocution lessons maybe.

She takes a long, almost manly stride toward the curb and Jonathan follows her. Her hair shimmers in the winter breeze, curls sprouting in every direction like a crowd of thorns. He calls out to her, "I'm Jonathan, by the way . . ."

She nods, as if she already knows this.

"What is your name?" he persists.

She turns her head around toward him and smiles gently, as if hesitant to reveal her true identity.

"My name doesn't matter," she finally says, and increases her pace. They are now walking down a narrow tree-bordered street of high brick walls and concealed gardens. It's all beginning to look familiar to Jonathan. He digs his gloved hands deep down into the pockets of his coat. How can it be so damn

cold in Venice of all places? He'd somehow never associated
Venice with this sort of weather.

Her slim ankles dance ahead of him as she makes her way
through the narrow Lido backstreets.

You had come to Venice in search of memories. Traces, images, thoughts of Giulietta somehow persistently lingering in
your mind from the time you had spent together here. Over
the past couple of months you had already roamed the winter pavements of Paris, Barcelona, Amsterdam, New Orleans,
Seattle, and New York on a similar pilgrimage to recapture a
past that was fast fading into the untouchable distance of time
and could no longer be held between your useless fingers. Not
just frozen shards of Giulietta, but of all the other women you
had known; some loved, some desired, lusted after, all lost or,
at any rate, left behind in the ebb and swirl of the ever-flowing
tides of feelings and dissolving days. The headlines and para-
graphs of what had been your life.

You could feel it in your bones: the night was coming.

Slowly but surely.

All-conquering.

And this was your pathetic way of raging against the falling darkness. Your only way.

Some would have called it ridiculous, but in a curious way
it all made sense. It was the sort of minor theatrical gesture
that the characters in the books and movies that touched you
most would do. There was even a French novel later made
into a film where the central character had done just that
before committing suicide. But his wandering peregrinations
had merely carried him through Paris, visiting acquaintances
on both sides of the Seine; men, women, past friends. You
had watched the movie over a dozen times when still in your

twenties. Not that you had any intention of topping yourself, of course, but wasn't there something so damn romantic about the idea of such a hopeless quest in search of the past and its parade of unforgettable women? And you were weak and so prone to giving in to temptations of every nature.

In your bones: the dull pain of a recurring toothache, the dizziness that swamped your senses on unwelcome occasions, the creaking in your joints, the hairs growing out of your nose and ears that you waged a losing battle against with your faithful set of tweezers, the shortness of breath, the blurriness in your vision when you woke in the mornings (this despite two cataract operations), the white pubic hairs sprouting on the left-hand side of your shriveled cock, the tired posture you witnessed all too often in the bathroom mirror, the tangled strands of gray hair that increasingly got caught in your brush, the incessant tiptoeing down the dimly lit corridor to relieve the pressure on your bladder at night, the tiredness that came so easily, the increasing unattractiveness of your aging body. But most of all, the terrible acceptance that, these days, there was nothing to look forward too any longer.

Yes, night was calling and its dark melody was becoming all too magically seductive to you.

Your travel agent had found you this exquisite small boutique hotel on the Lido, lost in a jungle of luxuriant shrubbery, a few minutes off the Via Marco Polo. Every room was full of antique furniture, heavy brocade, and curtains, like traveling back into an earlier century of indolence. It was a quarter of an hour's walk from there to the festival screenings held in a palatial congress center by the sea.

You had arranged to meet up with Giulietta after the opening movie. Prior to the screening you both had invitations to a formal dinner but were seated at different tables, far apart. She had been wearing a dress with an open back and your heart had experienced a pang of jealous pain on every occasion her neighbor at the table, a Rome editor she occasionally penned freelance pieces for, distractedly allowed his damn fingers to stray across her skin in a gesture of both affection and, it appeared to you, ownership.

You had, finally, made your way back in silence to your hotel. It had been a warm, humid September night. God only knew what she could be thinking, having rashly agreed some weeks before by e-mail to join a man she barely knew in his bed, a man double her age.

Maybe something buried deep inside your uncertainties was already telling you Giulietta would be your last adventure and you had to seize the day and not look such a gift horse in the mouth. What you didn't know is how she would make your heart melt, and how you would fall in love with her and turn all over again into a stumbling teenager in the thrall of it all.

Venice nights: Giuli's lanky body, the dark colors of the hotel room's heavy curtains, the tight dark curls of her pubes, the smell of her skin, her silences (and yours . . .), the sweat and intoxicating odors of lovemaking, halting breaths, sighs, cries. Early-morning yawns, open windows, and the smell of magnolia seeping in from the overgrown gardens outside, dark coffee in bed and vaporetto trips for mornings in the city, walks across a hundred bridges to discover a wildness of churches, the Arsenale, the grounds of the Biennale, further coffees in a small bar on Campo Santa Maria Formosa that Donna Leon had recommended, Bellinis at a bar that Hemingway had allegedly written about, an expensive meal at Florian's which all the guidebooks insisted should not be missed.

Late-morning screenings back on the Lido and then aimless afternoons hand in hand getting lost in the maze of La Serenissima, away from the familiar tourist tracks, the Ghetto, San Polo.

One evening, Giulietta wanted to go to the casino and was refused entry as the burly doorman would not believe she was over eighteen—yes, she did look that young—and she had left her passport and identity papers in your room. Giulietta laughed aloud but you blushed more than she did. Dirty old man caught with under-age prey! The bouncer's steely eyes pierced you through and through.

Neither of you filed much copy about the films in the competition and the Venice Nights section that year . . .

The exiguous lobby of Villa Stella is empty. When they enter the grounds of the hotel, Jonathan immediately recognizes the place. The overgrown gardens, the clean-cut façade.

Little has changed.

"Come," the young blond woman beckons him, as she lifts the oak panel that separates the granite-topped registration counter from the common area. She slides elegantly between the counter and a high-backed chair and turns to the wall where the room keys all hang and takes one. Maybe she is staying here, which would explain her relaxed familiarity? But how could she have known it was this specific hotel he was seeking?

"It's out of season," she says, as if answering Jonathan's question.

"And you have the run of the place?"

"You could say that." An enigmatic smile spreads across her lips.

She opens the door to the hotel room and Jonathan flinches.

"Oh . . ."

"What is it?" the young woman asks.

"Have you done this on purpose?"

"What?"

"This particular room?"

"I took the first key at random," she answers, the expression on her face unchanged. "There are only twelve rooms. One chance in twelve," she adds.

Jonathan shrugs his shoulders, content to go along with the fable.

The room is frozen in time, conjuring up too many memories and images sharp enough to puncture his heart and soul. All of a sudden, he loses his resolve.

"Would you mind if we came back later? Had a walk first?" he inquires.

"No problem."

They take the main road toward the sea, where the thin strip of land of the island borders on the Adriatic. Turn right at the Lungomare, walking down Gabriele d'Annunzio where it turns into Guglielmo.

The Hotel des Bains is shuttered and shielded by a barbwire fence. He has read somewhere it was soon to be remodeled into an apartment block. Its beach is also inaccessible, its golden sands lying wet and forlorn with scattered frayed deckchairs upturned here and there, like memories of a past, more opulent era.

"Sad, no?"

"Yes," Jonathan agrees.

"I've always wondered why Thomas Mann called his book *Death in Venice*. It should have been *Death on the Lido*, properly speaking."

"I know," Jonathan says. "Maybe it doesn't have the same

ring. People always think of Venice first. The Lido just hasn't the same romantic connotation."

This was where Aschenbach had coveted the adolescent boy Tadzio and allowed death to welcome him into its arms in the novella. Jonathan hadn't actually read it but he had seen the Visconti film. Though he would never admit to this publicly. There are a lot of classics he hasn't read.

"I only saw the movie," the young woman says.

"Me too."

"Philistines, eh?"

"Absolutely," Jonathan says. They both laugh.

"Anyway," she continues, "Aschenbach died of cholera, not a broken heart. A fanciful notion, but quite unrealistic."

There is a spark of mischief in her eyes.

They continue down the road, walking parallel to the sea. The gray sky chills his bones to the core. It looks as if it will soon begin raining. He tightens his black cashmere scarf around his neck.

They reach the Excelsior Hotel, which is also shuttered for the winter season. The main film screenings take place at festival time in the bowels of this luxury hotel.

"Did you know that Venice no longer even has a single cinema?" Jonathan says.

"Really?"

"Yes. A city that hosts one of the world's major film festivals doesn't even have a functioning cinema throughout the year. No demand. Not enough people. The population is steadily falling. Young people don't want to stay in Venice any longer. Tourists don't come here to see movies. They have other desires."

"Interesting," the young woman replies. "So what do you think brings people here in such numbers?"

"The beauty of decay, the weight of history, I don't know
. . . Maybe it's just habit, like lemmings. They reckon it's a
place everyone has to see at least once in their lifetime. Before
they die."

"I thought that was Naples."

"Both," Jonathan says. He's never been to Naples. Nor
even wanted too.

A gust of wind surges past him, moving between the sea
and the lagoon. He shivers yet again.

"Can we turn back?" he asks her. "This is getting too cold
for me. And at this time of year, all this is just too desolate."
He points to the abandoned beaches and shuttered buildings.

"It's just winter," she responds. And swivels around.

He remembers how warm the hotel had felt earlier, even
though it was empty.

"Did you come for the churches?" she asks you.

"No."

"Did you come to Venice for the canals and the art?"

"No."

"For the glass baubles from Murano, the food, the way
the evanescent light plays on the slow-moving waters of the
canals and the lagoon, the history, the gondolas, the teeming Rialto Bridge markets, the way the water slops against the
stone walls of the canals when the tide rises . . . ?" A litany of
questions.

"No, no, no . . ."

And you don't have the courage or the audacity to tell
her you have only returned to Venice to confront your own
history, your memories, to wallow in the past, to understand
once and for all that some things will never be the same again
whatever you say or do. To finally come to terms with the fact

that Giulietta was your last great adventure. And there can be no other. As if life has given you x number of chances, and you have taken them all, run out of numbers.

But then you guess she knows all this already.

You now sit in the hotel room, half a buttock uncomfortably perched on a corner of the same bed in which you and Giulietta had once made love in every conceivable position, while the young woman from the vaporetto stands by the door, observing you in silence, a detached interrogator in the house of love.

"Do you even have a name?" you ask her.

"Do you want me to have one?"

"Yes, I do."

She pauses for a moment. Ponders. Decides. "Make it Emma."

"Your real name?"

"Does it matter?"

"Not really, but it feels less awkward you having a name, I suppose."

"Makes sense, I agree," she nods.

"Emma?"

"Yes?"

"Who are you and what the fuck do you want?"

"Admirably to the point."

"And about time too. So?"

"Jonathan, you know who I am."

"I don't."

"Yes, you do," Emma asserts. "Just think. Hard. Come on . . ." Then smiles at you. A smile chock-full of compassion, sadness, and finality.

You blink. Your jaw loosens.

Deep down inside, you know who Emma really is. Could it happen any other way?

Did you think she'd just arrive on the scene knocking on the door like the long-expected killers in a Hemingway short story, or dressed in a red vinyl coat like a Venice-haunting dwarf in the movies?

And again, ask yourself, isn't it right that she should be a sumptuous long-legged blonde, with tousled hair, emerald-green eyes, pale skin, and cheekbones to kill for? The saving grace of fate, or mere coincidence?

"What now?" Jonathan asks.

Through the open curtains of the hotel room, he can see the evening darkness take hold of the sky and, beyond the Villa Stella's shrubbery, descend on the Lido. If he closes his eyes, he can imagine the pinpoint myriad lights across the lagoon illuminating the floating city. The thought occurs to him that he's never been to Venice at acqua alta when the water surges across Piazza San Marco.

There are so many things he's never seen or done.

"Do you want to keep the light on or should we switch it off," Emma asks, a note of tender concern in her voice.

Jonathan deliberates with himself just one brief moment.

"I think I'd like to keep the light on," he replies. "It would be nice to see everything. Clearly."

"Good choice," she says.

Once again he finds himself sitting on the corner of the bed while Emma stands just a few feet away, watching him, a halo of dying light circling her hair as the day retreats in the distance.

Jonathan sighs. Takes a deep breath. The room is relatively small. There are few hotel rooms he can remember passing through in his travels that were truly large, for reason of budget. He'd feel lost in a large room. It also made him feel closer to them. The women. Cathleen in the Radisson at Heathrow; Claudia in the Hotel de l'Odéon in Paris; Ingeborg at the Prince Conti in New Orleans; Marilena in the Holiday Inn Towers in Chicago, or Nicole in that Seattle skyscraper of a joint whose name has now faded back into the abyss of memory; and New York, New York, Lisa in the Algonquin—the smallest room of all—and Giulietta at the Washington Square Hotel. And Giulietta again at the Condal in Barcelona, and the Pensione Dezi in Rome, and the rented one-story villa by the lake, and here and there and everywhere, he can't even recall the full catalog of places they visited together after the initial encounter here at the Villa Stella. All the rooms of his life.

Emma stands motionless. He can smell her perfume. An ever so fleeting touch of Anais Anais tempered with a darker note that softens the floral peaks of the fragrance, no doubt the intrinsic odor of her skin, a smell unique to her. An obscene thought flashes across his mind, speculation on the way her cunt might smell, a subtlety of juices and heat and ardor. Or taste.

Emma moves.

Toward him.

Slowly, on a carpet of air.

Her fingers graze his cheek and he can feel the coldness. She extends her other arm and her palm cups his chin and the dull toothache he's been living with for the past fortnight fades away under her touch.

She unbuttons his shirt.

Jonathan rises from the bed and now faces her as she calmly, and deliberately, continues to help him out of his shirt one button at a time.

Close to her, he can feel the tiny tremor of her breath. He

looks deep into Emma's eyes. They are mirrors and bottom-less abysses. Her lips part. He moves nearer. Their mouths meet. Her tongue unfolds and shyly pierces his willing barrier. A slight taste of sugar, but far from unpleasant, unlike women who munch gum or smoke, which he's always found disagreeable.

Jonathan's tongue in turn ventures forward, inching barely inside her, and meets her teeth. Instinctively, his hands leave his sides and he hesitantly touches her, one hand in the small of her back, the other cradling her neck. Emma doesn't protest.

His exploratory movements become bolder. The practiced habits of a lifetime.

He reverently lifts her top. Her skin has an unbearable softness with the ability to turn all his senses into mush. His hand descends and tiptoes across her rump. Pliant but firm, tight oval cheeks shuddering slightly under his tactile exami-nation.

Porcelain horizons of pale white skin are unveiled, layer by layer, dimension by dimension.

In this very room where Giulietta's flesh had also been revealed to him, similarly pale but with a different, less milky variation in shade, just the hint of an olive tone, the texture of her sexual geography one more variation in the infinite palette of women's nudity. He knows he shouldn't be comparing, but it is difficult not to do so. Like a photographer or a filmmaker dissecting every image, every single sensation as it unfolds, a topographer of desire on a quest for the absolute.

His eyes are drawn to the back of Emma's calf. Unblem-ished, where Giulietta displayed a pale brown birthmark in the shape of an island, an inch or so across. His gaze lingers along the utterly smooth desert of her mons, where Giulietta sported a terribly exquisite jungle of jet-black curls.

They are now both naked.

He is rock hard.

Where, comparing again—damnit—in the final months of the affair with Giulietta he'd all too often required pharmaceutical blue assistance to maintain his hard-on, not for lack of desire but because of the passage of time and its effects on his body. A fact he'd always carefully hidden from her, with furtive trips to the bathroom to get the pill from his shaving kit, or the pretext of a sudden headache and the need for the relief of an aspirin.

Emma's body is perfection incarnate.

As if every woman he has ever known has come together, a female version of Frankenstein's monster dedicated to beauty, a magical cocktail of features, highlights, and idiosyncrasies. A perfection full of imperfections, but tailored to his unwritten preferences.

The way her eyebrows curve, the distance between her eyes, the height of her delicate, small breasts and the size and indefinable color of her nipples, the puckered depth of her belly button, the circumference of her long thighs and the alignment of her toes, the alluring angle of the empty space between her legs, beneath her love delta, and when she turns briefly, as if displaying herself fully to his voyeuristic gaze, the barely there, almost invisible shimmering blond down in the small of her back illuminated by end-of-day shards of light streaming through the window pane.

"Come closer," Emma says.

They collide in slow motion.

Jonathan holds his breath as once more their lips touch and a growing tremor begins to course through every synapse in his body. One of the young woman's hands slithers with utter delicacy down his back as he feels the nubs of hardness of her nipples digging gently into his own chest. The mast of his penis cradling against the velvet skin of her cunt. Like a perfect fit.

She pulls him down with one quiet and simple gesture and they fall, tangled, on the bed.

They make love.

Her grip below is domineering but expert, her mouth sucks the breath out of his lungs as they kiss with desperation, and then, just as he is gasping, she exhales again and the come-and-go of the tide that binds them continues. They fuck, they tumble, they squirm with pleasure, they fight for mutual domination.

He feels himself thrusting deeper and deeper inside her until there is no way forward as he expands within her walls, occupies her fully, her damp innards roughly caressing every square inch of his stem.

Jonathan closes his eyes. Abandons himself to the power of desire. Throughout she is silent, almost as if she is observing his thrashing, his animal reactions to her body, encouraging him, steadying him, mounting him. The faces of others he has known flash like lightning in a storm in front of his eyes. The tornado rises. Higher and higher.

Soon, the pleasure becomes so intense it is almost like pain. His breath is short, his heart is pumping out of control like a runaway train, his skin feels on fire.

"Yes, yes, yes . . ."

He explodes.

Inside her.

Inside.

He feels all the tiredness, the final ounces of energy fade away, like a bird taking elegant flight. His body relaxes.

His chest hurts now, but his slowing heart both roars and is at peace.

The young woman disengages from him at last, now a harbor for his seed.

He opens his eyes and looks at her.

Nude.

Pale.

Hypnotic.

He wants to say something but the words don't come. His left arm feels numb.

His eyes flutter. Trying to communicate.

"There, there," she says.

And the sound of her voice is as soothing as silk.

"Peace," she says.

Beyond her head, he catches a final glimpse of the window that overlooks the Villa Stella gardens.

It's dark.

It's night on the Lido.

His vision blurs.

All is peace. All is dark.

She rises from the bed, looks down at him, observes the sheen of sweat that covers his sprawled-out body, his fast-shrinking cock. She bends down, her small hard breasts grazing his damp chest hair, and, with absurd generosity, closes his eyes.

In the rising gloom of the room, she looks at Jonathan one last time. "Venice was a good choice, my love," she whispers softly.

She dresses.

Leaves the room. The hotel. The island.

It's early morning before the first vaporetto of the day on line one arrives at the departure pier. The sky is gray and desolate still as she boards, the sole passenger.

She sits at the back, now dressed in black.

Soon, she will be moving up the Grand Canal, past the Doge's Palace and San Marco and the stately procession of bridges, oblivious to all the beauty of the ethereal morning light falling on the waters.

Venice, she knows, has two islands for the dead embraced within the compass of its lagoon: San Michele, where locals and celebrities are buried; but also Poveglia, where the forgotten lie, a shore of ashes that began with the bubonic plague centuries ago, white bones and dust washed over by the waters, a place of charred remains which the fishermen studiously avoid.

For a brief moment she wonders whether Jonathan would feel at home there.

But another collection beckons. A man called Conrad who lives in London, and is on a visit to Aosta.

Time doesn't even wait for angels of death.

The vaporetto turns the bend.

PANTEGANA

BY Michelle Lovric

Santo Stefano

I'll admit this much.

The girl's death was my fault as much as anyone's.

In the middle of the blindfold hopscotch, as lightning rasped through the raindrops, I nipped her ankle where the hem of her nightdress clung. She squealed and flung her lighted candlestick up in the air. Unfortunately, her umbrella was made of wood and canvas. Protected from the rain, the flame from the flying candle gushed up the umbrella's shaft and snatched the fabric between the spindles.

Still, she might have lived—if only the watching man had rolled her to the sodden flagstones and beaten the flames from her hair.

And yes, perhaps he might have done it, if he hadn't just had the six silver blades of a gondola ferro impaled between his shoulders.

Let us imagine a row of stars at this point, and turn from this scene so redly saturated in treachery. We've all got memories. And *Il Gazzettino* immortalized it in diagrams for days afterward. I made a nest of them, down where I sleep; the same place where I keep the crabs I've snatched until they've melted to a quiet pungent death.

It didn't take long for the crabs to melt, not that particular August. It was the worst I could remember, and I'm not young. There was a heat to make hell seem like a spring holiday. For days, it had been hot enough to sear the thin skin of your ears: a mummifying, thrumming, compassionless heat. My eyes hurt from the burned-out sun that sequinned the tired water with cheap gold. Nor was there any relief after sunset. Those sultry evenings, the mosquitoes stage-whispered incessantly about the ambushes and massacres they were planning for the early hours. The flowers browned in their window pots; tides lingered so low that the seaweed rotted; refuse seethed in the bins. All around us, the air hung thicker with death than the inside of a crematorium chimney. We craved a thunderstorm. We were addicted to the thought of it. Instead, the sky taunted us with nothing but occasional and thin emissions of rain. Even the raindrops arrived parboiled.

Remembering that heat has addled my memory, and I've forgotten what I was telling.

Ah yes. But why did I bite the girl?

I'm fond of an ankle; a female ankle.

It is harder to change your nature than to change the object of your affection. Ankle by ankle, I'd been involved with dozens of girls in Venice, not a one of whom saw me crouching in a flowerpot or still as stone behind a drainpipe as she passed. I blend with marble like grouting. People will walk into a room where I am and say, "Oh, no one here."

Usually, I let them continue to think that's the case. If I don't, the consequences can be unpleasant, or violent, for me.

I used to watch that girl walking down our calle. There was a jagged little lilt to her gait. Evidently an old injury to my affectioned part—a fall years ago, perhaps, an undignified crumple in a gutter on a night of wine.

Her ankles were bare from April till October. She painted her toenails in the summer, the color of dried blood. I'm fond of a drop of blood, female blood.

I get it when I can, which is a lot, if you know me.

But how did it come to this? That one August night in the whipping rain I bit the object of my affection, and so caused the girl's death? And witnessed the impaling of her murderer?

There's little crime in Venice, as there's nowhere for a criminal to run. Few can walk on water; even if some plumbers think they can.

And it was one of that breed, a man with a knife and an ego like God's, who abducted the girl from her ground-floor apartment a few minutes before she died. I heard him arrive, quietly singing his favorite song, improvised from the names on the doorbells along our street. This is how it went (but you must imagine the words rolled through his shaggy tonsils, and perfumed with his asshole breath):

Fuck you, the Misters Gasperin
Fuck you, the Misters Olivetti
Fuck you, the Misters Lovisi
Fuck you, the Misters Zanetti . . .

When he rang the bell, I heard the girl stumble toward the door, which was right beside the flue where I'd been napping. My heart beat faster than two wristwatches, for I'm frightened of the same things as the next guy: loud noises, barbwire, poison, a bigger fellow than myself.

"Chi è?" she asked. ("Who is it?")

"Io," he said, unfurling that canvas umbrella. ("Me.")

She was a girl to whom any number of men might have made this reply. From my hole in the wall I saw her open the door and peer out the threshold, balancing her bare feet, with the varnished toes, on the stripe of greasy Istrian stone, speckled by lamplight and flung raindrops. He was on her in an instant.

"Out," he said, with the knife at her throat. "Come with me."

I was not the only witness to the scene.

"Oho, what have we here?" croaked my whiskery companion.

You see, there was a woman, a gondolier's widow, my hostess and landlady at that time. We shared a little hutch carved out of the damp ground floor of a grand palazzo near Santo Stefano. Discontented years had reptiled my landlady's skin, thickened her neck, and drawn the corners of her coarse mouth downward. Her eyes had popped in the constant search of something to disapprove of, until she resembled a pinkish stippled toad in a wig. And while the old lady may have looked like a flesh-colored amphibian, she was strong as an ox, and stuffed stiff as a teddy bear, not with wool or sawdust, but with spite for all her fellow humans.

Perhaps she had loved her husband once, for she lived surrounded by the memorabilia of his profession. The dried corpses of flowers were arranged in a silver gondola vase, though the metal had long been blackened by the gases emitted by her drains. Her knitting bag hung from the old gondola's wooden forcola. She even crammed her dimpled rear end into one of the gondola's little tasseled stools when she watched the television programs she hated. More than anything she despised *Festa in Piazza* and its faux square filled with cheerful dancing couples. She never missed a show. And she cursed it volubly all through. She hated the wide-eyed presenters, the aging singers, the bored musicians, and the underage dancers. She hated the audience, the director, and the advertisers. Most of all, she hated the cameraman, who could not keep his lens from jiggling in the crevices between the breasts and thighs of the dancing girls.

But I have left the poor girl and the plumber on the door-step in the rain!

So—the old woman woke promptly on the clanging sneer of the doorbell. In her iron cot, she slept little, so restless was her desire to find something new to be disgusted by. God had granted this woman a blessing: a next-door neighbor who was not a good girl. She was the delicate, dirty kind of girl who appealed to gangsters.

As she rushed to her spy-mirror, the old woman snagged her own nightdress on the ferro of her husband's gondola, which hung on the wall. With a curse, she lifted the offending curved comb of steel from its hook, and tucked it under her arm.

"Non si sa mai," she muttered. ("You never know.")

A twitched curtain and the spy-mirror revealed the face of the man at the next door. It was her son-in-law, the gangster. He played the amiable plumber, the joker, the hand-waggler, the punster, the clown. But he was one of those outlaws who bring misery, poverty, and ill health to hundreds of lives by brutishly shoddy work charged at crippling rates. His custom-ers were rightfully afraid of him. In Venice, we have water flowing through us the way other cities have faith. For Vene-tians, a plumber is a kind of priest. A rotten priest is a more fearful object than a rotten burglar. The betrayal is more com-prehensive. So it is in Venice with plumbers. A bad plumber is like a priest who corrupts little boys and frightens them into silence with the potency of the church. A truly bad plumber is il male impersonificato, a friend to flood, mold, and stink, an eager but ineffectual fondler of tools, a house haunter who manifests in sleepless, dripping nights, in a nameless sense of dread in the boiler room. This plumber was of that degree of badness, as ripe a son of Beelzebub as ever fissured a mains pipe with a careless nail. You could see it in his walk, smell it in his clothes. And see it on his face—which was flattened with sin, as if someone had pulled a stocking over it.

The old lady had suffered her own plumbing to be ruined by this hydraulic son-in-law of hers. She knew that he betrayed her downtrodden daughter too. The wife of that plumber suffered more leaks than anyone, more sodden days. Her faulty water-gates strained the Venetian floodwater straight into her carpet. Her lavatory oozed slow slime like contempt.

Now, like myself, the old woman had seen her son-in-law at the next-door apartment before. She knew that he had also inflicted his plumbing on the dirty, delicate girl. The old lady had witnessed the plumber leaving the girl's apartment on a number of smudged dawns. She had spied him arriving at several stagnant lunch hours, disappearing from the throbbing hot light of the calle into the dark doorway. She had also observed how, as he left on the previous day, he had passed another gangster swaggering in the direction of her door. He had waited in a crook of the calle until he had seen the other gangster receive a delicate, dirty admittance to the girl's door.

Now the old lady used her spy-mirror to watch the man with the knife march the girl down our calle. She waited until she saw them turn right, not left, at the crossroads. Then she dived into one of the fetid, flowered bags of viscose that she wore by day, picked up the ferro, and waddled after them. As did I, keeping a careful distance from the old woman, for she had several times beaten me with a broom handle, and once thrown a pot of boiling water on my back. It's still bald there.

A man with a knife force-marching a girl—from my hidden places, I have seen all this and worse. A man handing a girl a piece of chalk, and forcing her to draw a hopscotch outline in the rain—no, that was new. As was his blindfolding her, passing her a candle for one hand and an umbrella for the other, and lighting a cigarette for himself as he sat by the well under the dry of the canopy with the knife between his knees.

What did he mean to do to her? Humiliate her for preferring another gangster to himself? A special plumber's revenge: make her catch her death of cold in the rain? Or was it that visions of the day's slackened pipes and betrayed boilers swirled in his head, robbing him of sleep, reminding him of the girl's preference? Was it the maddening clench of August heat? Or the light rapping of the rain, the musical notes of the liquid which was his life's work, that had woken him and sent him out on the flowing streets to do more gangstering and worse than the other fellow?

In the early hours, Venice is lonely as a lake. The heat had stoppered up even the tiny trickle of humanity that you might encounter in Santo Stefano at two in the morning. From the corner of the Palazzo Loredan, the old woman and I had a private view of the blindfolding, the chalking of the hopscotch, the handing over of the candlestick, the pathetic sobbing and hopping of the delicate, dirty girl in the nightdress. We saw the first shaft of lightning finger the ground. We saw the first raindrops weaving through the air. We had the best view of the man with the knife between his knees, seated comfortably just a few yards away. With his back to us. We saw the smoke from his cigarette rise above the silhouette of his thick pipe of a neck and his shaggy cistern-shaped head.

The last time the old woman and I had seen that thick pipe of a neck from this angle, it had been bent over her boiler. Over his shoulder, he had tossed the news that the boiler was comprehensively dead and that a new one would cost her three thousand euros. He had installed that boiler less than a year before, a Caliban of boilers, a monstrosity bred from the blackened, broken organs of other boilers he had wrenched, kicked, and beaten to death. For that, he'd put the bite on the old lady for four thousand euros, a whole cushionful and change.

"Cash," he'd sneered. "Unless you want to pay the tax. And that's with your *sconto affettuoso*, mind. What do you say?"

An affectionate discount. What did she say? Here was his answer, at last. The girl was still hopping when the old woman did her work with the silver-pronged *ferro*. I was excited by the grunt and thrust and the smell of blood. Perhaps that was why I ran across the square to perform my instinctive act upon the ankle of the girl. Blood begets blood. It always has. Or perhaps I wanted to alert the girl to the fact that her tormentor was no more. I could not have foreseen the umbrella enfolding her like a tulip with petals of fire. Or the savory steam that would rise from her crisped corpse. Or the blood of the plumber, diluted by rain, palely loitering in a pool around her body.

"*Che cagnón*," muttered the old lady. ("What a terrible stink.")

Together, like friends enjoying a horror movie in the dark barrel of a cinema, the old woman and I took in the blaze. I even nestled up to her, for the comfort of flesh against my trembling fur. Finally, we turned our backs on the burnt girl and the impaled man and walked back toward the apartment.

Suddenly, pink lightning sewed up the sky in great clumsy stitches, like a battlefield surgeon. A monstrous thunderclap sent us both squealing to the bridge. The rain was thickening into something more useful, scampering furiously over all the roofs of Venice. Steam rose from the baked stone of the streets. The both of us were sneezing and shaking the droplets out of our whiskers. By the time we arrived at our door, the storm had fully opened its heart: thick shafts of silver stabbed the street, bayonets of water, crushing the flowers and filling the leaf-clotted gutters.

The old woman opened the door for me. I scuttled in ahead of her, expecting her boot in my buttock or a broom on my snout at any moment.

I was wrong.

"Mangiamo qualcosa insieme, vecio," she burbled in a cordial manner. ("Let's have something to eat together, old chap.")

I stared at her uncertainly. This was the first time she'd ever acknowledged me, although she'd long relied on me to clean up what she spilled on the linoleum.

She consulted the fridge and dropped a rind of gorgonzola wetly on the floor for me. I wasn't too dainty to swallow it. Something red was thrown in my direction. Automatically, I closed my jaws around it, and felt the miniature abrasions of a strawberry on my tongue.

Eating put the heart back in me. I looked across at her ankle.

No, I mustn't, I realized. *She and I are married now. By what happened out there.*

Next to our door, the rising black water sucked fervently at the steps, and an illegal soil pipe, installed by the plumber, fed it with filth.

DESDEMONA UNDICESIMA

BY ISABELLA SANTACROCE

Piazza San Marco

Translated from Italian by Judith Forshaw

I

I am not mad. I was watching them come out of the water, as stately as empresses, and I, at the window, was alone. I am afraid.

My name is Desdemona Undicesima; you are reading my words. You should know that these words belong to a dead woman, and I dedicate them to you, for always.

If you were here, in this room, you would see my eyes. And in them Venice.

It was November 5, 1911, there were motionless gondolas under the moon, then the fog descended.

It is so difficult not to lie. Do you love me? Don't be sad; I did not suffer. It was nice thinking that I was far away. Because this is what happens when you determine the outcome of your actions, of the voice you have and that you will never hear again.

I killed myself on November 5, 1911 at midnight in room number 5 of the Grand Hotel Bellosguardo. I was wearing a purple dress and pale velvet slippers. I was hungry. I could hear a child crying in her sleep. The rest was silence.

I had arrived in Venice a month before with my husband. I remember precisely a fork placed on the table. It was gleaming. My husband was laughing, saying: "My dear, don't you think Venice is mysterious? Look at this fork; it has the sun inside it."

I do not remember my reply, perhaps I stared at his hands, the way he had of moving them, it was odious. The thing that used to frighten me most about my husband was his hands; they seemed to belong to another man, a man who had killed without shedding a tear.

Are you listening to me? Now imagine that my voice is in these words. Put your right ear to them and listen.

Three numbers. Now say, "Three numbers."

The first is number 5, the second is number 13, the third is number 7.

You will feel my breath on your face. Do you feel it? I am close to you now.

Death is warm. Death is a noise that ends.

Listen to me.

I adored Venice. I would gaze at her in a book. There were photographs, and she was so beautiful that my face was stained with tears. I saw Ophelia painted by Millais when I looked at her. That is what I saw, and I wanted to reach her, to lie down beside her, with the sun in my eyes.

For so long I insisted. My darling, take me to Venice.

My husband would yawn, saying: "Venice is duller than you." Or he would say: "Venice is foggier than you." Or he would say: "Venice is gloomier than you." Or he would say: "You are Venice; look at yourself in the mirror and you will see her."

The long walks in my mind. I have only ever walked in my mind. I used to leave in the morning, and sometimes I would not return. I would stay closeted inside her for days. I would walk continuously; it was almost never-ending.

A labyrinth of bones.

My husband did not hate me; he did not understand me. Incomprehension is more unbearable than hate, because it does not exist.

We had no children; I would have liked to be a mother. I wanted a baby girl. I would have called her Cassandra. And I used to imagine that she had perfumed hair, and then sweet lips, full of kisses.

I had drawn her in my journal. Every day I perfected her. My daughter had become resplendent.

I took her too to Venice.

We left on October 2, 1911. It was raining. The tree trunks were shiny.

I had managed to convince him. I had said to him: "My darling, I have waited so long, give me this present, and I will never forget you."

He had looked at me. There was something in his gaze, perhaps anger.

He had replied: "My dear, we leave on the second of October, but promise me you will stop loving me so, you unnerve me."

Men. Cruel beasts.

On October 2 it was raining. The tree trunks were shiny. There was singing; only I could hear it. Nightingales and then a childish voice, frail.

My husband was driving. I stared at his gloves, then his profile. I asked myself: Who is this man?

We arrived in Venice on October 5 at four thirty p.m. I was having difficulty breathing.

How much water, I thought. How much water there is here. Venice is the stomach of a pregnant woman, I thought. Inside her is my daughter.

I wanted to call her, to shout: Cassandra, where are you?

To write is hellish. I am writing, and it is hellish. Hell is where a true writer lives. Writing is evil, darkness, black.

I am looking at you. Do you see me? I am wearing a purple dress, pale velvet slippers. I am sitting in room number 5 of the Grand Hotel Bellosguardo, a child is crying in her sleep, the rest is silence.

Listen to me.

A gondolier, his name was Ludovico, it was he who ferried us to the Grand Hotel Bellosguardo.

My husband was grumbling. He was saying: "Venice bores me. I need something to drink."

We entered room number 5, my husband with a glass in his hand.

I said to him: "My darling, this room is very elegant. I like it."

He dropped the glass to the floor, then he said: "Now I like it too."

I wanted to kill him. I looked at a golden paper knife.

Love is a surgical operation without anaesthetic.

Love is a deep pain.

I unpacked the suitcases. My husband was sleeping. His shadow was moving on the curtains. There was a gentle wind.

I went into the bathroom, I masturbated slowly. I could see myself reflected in the washbasin tap, I was pathetic. I could see a woman caressing herself, it was me. I wondered: Who is that woman? She must be an unhappy woman; she has graveyards and festivals in her eyes. This is what I thought.

The night, when it arrived, I remember it being immense and mirrored in the water. I was watching it as I breathed in the funereal perfume of my fate.

Three fates exist; when the last one arrives, the perfume begins.

That evening we dined in a romantic restaurant.

I was staring at a fork placed on the table. It was gleaming. My husband was laughing, saying: "My dear, don't you think Venice is mysterious? Look at this fork; it has the sun inside it."

Listen to me.

At ten o'clock we walked, we crossed bridges. The gondolas—black, accursed swans—seemed to watch us.

It was then that I saw them for the first time. They were three violet shadows, they were rising from the water like stately empresses.

I said to myself: You see the invisible because you need to dream.

And yet someone was speaking to me. They were saying: Something will happen soon, you must protect yourself. Tonight you must sleep with a small stone held tight in your hand. You will find it resting on the third step.

As we returned to the hotel, I saw a star become a river.

As I went back to the room, I saw a small stone resting on the third step.

I picked it up. My husband said: "It's dirty, it's covered with germs, throw it away."

I did not reply.

"I told you to throw it away. It's dirty, throw it away."

"My darling, don't worry, soon it won't be here anymore."

"You're lying, you always lie. You're a whore. Admit it. How many times have you been unfaithful to me, and with whom? Are they men I know? Tell me. If you don't tell me, I will strangle you. Answer me, Desdemona. I want to know the truth."

"My darling, I have never been unfaithful to you. You know that, I love you."

"You're a liar, you have the devil in your blood. You disgust me."

I did not reply. I was hungry.

We made love. My husband was grunting like a pig.

I counted. 101, 102, 103, 104, 105, 106, 107, 108, 109, 110. I knew that when I got to 150 I would feel his semen enter my blood.

150: I felt his semen enter my blood.

340: I fell asleep, holding the small stone tight in my hand.

In the morning the Stevenson family arrived at the Grand Hotel Bellosguardo.

I heard their voices.

They opened the door of room number 6.

My husband and I had breakfast wearing large dark glasses. The Stevenson family sat down at the table next to us.

Mr. Stevenson was wearing a black jacket. A horizontal scar adorned his left cheek.

Mrs. Stevenson was wearing a provocative dress. It revealed a glimpse of her nipples.

There was a five-year-old girl with them. Emily.

My husband was looking at Mrs. Stevenson's nipples.

I was looking at Emily's mouth. It looked like a rotting strawberry.

I knew, my hands were trembling.

A voice fell from the ceiling and landed in my glass. I watched it floating there. It was saying: "Desdemona Undicesima, go now to your room, take your journal, and cut your daughter Cassandra in half."

I got up. My husband was devouring Mrs. Stevenson's breasts with his eyes. Mrs. Stevenson was aroused.

"My dear, where are you going?"

I did not reply.

I could see my body passing through time. I could see it becoming the hand of a porcelain clock.

Are you still listening to me? Come with me. I do not want to be left alone. Read these words carefully: You are a murderer. Do you know why? Because you have become my name. You are Desdemona Undicesima now.

How are you, Desdemona Undicesima? Do you know what you are doing? You are taking my journal in your hand, you are looking through the pages for my daughter, and you are killing her.

I watch you. Cassandra is five years old, she has perfumed hair and a mouth full of kisses. You kill her with a golden paper knife, you tell me to be quiet, not to cry out.

I watch you as you cut her throat, and do you know what I do? I laugh at you.

The reader, the celebrated reader, or rather the person who reads. The writer, the celebrated writer, or rather the person who writes.

I was the writer, you were the reader. I am no longer the writer. You are no longer the reader. Now we are all Desdemona Undicesima.

Tell me. Tell me who you are or I will strangle you. Tell me: I am Desdemona Undicesima and I have killed my daughter.

The mind, an incomprehensible and grotesque landscape.

There are no cities. We live in our mind.

Now you are writing with my hands, and you are reading with my eyes. And now I am writing with your hands, and I am reading with your eyes.

We love each other, because it is impossible not to love oneself.

Listen to me.

Mrs. Stevenson used to sing in the morning. It was her

childish and frail voice that I had heard as I traveled to Venice, looking at the shiny tree trunks in the rain.

At night, she and her husband would grunt like pigs.

How much loneliness there is in sex. Sex: a cage with a crying pig inside it.

I remember vividly the seventh day in Venice.

Ludovico, the gondolier, was smoking. He was saying: "Piazza San Marco is as beautiful as you are, madam."

My husband had lifted up my skirt. He had done it because he was in love with Mrs. Stevenson, and he wanted me to be unfaithful too.

My husband said: "Ludovico, do you like my wife? If you want, you can kiss her."

I was lying among the sounds of the water. Ludovico kissed me. He had his hands under my skirt.

I do not remember for how many hours I remained motionless. Then it was evening.

My husband said: "Goodbye, Ludovico."

It was difficult walking. How much pain, I thought. How much pain there is here. I am the stomach of a pregnant pain, I thought, inside me is the infinite.

My stockings were ripped, I went into the bathroom, I waited for my husband to fall asleep.

When you achieve your dreams, they vanish. I had dreamed of Venice for so long, and Venice was no longer there.

I was looking at the darkness of the night from the window, I was thinking about dahlias, about when they bloom under the light. It seems like their petals are reaching out for caresses, and then the wind blows. I was thinking about the beauty of leaves, about when they fall from the branches and fly away like plucked feathers. And I was thinking about myself, about when I was small and I knew nothing of sin.

I was looking at the darkness of the night from the window, and then, once again, I saw them rise from the water, as stately as empresses.

They were three long violet shadows, they seemed like bodies that pass through time, the hands of a ceramic clock.

I put on my cloak and went out.

I sat down in front of the canal. A stone bench.

The shadows were dancing, stirring up the mist. I called to them. I said: "Come to me, talk to me, don't be afraid, and I will not be afraid of you."

The music, it was very loud. It started at that instant, as a rat was running through the dark, and its luminescent whiskers were squeaking like chalk on a slate.

"Come to me, talk to me, don't be afraid, and I will not be afraid of you."

I repeated this as I watched them dance, and I still did not know that I was about to meet my past.

"Desdemona Undicesima, do you remember us?"

"Yes, I remember you."

"Desdemona Undicesima, do you know why you are here?"

"Yes, now I know."

"Desdemona Undicesima, answer us: Why are you here?"

"I am here because there are three fates, and when the last one arrives, the perfume begins."

II

Nothing that happens is important. The importance of what should happen lies in what doesn't happen. But once what should happen has happened, what is left? Wind, just wind.

And it is because of this that living has no meaning. Because living is happening continually.

Similarly love, and dreams. What is left of them when they have happened? Wind, just wind.

What point is there in someone knowing now who those violet shadows were who rose from the water like stately empresses. What is the point of me explaining why by meeting them I met my past? And what is the point of me revealing why they asked me: "Do you know why you are here?"

And what is the point of me revealing why I answered: "Yes, now I know."

I could do it, I could explain everything, reveal everything. But what would be left? Wind, just wind.

I was in Venice, and Venice was no longer there. This is all I will say.

The Stevenson family was there: the Stevenson family had become Venice; later, my eyes would become Venice.

I made friends with Mrs. Stevenson on October 16 at eight thirty p.m.

"A pleasure, I am Odette Stevenson. This is my daughter Emily. The gentleman at the table is my husband Robert. I wanted to say that we would like it very much if we could spend some time with you and your husband. Tonight we are going to take a little trip in a gondola. Would you like to come with us? Our daughter will stay in the room, she goes to sleep at ten o'clock. We don't. We need adventures. We are a daring couple. Have you noticed how erotic Venice is? It would be a pity not to take advantage of it. My husband and I are electrified, almost as if we're reliving the early days of our romance. I am sure you know what happens in the early days of a romance, when two people still don't know each other well and they need to find out about each other. That indescribable thrill and bodies seeking each other out. Do you remember the caresses? I do. When my husband used to caress me I would turn to fire . . . Emily, don't listen. You're too young, go to your father, ignore me . . . Emily, why aren't you going? You know, I hate you. You are insufferable and ugly, I am ashamed to be your mother. Your mouth looks like a rotting strawberry. You disgust me, Emily, go to your father, forget about me."

III

The Stevensons were coming into our room like cobras. I could hear Emily crying in her sleep.

They were falling onto our bodies, and the room was beginning to shake.

I could see the chair moving, brushing against the curtains, then the violet shadows were coming in to watch us.

Only I was aware of their presence. Dark forces were everywhere.

Only I knew. Wind, only wind.

While everyone was grunting like pigs, voices were falling from the ceiling, filling my mouth. They were saying to me: "Enter your mind and travel across it. Do not stop, do not turn around. Go forward until you reach the gate. You will see Cassandra's hands opening like dahlias under the light."

I entered, and her hands were there. They were caressing me, and then the fog was descending.

Are you listening to me? You are still here, I know. You too have seen. What do you feel for me now that you are me? You are afraid, I know. You feel dread, because understanding is dread. The light is the darkness. The light does not exist, it is an invention of the darkness, a clever lie of the darkness. Good is evil. Good does not exist, it is an invention of evil, a clever lie of evil.

Life is death. Life does not exist, it is an invention of death, a clever lie of death.

Listen to me.

Twenty nights, twenty nights with the Stevensons. Odette's arms were scratched, there were cuts on her thighs, saliva trickled from her mouth. She reached orgasm as she gripped my head. My husband was saying to her: "I love you, Odette."

All the while I could hear Emily crying in her sleep.

When everyone was falling asleep, I was going out. I was sitting in front of the canal. Among the shadows.

I was watching the sky, and the stars were becoming rivers.

I was wondering: How much more time will it take before it appears?

The shadows were answering: "You must decide that."

I was returning to the room, I saw my husband entwined with Odette and Robert, then the fog was descending.

Listen to me.

I was a happy child, but when I was five they stole my happiness, and I knew nothing more of it.

I was playing with a shell. I was putting my ear to it, and I could hear the sea.

I had short hair, large eyes, I do not remember anything more. Perhaps I remember my dreams, they were vast.

I was alone in the house, they opened the door, they looked at me, they said, "Come with us," then the fog descended.

It was raining, the tree trunks were shiny, someone was singing. A childish voice, frail.

The following day my happiness had vanished.

Years passed without any memories. So many nameless years. I no longer knew anything about myself, I had vanished along with my happiness.

However, something was left, my vast dreams, they survived even without me, and they looked for me ceaselessly.

When they found me I said: "All right, I will return, but

promise me you will stop loving me so, you unnerve me."

Listen to me.

I was twenty-three, it was October 2, 1905. It was eight o'clock, it was Wednesday, I met my husband.

He said to me: "What is your name? You look sad."

I replied: "My name is Desdemona Undicesima, call me Desdemona."

He asked me: "And why are you so sad?"

I replied: "Because you never came."

The early days of our romance, when he used to caress me, I would turn to fire. It was so nice to love each other, to become butterflies in a sugar sky. And our hands, a blaze that rose up into the air, like a stately empress.

I loved my husband's strength. He seemed indestructible. So different from me. But his hands frightened me, they seemed to belong to another man, a man who had killed without shedding a tear.

We used to kiss each other; he would say to me: "I love you, Desdemona."

Then the memories came, and then I began to want a daughter.

I called her Cassandra.

I would daydream about holding her in my arms. I could sense her smell.

I bought three dolls, and then a teddy bear, and lots of strawberry sweets.

I would picture her cradle with little hearts embroidered on the pillow.

One day I said to my husband: "Why doesn't she come?"

He replied: "It is your fault, you are too sad."

He had started to be unfaithful. I discovered it on November 5, 1906.

In his jacket pocket I found a note, on it was written: *My love, I love you as I have never loved another man. Come back to me soon. You are wonderful, you have the sun inside you.*

For a few minutes I was unable to move.

I was wearing a purple dress and pale velvet slippers. The rest was silence.

I went into the bathroom, I masturbated slowly. I could see myself reflected in the washbasin tap, I was pathetic. I could see a woman caressing herself, it was me. I wondered: Who is that woman? She must be an unhappy woman; she has graveyards and festivals in her eyes. This is what I thought.

Love is a surgical operation without anaesthetic.

Love is a deep pain.

Cut me. Tell me that you love me. Do you love me? Don't be sad, I am not suffering anymore.

Death is warm.

Death is a noise that ends.

Do you know what happens? You see a sunset on your arms, and nothing deserts you, no one deserts you, because at last you are alone, forever.

You don't have to wait for anyone, because no one will arrive, and no one will go away, because at last you are alone, forever.

There are no more lies, because in death there is truth.

Listen to me.

When my husband started to be unfaithful, I began to draw my daughter.

I drew her on the last page of my journal. Every day I perfected her. Cassandra had become resplendent.

One afternoon I opened a book; Venice was in the book, and she was so beautiful that my face was stained with tears. I saw Ophelia painted by Millais when I looked at her. That is what I saw, and I wanted to reach her, to lie down beside her, with the sun in my eyes.

I said to Cassandra: "When you are five, I will take you to Venice."

She smiled, and she was so beautiful that my face was stained with tears.

My daughter, you killed her. Do you remember? You cut her throat, and I laughed at you. And do you know why I laughed at you? Because I hated her.

I never hated anyone so much.

I never hated anyone so much.

I never hated anyone so much.

I never hated anyone so much.

I never hated anyone so much.

I never hated anyone so much.

I never hated anyone so much.

I never hated anyone so much.

I never hated anyone so much.

I never hated anyone so much.

Do you understand?

I never hated anyone so much.

Every day she looked at me with unbearable eyes. She asked me for help. She said to me: "Please don't hurt me." She said to me: "I am only a child." She said to me: "Let me play with the shell." She said to me: "I don't want them to open the door." She said to me: "I don't want my happiness to vanish. Keep me safe."

Every day I said to Cassandra: "When you are five I will take you to Venice."

Every day I said to my husband: "My darling, take me to Venice."

He would reply: "Venice is duller than you." Or he would

reply: "Venice is foggier than you." Or he would reply: "Venice is gloomier than you." Or he would reply: "You are Venice; look at yourself in the mirror and you will see her."

The long walks in my mind. I have only ever walked in my mind. I used to leave in the morning, and sometimes I would not return. I would stay closeted inside her for days. I would walk continuously; it was almost never-ending.

A labyrinth of bones.

My husband did not hate me; he did not understand me. Incomprehension is more unbearable than hate, because it does not exist.

I know, you want to go. You can't. Do you remember the numbers?

The first was number 5, the second was number 13, the third was number 7.

You have said them, you have to stay.

I'm sorry, you will descend with me. Hell is waiting for us. Do you prefer heaven?

You should know that heaven does not exist. Heaven is an invention of hell, a clever lie of hell.

Listen to me.

I lied for years, but it wasn't my fault. It was my dreams that forced me to, if I didn't they would vanish. Dreams need lies to continue to exist.

If your dreams vanish, what is left? Your memories remain, and my memories will kill any dream.

I started to lie when my memories returned. They said to me: "We are here, now we will enter inside you, but you mustn't let on, pretend you don't know us, lie, only by doing this will you be able to stay alive."

My dreams then said: "Follow the advice that your memories gave you, otherwise we will vanish, and you will die."

I did it. I began to lie, and in that moment I became a mother.

Listen to me.

Do you know what smell the Stevensons had? They stank of rotting strawberries.

Odette was kissing me, clinging like a monkey to my body while my husband was entering her. Her husband Robert was saying: "How beautiful you all are, you look like you are dead."

Sometimes we would have trips at night in a gondola. Ludovico rowed, smoking his evil-smelling cigarettes, then he lay down beside us, under a blanket, in the cold.

Around us the violet shadows were dancing, stirring up the fog, and the stars were becoming endless rivers.

On November 3 the shadows said: "You cannot continue lying. Not anymore. Not now that Cassandra has been killed."

I was walking through one of the Grand Hotel Bellosguardo's long corridors. I was looking at its wooden green damask walls, decorated with small pictures depicting running stags. In the air the smell of jasmine was so strong that it brought on attacks of dizziness that with immense effort I tried to tame, pretending they were friendly dogs.

All of a sudden an overwhelming giddiness forced me to stop, and at that moment the shadows surrounded me, saying: "You cannot continue lying. Not anymore. Not now that Cassandra has been killed." And then they added: "You know who the Stevensons are. You have never forgotten them." It was November 5, 1887. They opened the door, they said: "Come with us." Then the fog descended.

I sat down on the floor, I saw a glass rolling. I recognized it. It was the glass that my husband had dropped. It was coming toward me, changing into a shell.

I took it in my hand; putting my ear to it I heard the sea.

"I am only a child," I whispered. "Let me play with the shell."

A door opened. "Come with us," they said.

While they were hurting me, that woman was singing, she had a childish voice, frail.

There was a window above me, it was raining, I could see the tree trunks, they were shiny.

Listen to me. I am talking to you. If you are afraid you can go. Forget the numbers you have spoken and go. I don't want you to watch me now, leave me alone. I will enter into my blood, as light as a feather.

Why are you crying? There is no sense in crying, because everything has already happened, I am merely telling the story. It has already happened, do you understand? And do you know what is left? Wind, just wind.

Do you hear it? It is so strong. Do you remember?

I was looking at the darkness of the night from the window, I was thinking about the dahlias, about when they bloom under the light. It seems like their petals are reaching out for caresses, and then the wind blows.

I am that dahlia now, and the wind is blowing.

Will you stay with me? Please don't go, stay here. I want you to watch me enter into my blood, as light as a feather.

Do you remember?

I was thinking about the beauty of leaves, about when they fall from the branches and fly away like plucked feathers. And I was thinking about myself, about when I was small and I knew nothing of sin.

Listen to me.

It was November 5, 1911. The Stevensons came into our room like cobras. I could hear Emily crying in her sleep, the rest was silence.

The room was shaking.

I saw the chair moving, brushing against the curtains, then the shadows came in to watch us.

Only I was aware of their presence. Dark forces were everywhere.

While everyone was grunting like pigs, voices fell from the ceiling, filling my mouth. They said to me: "Enter your mind and travel across it. Do not stop, do not turn around. Go forward until you reach the gate. You will see Cassandra's hands opening like dahlias under the light."

I entered, I saw her hands. They caressed me, and then the fog descended.

I left. I started to count. 1, 2, 3, 4, 5, 6, 7, 8, 9, 10. When I got to 20 I got up from the bed.

20: they were grunting like pigs.

25: I picked up the golden paper knife.

35: I put on a purple dress and pale velvet slippers. I was hungry.

I moved toward the window, I looked at Venice. How much water, I thought. How much water there is here. Venice is the stomach of a pregnant woman, I thought. Inside her is my daughter.

I wanted to call her, to shout: "Cassandra, where are you?"

I whispered: "Cassandra, where are you?"

My voice, a lament of wolves wounded by an iron heart.

It was then that she appeared. She had short hair, large eyes, vast dreams, and she was so beautiful that my face was stained with tears.

She was suspended in the air, while the stars became endless rivers.

"Come to me," she said.

I was watching her playing, she had a shell in her hand.

"Come to me; if you come here, the door will not open," she said.

"Come here," she said, "put your ear to the shell, you will hear the sea."

I know, I should have killed the Stevensons. I did not do it. I did not want it to happen, I did not want them to become wind, just wind.

I called to them, I said: "I remember you. You will not come in again."

They laughed at me.

I cut my throat.

My husband was screaming.

How much blood, I thought. How much blood there is inside me.

Then the fog descended.

Listen to me. I know you are still here. I can hear you, I can hear your breathing. Stay here for a while.

I want to tell you that you should not be sad, I did not suffer.

Death is warm.

Death is a noise that ends.

You see a sunset on your arms, and nothing more deserts you, no one deserts you, because at last you are alone, forever.

You don't have to wait for anyone, because no one will arrive, and no one will go away, because at last you are alone, forever.

And there are no more lies, because in death there is truth.

PART III

TOURISTS & OTHER TROUBLED FOLK

VENICE APHRODISIAC

BY PETER JAMES

Canal Grande

The first time they came to Venice, Johnny had told his wife he was on an important case; Joy had told her husband she was visiting her Italian relatives.

In the large, dingy hotel room with its window overlooking the Canal Grande, they tore off each other's clothes before they had even unpacked, and made love to the sound of lapping water and vaporetti blattering past outside. She was insatiable; they both were. They made love morning, noon, and night, only venturing out for food to stoke up their energy. On that trip they barely even took time out to glimpse the sights of the city. They had eyes only for each other. Horny eyes, greedy for each other's naked body. And aware of how precious little time they had.

Johnny whispered to her that Woody Allen, whose movies they both loved, was once asked if he thought that sex was dirty, and Woody had replied, "Only if you are doing it right."

So they did it right. Over and over again. And in between they laughed a lot. Johnny told Joy she was the sexiest creature in the world. She told him no, he was.

One time, when he was deep inside her, she whispered into Johnny's ear, "Let's promise each other to come back and make love here in his room every year, forever."

"Even after we're dead?" he said.

"Why not? You're stiff when you're dead, aren't you? Stiff as a gondolier's oar!"

"You're a wicked woman, Joy Jackson!"

"You wouldn't like me if I wasn't, you horny devil!"

"We could come back as ghosts, couldn't we, and haunt this room?"

"We will!"

Two years later, acrimoniously divorced and free, they married. And they honeymooned in Venice in the same hotel—a former palazzo—in the same room. While they were there, they vowed as before to return to the same room every year for their anniversary, and they did so, without fail. In the beginning they always got naked long before they got around to unpacking. Often, after dining out, they got so horny they couldn't wait until they got back to the hotel.

One time they did it late at night in a moored gondola. They did it beneath the Rialto Bridge. And under several other bridges. Venice cast its spell—coming here was an aphrodisiac to them. They drank Bellinis in their favorite café in Piazza San Marco, swigged glorious white wines from the Friuli district, and gorged on grilled seafood in their favorite restaurant, the Corte Sconta, which they always got lost trying to find, every year.

Some mornings, spent with passion, they'd take an early water taxi and drink espressos and grappa on the Lido at sunrise. Later, back in their dimly lit hotel room, they took photographs of each other naked and filmed themselves making love. One time, for fun, they made plaster of paris impressions of what Joy liked to call their *rude bits*. They were so in lust, nothing it seemed could stop them, or could ever change.

Once on an early anniversary, they visited Isola San Michele, Venice's cemetery island. Staring at the graves, Johnny asked her, "Are you sure you're still going to fancy me when I'm dead?"

"Probably even more than when you're alive!" she had replied. "If that's possible!"

"We might rattle a bit, if we're—you know—both skeletons."

"We'll have to do it quietly, so we don't wake up the graveyard."

"You're a bad girl," he had said, then kissed her on the lips.

"You'd never have loved me if I was good, would you?"

"Nah," he said. "Probably not."

"Let me feel your oar!"

That was then. Now was thirty-five years later. They'd tried—and failed—to start a family. For a while it had been fun trying, and eventually they'd accepted their failure. A lot of water under the bridge. Or rather, all 409 of Venice's bridges. They'd seen each one, and walked over most of them. Johnny ticked them off a coffee-stained list he brought with him each year, and which became increasingly creased each time he unfolded it. Johnny was a box ticker, she'd come to realize. "I like to see things in tidy boxes," he used to say.

He said it rather too often.

"Only joking," he said when she told him she was fed up hearing this.

They say there's many a true word spoken in jest, but privately, he was not jesting. Plans were taking shape in his mind. Plans for a future without her.

In happier times they'd shared a love of Venetian glass, and used to go across to the island of Murano on every trip, to see their favorite glass factory, Novità Murano. They filled their home in Brighton, England with glass ornaments—vases, candlesticks, paperweights, figurines, goblets. Glass of every kind. They say that people who live in glass houses shouldn't throw stones, and they didn't. Not physical ones. Just metaphorical ones. More and more.

The stones had started the day she peeked into his computer.

Johnny had been a police officer—a homicide detective. She had worked in the divisional intelligence unit of the same force. After he had retired, at forty-nine, he'd become bored. He managed to get a job in the fulfilment department of a mail order company that supplied framed cartoons of bad puns involving animals. Their best-selling cartoon strip was one with pictures of bulls. *Bullshit. Bullderdash. Bullish.* And so on.

Johnny sat at the computer all day, ticking boxes in a job he loathed, dispatching tasteless framed cartoons to people he detested for buying them, and then going home to a woman who looked more like the bulls in the cartoons every day. He sought out diversions on his computer and began visiting porn sites. Soon he started advertising himself, under various false names, on Internet dating sites.

That was what Joy found when she peeked into the contents of his laptop one day when he had gone to play golf—at least, that had been his story. He had not been to any golf club. It was strokes and holes of a very different kind he had been playing, and confronted with the evidence he'd been forced to fess-up. He was full-frontal, naked, and erect on *eShagmates*.

Naked and erect for everyone in the world, but her.

And so it was, on their thirty-fifth wedding anniversary, they returned to the increasingly dilapidated palazzo on the Canal Grande, each with a very different agenda in their hearts and minds than those heady days of their honeymoon and the years that followed.

He planned to murder her here in Venice. He'd planned last year to murder her during a spring weekend break in

Berlin, and the year before that in Barcelona. Each time he had bottled out. As a former homicide detective, if anyone knew how to get away with murder he did, but equally he was aware, few murderers ever succeeded. Murderers made mistakes in the white heat of the moment. All you needed was one tiny mistake. A clothing fiber, a hair, a discarded cigarette butt, a scratch, a footprint, a CCTV camera you hadn't spotted. Anything.

Certain key words were fixed in his mind from years of grim experience. *Motive. Body. Murder weapon.* They were the three things that would catch a murderer. Without any one of those elements it became harder. Without all three, near impossible.

So all he had to do was find a way to dispose of her body. Lose the murder weapon (as yet not chosen). And as for motive, well, who was to know he had one? Other than the silly friends Joy gossiped with constantly.

The possibilities for murder in Venice were wide. Joy could not swim and its vast lagoon presented opportunities for drowning—except it was very shallow. There were plenty of buildings with rickety steps where a person could lose her footing. Windows high enough to ensure a fatal fall.

It had been years since they tore each other's clothes off in the hotel room when they arrived. Instead, today as usual, Johnny logged on and hunched over his computer. He had a slight headache, which he ignored. Joy ate a packet of chocolate from the minibar, followed by a tin of nuts, then the complimentary biscuits that came with the coffee. Then she had a rest, tired from the journey. When she woke, to the sound of Johnny farting, she peered suspiciously over his shoulder to check if he was on one of his porn chat sites.

What she had missed while she slept was the e-mails back

and forth between Johnny and his new love, Mandy, a petite divorcée he'd met at the gym where he'd gone to keep his six-pack in shape. He planned to return from Venice a free man.

The Bellinis in their favorite café had changed, and were no longer made with fresh peach juice or real champagne. Venice now smelled of drains. The restaurant was still fine, but Johnny barely tasted his food, he was so deep in thought. And his headache seemed to be growing worse. Joy had drunk most of the bottle of white wine, and on top of the Bellini earlier, into which he had slipped a double vodka, she seemed quite smashed. They had six more nights here. Once, the days had flown by. Now he struggled to see how they could even fill tomorrow. With luck he would not have to.

He called the waiter over for the bill, pointing to his wife who was half asleep and apologizing that she was drunk. It could be important that the waiter would remember this. *Yes, poor lady, so drunk her husband struggled to help her out . . .*

They staggered along a narrow street, and crossed a bridge that arced over a narrow canal. Somewhere in the dark distance a gondolier was singing a serenade.

"You haven't taken me on a gondola in years," she chided, slurring her words. "I haven't felt your oar much in years either," she teased. "Maybe I could feel it tonight?"

I'd rather have my gall bladder removed without an anaesthetic, he thought, but did not say.

"But I suppose you can't get it up these days," she taunted. "You don't really have an oar anymore, do you? All you have is a little dead mouse that leaks."

The splash of an oar became louder. So did the singing.

The gondola was sliding by beneath them. Entwined in each other's arms was a young man and a young woman, clearly in love, like they had once been. Like he was now with Mandy Brent. He stared down at the inky water.

Two ghosts stared back.

Then only one.

It took Joy some moments to realize something was wrong. Then she turned in drunken panic, screaming for help, for a doctor, for an ambulance. A kindly neurosurgeon told her some hours later, in broken English, that there was nothing anyone could have done. Her husband had been felled by a massive cerebral aneurysm. He would have been dead within seconds.

Back in England, after Johnny's body had been repatriated, was when Joy's troubles really started. The solicitor informed her that he had left half of his entire estate, which was basi-cally the house they lived in, to a woman she had never heard of. The next thing she knew, the woman was on the phone wanting to discuss the funeral arrangements.

"I'm having him cremated," Joy said.

"He told me he wanted to be buried," Mandy Brent in-sisted. "I'd like that, I'd like to have somewhere I can go and sit with him."

All the more reason, thought Joy, to have him cremated. But there was another, bigger reason she had been thinking of. Much bigger!

The following year, on what would have been their thirty-sixth wedding anniversary, Joy returned to Venice, to the same room in the dilapidated former palazzo. She unpacked from her suitcase the small gray plastic urn and put it on the windowsill, and stared at it, then at the view of the Canal Grande beyond.

"Remember what we said to each other, Johnny? Do you? That promise we made to each other? About coming back here? Well, I'm helping us to keep that promise!"

The next morning she took a vaporetto across to Murano. She spoke to the same courteous assistant, Valerio Barbero, in the glass factory, Novità Murano, who had helped them every year since they had started coming. Signore Barbero was an old man now, stooped and close to retirement. He told Joy how very deeply sympathetic he was, how sad, what a fine gentleman Signore Jones had been. And, as if this was quite a normal thing for him, he accepted the contents of the package and her design without even the tiniest flicker of his rheumy eyes. It would be ready in three days, he assured her.

It was. Joy could barely contain her excitement on the water bus ride back to the mainland. She stopped in St. Mark's Square to gulp down two Bellinis in rapid succession, to put her in the *mood*, she decided.

Then she entered the hotel room, hung the *Do not disturb* sign on the door, and locked it from the inside. She untied the pretty blue bow around the tall box, and carefully opened it, removing the two contents.

The first item was the plaster of paris mold she had taken of Johnny's rude bits, all those years ago, when he had been particularly drunk and even more aroused than usual. The second was the exquisite glass replica, now filled with the gray powder from the urn.

Slowly, feeling pleasantly tipsy from the Bellinis, she undressed, then lay on her back on the bed. "Remember, Johnny?" she whispered. "Remember that promise we made each other that very first time we came here? About coming back and making love here in this room every year forever? You were worried, weren't you, about not being able to get stiff enough for me after you were dead? Well, you really shouldn't have worried, should you?"

She caressed the long, slender glass. Hard as rock.

Stiff as a gondolier's oar.

Just like she remembered him.

DRIFTER

BY EMILY ST. JOHN MANDEL

Ponte dei Sospiri

When Zoë's husband died she decided to travel. She was twenty-eight years old and had seen very little of the world, and this seemed like the best possible moment to leave Michigan. A friend from art school had been to the Arctic in the summertime once and she'd told Zoë about the landscape's clear beauty, the wildflowers, ice-blue lakes, and slate mountains. Now it wasn't summer, but that was almost the point. Zoë boarded a series of flights to the Northwest Territories and found herself in a lunar kingdom of shadows and ice, scoured landscape. The sun behaved strangely. The days were short.

"Trying to lose yourself?" Zoë's brother asked, when she called from a hotel in Inuvik to tell him where she'd gone. Zoë's husband Peter had been dead for four weeks. She had given up the apartment, sold or given away all of her belongings. People were concerned.

"Trying to find myself," she said, which wasn't at all true but had the desired effect of slightly reassuring her family. Losing herself wasn't enough. Zoë wanted to erase herself. She wanted extremity. She wanted to be eradicated but she didn't want to die. When she left the hotel she felt swallowed up by the landscape, by the absolute cold. By night she stared through the hotel room window at the northern lights, colors shifting across the breadth of the sky. She liked it here but she was restless and she'd heard of a town that was even farther north: Tuktoyaktuk, on the edge of the Beaufort Sea.

"The ice road just opened," a man behind the counter in a coffee shop told her when she asked about it. "Should have no problem getting up there." He looked at her doubtfully. "You got a 4x4?"

"No," Zoë said. She'd sold her car before she left Michigan.

"I know a guy who's going up tomorrow. Probably take you with him if you split the cost of gas. I'll ask him if you want."

"Thank you. I appreciate it." What she truly appreciated was the way the man in the café didn't ask why she'd want to go to Tuktoyaktuk this time of year, or what she was doing in the far north in the first place. Over the weekend she agreed on a fee for gas expenses and got into a truck with a silent man in his fifties who navigated them seamlessly down a ramp onto the frozen MacKenzie River.

Zoë had heard the phrase "ice road" in the café without thinking about what it might mean. It meant driving on ice. Driving in slow motion with chains on the tires, fifteen kilometers an hour with the lights of enormous rigs shining ahead and behind them in the four p.m. darkness. They drove up the river to the northern edge of the world and then turned right and drove for a time over the frozen Beaufort Sea.

The village itself was like Inuvik only smaller, darker, more utilitarian, little windows shining bright in the permanent twilight. Daylight lasted four hours but the stars here were brighter than any she'd ever seen. She felt that she'd traveled beyond the edge of the world and landed on some colder planet farther from the sun. Aurora borealis in the sky most nights, shifting vapors of green and yellow that she watched by the hour, sitting alone by the hotel window wrapped in blankets with the lights out. On the third day she rented a snowmobile, got a cursory driving lesson from the man who ran the rental business, and drove a little way out of town.

Zoë liked the sound of the machine, the din and the forward momentum, but it wasn't a smooth ride and she felt as if her bones were rattling. She stopped by the sea. She could go no farther. She climbed off the machine and walked a few paces to look out at the horizon, blue shadows of icebergs. The sun was low above the ice, the few scattered lights of Tuktoyaktuk shining in the near distance.

"I am not unafraid," she whispered, to Peter, to herself. She had said this first, in the dazed weeks just after the diagnosis when they were trying to come up with words to frame the catastrophe. They had repeated it to each other in the final nine months that followed, a private phrase that conveyed hope and stoicism and terror in equal measure. The cold was getting to her now, her fingers numb inside her gloves. She turned and for a fraction of a second Peter was standing there beside the snowmobile, smiling at her in the fading light. He was gone in less than a heartbeat, less than a blink.

"Oh God," Zoë whispered, "oh no, please, please . . ." It took a moment to restart the snowmobile; she kicked at it frantically, not daring to look up. There was movement at the edge of her vision, faint as a curl of cigarette smoke. She heard Peter's voice as though from a long way off, but couldn't make out what he was saying. The cologne he used to wear on special occasions hung sweet and clear in the freezing air. The snowmobile jerked into motion and her tears froze on her face. She left all the lights on in the hotel room that night and packed up to leave the north in the morning, a slow process at this time of year, performed in increments over a number of weeks. There were several runways that had to be navigated to get from the Arctic Circle to the warmer parts of the continent, and most of them were frozen over. There were long delays in northern airports, sometimes for days at a stretch. She slept on benches, ate out of vending machines, washed in public restrooms, and felt somewhat deranged. Her reflection was pale and hollow-eyed in mirrors and darkened windows, hair standing up in all directions. It wasn't until she was sitting in the airport in Edmonton two and a half weeks later, drinking coffee after a sleepless night and staring out at an airplane that would take her farther south as soon as a storm cleared, that it occurred to her to wonder why she'd been afraid of Peter's ghost.

Zoë arrived in the Toronto airport and spent some time considering flights back to Michigan, but she had no desire to return just yet and the situation seemed to call for a new continent. Zoë and Peter had made a good living dealing coke to college students and she still had a few thousand dollars at her disposal, so she flew from Toronto to Paris and lived for some time in a marginal neighborhood, trying unsuccessfully to learn French. But the lines and beauty of Paris reminded her too much of the architectural paintings Peter had been working on when they'd met at art school and her money dwindled rapidly there, so she left France and began a slow, directionless slide across the continent, heading mostly south and east.

Zoë didn't have much money now. There were dark little places in winter where she didn't speak the language, and she occasionally forgot which town she was in. She found a job busing tables in Slovakia for a while. She heard there were resort jobs to be had on the Croatian coast, so she made her way through Hungary and then worked for some months as a waitress near the Adriatic Sea. On the day she saw Peter walking across the town square she packed her things and resumed a halting eastward migration, through Bosnia and Her-zegovina, across a corner of Serbia and through Albania, to-ward Greece. It was important in those days to keep moving. She saw Peter sometimes, always at a slight distance, moving through crowds in various countries. Not looking at her, not sick anymore, seemingly in somewhat of a rush. She was per-fectly aware every time that it couldn't possibly be him—Peter was buried in her family's plot in Ann Arbor—but that didn't make her see him any less often.

"I'm worried about you," her brother said. He persisted in keeping in contact, which was thoughtful but also somehow annoying. She was trying to drift across a landscape without remembering and he kept pinning her to home.

"There's no need to worry," she replied. "I'm just traveling a little."

"When are you coming home?"

"I don't have a home," she said. "I'm like that song. I'm a rolling stone."

"Have you been drinking?" he asked.

She didn't see that this was any of his business. She took a long pull of whiskey before she answered him. "Of course not. And even if I *was* drinking, what difference would it make? Haven't I always been the black sheep?" This was in Albania, at a pay phone in the lobby of a rundown hotel near the Greek border. The clerk glared at her from behind the front desk but said nothing.

"It doesn't matter what you've always been," her brother said. "All that matters is that everyone's worried, Zoë, we all love you," and she understood from his voice how tired she'd made him. "We all want you to come home."

"I'm sorry," she said. "I lost Peter there."

* * *

In Greece, after two years of travel, she discovered that she could sell landscape paintings to tourists. Zoë disliked painting landscapes. She had other interests. On the days when she painted landscapes she spent a lot of time swearing at the canvas. In her last three years in the United States she'd taken to painting extreme close-ups of liquid in glasses and she'd felt that she'd found something, if not her mature style than the style that might lead to it. She'd loved the way glass and ice and liquid caught the light, the warmth of red wine in a low-lit room, the suspension of bubbles in champagne, in seltzer, lime slices trapped among ice cubes with tiny bubbles clinging silver to the peel. Her work had been shown in galleries. She'd entertained thoughts of a brilliant future. It was difficult to paint landscapes again after all these years of ice cubes and extreme martini-glass close-ups, after the two years of traveling and not painting at all, but on the other hand she was nearly out of money.

She lived in a dilapidated inn by the sea, where she cleaned and helped the cook in exchange for a room, and sold paintings to tourists for food money. Her life wasn't unpleasant. She had come to realize the value of southern countries: she would never have imagined this quality of sunlight, the way it bleached the landscape, the way it seemed to pass through her, the way it burned away the darkest parts of her thoughts. She spent a lot of time on the beach with a fifth of whiskey, disappearing into brilliant light. She attracted frowns from passersby but she didn't think it was such a terrible thing, actually, drinking a little by the sea. She didn't see why people had to be so judgmental about it.

Zoë had been in Greece for six months when she decided to keep moving. She knew she wanted to remain in a southern country and she spent a long time studying maps of India, but she was afraid of malaria and she wasn't sure how a person would go about getting vaccination shots in Greece. She'd always wanted to see Venice, so she spent two weeks trying to sell the last of her landscape paintings, abandoned the ones she couldn't sell along the beach in the early morning, took a bus to Athens, and then a cheap flight to Rome. She did crossword puzzles and read the *International Herald Tribune* all the way to Italy, where she found upon arrival that she had just enough money left to get to Venice by train.

It was September and a tide had overtaken the city. The water had risen over the streets and tourists moved slowly on walkways, wearing strange boots that looked like bright plastic shopping bags tied up to their knees. In a doorway near the train station she counted the last of her money. Eighteen euros and eighty-seven cents. Her bank account was empty, and she had no credit cards. She didn't want to spend money on a vaporetto so she made her way on foot through the drowning city, trying not to think about how little money she had or what might become of her now. There was an unexpected pleasure in wading through the water and getting her shoes wet, childhood memories of splashing in puddles with her dog.

Zoë came upon St. Mark's Square, turned now into a shallow lake. She waded out over the cobblestones in water up to her knees and stood before the domes and archways of St. Mark's Cathedral, pigeons wheeling through the air above her, and this was when she realized that she'd had it wrong: it wasn't that she'd always wanted to come to Venice, it was that Peter had always wanted to come to Venice. He had painted this cathedral from photographs a dozen times. He was everywhere.

She turned away and left the square, but within minutes she had landed in another of Peter's paintings. She looked up from a bridge and was ambushed by memory. Detroit, the year before Peter got sick, their apartment filled with canvasses, a Sunday afternoon: "It's called the *Bridge of Sighs*," Peter said, and stepped back from the easel so she could see what he'd done. All this time later here it was before her, an enclosed white bridge with two stone-grated windows high over the canal, somehow dimmer in life than it had been in her husband's luminous paintings.

She crossed the bridge and spent some time wandering, watching the movement of boats from the flooded sides of canals, from the arcing bridges, these crafts gliding on the water streets. She came upon a narrow canal that Peter had never painted, a place where the water hadn't reached the level of the promenade, and for the first time all day she was perfectly alone. She had lost track of where she was. A residential quarter far from St. Mark's Square, houses crowded tall and silent on either side. The water of the canal was almost still.

Zoë sat on a step and pulled her knees in close to her chest. She would have to buy food soon and then the eighteen euros would deplete still further. She'd been dimly aware of how little money she had when she'd bought the train ticket but it somehow hadn't registered, all she'd really thought of was the next destination, and now she didn't have the money to either get out of Venice or stay here. She could call her family, but she knew they'd only buy her a plane ticket back to Michigan. She could go to the American consulate, but what would they do except return her to the United States? She was looking at the rippling shadows the houses cast on the canal in the end-of-afternoon light, thinking of how she'd paint this water if she still had money for paint, and this was when she became aware of footsteps. A tall man in jeans and an expensive-looking sweater, dark curly hair and sunglasses that reflected her own pale face when he looked at her. He stopped before her and said something that she didn't immediately comprehend.

"Parla inglese?" she asked, in what was meant to be a steady voice. It came out wavery.

"Can I be of any help at all?" he asked.

There was a fleeting second when she thought she smelled Peter's cologne in the air.

"I don't know," she said. No one else was on the street, and she wondered if he'd followed her here.

"You're quite wet," he said gently.

Her jeans were in terrible condition, now that she looked at them; soaked past the knees and filthy. Her tennis shoes were waterlogged.

"I went wading," she explained.

He extended a hand. "Rafael."

"Zoë."

"Zoë, may I buy you a cup of coffee?"

"You may," she said. There was no reason why not. She wasn't one to decline offers of coffee from strange men. She hadn't had coffee all day, or food for that matter, and it was nearly evening. "Would you mind buying me dinner instead?" she asked.

"Tell me about yourself," Rafael said. He had taken her to a small dark restaurant not far from where he'd found her, a place so narrow that she might have walked past it without noticing. The street outside was shadowed and still. He'd led her to a table in a far back corner, and now he was sipping red wine while she attacked a plate of pasta.

"I'm a painter," she said. "I *was* a painter, I mean."

"I see. And where are you from?"

"The United States. But I've been traveling for a long time."

"You're traveling alone?"

"I am," she said.

"Do you have any family?"

"A brother. I haven't spoken to him in a while." Memories of a pay phone in a hotel lobby in Albania, the desk clerk glaring as she capped the whiskey.

"There's no one else?"

"My parents died in a car accident when I was little." This wasn't at all true—her parents were a seldom-thought-of presence in the suburbs of Ann Arbor, probably worried about her, faded to shadows now—but wasn't she free to reinvent herself? This wasn't her continent. "I have no children."

"But you're married," he said. She still wore the ring.

"He's dead."

"I'm sorry. How long have you been traveling, Zoë?"

"Two years? Maybe three. I haven't really kept track."

"A drifter." Rafael smiled to soften the blow of the word.

She had been reaching for her wine glass, but found herself stilled by the idea. Memories of Greece, of Slovakia, of the Arctic, dark cities. "I suppose," she said. "Yes, I suppose you could say that."

"I have a confession to make." Rafael had taken off his sunglasses. His eyes were blue, and she thought him handsome; there was an easy grace in every movement, a confidence in his gaze. She liked his smile.

"What sort of confession?" She was interested in the confession, but more interested in her pasta. It was the first time she'd eaten that day and she was having a hard time chewing slowly.

"I followed you for a while before I approached you."

A quick bright star of light caught in an ice cube as she raised her water glass to her lips.

"Really," she said.

"And my interest, if I may be entirely candid, was partly economic in nature. You appear to be—forgive me for speaking so bluntly—a girl of limited means."

"You could say that." Zoë was aware of her appearance. She knew she hadn't been paying enough attention to it. The cuffs of her sweater were fraying and a seam was coming apart at the shoulder. It had been some time since she'd washed her hair.

"It happens," he said, "that there's a job I need done. It would take no more than an hour of your time."

She had all at once the same feeling she'd had those years ago on the ice outside Tuktoyaktuk, when for an instant she'd thought she'd seen Peter standing on top of the snow and she'd been seized by a desperate desire to flee. Rafael's questions, she couldn't help but notice, seemed designed to establish that she was alone in the world. Put down your glass, she told herself. Stand up from the table, thank Rafael for the meal, and walk out of the restaurant.

"What kind of job?" she asked, instead of doing any of these things.

"A simple delivery."

"Of what?"

"A small package," he said. "It happens to be a matter of the utmost delicacy. You'll deliver a small package to an address near here, and in return I'll pay you a hundred euros."

"In advance."

"Half in advance, half when you return." He glanced at his watch. "I'll be waiting for you here, at this table."

"We're doing this now?" she asked.

"In thirty minutes," he said.

"Why would you send someone you don't know, if it's a matter of utmost delicacy?"

"You're at hand," he said. "All you have to do is knock on the door, and tell whoever answers that you have a message from Rafael. You'll step into the building, give them the package, and you'll be on your way."

"And you'll pay me a hundred euros for that?"

"It's important to me to see that the package gets delivered, but it isn't possible for me to do it myself."

"I see." There were things she could accomplish with a hundred euros. She could pay for a hostel for a few nights, and perhaps that would be long enough to find a new job. It was suddenly possible that she hadn't reached the end after all. She wanted very much not to go home.

The package was a rectangular box no larger than a deck of playing cards, wrapped neatly in brown paper. Rafael slid it across the table following the dessert course, extracted fifty euros from a wad in his pocket, and pressed the money into her hand. "The rest when you return," he said. He nodded at someone behind her, and when she looked up a man who had been sitting at the bar when they came in was standing by her side. "My friend will walk you to the address."

She felt unsteady as she stood. Perhaps she'd had slightly too much wine. Rafael's friend said nothing, only nodded to her and set off for the door.

"Goodbye, Zoë," Rafael said. He winked at her. She looked back as they left the restaurant, and he was speaking softly and urgently into a cell phone.

Zoë held the package in both hands. It was curiously light. She was worried that it might be fragile, and it was certainly important; Rafael's friend kept glancing at it as they walked.

She wondered if it could possibly be jewelry—a blood diamond? She wanted to ask, but she feared the question was indiscreet and he seemed to be a man not given to talking. Her feet were cold and wet in her sneakers. At least the tide had receded. They were in a corner of Venice that seemed all but deserted, buildings pressed close on either side of the street. Night had fallen and the streetlamps were few and far between, pools of light spilling over cobblestones and walls.

"Here," Rafael's friend said. It was the first word he had spoken to her. They had stopped before a narrow stone building. He rang the doorbell and was gone almost instantly, sliding into the shadow of a nearby doorway. She knew he hadn't gone far but she felt acutely alone on the silent street. The graveyard stillness of a city without cars.

The man who opened the door was very old, stooped and blurry-eyed in an impeccable black suit. It seemed to Zoë that he couldn't see her very well.

"I have something for you," she said. "A message from Rafael."

He considered this for a moment before he stepped back to let her enter. She found herself in a dimly lit foyer, wall-mounted lamps casting shadows on the walls, a black lacquered sideboard with a potted white orchid gleaming in the half-light. She was painfully aware of how dirty her clothes were, how ragged and wet. He closed the door behind her.

"Here," she said, and tried to give him the box, but he shook his head and gestured for her to follow him. She thought about turning and slipping back out into the street, leaving the box by the orchid and running away, but she was seized by curiosity. She wanted to see what came next. She wanted to do the job correctly and return to Rafael for the other fifty euros. It had perhaps been a mistake to leave her backpack with him, in retrospect. The wine she'd had with dinner was wearing off quickly.

The butler moved slowly down the hallway before her. His thinning hair soft and wispy at the back of his head. She wondered who he was, if he had a family, if he knew Rafael. Her shoes were making embarrassing squelching noises on the carpet. He opened the last door on the right and she stepped into a long, low room, a study. There was a massive black desk at one end, chairs and a sofa at the other. A man in his early thirties sat in an armchair reading *La Repubblica*. Everything about him looked expensive, from the high shine of his shoes to his carefully tousled hair. His shirt was pink. He made a show of folding his newspaper unhurriedly when he saw her, but she noticed that his hands were shaking.

An older man was walking away from her, and she had the impression that he'd been pacing. He pivoted sharply when the door closed behind her, but said nothing. The butler had retreated into the hall.

"Hello," Zoë said, but the two men only looked at her. "I have a message from Rafael," she said.

She held out the box. The older man came toward her and she saw the strain he carried, bloodshot eyes and slumped shoulders, a two-day beard. His suit was expensive but his collar was in disarray, he'd pulled his tie loose, nails bitten to the quick. He took the box from her hands and held it for a moment as if weighing it. She watched the color leave his face. He set the box on a low marble coffee table before the man in the pink shirt, sank down into the sofa, and closed his eyes.

The man in the pink shirt glanced at Zoë. He unwrapped the box carefully and removed the lid, pulled back the layer of gauze within. He let out a strangled sound in his throat.

The box contained a human ear. It had been washed clean

of blood and it was small and waxy, blue-white, a porcelain seashell with a pink stone earring in the shape of a rose still attached to the earlobe. As she stared, the man in the pink shirt put his hand on the other man's shoulder and murmured something to him. The older man was still for a moment, as if it took two or three heartbeats for the words to absorb, and then he began a slow downward movement that reminded Zoë of a marionette being lowered on its strings; he slumped forward on the sofa until his head was nearly at his knees, curling in on himself; he pressed his hands to his face and began silently weeping.

The man in the pink shirt sat still for a moment, looking at the ear. He carefully replaced the gauze, set the lid back on the box, carried it away to the far end of the room, and put it high on top of a bookshelf. Zoë stared at him, waiting, trying to guess what might happen now. His face was expressionless when he turned to her.

"I didn't know," she said.

"It's a beautiful night," he said. His voice was hoarse. "Let's go for a walk."

He opened the door and ushered her out into the dim corridor. When she glanced back into the room the older man hadn't moved. The back door of the building opened into an empty courtyard, houses silent all around them. She breathed the cool air and thought about running—but where could she go? The courtyard was enclosed, and anyway, they were already in motion, the man in the pink shirt holding her arm. He was leading her to a wooden door in the far wall, their shadows moving black over the cobblestones. Light escaped here and there through the cracks between shutters. She could hear a television somewhere, voices rising and falling, canned laughter. When she stepped through the wooden door she found herself on the edge of a canal, water lapping near her feet. The man in the pink shirt stepped through behind her and closed the door. Something caught the light just then, the quick sharp gleam of a gun in his hand. She wasn't sure where it had come from.

There was no one else by the canal, and the buildings on the other side were dark. He took her arm again and they walked together, an unhurried stroll down the length of cobblestones with the water rippling black beside them. The slight pressure of the handgun against her ribs. She felt strangely detached, a sleepwalker in a long dream. Her thoughts wandered.

Once in Michigan she'd been held up at gunpoint. This was when she was dealing coke to art school students, and she knew it was dangerous, but no transaction had ever gone bad before and her guard was down. She knew as soon as she walked into the apartment that everything was wrong; the squalor, the way the girl sitting on the sofa was staring at her, the cigarette burning in an overflowing ashtray, the way the door closed just a beat too quickly just as someone said her name—*Zoë, I'm real sorry about this, we're just going to take the money and the coke, no one's going to hurt you*—and then she'd heard the click of the safety catch. *Okay,* she said quietly. *Okay.* She raised her hands. The colors of the apartment were florid, a fever dream of red and purple and orange, and she found herself staring at the curtains and trying not to look at the girl on the sofa, who smelled bad when she leaned in close to pull the wad of money out of Zoë's jacket pocket, and then later out on the street unharmed she'd felt so alive, so giddy that she started laughing even though she'd just been robbed and snow was falling through the haze of streetlights; she looked up and she felt it, felt it fall on her face—

"I told Rafael that if he did this, I would kill the messenger," the man said softly. He sounded apologetic but he wouldn't meet her eyes when she glanced at him. His grip tight on her arm, their footsteps quiet on the stone promenade. Time was moving very strangely. She felt that perhaps she'd always been walking beside him.

"But I didn't know what was in the box." She heard her own voice as if from a long way off.

"It is a request for payment," he said. "It's an escalation. It's a message that demands a reply."

"Whose ear is it?" she asked, but he didn't answer.

In Greece she bought a postcard of her village by the sea, the little place where she was living with the white buildings and the church and the endless light, and she sat on the beach at the end of a difficult day and wrote a note to her brother: *Jon, it's Zoë. I'm sorry for your worry and I just wanted you to know I'm still alive, I hope you're alive too, I wish I knew you better, I'm sorry we were never close—*

"We're close now," the man said. They were nearing a dead end. A boarded-up restaurant with a wide awning that reached across the width of the promenade, where once there must have been café tables shaded from the sun, and on the other side of the awning the promenade ended in a brick wall. They stepped into the awning's ink-black shadow and Zoë realized that they were all but invisible to anyone who might be watching from a window, now that they'd passed out of the light.

She'd had a dog when she was little, Massey, a cocker spaniel with ears like silk who quivered with joy when she came home from school, and when it rained they splashed in puddles together—

"Here," the man said.

They had stopped by the brick wall. Zoë turned to look at

the canal, all rippling moonlight and black. Darkened build-ings rising up on the far side, moored boats. What was strange was that she wasn't frightened. She could hear nothing outside of herself but the sound of the man in the pink shirt breathing beside her, the movement of water. Both of them were wait-ing, but especially her.

"Step forward," the man said softly, "toward the water," and she inched toward the canal until her shoes were at the very edge. She felt the metal against the back of her head, the click of the safety catch being released. There was an in-stant when it seemed that nothing had happened, but then the moonlight expanded and became deafening and there was only pure sound, the gunshot flashing into blinding light—

Her brother making a snow angel in the playground—

Massey chasing a squirrel in the grass—

"It's cancer," the doctor said, and Peter gripping her hand so tight—

Prom night in Ann Arbor, the headlights of cars pulling up in front of the auditorium, the slippery tightness of her green silk dress—

Blue ice shadows on the Beaufort Sea—

"You have a fever, sweetie, no school for you today," and a cool hand on her forehead, her mother's voice—

"Stand up," Peter murmured. His hand on the back of Zoe's head, where the bullet had entered her. "Stand up, my love. Let me look at you."

RENDEZVOUS

BY TONY CARTANO

Calle Larga XX11 Marzo

Translated from French by Maxim Jakubowski

I recognized him immediately, a few steps behind me in the line at the Alitalia first class counter at Charles de Gaulle airport. Even if I hadn't been on the lookout, how could I have missed him? His face was striking, disturbing even. A messenger of bad things. An evil incarnation. Like an avenging archangel, a carrier of death.

The photographs of him one could find in the newspapers or in the press agency dispatches were somewhat softer in nature, less worrisome than reality. He held himself like a dandy, regal, majestic, almost Christlike.

What I hadn't known was that on that very day, he would be standing a few meters away from me, ready to embark on the same flight to Venice. Maybe I should have expected it, at least had some strange premonition. Shouldn't I? As, under the pretense of a story for my newspaper, I was making this journey to go and meet up with his wife.

Skin like crumpled parchment, clean shaven, almost translucent. Invisible features, as if washed away by some heavy, unexplainable form of makeup. He was like an apparition. Only his bushy, silver eyebrows betrayed his age. A well-built sixty-something, it was public knowledge. With his wide-rimmed white felt hat, the man could not avoid attracting attention. But in the passenger line he was ignored and no one took notice of him. Apart from me, of course.

Harry Menikov. That was his name. Anyone with an interest in the arts would have known he was one of the most important gallery owners on the planet. He had places in New York and Peking, as well as London, Paris, and Venice. He was much feared and his wealth seemingly knew no limits. A two-million-dollar canvas by an established master was no more than a bagatelle as soon as he decided to buy it. What was less certain was where his initial wealth originated. There were different versions in circulation, each fed by the spice of media frenzy. An obscure defector from Eastern Europe, he had carved a niche for himself with the support of a network of sometimes highly dubious contacts, reaping the benefit over the past several decades of the crème de la crème of Russian oligarchy. As for his enlightened taste in matters of art, he was the only one to know its precise provenance and actively took advantage of this particular secret in order to embellish his own legend every single day.

Victoria was his third wife.

In this respect, the gossip magazines had seldom been less than generous in providing photos and details of Mr. Menikov's sentimental goings-on.

The sole daughter of a dignified bourgeois Boston family, she had been a brilliant Harvard student, specializing in modern painting, with a PhD dissertation on the Long Island artists of the likes of Pollock and De Kooning. It was at the opening of a show devoted to the latter that she first came across Harry Menikov. He quickly gave her a job as an assistant at his Madison Avenue gallery. The sort of offer someone straight out of college couldn't turn down. Victoria could not have known then the sort of tyranny he would inflict on her from that moment forward. In every which way. She had told me of some of the methods he'd used to "convince" her to give in to his will.

"I surrendered to fascination. It was all very good resisting, telling myself I should be stronger, but I was never able to carry out any of my plans of escape . . . He married me. I then swore he would never own me again. But it was already too late . . ."

We had just made love in the bedroom of the small Mayfair apartment the billionaire had left at her disposal. It had been less than two weeks ago. Her husband was expecting to meet up with her later, in Venice. There was nothing paradoxical about this: the illusion of freedom he granted her was, as far as she was concerned, merely a clever fabrication to mercilessly abolish in her mind any thought of independence. She didn't even know where he was right then. New York, Miami, Los Angeles? As a rule he never disclosed his itinerary in advance. Victoria, for her part, had explained her London stopover away on some fashion sales and an unlikely encounter with a girlfriend back from the Harvard days. Harry had merely grumbled in response.

She was thirty years old. She was beautiful, her sensuality barely dented by the Menikov experience. But small, carefully concealed signs would often betray her growing defiance and distress.

"Are you scared?" I asked her.

"Yes . . . He's capable of the worst."

We had met up at the Royal Academy at the Giacometti retrospective. We had a drink together, but as I was about to order a second round, she almost ran away when I told her I was a journalist specializing in the arts for the culture pages of a French daily.

"You're not going to write about me, are you?"

I had great difficulty reassuring her and getting her to accept my invitation to dinner.

Strangely enough, right at the moment when the whole encounter was at risk of turning into something of a catastrophe, she said: "I may be crazy . . ."

"Or someone wants you to believe that."

"Yes . . . I may be crazy but, I don't know why, I totally trust you. It's been such a long time since I've felt that way . . . Okay, let's go."

When I had left her early the next morning, she made me promise to get in touch with her in Venice. She was traveling there the following week for the inauguration of a foundation Harry had decided to set up on the Isla San Pietro in a palazzo being restored and widened, deliberately close to the pavilion halls of the painting Biennale, possibly in order to annoy the likes of Guggenheim and Pinault. Malicious enemy tongues had cast doubt on the viability of the project, stating that this time the mogul was in beyond his depth and likely to take a heavy fall.

Victoria wrote down her cell phone number. I gave her mine.

Back in Paris, it was easy for me to convince my editor of the necessity of an assignment to the Venetian lagoon, so I could write something up about the mighty Menikov's latest folly.

Walking through the security portal, minus shoes and belt, on my way to the departure gate, I had felt for a brief moment the unpleasant sensation of being stark naked. A nudity that owed nothing to the security measures, but stemmed from a sudden and unexpected sensation of fragility. I had tried to tell myself that this sense of unease was due to my divorce a year earlier and my yearning to see my nine-year-old son more often. The bouts of dejection took hold of me much too frequently and out of the blue. I often tried to understand these mood swings, this unstoppable double-bladed force carrying me forward, punctuated by both despair and a renewed appetite for life . . . But the truth was, I had known as soon as I saw him in the line that it was the presence of Harry Menikov, now a few meters behind me, that was troubling me. There was no reason for him to be on this flight, with me.

Normally he would have traveled on a private jet, framed by his bodyguards.

X-ray inspections, body searches, they were all of no consequence. I had been found out. The look in his eyes, oh the look! He knew, the bastard!

A little later, on the plane, I became certain of it. It was no longer a fantasy. Sitting in the last row of the first-class cabin, his face partially concealed under the brim of his hat, he kept on watching me. I shuddered. What did he want with me? I had no need to turn around to experience the sharpness of his eagle eyes twisting like a knife between my shoulder blades. I was the sole reason he was here, just me. He didn't give a damn about his foundation in the Doge's city. Right now his only prey happened to be me. As much as I tried to loosen my shirt's collar, my breathing became heavier and I could feel drops of sweat dripping down from the base of my neck. How was I going to escape him?

A manhunt. For me, until now, it had been a word that was fully part of the worst clichés of mystery writing, a literature I was a great consumer of by the way. And now I was facing those circumstances myself; it was brutal, incomprehensible. Everything was getting mixed up in my head, memories of novels and the incontrovertible evidence of reality. I was questioning my past, refusing my future, and the present day was like a many-faceted mirror I was unable to interpret.

I was becoming conscious of my fragility. I was a journalist, not a race-car driver or someone familiar with the hide-and-seek maneuvers of veteran spies; even as a child I had shown no interest in those silly games where you pretend you are invisible. Maybe I was wrong. Maybe I should have believed those maneuvers would come in handy one day. Now, under pressure, my only reaction had been a bewildered amateur's: carrying my small piece of luggage on wheels onboard. This way, I told myself, I could try to lose him amongst the crowds of tourists congregating around the gaggle of guides on arrival at Marco Polo. I had noticed that Menikov, on the other hand, appeared to carry no luggage. Like all wealthy men, he had no need of anything, just a handful of banknotes and an assortment of gold cards in his pockets.

Wow! I had a solution. A man like him would treat himself to a private water taxi to cross the lagoon and reach the historical center. Normally, I would also have treated myself to this and put it on my expense account rather than take the vaporetto. The moment was ripe for this: rush through the arrivals hall all the way to the ticket counters for the buses going to the Venice land station.

It worked! "There's one leaving in three minutes, over by the exit, thirty meters to your right."

"A single ticket, per favore, subito!" Wonderful! There were only three or four of us climbing aboard. The driver advised me he would be making a five-minute stop at the entrance to the city, where I would locate all the necessary connections to reach my final destination.

"And if you're interested," he added, "for a little bit extra I can take you all the way to Padova."

I smiled back at him. Finally at peace, relieved. As soon as the bus drove off, following a rapid glance backward to check that I was not being followed, I took out my cell phone and sent a text to Victoria.

A thin curtain of rain had begun to fall. Nothing unusual for early April. In my naïve ingenuity I thought it would help muddy the waters. And anyway, I didn't feel much like a tourist. I already knew Eternal Venice, and on that particular day I didn't give a damn about her.

When the bus came to a stop, I stepped off with my luggage, looking all around me to make sure everything appeared normal. During the flight, I had turned down the meal offered by the flight attendant. Now I was both hungry and thirsty, so I walked into a café and purchased a panini and a beer before exiting onto the esplanade. The fine drizzle had ceased, leaving a gray sky in its place. Sitting on a stone bench, surrounded by the real people of Venice, workmen, suburbanites, I fed myself quickly, impatient to be able to smoke a small cigarillo in peace.

Hell and damnation! I'd barely had time to take a few puffs when the next bus from the airport arrived, occupying the vacant parking space of the one that had just brought me here. A few passengers disembarked. Amongst them, unmistakable hat, Armani suit, the by now terribly familiar face. It was him! Menikov! How could he have followed me here?

He lit a cigar, much thicker than mine, moved away, and walked up and down the esplanade, without a single glance in my direction.

I had a sudden urge to call out to him, confront him, throw at punch at him. But something more powerful inside of me was keeping me rooted to the spot. I threw the butt to the ground. Ran toward the bus driver who was finishing his own cigarette. "You're going on to Padova? Let me have a ticket!"

"We're leaving in under a minute," he answered.

"So close the damn doors," I demanded brusquely, climbing onto the bus. He calmly ended the exchange by telling me he was the one who was "in charge." If only he had been! He made his way back to the driver's seat and started the engine. "Grazie! Grazie mille, signore!"

As we began moving off, I noticed Menikov still smoking next to the line of stationary cabs. My throat tightened. Of course, he would just hail a cab and follow me again. Why? Why was he so concerned about little me?

A detour of ten kilometers or so to try to get myself back on track, to forget all about this crazy affair. Art was my only concern, both in dream and in reality. I had no further need for colorful nightmares. This was not real life, even if through my own mistake I'd almost forgotten that damn fact.

I glanced at my cell phone. No message from Victoria.

Let them both go to hell!

I pulled out my laptop: Padova, a map of the town, a hotel, an indispensable visit to the sublime Giotto frescoes in the Scrovegni Chapel which I'd only ever seen in reproduction. I made a reservation for a visit the following day at ten thirty in the morning. The joys and temptations of the Internet. At least this silly situation I'd gotten myself into would not prevent me from enjoying visions of sheer beauty. Even if it was for the last time . . .

Are you crazy or what? There you go again with your stupid fantasies. This persecution complex you have. Okay, stop right now, everything is fine, I kept on telling myself. Following a good meal, washed down with a red Veneto wine, a peaceful night, it would all become so much clearer. Forget about the rest. It was all merely an illusion.

Vice. It had always held a fascination for me.

As could be expected, there were all these scenes from the Gospels, each one more spectacular than the one before. Blue backgrounds worthy of damnation . . . The Annunciation, the Wedding at Canaan, the Road to Calvary . . . Mary's intense pain overlooking the face of her son already in the throes of death . . . So much emotion!

But the vices! Like a terribly modest graphic novel unrolling in a strip below the mighty frescoes. The buffoonery of Folly. A young woman throwing her legs up in the air to signify Fickleness. Wrath hopelessly tearing itself apart. An old man holding a sword and a spear representing Injustice. I slowed down to take a closer look at him. Before being drawn to Envy, personified by a blind man with a snake's tongue. Then, utterly fascinated, I focused on Despair. Where the Devil was savagely pulling out the soul of a suicide from his body.

I was concentrating so hard on the paintings, I didn't notice the presence of a man immediately to my right. Just standing there next to me. It was him! He was silent. Watching the painted image with no less an intensity than mine. We both just stood there, not making a sound. Out of the corner of my eye, I risked a quick glance at him. He responded by turning his face toward me, his eyes peering straight into mine, watching closely for any reaction in my frozen features. I promptly moved away, toward the panels illustrating the Virtues on the other side of the room. He did not follow me, walked back to the large wall of the Last Judgment. He stretched his creased saurian neck upward, as if trying to absorb in a single glance the cohort of angels and seraphims opening the doors of the

Heavens under the very noses of the damned who were haloed by a river of fire by Avarice, Lust, and Pride.

All of a sudden, Menikov moved away toward the exit without waiting for the official end of the tour. By the time I reached the Eremitani gardens, a late straggler, he had disappeared. Nowhere to be seen.

How could I have not noticed him on the way in, as the number of visitors was strictly limited to twenty-five for each tour? He must have slipped in at the last minute while we were negotiating the climate-controled security chamber next to the chapel. Sitting right at the front, facing the screen on which a documentary feature about the historical background of the place was unfolding, I probably hadn't made a note of him at the back. Lack of instinct. Which was in all likelihood one of the things that made us so different from each other, I told myself. On one side of the divide a natural predator, on the other an advocate of peace, of goodwill between men; not that my own life had been perfect by any measure with regard to the latter . . .

Was I wrong? And what if good old Harry was not following me, had nothing to do with my travels? He hadn't even bothered to wait for me. After all, Mr. Menikov had as much a right as any other to visit the Scrovegni Chapel. Who was I to make accusations? He was surely a master of his own destiny.

I even began to imagine, professional duty rising in my conscience, the incredible interview I could have written up following this unexpected encounter. *Giotto and Menikov: A Summit Meeting.* A hell of a feature.

Great idea. Positive, at last. You're a journalist, not a private detective. Do what you do best.

But there was a detail that escaped me. I was convinced of that. I had thought I knew all there was to know about the guy's biography. The reported facts at least. But I still felt I had to conduct some additionnal research.

Back at the hotel, I threw myself at the laptop. Navigating between websites, I found the information I had been missing.

First of all, Harry Menikov was very religious. When he was in Italy, he never failed to visit the tomb of Sant'Antonio di Padova and leave an offering. It apparently had something to do with losing someone he loved when he was young.

In addition, some years back he had acquired a Palladian villa on the shores of the Brenta, in the Mira area some fifteen kilometers away from the Venice lagoon, where he enjoyed coming to visit.

I imagined this was where he kept Victoria a prisoner, surrounded by an army of servants and right-hand lackeys.

What if I were to go there? I could rent a motorboat to travel down the river. No, the Internet told me this would take hours, because of the locks. So there was just one thing I now had to do: reach Venice as soon as possible, by taxi this time, and warn Victoria of my arrival.

At Piazzale Roma, I took a motoscapo to navigate down the Grand Canal. Toward the end of my journey, having reached Calle Larga on foot, pulling my small case on wheels behind me, I came across a police cordon. Three Alfa Romeos belonging to the carabinieri were blocking the street, their warning lights ablaze. The last time I'd had a problem reaching my favorite hotel had been some years earlier when menacing floodwaters, so familiar to Venice, had risen to fifty centimeters, forcing visitors to wear boots or plastic trash bags all the way up to their knees. But that wasn't the case on this occasion: yesterday's thin rain was long gone, and the sky was pure blue but for a few luminous clouds. The obstruction was all human, nothing to do with the weather's vagaries. Something had happened. Something serious enough to warrant three police cars parked in front of the Saturnia's doors, as well as the stirrings of a crowd, curious passersby, the flashes of some journalists' cameras, a curious mob always attracted by the bizarre and any inkling of morbidity.

I hesitated briefly before pushing my way through the febrile crowd.

I was weighed down with anxiety, to say the least. A forceful feeling of diving into a tragic new universe. A cinematic denouement from a Vittorio de Sica neorealist movie or a bloody and sensational Puccini operatic moment.

Memories of *Tosca*, seen at the Fenice some years earlier with my then wife, were rising up in my throat. Passing under the hotel's porch, I struggled with a deep feeling of sickness, and almost stepped back. But it was too late.

At the reception desk, after I'd identified myself, the clerk gave me a lugubrious look, all lowered brow and funeral-faced.

"These gentlemen are waiting for you," he said, indicating two policemen in civilian garb smoking cigarettes in the hall, quite unbothered by the recent antitobacco laws.

One of the men approached. "Signore, you have to come with us. We have some questions we would like to ask . . ."

Just the sort of universal cop talk you'd expect anywhere.

"The body of a woman has been found in the room you booked. We don't know yet if it's a suicide or murder . . ."

I didn't have the strength to object or even attempt to fathom the situation.

They took my by my arms, one on each side. As if I were about to flee!

"Can I contact my embassy?" I simply asked.

How funny that right there and then I remembered that

in three days it would be my forty-second birthday. And to think that, in all likelihood, I would be spending it in prison.

SIGNOR GAUKE'S TONGUE

BY MIKE HODGES

Palazzo Ducale

L enny Gauke knows he's being followed. From his window seat he cautiously studies the reflections of the
other passengers as they take their seats in the car-
riage. He smiles to himself: it's obvious none of these inno-
cents are potential assassins, just excited tourists. Although
he's never before had dealings with the Mafia he knows a lot
about its internal structure and over the years has come to
admire its effectiveness. The superimposed "family" concept,
with its straitjacket of ruthless sentimentality and emotional
entanglement, is brilliantly effective. He sees it as the perfect
template for running every human enterprise, from country to
corporation, including his own. A freemason since his early
twenties, Lenny Gauke is already imbued with the code of
silence and secrecy. Omertà, however, is but one attribute he
shares with the mafiosi: he has also committed murder. Just
one.

As soon as the train pulls out of Milan station Gauke
promptly leaves his seat, hurries along the swaying corridor,
and disappears into the bathroom. Once the door's shut and
locked he doesn't, as you might expect, unzip his fly or drop
his pants but instead steadies himself in front of the wall mirror. His eyes, like peepholes onto a clear blue sky, immediately suck up the likeness before them. It always pleases him
to remember that every image entering his head arrives upside

down, and it's his brain that twists it the right way up. He leans forward to study his forehead, wishing for the umpteenth time he had X-ray eyes to observe the workings of his labyrinthine brain—a brain that's served him so well. Until now. Interestingly, his image, as reflected in the mirror, is also in reverse. All this matches Lenny Gauke's take on life.

His gaze finally shifts, albeit reluctantly, to his waves of white hair deranged by the strong wind gusting along the station platform when he boarded the train. With a sleight of hand worthy of a conjuror, a tortoiseshell comb appears and is soon streamlining the locks back into place. He rarely does this without thinking of his mother: even into early manhood she would take every opportunity to have him sit in front of her dressing table and lovingly brush his luxuriant hair. The train lurches as it crosses some points and he has to grip the basin. His attention is thrown back onto his face and, as if to poke fun at himself, he shoots out his pink tongue. He waggles it playfully, then turns away to unlock the door and leave. Back in his corner seat he puts on his inflatable neck pillow, and sleeps like a baby for the rest of the journey.

He wakes when the train brakes sharply several times before slowly entering Santa Lucia station. It's his first visit to Venice and his arrival coincides with the last rays of a dying sun. As a consequence his first sight of the city's breathtaking Canal Grande is depressingly funereal: a mosaic of long shadows edged with spires, domes, and towers that, in black silhouette, resemble tombs and mausoleums. It's as if he's disembarked directly into a cemetery. Gauke rather likes that idea. He cuts through the ponderous mass of human flesh descending onto the platform and moving slowly toward the exits. Suckers! The wheels of his suitcase stutter like an automatic weapon as he hurries across the concourse toward the waiting vaporetti.

He's reserved a suite in a five-star boutique hotel "reeking of old-regime opulence," as one guidebook put it. With opulence being the key to Gauke's entire life, he immediately feels at home in the Gritti Palace. The receptionist (the plaque on the counter identifies him as *Umberto Ziani*) consults the computer and locates his booking.

"For just three nights, Signor Gauke?"

"Correct." His eyes rest on the plaque and he quietly adds: "Umberto."

As Umberto photocopies his passport Gauke wonders if he'd been wrong not to travel under a different name, grow a beard, dye his hair, insert an earring into his nose. The thought causes an involuntary shudder of his head: no, he'd decided against all that nonsense months ago. The idea of being cornered, looking like some bum on the run, was too humiliating for serious consideration.

The young porter summoned to show him his suite releases the catch on the handle of his suitcase and sticks it loudly into its innards, like a stiletto. His immaculate white gloves flash as he lifts it onto the golden luggage trolley.

"You been to Venice before, signor?" the man asks as they travel up in the elevator.

"Many times."

Gauke wraps himself in lies. Much as the linen binding an Egyptian mummy is there to preserve the person inside, so it is with Gauke. Indeed, it's ironic that this habit took root early in his childhood, dealing with *his* mummy. So overweening was her love for him that he rapidly learned, in a desperate act of survival, to use falsehoods as a shell to protect the formation of his secret inner self. Lying is a habit he perfected and never lost. The elevator reaches the first floor and they move along the corridor. Gauke stops at a door to read the name of the suite.

"Know who Ernest Hemingway is?"

The boy looks puzzled. "Mi scusi, signor?"

Gauke tut-tuts and wags his finger disapprovingly. "No mi scusi, kid. He was a famous writer. Americano. Often checked in to this hotel."

They reach a suite farther along. The porter opens it up, letting Gauke enter first. "Spent my honeymoon in this very suite." He strides across the sitting room, his handmade shoes sinking into the Oriental carpet. At the huge picture window he holds back the damask drapes to get a better view of the canal below. "Over forty years ago."

"Your wife, she—"

Gauke cuts the boy's words off sharply: "My wife's dead."

He catches sight of himself in the ornate wall mirror on the far side of the room and smiles. Gauke is one of those among us prone to private smiles, causing the uneasy observer to ponder the reason for such apparent inner happiness. On this occasion he's wondering if his wife, Eve, has realized he's no longer in their apartment, let alone their country. Eve is a busy woman with many interests (including some demanding charities) so it's possible she hasn't yet noticed his absence.

Gauke finds his wallet and fishes out an excessive tip which he gives to the wide-eyed porter.

"Mille grazie, signor."

"Prego."

On his way to the door the porter turns when he's called.

"Hey, kid! Smart guy, that Hemingway. When he saw the game was up he did the final check-out. Into the void." He shapes the index finger of his right hand into a gun barrel and holds it to his head. "Booom! Blew his brains out with a hunting gun. Big balls; big gun." His laughter follows the boy as he retreats from the room and quietly closes the door behind him.

Gauke is still laughing as he showers. When he emerges a bottle of Taittinger Comtes de Champagne waits in an ice bucket, compliments of the hotel. He pulls the bottle out as he dries his hair and checks the vintage. It's 1998. Satisfied, he pours himself a glass, switches on the television, and finds CNN. The pair of smiling newscasters, sitting like conjoined twins, have the personality of action dolls. He momentarily imagines a giant hand dressing them before placing them in the frame. Still, he watches the world news intently from start to finish before dressing and leaving.

Gauke has what used to be called, and maybe still is, a photographic memory. That intuitive ability, married to the acquired one of speed-reading, accounts for his lethal precision in all forms of commerce. He realized, as he indelibly absorbed no less than three guidebooks (including maps of the city) on the flight to Europe, just how the personality of Venice, with its maze of intertwining alleys and secrets, mirrors his own.

Even though darkness has fallen, and a swirling fog is seeping into the city, he walks the streets, crosses the bridges and piazzas with the confidence of one born and bred there. The somber ugly church of San Moise looms out of the darkness, revealed by weak flickering streetlights. Buried inside, he remembers from a guidebook, is John Law, the Scotsman who created one of the very first financial scams graced with the title "bubble." Although many distinguished names— Richard Wagner, Robert Browning, Sergei Diaghilev—have been chiseled into Venetian gravestones, it amuses Gauke that a fraudster, John Law, is among them. He died in poverty, a state that has always terrified Gauke. He quickly shakes the thought from his head; unpleasantness features little in his life. Emotionally he's fitted with a very effective garbage disposal unit. Turning into Calle Vallaresso he's treated to the distant lights of the San Marco pier bustling with traghetti crisscrossing the Grand Canal. The phantom taste of that first cold prosecco excites him.

A single table waits for him in Harry's Bar. Even if the ghosts of the jet set that once frequented it, of Hemingway, Welles, Capote, and Churchill, had bowed out before the avalanche of the nouveaux riches, Gauke had still wanted to experience the place. Already crammed with guzzling customers, he wouldn't have made it past the front door if a booking hadn't been made. One of his investors, an heiress and the distant relative of a Venetian count, had pulled some strings. Silk strings. His table is against the back wall: a prime position from which to observe the antics of his fellow consumers. Gauke's adult life has been spent scrutinizing the behavior of the wealthy—this evening is no exception. The prices listed in the menu confirm that your pockets need to be deep to eat here. No matter. He orders carpaccio and cucina Veneziana, then sits back, sips his drink, and lets his sky-blue eyes scan the posturing on display.

Filthy rich?

Stinking rich?

Eating alone in a restaurant frequented by the wealthy, as Gauke often does, witnessing them with their noses in the gilded trough, allows the observer uninterrupted time to appreciate just how grotesque, vacuous, vain, tasteless, and ignorant most of them are. He has every right to hate and destroy them; to strip them of their wealth; to deflate the thing he loathes most about them—their goddamn complacency.

Tonight Gauke is like a pathologist dissecting not only the scene beyond his table but the lonely voyeur sitting behind it. He begins to cautiously apply his scalpel to himself. Where had he gone wrong? When did it all go sour? At college he had studied philosophy. Why? He simply can't remember. Was he that ideological? Maybe. It must have been short-lived because the net result of three years studying ethics, semantics, epistemology, and metaphysics was one obsession: money. That was the only reality that interested him.

His time at Harvard, however, was not wasted when it came to that most valuable of attributes for the ambitious: *connections*. This network of influential contacts, sustained by his silver tongue and its ability to inspire trust, was the springboard from which he was able to dive into a vast pool of liquid funds. If he had ever been ideological, he'd certainly executed a perfect volte-face and entered without a ripple. At first even he was surprised at the level of greed he found among the wealthy. Greed soon became his bait; greed became the trump card he played every day of his professional life. For over thirty years he's had to stomach a constant diet of undiluted avarice; watch dollar signs eternally spinning in rapacious eyes; peer into the unfathomable depths of insatiable covetousness.

Gauke hungrily polishes off the thin strips of raw beef in the exquisite knowledge that carpaccio was reputedly first created in this very bar. The waiter now places the main dish in front of him: a stew of wild boar, peacock, and venison. Picking up his knife and fork he hesitates, not sure if it's his contemplation of this money-grubbing world, or sight of the cooked meats, that causes him to suddenly gag with nausea. He calls the waiter back.

"Il conto."

* * *

Outside, he breathes in deeply, seemingly unaware of the thick damp fog enveloping him. A violent fit of coughing grabs him, shaking the gathering vomit from his mouth. Not since childhood has he felt so forsaken; never before has his pursuit of loneliness become so apparent. His vibrating frame shifts from coughing to crying. The sound of his sobs is lost in the fog; not even God Almighty could hear or see him. It's as if Lenny Gauke no longer exists.

The journey back to the hotel is painfully slow and frightening. Hands reaching out like a blind man, he feels his way along walls, over bridges, bumping into railings and, occasionally, people. Each time he calls out, asking where he is, but nobody bothers to reply. He hears the water lapping in the canals and makes sure he veers away from the source of the sound. Moisture clings to his face and hands, saturates his clothes which adhere to his body. Hours pass. Close to collapse he suddenly, and inexplicably, finds himself in front of the Gritti Palace. The hotel just emerges from the fog like a photograph in a developing tray.

The staff manning reception are immediately alert to his return, as if they were waiting specifically for him. They whisper conspiratorially while one selects his key. It's Umberto. Gauke detects a distinct change in his attitude from when he checked in some four hours earlier: the man's eyes never once meet his and the receptionist makes no comment on his distressed appearance. He wonders if it's just paranoia on his part. Trying to control his chattering teeth, his voice hits a strident note, more of a bark.

"Have a bottle of Black Label whiskey sent up to my suite, per favore."

Umberto summons a look from the coldest regions of the Alps. "A bottle?"

"A bottle!"

Steaming hot water cascades loudly into the bath and Gauke barely hears the knock. The security chain is already in place when he partially opens the door. It's the boy porter again, this time with the scotch. Even he has lost his bounce, entering cautiously and retreating as soon as Gauke has signed for it. He doesn't even hang about for another gratuity.

Gauke is now convinced something momentous happened during his hellish outing to the bar. He makes sure the door is secure, turns the bath taps off and the television on. Pouring a large glass of whiskey, he settles down to watch the news. He sneezes. Instinctively he finds himself worrying if he's getting a cold—until a remote smile betrays the fleeting thought that it doesn't matter, as it won't have time to develop.

The television spews out reports on the multifarious horrors of human behavior perpetrated that day around the world, holding no interest for Gauke. When it reaches the sports coverage at the end of the newscast he withdraws to the bathroom, disappears in a cloud of steam, and sinks into the hot water. The sound of the television is relayed from hidden speakers. He empties the glass of whiskey in great gulps before sliding under the water; his abundant long white hair floats to the surface, waving like an exotic plant.

"*News is coming in of a body found in a sports car owned by prominent New York stock broker and investment advisor Leonard Gauke.*" The voice of the newscaster is drowned as the man himself noisily bursts to the surface. Great globs of water spill from the tub to the floor, saturating the bath mat. "*The victim is believed to be the brother . . .*"

By the time Gauke reaches the television, naked and dripping wet, the item is over and a weather forecast is in progress.

He fills the tumbler with whiskey and sinks it down. Was that a knock on the door? He kills the sound of the television. There it is again, a gentle brief knocking on his door. He pads quietly across the room and looks through the security spy hole. The corridor appears to be empty so his visitor must have left, or is standing beside the door with his back to the wall. Now the telephone rings. When he reaches the receiver the caller hangs up, leaving him listening to the tone of a dead line. He sees his naked frame in the same mirror he'd smiled into when he first arrived. This time he doesn't smile. Instead he retrieves from the bathroom a huge white bathrobe and wraps it around himself.

When he wakes he finds the whiskey bottle empty. Slithers of cold dawn light percolate past the heavy curtains onto the sofa that he'd collapsed on. The muted television is showing images of himself, Eve, his two daughters, his only son, his brother and his two sons; Gauke, like the Mafia he admires so much, employs mostly family. Unused to heavy drinking he has a hangover so painful he decides against turning up the sound. Besides, the pictures tell their own story. It amuses him to watch the newscasters tossing fact after fact to each other like a shuttlecock.

Well into the news item they cut to a faded picture of Charles Ponzi from the 1920s, and Gauke knows he's being compared to the man after whom his particular scheme for defrauding investors has been named. He knew Ponzi was an Italian immigrant, and wondered if he'd come from Venice. Closely watching the newscaster's mouth he could tell she was saying that he, Lenny Gauke, had masterminded the largest Ponzi scheme ever. All too true. And it had paid for, among many other properties and possessions, the seventy-foot rac-

ing yacht now on the screen. There's its name filling the
screen—*Making Waves*—an apt one under the circumstances.

Gauke groans when the shot is replaced with one of med-
ics removing a body and bringing it to the quayside. He adored
his brother Arthur. It was he who had made, at Lenny's be-
hest, the arrangement with the Mafia; he who had paid them
for services still to be rendered; he who was intending to report the Ponzi scheme to the authorities. "You've run out of
road, Lenny," was how Arthur had put it. For all these reasons
he'd had to shoot him. Incarceration for either of them was
not an option. Incapable of seeing his brother suffer, he'd put
him down like he was a favorite pet.

There's a knock on the door. Moments later the phone
rings. Gauke reacts to neither but hurriedly starts dressing. He
drags a chair to the window and waits. Eventually a vaporetto
full of new arrivals docks at the hotel pier. As they begin to
disembark Gauke stands, quickly pulls the collar of his coat
around his ears and a baseball cap tightly over his eyes. He
quietly releases the security chain, eases open the door, and
slips into the empty corridor. By the time he reaches the foyer
the party of guests has engulfed the receptionists. Moving rapidly he circumnavigates the gaggle of people, scuttling unno-
ticed from the hotel.

Nothing prepared him for the vast herd of gawping visitors
crushed into the Piazza San Marco. The Venice he'd chosen
to come to was no longer the Venice of his imagination. That
invisible city in his head had been conjured some forty years
earlier, long before the devastating tsunami of tourism had hit
it. Only then did he recognize the time warp he'd inhabited
for so long: fraud had preoccupied him to the exclusion of all
else. Reality comes crashing in as he watches in horror the
day trippers swarming into the square. Against a setting of

such wonder and beauty, man appears ugly, very ugly. That, however, he *was* prepared for.

For someone accustomed to receiving preferential treatment wherever and whenever he appears in public, to being feared and fawned over by rich clients, much like the doges whose Palazzo Ducale he can see in the distance, the indignity of being jostled by this crowd of nobodies is unbearable. He'd foolishly expected to walk straight into the Basilica of St. Mark, contemplate in peace the famous mosaics, seek spiritual succour alone in the presence of Tintoretto's *Paradiso*, but that was not to be. Gauke immediately dismisses any idea of waiting in line and consequently gets to contemplate nothing except his own misery.

In a pathetic attempt to hide his lonely status he hovers uncertainly on the outskirts of the square, close to the campanile, where a guide's sing-song voice catches his attention. The woman explains in execrable English that, like much of Venice, these watch towers were built on mud flats and, again like much of Venice, are very unstable. The most famous of them, the Campanile of St. Mark's, was originally built in 912 and quickly became so much part of the city that it seemed eternal. "One eighteenth-century guidebook," here she reads from her notebook, "described the tower as never showing the slightest sign of leaning, shaking, or giving way. Then, early one July morning in 1793, it suddenly made a slight shudder, silently shook itself, and slowly collapsed."

He wanders aimlessly toward the other side of the square, savoring the words the guide had chosen. Like the old tower in the Piazza San Marco, his ivory one had just shuddered, shaken, and collapsed without warning. What had possessed him to embark on the fraud all those years ago? Surely he'd known from the start the bubble would eventually *have* to burst. Had he been so delusional as to think otherwise? Or just plain arrogant? Or was it the sheer stupidity of the investors that first began to intrigue, even amuse him. As he'd pumped up his promised returns, making them increasingly ludicrous, even mathematically impossible, the more they clamored to be his clients, part of his elite inner circle. The inanity of the rich, their moronic smugness, their compulsive fixation with money, had finally poisoned him. He began to despise them; he wanted to hurt them, destroy them, make them experience destitution and poverty. Like his parents had.

This brooding is abruptly broken by a change in the light. The sun has come out. Yes, Venice is proving to be the right choice after all.

Now the familiar smile returns as he again looks across at the Doge's Palace. He recalls what lies in store there for the visitor, and has no desire to share it. Its gilded exterior is a beguiling façade for the horrors that still haunt this city. He's thinking of the dungeons: the sweltering Piombi under the roof, or the damp hellish gloom of the Pozzi in the bowels of the building. Just thinking of Venice's secret police curdled blood across medieval Europe. The Council of Ten and the Council of Three dispatched agents across every land in pursuit of revenge; nobody escaped. "The Ten send you to the torture chamber," the Venetians used to say, "the Three to your grave." He nods in agreement with himself: it's better for Arthur to be dead than suffering the torture of a life sentence in jail.

The warm sun encourages him to dream and drift. Morning turns into afternoon, and afternoon into evening, as he walks across piazzas, over bridges, onto piers and vaporetti, crisscrossing the Canal Grande, finally shedding all sight of tourists and their trappings. So intense is his curious state of euphoria that every sight, sound, and smell dissolves into a ghostly sensual pentimento. He even forgets that behind the city's Renaissance veneer, the splendor of its façades, there lies a layer of squalor. Slums sit like diseased pockmarks across the city, and it's in one such place that Gauke's dreaming and drifting comes to an end. Born in a slum, like a homing pigeon, he's back in one.

For some reason he had assumed they would shoot him. Only when two tattooed muscular arms loop over his head does he realize he was wrong. He was to be garroted. A wire glints in the sunlight as it closes on his throat, cuts into the flesh, severs his esophagus, then the carotid arteries. Blood spurts against the decaying wall of the alley he's being dragged into. As he loses consciousness his admiration for the Mafia soars. Efficient, effective, and economic. Why waste a bullet? The assassin backs away, letting him fall to the muddy cobblestones. Bulging from their sockets, his eyes are wide open as he hits the ground. Lenny Gauke's world, as he finally sees it, is the way he always knew it was: *upside down*.

The next morning urchins find his corpse among a mangle of rusty cans, broken bottles, bent bicycle wheels, plastic bags, and used condoms. The canal, gently lapping at the end of the alley, is washing over his fancy handmade shoes. Perversely, the boys are not so shocked by the gaping wound in his neck as by the black bloated misshapen object sticking obscenely through the blood caked about his mouth. Only later does the pathologist confirm that the obscene object was, in fact, Signor Gauke's tongue.

PART IV

An Imperfect Present

TOURISTS FOR SUPPER

by Maria Tronca

Santa Maria Formosa

Translated from Italian by Judith Forshaw

The tide was rising quickly. In less than half an hour three-quarters of the city would be flooded and the water would flow over and submerge everything below sixty inches. The acqua alta was bad; it had been going on for three days and gave no sign of wanting to end its siege of La Serenissima and its tired, infuriated residents. And the tourists, who were charmed and excited to start with, were just as frustrated and irritated after the second day.

The female, on the other hand, was happy. By now she was finding it hard to run with her pregnant bump—it weighed her down and made her slow—and it was more comfortable and she could move more easily if she swam. Another couple of days and she would give birth. On her own. She stuck her head through the wide crack in the wall and quickly looked to the left and right. No one, just water, silence, and beauty. She loved this city, still and eternal, tasting of salt and mold, with its foundations covered in algae and the great marble palazzi built on millions of upside-down tree trunks. They said that the city was dying, suffocated by the tourists and the greed of shopkeepers and restaurateurs, gondoliers and taxi pilots. They said it was sinking, that its population was decreasing, and soon it would become a ghost town, a huge open-air museum, a theme park for grown-ups, the Disneyland of art. But she would not have chosen any other city in the world, and she was happy that her babies would be born here. She sighed as she thought about her husband; he had been gone for three days and she did not want to believe that he had abandoned her. Something must have happened, but she didn't have the faintest idea what that something could be. She sighed again, and with that small amount of agility she had left, she plunged into the water. The tide now covered the entire foundation of San Giovanni in Laterano and was creating a single, very broad canal, making the black iron railing that stood there, in the middle of the water, look surreal, pointless, and isolated. The female with her blue-black fur swam underwater until she reached the wall of the palazzo opposite the one where she had stayed all day, safe. She was hungry but the acqua alta, helped by the current, would deliver supper to her door—she just had to wait for the first bag of trash to be swept past by the tide and she would be okay for the following day as well. She resurfaced and checked the wall of red bricks for a wide enough crack; it was hard to breathe and she could feel her babies moving incessantly inside her. A tear merged with the beads of water on her water-repellent coat, but she held back the rest and made herself think only about supper and about her little ones and all the things she would teach them. She calculated the route she needed to follow and plunged under the water again, swimming toward the palazzo's canal-side entrance. She reached the bottom steps, which were completely submerged, and headed for the lower cornice running along the wall; it supported one end of the drainpipe, a staircase that would lead her to the crack where she could rest. A sudden and excruciating spasm in her abdomen took her breath away and immobilized her under the water; she was just a few yards from her destination but it seemed an infinite uphill distance to cover with that pain. She looked in front of her; the steps seemed to be the only solution—they would take her to the courtyard inside the palazzo and she was bound to find some hidden corner where she could give birth. She moved slowly; the pain had faded and she began to breathe again, but she was scared she might have a second spasm, stronger than the first. The large rectangular courtyard was flooded and at first glance it didn't seem to provide any cover; she felt trapped and her fear made her nauseous. A distant squeak made her prick up her ears; perhaps there was someone who could help her. She floated motionless in the water, straining to catch even the smallest change in the still silence; the merest vibration would have been enough, but she could hear only the sound of the small waves that lapped against the brick and cement walls and the simmering of the rising water.

She thought she must have imagined it.

She shook herself out of her immobility and moved toward the center of the courtyard. On the right, beyond a marble wall, a staircase opened up; just looking at it made her feel short of breath and exhausted. And it was dangerous to venture so close to humans; they were savage, dangerous animals. But deep down she liked them, especially when they laughed and sang. It was a pity they were so scared of her kind, especially as their fear was totally unjustified.

The female shuddered and peered again at the stairs that rose up into the dark. Yes it was dangerous, but there was no other option. She started to quickly climb the wide steps, but the overpowering smell of food and the warmth that radiated from an apartment on the first landing made her stop. She was tired and hungry; she was frightened and could burst into tears at any moment. A blade of light shone through the crack under the door; the female drew nearer and nestled her damp nose between the wooden door and the floor, sniffing at the heat and the scent of home and food. An imperceptible noise chased her away to the next flight of stairs. She hoped at last to find a place to rest and some peace at the end of her climb, but her path came to an abrupt end on the seventh step, which opened under her paws and swallowed her up.

Signora Adele cleared the table, washed the plate and glass and the small pan in which she had fried an egg, cleaned the stove top where some oil had splashed, and swept up the few crumbs on the tablecloth. She went and sat down on the sofa in the living room and switched on the television hoping to catch a nice romantic film, possibly something from her youth. But she knew it was virtually impossible that her sort of film would be on, at least at that time of day. They broadcast them toward the end of the evening and sometimes late at night, hours after she usually went to sleep, and she never managed to stay awake for them. And anyway, sometimes it turned out not to be a love story at all. She didn't like detective films or gialli, let alone horror or war films. They upset her and she found them too frightening. Signora Adele needed things that were romantic and nice; pleasant, pretty images; gentle and harmonious sounds. She was a simple and sensitive soul; she loved poetry and the theater, two things that hardly anyone was interested in anymore. Once upon a time they used to have plays on television, often even Goldoni's, in Venetian, and she used to watch them all. When she was younger she went to the theater every week—she had season tickets—but then her husband died and she had started to suffer from osteoarthritis in her knees.

Little by little she had stopped going out: she found it

difficult to move up and down the stairs, and there was no elevator in her building. But even if there had been one the situation would have been the same: with all the bridges in Venice there was no avoiding steps. They delivered her groceries from the nearby delicatessen, a lonely survivor—along with the wine merchant and the butcher—of the string of small shops that until five years before had lined the entire length of the street. The bakery had gone, and the dairy, the fishmonger, and the grocer. And also the cobbler, the haberdasher, the health center, and the ironmonger. Now there were just glass and mask shops, second-rate garbage that was made on the other side of the world and was all identical. And bars, restaurants, hotels, and B&Bs. Prices had rocketed and houses had been deserted; families had moved away to the mainland, replaced by the tourists who swarmed into the city. Their numbers had grown every year and they brought with them a huge amount of money and filth. And vulgarity. All they wanted to do was eat, drink, sleep, and buy souvenirs, and to keep them happy the shopkeepers had been driven out, families evicted, and the city condemned to death. And not just any city—La Serenissima: the most beautiful city in the world. Unique, one of a kind.

When Signora Adele stopped to think about it for more than a few minutes she felt ill; it made her anxious, she had difficulty breathing, and she got the unpleasant sensation that her living space was shrinking. Her own home! Too many people, too many heads, legs, arms moving along like a single entity, too many mouths talking, singing, shouting, making an unbearable din. Too much litter, ice cream dropped on the ground and melting on the street, bits of discarded pizza along with bottles and cans in every corner. She saw it all from her window: she didn't have to go outside, all she needed to do was look out and watch the flood of people that flowed every day through the alley where her building stood. Thank goodness some of her windows looked out onto the canal, where there was simply peace and quiet and the smell of the ocean and seaweed. The gondoliers didn't pass under her windows: she heard their voices from far away and the songs with which they entertained the tourists—it was almost pleasant. It took her back to when courting couples, people on their honeymoon, and even Venetians used to ride on the gondolas. There were none of those horrible water taxis then, speeding along the canals and across the lagoon, shaking the foundations of the palazzi with their noise and the waves they left in their wake. Signora Adele was extremely upset by the barbarian invasion and was unable to accept the fact that her city was now being held hostage by people she thought were vulgar and greedy, who were destroying its beauty and had delivered it into the hands of the tourists.

There was nothing she wanted to watch on television so she switched it off and went to the window that looked out onto the street, pulling her checked flannel dressing gown around her and straightening the woolen shawl on her shoulders since it was especially cold that evening. Signora Adele was a large woman—tall and plump—she was seventy, and apart from the osteoarthritis in her knees, she felt quite well. The hairdresser used to come to her home twice a week, and once a month she would touch up the color, a dusty pale blue verging on silver that brought out the blue of her eyes, by now rather watery but still pretty.

The street was silent now; the odd person walked past every so often—young people going to and from the Rialto and the area around the Erbaria, which was full of clubs and tourists enjoying a night out. At the end of the street she could see the dome of Santa Maria Formosa, the church she had attended since she was a girl. Nowadays people watched mass on television—it was all the same to them. When she was young, Signora Adele was always out and about: she did ironing and had clients all over the city. She loved walking along the alleys, constantly finding new shortcuts through tiny passageways or hidden canal-side paths. She knew every corner of Venice; she knew about places that perhaps not even the old people who had lived there all their lives were aware of. She used to meet Alvise, her late husband, every evening in Piazza San Marco, between the two columns that watch over the Bacino, and they would stand in silence at the water's edge, gazing at the lights of the Giudecca glittering on the opposite shore. Signora Adele rested her head against the cold glass of the window and let a single tear run down her lined cheek.

That evening she felt a bit more sad than usual, and the only thing that comforted her was the thought that tomorrow would be the first day of the carnival. The city was already packed with tourists who couldn't wait to put on their stupid, and stupidly expensive, costumes and strut about, showing off to other idiots dressed up like clowns. They paid a fortune to rent the costumes and she didn't understand how they could derive any pleasure from it. In her day, everyone made their own masks; they asked their parents, their relatives, and their friends to help. They put some thought into their costumes, which they sewed piece by piece; usually they were simple, patched, a bit amateurish, but how satisfying it was to wear something that you had made yourself! What fun! The delirium of masks that jostled and thronged in the alleys lasted for a week, blocking the streets and making it almost impossible for the poor residents to get around, and every year there would

be a few silly people who would find themselves without anywhere to sleep. And they would arrive at her house, drawn to
the notice that she had stuck on the wall above her intercom:
ROOMS FOR RENT. During the carnival she put up a larger
sign that covered all the other doorbells as well; in any case,
she was the only person who still lived in the building. All the
other tenants had moved out and the owner was just waiting
for her to die so that she could turn the building into a hotel,
or sell it to some rich Russian or Chinese or Arab who would
do the same thing. Damn them!

She was the last port of call for exhausted youngsters with
enormous backpacks, for adventurous couples or elderly people who had lost the rest of their group and were too tired
to walk another step. All of them naïve, unwary, and stupid.
Leeches, parasites.

Signora Adele trembled with excitement every time she
heard the doorbell ring; she knew it was one of them and she
looked forward to saying yes, there were vacancies, as many
as they wanted. And what a thrill she felt when she saw their
tired faces break into smiles of relief and gratitude; what a
pleasure it was to take them off the streets. Forever.

If it was lunchtime or dinnertime, she cooked for them,
insisting that they accept, or else she offered them a coffee,
a tea, a tisane. Anything in which she could put her magic
white powder, odorless and tasteless, that took them out of action in about five minutes. And when they had finished eating
and drinking, and couldn't nurse their drinks any longer, she
brought them to see the room.

"Excuse me, I'll show the way," she would say.

She would open a small door, switch on the light, and
move aside to let them enter. Usually they were already half
asleep, their eyelids drooping. They would take a step through

the doorway and then fall, sometimes without even having time to cry out, and her little friends would finally have fresh meat. There was no floor in that room—it had collapsed many years before—there was a void that went right down to a basement, a storeroom that was always partially flooded and that she had transformed into a vast lair.

It was a friend of hers who had given her the idea.

"Why don't you put people up? You've got so many rooms, and it pays well!"

It had been a flash of inspiration, a bulb that had come on in her brain and lit up her life. It was a bad time—the building was emptying and the shops were closing one after another. The alleys were more and more dirty and crowded, the tourists more and more numerous, noisy, and rude. Signora Adele was angry, exasperated. Her hatred for that human scum had become so strong that she hadn't been able to sleep or eat, and what they were doing to her city made her feel physically sick. So she had decided to intervene, to do something to clean up Venice. In her own small way and according to her means. She would take in tourists, but in her own way.

Soon, another "sign" suggested to her the idea of getting her little friends to help. She had just been entering the house when she saw one plunge into the void, through the broken step. The squeak she heard from the other side of the door made her realize that it had ended up in the windowless basement. The first ones had arrived like that, by chance. They were hungry and frightened and Signora Adele decided it couldn't be a coincidence: it was a sign from heaven. So she had begun to attract more of them, putting out bait to make sure they found their way to the right spot and then fell down the hole. She caught them one at a time, and now there were lots and lots. She had no idea how many there were, but from their squeaking she thought there must be hundreds, and so she had stopped putting out bait. And now there was no need for bait; they reproduced quickly on their own. At first she had fed them: not only did she throw her leftovers into the pit, she had also bought food especially for them, then she had stopped. And she started to feed them with the flesh of the invaders.

She would smile with the contentment of a mother feeding her babies when she heard them squeak happily as their food arrived at last.

The drop into the void seemed to go on forever, and while she was falling, in the cold and musty darkness, she thought about the babies inside her and hoped for a miracle—a soft landing. She prayed she would not die, otherwise her little ones would die too. And God heard her and broke her fall with a soft, warm blanket of fur that enveloped her in an embrace that seemed to be moving. But it was also very noisy. The moment she landed she heard a cry—more of surprise and protest than of fear—that was repeated by a thousand other voices, creating a monstrous echo that reverberated off the walls of the mysterious place where she had landed.

Aaaah! But where . . . ?!

The female found herself in the water; the soft surface she had landed on had suddenly disappeared, its place taken by the black, cold tide.

She looked around and shook her head in disbelief; she blinked once, twice, three times to be sure that she wasn't dreaming. All around her there were hundreds of squeaking rats, frightened and startled by her abrupt arrival. Some of them were swimming underwater, others were scrambling up the brick walls and running around anxiously, worried and ready to defend themselves.

"But where am I?" she said, thinking aloud.

"Who are you?" questioned a chorus of voices.

"Yes . . . who are you?" other voices repeated.

"Where are you from?" asked yet more.

"What do you want?" demanded the echoing crowd.

"THAT'S ENOUGH!" shouted someone very near her, and suddenly the roar of questions died down and a silence descended.

The female was terrified and swam in circles looking at the gaping mouths that had been screaming at her and those unfriendly eyes staring at her. Her heart was beating fast and the babies were wriggling in her swollen stomach.

"Who are you?" the voice that had shouted before asked her gently; it was very close.

She turned and saw a kindly muzzle, adorned with long gray whiskers, and two dark, deep eyes that smiled at her.

"I'm Milly and I fell, I was going up some steps and all of a sudden the floor went from under my paws, I thought I was dead, I'm pregnant," she replied without pausing for breath. The silence was complete, but her last words had triggered thousands of exclamations of pity and sympathy from all the females.

"I'm Grazia. I'm in charge of this community . . . I'm the oldest and I welcome you on behalf of everyone here . . . Come along, you must be tired and hungry . . . There's somewhere dry where you can rest, but you'll have to wait for food . . . Follow me."

The large female headed toward one of the redbrick walls that enclosed the flooded basement and, as she walked, hundreds of rats drew aside to let her through. Each of them had a kind word, a welcoming touch, a shy smile for Milly, who was confused; her head was spinning and she wasn't at all sure that she was really awake.

Grazia led her toward a wooden structure, the base of which was submerged underwater; it had three rows of horizontal planks, each about a yard long. All the flat, dry surfaces were occupied by females and their young, and along the vertical posts that led to the various levels there was a steady stream of rats running to and fro. The old female rat climbed up to the top of what must have been a bookcase and came to a stop on the last shelf.

"Come along, Milly," she said as she motioned with her muzzle to the other rats to move. "It'll be nice and quiet here; it looks like you don't have long to go . . . As you can see, you're in good company . . ."

Milly followed her gaze and realized that the females who were living on the plank were all pregnant, or had recently given birth.

"Oh!" she exclaimed, her eyes wide.

"We call it the palace of life . . . Only mothers-to-be and new mothers with their babies stay here . . . They stay until their little ones are weaned and we take turns bringing food and water and we help with the birth when it's needed . . . Here you'll be safe, you can be quiet and just think about your babies."

Milly stared at her open-mouthed while the other females with their round stomachs came toward her and sat down around her, embracing her in a ring of protection and kindness. The tears she had held back for so long now blurred her sight and a flurry of silent sobs rippled over her pregnant body. She shut her eyes and crumpled like an empty sack. Someone lightly stroked her neck, then her shoulders, her bump and muzzle, and soon she felt a single, all-enveloping embrace from paws, noses, and tails that held her gently.

"My husband . . ." she murmured.

"What's his name?" asked a nice voice nearby.

"Rocco . . . I haven't heard from him in three days. He went out to look for food and didn't come back . . ."

"I don't think he's here, but I can ask my husband. Perhaps Rocco is somewhere like this, where he can't get out . . . like us. Calm down now—all these tears are bad for your babies."

Milly sighed deeply and dried her eyes on the fur of her paw; she turned her head and looked into two large, gentle hazel eyes with long lashes.

"Hi," said a little face, young and cunning, framed by a thick, reddish down. "I'm Ambra. Nice to meet you, Milly. I've got a feeling your babies aren't going to make you wait much longer." She glanced at Milly's enormous stomach that made her look like a ball with legs. And she smiled at her.

That led to more introductions.

"Hi, Milly, I'm Paola."

"A pleasure to meet you. My name's Enza."

"I'm Giovanna . . ."

"Martina . . ."

"Perla . . ."

They smiled at her and competed to move closer. She responded to everyone—"A pleasure. Milly"—immediately forgetting the huge number of names, all called out at the same time.

"That's enough now," said the calm voice of Grazia, "let her get her breath back . . . She has to rest . . . Ambra . . ."

"Yes?!" squeaked the cunning little face.

"She'll be next to you. Make room for her and tell her everything she needs to know. I think the next one will be here soon . . . It'll be better if she's prepared . . . And the rest of you—move! And look after your own bumps, and your children . . . Come on, back to your own spaces!"

"Okay, Grazia . . . Come on, Milly, over here . . ." Ambra's voice had darkened and she had lowered her ears against the side of her head, giving her an unhappy, annoyed expression.

The young red-haired female pushed her way through her companions—some with prominent bumps, others less so—and nests of babies who were suckling milk from their mothers or sleeping one on top of another.

As she followed, Milly noticed heaps of rags on the planks forming warm, soft nests. There were pieces of material of different colors and patterns, sleeves from shirts and sweaters, strips from skirts, fragments of pants, the cups of bras, and panties. They looked to her like the remains of a clothes shop where a bomb had gone off.

"How come you have all these rags?" she asked Ambra once they had arrived at her nest, at the end of the plank.

The red-haired female sat down heavily on a piece of gray wool that still had a button attached and rested a paw on her prominent stomach; with the other she beckoned Milly to settle down beside her. "They're from tourists," she told her in a hesitant voice.

"What tourists? Do you steal them?!"

"No, that is . . . We take them. They're no use to them anymore."

"Why not?"

"Because . . . they're dead . . ."

"Eugh! But dead how? Do you undress the dead bodies?!"

"No, Milly . . . we . . . God, why do I have to tell her?! The thing is . . . we eat them."

The female with the blue-black fur raised her paws to her mouth, stifling a shriek of horror, but she wasn't able to hold back the nausea that overwhelmed her. She leaned over to one side and vomited. No one protested, there wasn't even a grumble, and Milly became aware of an unnatural hush that had fallen, not just in the palace of life but in the whole of the large basement. Even the babies had stopped their shrill squeaking. Everyone was listening to what Ambra was saying.

"I'm sorry," she murmured, "but we don't have any choice . . . We're prisoners. Either we eat them or we all die."

"But how . . . ? Why . . . ? Who . . . ?"

Ambra sighed and grimaced, though she meant it to be a smile. "Above this basement there's a woman's apartment . . . Look up, there . . . see? There's no ceiling."

Milly nodded, unable to make a sound.

"It used to be the floor of one of the rooms of the house, but it caved in who knows how long ago. The door you can see opens into her home and it's always closed, except for when . . . the tourists arrive and fall down here. I don't know how she does it or why, but she does. These are their clothes. We take them, divide them up, and use them for our nests."

"But why don't you all leave? No, wait. How did you all end up here?"

"I don't know about the first ones—perhaps she caught them. The others, all of us, were born here and had babies of our own. There's over a thousand of us now, and even though this place is huge, there'll come a time when there won't be room for everyone. Grazia says we should start to think about limiting the number of births . . . It's been awhile now since anybody's arrived, but now it's carnival and lots of people visit . . . I know it's awful but they're the only source of food we have, and their clothes keep the babies warm."

"I can't believe there's no way to escape, to get away from this horror. You can't have looked very hard, there must be a crack, a hole . . . something!" There was a touch of hysteria in Milly's voice.

"We've searched this place inch by inch, my dear," said Grazia in a voice that was resigned and sad. "We've even tried digging, but we found only stone and petrified wood, as hard as rock."

"And me?"

"What about you?"

"How did I get here?"

"From the broken step, I imagine . . ."

"But if there's a way in, there's a way out, isn't there?"

"No . . . the basement wall that ought to go up to the steps has a gap in it; the bit that joined them has collapsed too . . . It's a very old building and it's falling into ruin, one brick after another . . . We're stuck here . . ."

"No, there has to be a way. Doesn't the woman ever go out?"

"No . . . we watched her for days, from under the door. They put her groceries in a basket she lowers from the window . . . She's always in the house, on her own. Her imprisonment is voluntary, unlike ours."

"Yes, but . . . you can't keep on eating people!" Milly was talking to herself, she was thinking aloud, and in the huge flooded cellar there still hung a thick, heavy silence. "I know you do it to survive but it still isn't right and I think you haven't really tried to get out . . . After all, you're doing okay here . . . and I imagine you eventually get over the sense of guilt and get used to the horror. You're behaving just like them, humans, when they're at their worst . . . But we're not like that—we love them, even if they hate us and despise us, even if we disgust them . . . We love their funny ideas and their high spirits, we're their friends . . . even if they're our enemies. We don't eat people, no, we don't eat them—"

Suddenly, all the ears that had been turned toward her

pricked up and rotated slightly, all in the same direction: the door into the void. Signora Adele was talking to someone, and in the background they could hear the sound of saucers, cups, and teaspoons, of biscuits being broken and jaws crunching them.

"They're about to arrive," said Grazia in a solemn voice, but Milly noticed that her eyes were gleaming. She looked around her and saw that the other rats had the same expression of deep sadness but also great expectation.

"How long has it been since you've eaten?" she asked Ambra.

"A long time . . . too long," she replied, keeping her gaze fixed on the door. "You're right," she added a second later, looking Milly in the eye, "we're monsters and we shouldn't feed on them, but I'd eat anyone to make sure my babies survive . . . You know that most of the time they're still alive?"

Milly felt sick and retched again; this time she held it back but an expression of incredulity and horror was etched on her face.

"We kill them right away, we aim for the jugular or the aorta . . . They don't suffer much . . . Once no one arrived for months . . . Do you want to know what happened?"

"N . . . no . . . wh . . . what?"

"Carnage . . . We ended up eating each other and—"

"Stop it!" shushed Milly. The tears that were filling her eyes streamed over the fur on her muzzle and she shrank into the redbrick wall against which the bookcase rested.

Ambra stopped talking and turned to stare at the door, waiting.

"Get ready!" Grazia suddenly cried, and all the rats moved at the same time as if they were one. An immense furry army cleared the center of the mirrorlike black tide that covered the floor of the flooded cellar, leaving it empty, ready to swallow up the next lavish meal. They settled along the walls, quickly scrambling up, almost to the ceiling. Only ten or so remained in the dark water; they were the ones who would finish off their wounded prey. The first to feed would be the females who were pregnant or had recently given birth, then the elderly and the weaned babies, and finally the adolescents and the adult males.

The door opened slowly, creaking on its rusty hinges, and a shaft of light entered the dark basement, lighting up a slice of the submerged floor. It was then that Milly realized there were things floating on the water. They were light in color and smooth, some long, others rounded or slightly pointed. It took her a few seconds to work out what these strange objects were, and when she did she hid her face in her paws. She hadn't noticed them before because it had been too dark and the rats had completely covered the surface of the water, but now that it was almost empty she had seen them and recognized them: bones from thighs and forearms, knuckles, vertebrae, and skulls. The leftovers from the rats' meals. The only traces of the passing of human beings from that hell.

The influx of light was accompanied by Signora Adele's laugh, followed by two other cheerful voices.

"Here we are! Please, come in . . . Oh, how silly! I forgot to turn the light on. Can you do it, please? The switch is there, on the right."

A hand and a foot came into view at the same time, and immediately after that a body tumbled down into the void, followed by another who had been gently pushed by Signora Adele. The thud was hideous and the splash reached as high as the third level of the palace of life, where Milly was curled up into a ball, her muzzle buried in the heap of rags that made up her nest and her paws covering her ears. She didn't want to see or hear; she would have liked to have been a thousand miles away from there, even all alone in the night, in labor, without anywhere to go or anyone to help her. Even hell would have been better than this slaughterhouse.

The man and the woman, two elderly people, barely had time to scream—"Ooooh!" and "Aaaah!"—more in astonishment than fear. Then they landed heavily on the fifteen inches of icy, slimy water and had no idea where they were or what was happening to them. Ambra was right: their deaths were quick and virtually painless. Milly heard all the rats talking at the same time, creating a monstrous collective squeak. A few were excited and relieved because food had finally arrived, some were crying, and others were giving directions. And above it all, the voice of Grazia was telling them what to do. The palace of life began to shake and Milly opened one eye to take a peek. All the females were leaving their nests and descending to the water to go eat. The operation was extremely orderly and swift as all the rats went to feed on the tourists. She, however, did not eat, and even when she met the eye of Grazia, who kindly invited her to have something, she stayed where she was, on the top level of the palace of life, demurely hungry.

When all the rodents had finished eating, there was very little left of the two bodies: just the skeleton of one, and a bit more of the other.

In the meantime the tide had started to recede, and within a couple of hours there would be left in its place a thick layer of dark sludge in which the white of human bones would be clearly visible.

Milly touched her swollen stomach and sighed; she could not understand why she hadn't already gone into labor after all this emotional turmoil. She closed her eyes and fell asleep almost at once; her last thought was for her husband and the two tourists who were resting in peace in the bellies of the rats.

Signora Adele was furious: that fat bitch had broken the handle of the door to the "guest room." When she pushed the woman after her husband, who was already falling into her darling little friends' lair, that idiot had tried to grab hold of her, and then snatched at the door handle. And since she was obese she had nearly wrenched it off, which meant that Signora Adele couldn't close the door anymore—it remained slightly ajar. That moron had deprived her of one of the few pleasures still left to her: watching her friends welcome the guests she gave them as a gift. The handle almost coming off had distracted her and put her in a bad mood, and Signora Adele had slammed the door violently and went to sink into her favorite armchair, the one with the floral velvet upholstery that was so threadbare it was almost transparent. And she didn't get to enjoy seeing them have their meal. She regretted this now and she was twice as angry. She fervently hoped she would be able to do it again with the next tourists; she was certain more would arrive the following day. The city was a masked hell, and among all those crowds there was sure to be some other fool with nowhere to stay. She went into the kitchen and poured herself another cup of tea; those two bastards had eaten almost all her biscuits. They were uncouth and coarse. *Two ignorant scumbags*, thought Signora Adele as she switched on the television and collapsed again into her armchair, turning the volume up so she couldn't hear the noise of the masked revelers passing under her window.

A whimpering squeak woke Milly; she rubbed her eyes with

her paws and poked her muzzle out of the nest of rags. The basement floor was completely carpeted with rats sleeping almost on top of each other. Legs and tails intertwined, one head a cushion for another. The darkness was as deep as the silence, but Milly noticed that a sliver of light seeped from the door into the abyss—it hadn't been there before. She looked more closely, trying to work out where it came from, yet she couldn't: it was too far away for her to identify the source of the glow. But she desperately wanted to find out. Trying to make as little noise as possible, she crept out of the nest of rags and went down to the bottom level of the palace. The water had receded completely and it was a nuisance having to walk through the mud—it was smelly and sticky—but she braced herself and quickly crossed the room to get to the redbrick wall that would allow her to scramble up to the top. She had to climb only halfway up to realize that the door had been left ajar. She thought it was a sign, an opportunity not to be missed. She rapidly climbed down again and went back to her nest; she had to think and organize the escape. After about an hour she went to look for Grazia. She found her near one of the wooden struts of the palace of life; she drew closer and sat next to her, out of breath and with her paws on her stomach.

"Have you seen it too?" the elderly female asked her all of a sudden, making her jump.

"You mean the light? Yes . . . the door's slightly open . . . We can leave."

"Leave? How? And go where? Milly, it's pointless."

"Hang on a minute, let me speak . . . I've got a plan."

"Let's hear it," Grazia said in a tired voice, still half-asleep.

"You said they put her groceries in a basket that's lowered from the window, didn't you?"

"That's right."

"Good. Well . . . I've thought it over: one of us will go into her house and stay there until she opens the window to get her food supplies . . . then they'll come and tell us and we'll go up to the door—we'll push it open and we'll escape through the open window."

"But you realize that it'll be chaos? Do you know how many of us there are? Over a thousand!"

"It doesn't matter what happens . . . and anyway I've given it some thought—nothing really bad can happen. People will scream, run away, feel sick, and throw up. And that's all . . . We'll dive into the canal and disappear. We're fast . . . and no one is about to give birth—except me—and almost all the babies are weaned . . . We can do it . . . please . . ." She looked at Grazia with eyes full of hope and determination. "I'm going anyway, with or without you, and I'll take along anyone who wants to come . . . with or without your permission . . ."

"Oh my Lord!" Grazia exclaimed, shaking her head with an air of resignation. She stood for a while looking at Milly and understood that she would do things her own way regardless.

"Okay, we'll put it to a vote. If the majority agree with your idea, we'll all go. If not, anyone who wants to can follow you . . . but the others will stay."

"That's fine," whispered Milly, hoping that every single one of the rats would raise their paw and vote yes, even if in her heart she didn't believe it would happen.

"General assembly! Wake up, lads," Grazia said without needing to raise her voice. Lots of the rats moaned, turning over onto their other side, others got right up, and most opened their eyes slowly, stretched, and sat up, sniffing the air and directing their muzzles and ears toward Grazia, who had climbed up to the first level of the palace of life so she could be seen and heard by everyone.

The large gray female slowly explained the plan, and when she had finished Milly sensed that the hundreds of eyes that had previously been fixed on Grazia were now resting on her, a few of which were hostile.

"I'm going with her," concluded the matriarch, "but you can all do what you want, according to your own conscience."

The voting was quick and the result unequivocal: 1,064 yes, 15 no, 35 abstentions.

Milly was overjoyed and let out a squeak of exhilaration and delight that triggered a surge of excited applause.

Pippo was chosen as the "lookout," a young rat with dark brown fur, two lively winking eyes, and a pair of enormous ears that were never still, just like his nose, which was continuously sniffing the air. He was fast and quiet and had a nice, honest face. After having talked to Grazia, who gave him his instructions, he turned for a moment to Milly, wrinkled his nose, gave her a half smile, and tweaked her ear. Then he ran away quickly, scrambling up the wall and disappearing into the crack where the shaft of light was coming through.

"We don't know how long we'll have to wait," said Grazia to all the rats who stood motionless, watching Pippo as he climbed the redbrick wall and sneaked into Signora Adele's house. "It could be just a few hours . . . perhaps even a day or two . . . but we should be ready to go at any time and the evacuation will have to be fast but, above all, orderly, otherwise there's the risk that someone will get hurt . . . When we go into the house we'll have to move right to the window, ignoring everything else, especially the woman who lives there. I don't know how she'll react . . . she's old, and she might even have a heart attack."

They heard someone murmur: "I wish." It was Milly.

Someone giggled, others glanced at her, but most remained attentive, listening to Grazia.

"I just hope she doesn't hurt any of you . . . Once we're outside, jump straight into the water, it's the only escape route we have. Good luck, all of you." She stood for a while on the palace of life, looking at the rats and smiling to reassure those who were the most frightened, then she climbed down and went back to crouch against the wooden base of the bookcase. The wait would be lengthy.

Signora Adele had an urge for frittelle e chiacchiere—the fried pastries and donuts that were the only good thing left about the carnival. She had dreamed about them and woke up with an intense desire that made her get out of bed quickly and pick up the telephone directory to find the number of the pasticceria that delivered them to her every year.

Pippo had hidden under the sideboard in the living room and had fallen asleep; the shuffling steps of the lady of the house woke him up and the young rat strained his ears and kept his eyes peeled. He could taste freedom in the air and couldn't wait to go back to being a civilized rat, respectable, and not a murderer who ate humans. He was one of the rats most responsible for inflicting the coup de grâce on the tourists.

After ordering the pastries and donuts, Signora Adele went into the kitchen to make coffee, licking her lips at the thought of the feast she was about to have.

Pippo made the most of the opportunity, slipped out of his hiding place, and returned to the basement, passing through the crack left by the partly open door. He climbed halfway down the redbrick wall and stopped, searching for Grazia. She was in the midst of the hundreds of muzzles raised toward him, waiting. He could feel the tension in the huge cellar flowing like electricity, a current snaking through the bodies of all his companions, permeating the atmosphere.

"She's ordered sweets; they'll be delivering them in a bit . . . Get ready. As soon as she opens the window I'll whistle," he said to the large gray female who had ascended to the third level of the palace of life. She nodded her head, and all the others did the same.

"Good luck, everyone. We'll see each other outside," whispered Pippo as he retreated quickly back into the house.

"In rows of five," Grazia said. "We'll leave in the same order that we set up for eating . . . Come on, start to get ready and climb."

The entry phone crackled after twenty minutes and Signora Adele, who was already getting annoyed by the wait, finally smiled at the thought of the sweet softness she was about to bite into.

Pippo dashed out from under the sideboard, leaned through the crack of the door, and let out a long whistle. The pregnant females and the new mothers, with all the babies hanging onto the fur of their backs and their sides, started to cover the final yards that separated them from the door.

Instead of going to answer, Signora Adele headed straight for the window, opened it, and looked down. The boy from the pasticceria was standing with his head tipped backward and his stare fixed on the shutters; in his hand was a packet wrapped in pink paper that made her mouth water just looking at it. "How much do I owe you?" the woman called down to him.

The first row of rats pushed with their muzzles against the almost closed door; it creaked, but the roar of cheerful shouting from the people in masks and children's toy trumpets covered the noise.

236 // Venice Noir

"Eight euros seventy," said the boy, edging closer to the wall of the building.

The rats entered the house but then stopped. Pippo was signaling them to wait.

"More expensive every year! All this money for a bit of flour and sugar. What crooks!" muttered Signora Adele as she moved away from the window to get her purse, which she had left on the round table in the living room.

"Now!" squeaked Pippo.

And a river of fur flooded into the room, running rapidly toward the open window and spilling outside like a waterfall. Signora Adele heard a strange noise, like hundreds of pins falling onto the floor; she turned around, frowning, and saw the surge of ears, paws, and tails that was flowing through the room and plunging out of the window. The bloodcurdling scream that came from her gaping mouth, contorted in a grimace of pain, had a domino effect: it was echoed by another scream, then another, and yet another, until it became a terrifying collective wail.

The rats ran; they were well organized, one row behind another, not glancing around, sniffing out only the water of the canal that awaited them with the promise of escape.

The packet that the boy was holding had fallen to the ground and was crushed by hundreds of feet that were fleeing in a panic. The people in their masks were shouting hysterically; they were pushing, falling, trampling each other, crying, and swearing; they were kicking and punching, trying to escape from the enormous furry serpent that stretched from the window, along the alley, and all the way to the canal. People fainted, others were hurt, and one person died—out of fear, revulsion, or possibly crushed because of the fear and revulsion of others.

Signora Adele held her hands over her heart, as if she feared it might break or leap out of her chest. She was crying and she kept on shouting: "NO, NO, NO, NOOO!"

When the very last rat abandoned her home, she became quiet. She closed her mouth and stood in silence, leaning against the table, her purse at her feet and her eyes wild and full of tears. She turned her head toward the window, then toward the "guest room"; she walked to the door to the abyss and peered down. The silence that rose from the deserted basement and the sight of the motionless floor, no longer teeming with life, caused her unbearable pain. No more tourists to punish, no more cleansing, no more hope for Venice. She closed her eyes and threw herself into the dark chasm, without making a sound; she now felt empty, even the hate that had kept her alive had vanished. Her last thought was for Venice, her beautiful city.

The dull thud made Milly jump. Her labor had started suddenly and she was the only one who hadn't escaped. She had taken refuge on the third level of the palace of life and had given birth to seven beautiful babies while all the other animals were fleeing the cellar. She looked over the edge of the shelf and saw the large body in an unnatural and undignified position that dominated the middle of the mud-covered floor. She closed her eyes and went back to licking her babies, who had already started to suckle. She felt weak and strange, and she was hungry. She wouldn't be able to move from there for another two weeks; she shuddered at the thought of the men who would come to see what had happened. The smell of the blood that had started to flow from the body of Signora Adele made her feel sick but also made her salivate. She knew she wouldn't be able to resist, nor did she have much time; soon they would come to recover that horrible woman's body. She shook her babies off her nipples and quickly climbed down from the palace of life; she moved close to Signora Adele and stood looking at her and sniffing the scent that came from the warm, succulent body.

"We don't eat people, we love them; they despise us and hate us but we love their singing and their high spirits." She had said this only the day before to Grazia.

"For my babies I'd eat anyone," Ambra had said to her.

You're right, Ambra, thought Milly as she sank her teeth into the soft, juicy flesh of Signora Adele's arm. *For my babies I'd eat anyone. And anything.*

LAGUNA BLUES

BY MICHAEL GREGORIO

Porto Marghera

1. Via Delle Macchine

T hink sludge.

Try to imagine an ocean of it.

It looks like wet cement, and is similar in color. A slick melding of light gray and sandy brown. My torchlight adds a yellow sheen that catches on kaleidoscopic rainbow traces of petroleum, oil, and other chemical waste.

And lying in the middle of the sludge is a naked body.

A man, I'm certain of it, ass pointing skyward, facedown. He might be skinny-dipping, right arm stretched far out ahead of him, left arm buried somewhere beneath his body. It could almost be a freestyle stroke, except that there is no physical tension in the buttocks, no sign of any muscular contraction in the back, no trace of any movement in his legs or his arms.

"He's never going to win a race," says Marcello.

Snapshot of a crime scene . . .

But let's hold on a second. Let's go back a bit, and try to fill in the larger picture. We need to know the where and why of the industrial sludge, the when and how of the naked swimmer. Isn't that what a murder investigation is all about? I'm filing my report now, so I can fill in some of those facts.

That night, we were on the patch that the duty roster calls "three bridges."

I'm on permanent night patrol; the only way onto the day shift is promotion, and there is little hope of that. The way it goes is this: Every night at a quarter to ten I drive out to the police barracks and the high-security court complex in Carpenedo from my tiny two-room flat in Piazzetta della Pace. At the barracks gate, I clock in, pick up the squad car and my partner, Marcello Pigozzo, and we drive a slow triangle that takes in the three bridges. We do the round trip as many as eight times in a night. It all depends on what happens.

So, first step, the three bridges.

I live near the town center of Mestre, the modern abortion on the mainland where all of us Venetians live these days. Many of the inhabitants work in Toy Town, but they're forced to live on the mainland, commuting there and back by bus. Venice was renamed Toy Town after the Stones bought a palazzo on the Canal Grande as an investment, and the price of housing rocketed into the stratosphere. Now, a cellar that gets flooded every time the tide comes in costs one hundred thousand euros minimum. A small apartment on the second floor of a decent building costs ten times as much. And if there's a terrace and a view of the lagoon, the price doubles. If there's a good, clear view, it triples. Nowadays, Venetians stroll around on Sunday, or on their day off work, just like the rich Americans and the Japanese tourists who stay at the five-star Hotel Daniele on Riva degli Schiavoni, which is only a "five-minute walk from magical Piazza San Marco." My mother was born a five-minute walk from Piazza San Marco, but she swears it was a shithole.

The three bridges. First step, second try.

Bridge number one is the dividing line, the so-called Cavalcavia that arches over the railway lines, taking you out of Mestre and onto the main road that leads south to Piazzale

Roma and the islands of Venice. It's ten or fifteen minutes away, depending on how fast you are driving. And that is also bridge number two: Ponte della Libertà, the combined road and railway bridge that crosses the Venetian lagoon. The Austrians built the railway bridge back in the 1840s. They didn't like the idea of having islands in their empire. Island people tend to be ungovernable. So, me and Marcello take a left toward Venice, then we turn off a mile or so down the road and enter Porto Marghera, the huge industrial zone on the northern edge of the lagoon that some government visionary dreamed up the day before tourism became the major industry in Italy. We take a slow run through the port, the factories, and the warehouses, hustling no one, checking that the business of the night is going ahead without undue disturbance. Sometimes, as many as two hundred girls are working the area, girls of every race and color, "girls" of every sex, Brazilian transsexuals for the most part. Romanian and African prostitutes outnumber the Brazilians, three to one. Then we double back, cross the traffic lights, check out Via delle Macchine and the heavy industrial plants down by the dark water's edge, before getting back out onto the Libertà bridge and driving across the lagoon to Venice. There, we circle Piazzale Roma, stopping sometimes for a coffee and a smoke, then we drive back across the bridge and keep going, all the way out to the ring road and the third bridge just beyond the Malcontenta. The Malcontenta was a summer villa that an architect named Andrea Palladio built on the banks of the River Brenta way back in the sixteenth century. It was an odd name then, but it fits the bill perfectly nowadays. I'd be unhappy too, if I had to live out there and breathe the traffic fumes.

Cavalcavia, Ponte della Libertà, Malcontenta: that's the three bridges circuit.

Last night we got as far as Via delle Macchine in Porto Marghera.

That was where we found the dead man swimming in the sludge.

Dead men are not at all unusual in Porto Marghera. Generally, they have been stabbed. As a rule, they are foreign sailors or randy widowers from Padova, a city thirty miles down the road to the west beyond the Malcontenta and the ring road. These characters pick up a girl, get wanked or blown, then they try to skip without paying, though they never get very far. The girl or her pimp will grab the offender, stick a stiletto in his guts, then empty his pockets of money, ID, credit card, house keys, car keys, whatever. It's a thriving industry that feeds a lot of bank fraud, house-lifting, and automobile recycling. At other times, drunken foreign sailors turn on one other in the dingy bars of Porto Marghera with flick knives or broken beer bottles.

On really bad nights, a truck-jacking goes wrong.

Porto Marghera is all about sealed containers and bonded warehouses. Everything that moves through the port is valuable. Stolen goods fuel the black market in the north of Italy, and as far south as Bologna. A ship comes in, and while it is being offloaded, one of the dockers makes a quiet phone call. Next thing, the truck is stopped by an armed gang as it is heads out toward the Malcontenta and the ring road. Next day, Acer laptops, Samsung mobile phones, or German washing machines are being offered around at half the usual retail price. On rare occasions, the driver tries to defend his load beyond the call of duty. If he does, he dies. The drivers know it; they just hand over the keys most of the time, and walk away from harm. Quite frequently, the tipster makes two phone calls, trying to double his take. The hijackers get hijacked by a rival gang—the Mafia of the Brenta versus the Mafia of Marghera—and then the shooting starts. The docker gets a bullet from whoever wins. You can't bet on two horses. The body count tends to be high.

But a naked man in a lake of sludge?

Me and Marcello climb out of the patrol car, and the sludge oozes over the tops of our shoes. There's nothing we can do about it. We switch on our flashlights and start wading through the shit. It looks like wet cement, as I said earlier, and it sucks at your feet. You have to go slow, or it pulls off your shoes. It feels even worse than it looks. It doesn't just soak your shoes and socks, it seems to eat its way inside them like hydrochloric acid. This sludge is a compound of all the nasty things we tell ourselves we should never touch: dirt and filth, untreated sewage, illegal industrial runoff, petroleum and oil scum, spillage from all the chemical factories and processing plants that give Via delle Macchine its name. It drains off into the lagoon eventually, poisoning the fish and polluting the mussels that are being cultivated in the shallow waters. This sludge is the sum of the liquid waste that heavy industry produces.

The dead man is half sunk in it.

I play my torch along the length of his nude body.

"No sign of a wound. No exit, no entry. What's your guess, stabbed or shot?"

Marcello looks at me. "Dead," he says.

He turns around and starts wading back toward the patrol car and the radio.

He's going to call for backup, the murder squad, forensics, an ambulance from the city mortuary. They should be here within fifteen minutes, then we can get back into our patrol car, turn up the heat to dry off our shoes, socks, and trouser

244 // Venice Noir

cuffs, and head out onto the three bridges circuit again.

He wades back.

"Done," he says.

We stand there looking down at the body, then Marcello offers me an untipped Nazionale. We light up, take a few slow puffs. We'll have to wait by the body. And it's way too early for the sirens. It's like standing on a moon that's soaking wet and very noisy. All around us we can hear the thump of heavy engines, the shrill whirring of machinery slicing through the night. The wheels of industry, they call it, though it tends to be steam hammers, swooshing pistons, and suction pumps in Porto Marghera.

Suddenly, there's a flash of light from the ENI oil refinery at the dead end of the street, down by the banks of the lagoon. A blue flame with an orange core surges twenty feet into the star-speckled sky. It lights up the wooden trestles of the mussel-farming rigs in the water close by, burns with a roaring fizz for a minute or more, then stops as suddenly as it started.

"Gas will be up ten cents tomorrow," Marcello says.

"What do you think happened?" I ask him.

"What happened where? They're burning off excess gas—"

"The body," I say. "What do you think happened to him?"

"Why don't you go and ask him?"

This is Venetian humour. Marcello doesn't give a fuck. What has it got to do with us? He flicks his cigarette away, and a ghostly flame flares up as it hits what looks like a pool of water, but isn't.

I look at the dead man instead.

My dream is to get off the night patrol and into criminal investigations. If I could work it out before the detectives arrive, maybe I'd stand a chance. The victim is stark naked, and he is lying in the middle of one of the most frequently traveled streets in Porto Marghera. No one has reported a thing. Not even an anonymous phone tip-off. He could have been there for five minutes or five hours. If he'd been there five hours, the cops on the three bridges shift before us should have seen him. *Should have* . . . Sometimes, we do the same thing. We skip a beat, park somewhere out of sight for an hour, smoking and dozing, then we write it up as a no-incident circuit. *And yet, the body looks clean.* Closer to minutes than hours. There is a spattering of mud like octopus stings across the back of his legs, but nothing else. If he'd been there an hour, with trucks passing by all through the night, there wouldn't be any white flesh left to see.

Twenty or thirty minutes, I estimate. *That's how long—*

"They're fucking slow tonight. You figure there's been a pileup on the ring road?"

"Who knows?"

I look back at the body. A naked john? It isn't likely. They pull up their zippers and feel for their wallets before they try to run. I take out a packet of Marlboro 100s and offer one to Marcello. A hit job? One of the Mafia warlords? One of the soldiers? We would need to turn him over and wipe the sludge off if we wanted to see his face, but I know Marcello Pigozzo won't go for that. It would be a dirty job, certainly, but there's the bigger question of tampering with a crime scene. We wouldn't get promoted if anyone saw us touching the body. No, we'd get the push instead. Then again, I think, if it was a crime boss, you'd shoot him. More than once. You'd riddle him with bullets, make sure he didn't live to come after you.

"No exit wounds. No bullet in the back," I say. "You think he was knifed?"

Marcello doesn't say a word, just turns his wrist and shines his flashlight on his watch. "Twenty minutes," he mutters. "It's already two o'clock. My feet are freezing. What the hell are those jerks doing?"

If he's been jabbed with a knife, I think, he's either a sailor or a whore's mark. Maybe both. I can't see his face, but I guess that he is a European. His skin is stark white against the gray-brown sludge, no sign of a suntan above the waistband of the underpants that he isn't wearing. A man who lives indoors, who never goes to the beach in Sottomarina or Jesolo, who never takes a foreign holiday. He works indoors too, maybe sitting behind a desk all day in an office. That's what I assume from the flabby bulge above his hips, his flaccid buttocks, the lack of muscle in his extended right arm.

He's not a sailor, though he might be an officer.

"You hear it?" Marcello flicks his cigarette butt at the puddle, misses, and it sizzles in the slime. Far off, you can just about hear the sound of an ambulance siren. *Nonny-nonny-no! Nonny-nonny-no!* "About fucking time," he adds. "I don't want to stand here much longer. Move an inch, and a stench comes up. Unless that's you farting?"

I hear a squad car somewhere, like a braying donkey a long way off.

Hee-haw! Hee-haw! Hee-haw!

"I think he's one of the money men," I say. "An important guy. They gave him a girl, told him to have some fun, then shot him though the temple while he was doing it. They burned his clothes, dumped the body out here. They knew we'd find him. They wanted him to be—"

"You should work for Radio Mestre," Marcello interrupts, moving out into the center of Via delle Macchine, holding up his hands, waving them high above his head as the headlights come racing toward him, watching as the squad car skids to a halt, slewing sideways into the mud, sending up a scythe of sludge that covers Marcello from head to foot.

My partner curses as the car door opens and the night inspector climbs out.

He's been warned. Inspector Zambòn is wearing yellow rubber boots and an old blue boilersuit. "You, just fucking shut it!" he snarls at Marcello, and he comes stomping over toward me, kicking up sludge like a kid playing in the mud. "Well, what do we have?"

"A body, sir."

It sounds obvious, but what else can I say?

"So I see," he says sarcastically. "No clothes? No ID? Tire tracks . . ." He pauses, looks out across the sea of sludge. It's like a plowed field. At least a thousand heavy-duty truck tires have traveled up and down Via delle Macchine in the last twelve hours. "No tire tracks worth the mentioning, I suppose. Forensics will be coming soon . . ."

Another siren sounds. It's close. A quick, repeated *blip-blip*, a flash of orange light, then it's on us. The large black Fiat van skids and slithers to a halt, far too close to the body, less than six feet away, causing the sludge to shift in a tsunami tidal wave. One minute the body is marble white, the next it's a gray-brown sludge, almost invisible except for the buttock islands.

"Who the fuck is driving that vehicle?" the inspector yells out. No one answers, so he turns to me. "And what the fuck are you doing here? Don't you have work to do?"

Two minutes later, we're back on the main road, heading for the Malcontenta, giving Piazzale Roma and Venice a miss. Marcello lives in Chirignago, which is just a short way off our regular route. I take him home. Top apartment in a block of eight. He's cursing like a savage. Fucking CID, fucking van drivers, fucking sludge. I follow him into the hallway. His wife Marisa takes one quick look, then smiles, hurrying off to get him clean clothes, telling him to take a shower, offering me a cup of coffee and a dry pair of socks.

Half an hour and we're back on the road.

"About that body," I say.

"Don't talk to me about that fucking body!" Marcello snaps. "I don't know, and I don't fucking *want* to know!"

We had a quiet night after that. Nothing happened. No one else disturbed our peace.

I couldn't forget the body in the sludge, though. It was an unforgettable sight. It was like walking into a modest church and discovering a fine marble statue that you didn't expect. Sooner or later, I would have asked Inspector Zambòn about it, though I never did get the chance. It was big news down at Mestre Central the following week. Zambòn had been suspended, the desk sergeant reported. Paid leave while he was waiting for the case to come up.

"That naked body in Marghera last Thursday night?" I asked, hoping. I couldn't help but wonder whether my guess had been right. A Mafia boss, a commissioned hit job, taken out by the opposition, something along those lines.

"He's been charged with corruption, according to the magistrate. Didn't you notice those fancy suits he was always wearing? He was taking money, hand over fist, the sly bastard. Been at it for years, apparently."

The Porto Marghera investigation didn't come to much, and I never did find out who was handling the case. I saw it mentioned in one of the local newspapers, *Il Gazzettino*, I think it was. *Mystery Man Found Dead*, the headline said. No name, no story, nothing. A body in Via delle Macchine, the newspaper noted dutifully. A middle-aged man. There was no sign of a wound. A massive blood clot to the brain was the probable cause of death. The corpse had been ditched, unclaimed, unwanted. The hack managed to squeeze the fact that the body was naked into the very last line.

He didn't bother to mention the sludge.

2. A Domestic Crime . . . or Three

They gave me two months of sick leave when I caught a bullet in the shoulder.

Ten days in the hospital in Mestre, then I was discharged. I had nowhere to go, and nothing to do, so I spent a week in front of the television watching any damned thing that came on, doing the rehabilitation exercises the physiotherapist had taught me, cooking, eating, sleeping, trying not to smoke too much, taking an occasional stroll, slowly going out of my mind. When I started hitting the red wine immediately after breakfast, I decided that I had to do something constructive.

But what?

My apartment is on the first floor of an apartment block in a quiet cul-de-sac beyond the city hospital, the swimming pool, the tennis club, and a bridge that crosses the canals. It's an assigned council flat. You don't need to be on the housing list if you're a policeman in Mestre. There are two other cops living in the building, but we are all very careful never to tell anyone how we got decent living accommodations so close to the town center. Piazzetta della Pace is an idyllic spot in its dead-end way. If I spit out of my bathroom window, I can hit the river. There are two of them, as a matter of fact, which converge right there outside my window. They are drainage canals, rather than natural rivers, and they have no names. They carry runoff irrigation water from the agricultural plain through the town of Mestre and out into the Venetian lagoon. A couple of years back, I lost my car when the canals overflowed and flooded my garage. Well, I looked out of the window one morning, my hand trembling at the thought of red wine on my tongue, and that was when I saw the opportunity awaiting me.

I hadn't been fishing for years, but I still had a rod and a tackle box in the garage.

There's no access to the river bank from the parking area behind my place, but I had noticed a gate in the chain fence of the old lady who lives in a rundown cottage next to the development. Her name is Amalia Bianchini, but I just call her Signora Amalia, like everyone else in the neighborhood. She's a kind of myth around here: all the kids believe that she's a witch, and their parents tend to avoid her.

I say hello whenever I see her, and I see and hear her quite a lot. She is in her eighties, a lean country woman with a narrow wrinkled face, bright blue eyes, gray hair that drifts in loose strands from beneath the black scarf that she always wears. Her clothes never change, summer or winter—that black scarf, an old gray overcoat, a pair of old rubber boots. She's the last of an ancient tribe in modern Mestre, a contadina, a peasant, struggling to survive in sprawling suburbia.

The town must have grown up all around her, slowly swallowing the countryside, covering it with ugly apartment blocks of three, four, or five storys. Whenever I leave for work, she stands up, eases her bones, waves at me, and says something totally incomprehensible in a language that died out many generations ago.

At least she smiles, which no one else in Piazzetta della Pace ever does.

Signora Amalia works all day in her large garden, growing fruits and vegetables, tending her vines, her hens, and the rabbits that she keeps in a shed. As I said before, when I don't see her, I often hear her. That is, I hear an agonized squawk, or a high-pitched scream, and I know what she'll be having for lunch or dinner. Hens lay eggs, and rabbits breed. She slays one or the other at least once a week. I saw her one day swinging a chicken around and around by its neck. It was brutal, mercifully over in a couple of seconds. Murder in the name of subsistence. You could call it domestic crime number one, though it sounds melodramatic. I couldn't slaughter a hen if you paid me. Another day, I saw her going into the rabbit hutch with a rusty roncola, which is a big curved knife, the peasant's scimitar. Could you slaughter a rabbit in cold blood, skin it, gut it, roast it in the oven?

I know what it was that got me into Signora Amalia's good graces.

She's a gattara. That is, she keeps cats. She always has two or three of them trailing at her heels. I like cats, but in my job I really cannot have one. Who would feed it when I'm asleep all day and out on patrol all night? Having said that, in recent months, I had noticed one cat in particular that followed her around. Whenver I was passing her gate, I would stop and play with it. Il Rosso was the name she gave to it, but I always thought of him as Big Red, a cross between a Persian and a ginger tom, an Angora ball of orange flames, with a tail to die for. Affectionate wasn't the word for Il Rosso. It was hard to tear yourself away when he started to purr, rolling onto his back, inviting you to stroke his belly.

I got out my fishing rod and tackle box, and I stopped outside her cottage, waiting until I caught sight of her in the garden. Long before the old lady appeared, Il Rosso came to greet me. He licked my hand, rubbed his head against my legs.

I hadn't felt so loved in one hell of a long time. He was such an affectionate, trusting creature, and he seemed to have taken a shine to me. I was down on my haunches, tickling his ears, when the old lady appeared.

"Signora Amalia, can I use your gate out onto the river bank?" I asked.

Ten minutes later, I was sitting on the riverbank with a can of worms, courtesy of the old lady. I'd been planning to use a lure, but she took me to her compost heap, turned over a sheet of cardboard, and uncovered a mass of earthworms that would have fed a thousand fish. I could use her gate anytime I wanted, she said. On one condition. I had to bring her back a fish. Or two, if I was really lucky. Well, I'm no big game hunter, and I hadn't been fishing for years, but catching fish from the spot where the two canals become one is like fishing in an aquarium full of piranhas. You threw in a worm, you pulled out a fish. It was, I must admit, almost too easy. Still, it kept me busy, it kept me away from the wine, and casting the line was the sort of exercise I needed for my wounded shoulder. Every time I passed through her gate and into the garden, Il Rosso came running, and old Signora Amalia was right behind him. I'd hand her a couple of half-pound perch, and Il Rosso would let out a meow of thanks. At least that's what it sounded like to me.

Maybe a week had gone by when I asked her if she was happy with the fish that I was bringing her. I was thinking of the cats, thinking of Il Rosso in particular, who seemed to be getting bigger by the day.

I have to try and give an impression of what she said—that is, of what I thought she might have said. The dialect was a problem, as I mentioned earlier. She smiled, she made a face. "They're a wee bit bony," she said. "They get stuck in your teeth."

It set me thinking. Did she mean too bony for the cats, or was *she* eating the fish that I had been pulling out of an open sewer?

The more I thought about it, the more perplexed I became. Those fish were big, and kind of swollen. There was a slimy puffiness to their bellies, which were olive-green instead of natural pearl. Those canals were chemical wastepipes, I realized. Thousands of tons of additives and fertilizers had been spread over the surrounding fields to produce bigger tomatoes, more grapes, a larger yield of maize. Those chemicals would leach through the soil, drain into the canals, and end up in the Venetian lagoon, where legends of monster catfish abound.

If Signora Amalia were to die, would I have poisoned her?

Signora Amalia didn't die, but I stopped going fishing. I started taking long walks instead. Next thing, I was jogging. I only had one thing on my mind. Get fit, and fast. End the tedium. Get back to work. I was jogging toward the gate of our apartment block in Piazzetta della Pace when it hit me. I hadn't seen Il Rosso for a couple of days. As a rule, he would squeeze through the bars of the gate and wait for me, until I stopped and paid him some attention. There was no sign of Il Rosso.

Had I poisoned the cat with my toxic fish?

That would have been domestic crime number two.

For a day or two, I let it go. A contadina would laugh in my face, I thought, if I, a townie, started making a fuss about a missing cat. Even so, I didn't have to wait very long before my curiosity was satisfied. The next day, as I jogged back toward my gate, Signora Amalia stood up straight and stared at me. I waved to her, and she shook a handful of radishes at me. I thought that she was being neighborly, and that she wanted me to have them.

I stopped by her gate, and the old woman came to meet me.

"No more fish," she said, and she frowned, as if she missed them. As if the cats missed them. That was how I preferred to think of it. As if Il Rosso missed them.

"I have to run," I said. "I have to get well. I need to go back to work."

"Eat radish," she said. "Eat cheese." I had seen her three goats, as well. I had seen her churning goat's milk in a bucket. Incredible as it might seem, this old lady was producing edible organic things that all her neighbors bought from the local Despar supermarket. "I owe you these," she said, holding up the radishes, offering them to me.

"What for?"

"The fish," she said.

I took the radishes, thanked her, turned away, then turned back. I couldn't stop myself. I missed Il Rosso. "What happened to the cat?" I asked.

"Which one?" There were two or three cats in her vicinity, but not the one that I was looking for. These were rangy, stringy spotted beasts, the sort you wouldn't touch for fear of the diseases they might be carrying.

"Il Rosso," I said.

She looked at me, and her eyes narrowed. They were distant, cold. "Il Rosso's gone."

"Gone where?"

She stared at me even harder. "You know where."

I was lost. What did she mean? Was she accusing me of having stolen her cat?

"I don't know anything," I said.

"Ehi!" she responded, her voice a lilting doubt. "If it's not you, then it's one of them." Her eyes flashed over at the building where I lived.

"One of them?"

"They're good, they are."

I didn't understand what she was saying until she made a gesture which is typical of the people in the north of Italy. She pushed her forefinger into her right cheek and gave it a rapid twist, as if she were drilling a hole. It means, *It's really tasty*.

"Il Rosso?"

"Ehi!" she said again, waving her finger at me. Then she spoke some more in thick Venetian: "Ghe son più bòn dei conigi!"

I went home and I thought about domestic crime number three. They're tastier than rabbits. That was what the old lady had said. Somebody had murdered and eaten Il Rosso. Signor Amalia laid the blame on me, or on one of the other people in the apartment block. And she was resentful too.

Was it because she had been planning to feed up, murder, and eat Il Rosso herself?

A week later, I had seen the doctor, been signed off, and I was back at work in time for the trial of the kid who had shot me. He was seventeen years old, sleek as a greyhound, eyes as cold as the dead fish from the canals behind my house. I had walked into a tobacconist's shop while a holdup was taking place. The kid didn't hesitate, he turned and fired at me point-blank. Then he stepped over my body and walked away, leaving me for dead.

I had seen the same look in the eyes of Signora Amalia.

Fortunately for me, she'd been holding radishes, not that roncola with the rusty blade.

A CLOSED BOOK
BY Mary Hoffman

Rialto Bridge

The woman with the fancy camera spent a long time at the edge of the piazzetta, adjusting the focus and firing off shot after shot. Some of the gondoliers looked up and glared. They were used to tourists taking souvenir photos; some of the men even offered to pose—but they charged for it. This woman, though, seemed too focused on herself to be collecting memories of a holiday.

"Giornalista," grumbled one of the older men, glaring into the zoom lens.

If this woman—English, surely, from the straggly brown ponytail and utilitarian clothes—was writing an article about Venice, like so many of her countrywomen, she should expect to pay for taking pictures.

But she wasn't a journalist.

After a last shot or two, she walked away from the water and perched at the first outside table she came to, belonging to the first overpriced café, and ordered a caffé latte, although it was nearly lunchtime.

She reviewed her morning's work, but was dissatisfied. Face after Venetian face scowled at her from the little screen on the back of her camera—old, middle-aged, the occasional thirty-something—stubbled, bald, fat, self-satisfied. There was no gondolier that fit her exacting standards. She sat back, stretching her long denim-clad legs in front of her, drinking her expensive coffee, crumbling the biscotto in her saucer.

The woman left an unnecessarily large euro note for the waiter and set off toward the Riva degli Schiavoni, without a backward glance at the gondoliers who had taken so much of her attention a short while ago. There were even more of them here in the busy waterway that ran under the bridge, alongside the Doge's Palace. She leaned on the north parapet of the Ponte della Paglia and looked away from the lagoon toward the ridiculously picturesque Ponte dei Sospiri.

A shrill voice floated up from the water behind her.

"If only you were half the man he is!" complained a woman to her husband.

The photographer turned for a better look at the gondolier who had provoked the comparison so unflattering to the tourist's husband, who was sitting scarlet-faced on the cushions of the vessel. In fact, literally the opposite was true, for the husband was obese and the gondolier trim and well muscled.

It was not clear what had led to the woman's outburst but it amused the gondolier so much that somewhere between the two bridges he lost his balance and tipped into the cold and murky water of the canal. The splash was galvanizing and the photographer hurried over in time to see him come up spluttering and shaking his hair. His fellow oarsmen laughed and clapped and the tourist in the gondola allowed himself a tiny smirk at his furious wife, who seemed now to have decided that all men were useless.

The little bar in Cannaregio had only one tourist in it but she attracted no more than a quick second glance from the regulars, since she was with Taddeo, who was a local. At that second glance they saw that she was buying, and that gave them quite the wrong impression.

Taddeo was having trouble with her name: *Kathy Hughes* was hard work for a Venetian tongue and he soon renamed her Caterina, which she liked, sitting up a bit straighter on the barstool and loosening her hair from its elastic band.

"So, Taddeo," she said, "have you fallen in before?"

He shrugged. Taddeo didn't feel his masculinity compromised; every gondolier got the occasional dunking. "It is a— what do you call it?—a sort of industrial accident."

"Like a prostitute's orgasm," the woman said.

Taddeo choked over his drink.

"I'm writing a book," she continued, as if that was the natural course of the conversation.

"You want to put me in it?"

"Maybe."

Taddeo preened just a bit.

"It's not a novel, though," she added, draining her glass of Campari. "It's a book of short stories."

It made no difference to the gondolier; he was more interested in the next round of drinks, which soon arrived.

"They're called *Scorpion Tales*," said Kathy.

Taddeo's English was pretty good but he couldn't quite grasp puns. "Where they have the stings," he said, nodding.

She let it pass; her stories *did* have a sting in the tail: that was the point of them. She wanted to impress him but she saw the limitations of his literary knowledge. He would not ask her if books of short stories were not a notoriously difficult genre to sell and she would not have to tell him that her father was the director of a successful publishing house.

"The thing is," she said, "I want to set one of them in Venice. But I can't get at it."

"Get at what?"

"The real Venice. It's all . . . tourist rip-offs," she explained.

"Gondola rides at eighty euros for a forty-minute stock trip up the Grand Canal, cappuccinos at ten euros, tatty masks, plastic fans, sweeties made of glass—nothing I can get my teeth into." She looked around the bar. "This is the realest place I've found since I got here."

Taddeo didn't want to disagree; he was hoping to get dinner out of this and maybe more. She wasn't really his type—not enough flesh on her—but a young foreign woman who wasn't his wife, well, that was irresistible.

Kathy wasn't looking for sex. She hadn't been photographing gondoliers to find the best-looking one; she wanted to find the different one. She loved the bar in Cannaregio and liked the restaurant even better. This was the real Venice at last. She had spent the evening getting Taddeo to tell her about crimes, the more gruesome the better. And as she got more and more out of him, the gondolier began to think he would prefer to be back home with Micola, his wife, after all.

"Caterina" was interested in all the most bloodthirsty crimes and Taddeo began to invent ones that he had only half-heard about, embellishing and extending with a drowning here, a strangling there. Then he told her about the famous murder in Cannaregio: "Just a little way from here—they got the murderer, at least *one* of the murderers. He's in prison. But he made it look like a Mafia crime, fixing the victim up like a sacrificial goat."

Then he had to explain incaprettare to her, the process of tying hands and feet behind the back in such a way that the more the victim struggled, the more the noose around his neck tightened. She liked that; he got the feeling there was someone she would like to do that to.

By now Taddeo was sweating. It was great to have a free

meal and plenty to drink but surely it wasn't natural for a young woman to want to talk about nothing but rapes and murders, crimes of passion, incest . . . Ah, incest. Heading her off from the murder of the greengrocer, he had chanced to mention a case of familial abuse from years back, simply because the perpetrator shared a first name with the fixed-up corpse.

Signor Giampaolo Volpe was a dentist with two daughters. After the death of his wife, Volpe turned his attentions to the daughters, first the older, then, when she fled, the younger. It all came out when the dentist's body was found floating in the lagoon. There was not a mark on him, so it could have been accidental, and the sisters, who had been estranged for some years, both had alibis.

As the stories poured out of him, Taddeo became a bit loose with the wine and all the food. The woman was taking notes in a little book she drew from her handbag; he wished that he could just stop. He was singing for his supper and not just a single aria; he was beginning to feel as if he had performed a complete *Tosca*.

At last the flow of words slowed to a trickle and he slumped in his seat.

"Can you take me out in your gondola tomorrow night?" she asked, merciless. "I'll pay twice what you normally charge."

The craft slipped silently through the back canals of the city, black hull sliding through black water. Taddeo was relieved that tonight she wanted no talk at all. There was no sound but the splash of his oar and no light but the lantern on the gondola and the eerie mezzotint of the scene under the full moon. It would have been peaceful if only Taddeo's passenger hadn't been so tense; she was not lying back on the cushions drinking in the romance of the lagoon city by night, but sitting upright and fiddling with the gold heart she wore on a chain around her neck.

"Take me to where they found the dentist," was all she had said when he'd led her into the gondola and wrapped her up with rugs.

He couldn't remember where that corpse had washed up so he took her to a place that looked right, a lonely minor canal where no gondoliers sculled tourists, where a little bridge reflected itself in the still water like a perfect circle.

"He was washed up against one side of the bridge," he lied.

The woman made him stop and she took lots more photos of the supposed site of the body's discovery before motioning him onward.

There were few people about in the little campi or on the bridges of the district they were gliding past. "Caterina" emitted a small, satisfied sigh; she was finding the real Venice.

Taddeo no longer found her even slightly attractive but she had very deep pockets and that had its own appeal.

"You are finding your scorpion stings?" he asked after a while.

"Oh yes," she said. "Drop me back somewhere central soon. I want to write them up."

Taddeo realized he didn't even know where she was staying; all he had was her cell phone number. He let her out near the Rialto as courteously as he could manage and she pressed a large bundle of bills into his hand. It was all he could do not to shudder at the coldness of her touch.

The woman typed furiously in her room. It was the last story in her collection and she sat back with a small smile when it was finished, cracking her knuckles. This one had a good sting. The best.

She sent an e-mail to her father, attaching the file. She didn't bother to revise what she had written; he would publish whatever she sent him. After a slight pause, she sent it again, this time to her sister in London. She backed it up on her flash drive and her cloud storage account. Then she permitted herself a larger smile.

Time for room service.

In a small cluttered office in Covent Garden, a computer beeped to let its user know he had mail. A rumpled, middle-aged man read the attachment with growing horror; of course the first story he had opened was "The Good Father." He did not need to see any more. He sat slumped, with his head in his hands.

Then took out his cell phone and dialed a number he had hoped never to use again.

Three days later it was all over the lagoon city and the police came to visit Taddeo.

She had been found in her room, strangled with the cable from her laptop, of which there was no sign. Her wallet was also missing though nothing else seemed to have been taken; the police didn't know about the flash drive or cloud account. An expensive camera remained on the desk and the police took that. It was only the cable that made them realize there had been a laptop computer. It had been used as a garrote, with a pencil twisted up in it to apply the necessary force for asphyxiation.

The staff at the Gritti Palace knew nothing, had seen no one suspicious, and said no visitor to her room had stopped at the desk. They were appalled at the blow to their reputation. But there were more visitors to the bar that night than usual. The barman, who scarcely remembered what Kathy Hughes had looked like, gathered a large number of tips as he embroidered his memories for their benefit.

Hardly anyone who knew her would have recognized the woman from the photographs the police showed Taddeo. Their methods were unorthodox but they hoped to shock him into a confession. Instead they sent him running for the bathroom where they could hear him vomiting copiously and comprehensively.

The black-and-white photos taken at the scene showed her lying on the carpet between the round table and the draped double bed, in front of long windows that overlooked the canal. Her tongue protruded from her darkened face and her eyes were stained with bloody spots. The only recognizable thing about her was the little gold heart locket on its chain; the murderer had not taken that.

"When did you go to the Gritti Palace?" asked the older of the two officers when Taddeo got back from the bathroom, his face several shades paler.

"I have never been inside the Gritti," said the gondolier. "Only picked people up or dropped them outside."

"You were seen," lied the younger detective.

"Whoever says that is wrong," said Taddeo. Then he had a thought. "Is that where she was found? I never knew where she was staying."

"You admit you knew her then?"

There was no point in denying it.

"I took her out in my gondola," he said.

"And you had drinks with her and dinner—more than once," said the older detective.

It was true. After the gondola ride by night, when she had been so silent and absorbed, he had seen "Caterina" twice more. Once she had asked him to do the usual tourist thing along the Grand Canal and had insisted on his giving her the standard spiel.

And then, yes, he had let her take him out to dinner again; perhaps that had been unwise. In fact, looking back at his short relationship—hardly a relationship!—with the murdered woman, he wished heartily that he had never set eyes on her. She had given him a lot of money and paid for every drink and dish they had shared, but now he was a murder suspect.

"How much do you know about this Kathy Hughes?" asked the younger detective, stumbling over the barbaric English name.

"Nothing! Almost nothing," he said.

"And yet you had dinner with her," the older man consulted a notebook, "twice. What did she talk about?"

"She didn't talk much. She wanted me to talk—about crime in Venice. She was writing a book, about scorpions."

"Scorpions?" The detectives exchanged dubious looks.

"She was interested in murders and rapes and things like that." Taddeo immediately realized it would have been better to say nothing.

"Well, let me tell you about her," said the older policeman. "She was English—that you know—twenty-seven years old. Unmarried. One sister, younger, called," he screwed his face up into a grimace, "Tabitha. Parents divorced. Mother's whereabouts unknown. Father lives in London. Interpol has sent the information to Scotland Yard so they can inform Signor Hughes about his daughter's death."

"She had been in Venice only a week," said the younger officer. "Had no friends or contacts here. The only person whose company she has been seen in is you."

Micola arrived back from a friend's house at that point. When Taddeo explained why the police were there, she shrieked at him.

"What did I tell you? That Englishwoman is trouble!"

She *had* said that. But then Micola had feared he was sleeping with her. Taddeo shuddered to remember how he had once contemplated doing that. Now all he could see in his mind were the obscene tongue and eyes.

The police wanted to question Micola too. And at the end of their interview with her, they arrested Taddeo on suspicion of the murder of Kathy Hughes.

He was not at the office when the news came, but in his tall thin house in Tufnell Park. The doorbell rang and there were two uniformed officers on the doorstep—one male, one female. He knew what that meant; anyone who had ever watched a TV crime series knew what that meant.

"Which one?" he managed to get out, meaning his daughters.

"Can we come in?" asked the policewoman, professionally gentle. "It's Kathy, I'm afraid," she continued, when the three of them were seated at his scrubbed-pine kitchen table. Her male colleague moved instinctively to the kettle.

But when the facts had been conveyed, the father stood up, passed his hands through his already disheveled gray hair, and said, like a character in one of those TV shows, "I'm going to need something stronger than tea."

Russell Hughes didn't even bother to offer them the malt. He poured himself a slug and knocked it back too quickly for something that expensive, and then poured another glassful which he just cradled in his big hands.

"What was your daughter doing in Venice, Mr. Hughes?" asked the policewoman. "Can you tell us?"

"She was on vacation, I suppose," he said.

"You suppose? When did you last see Kathy, Mr. Hughes?"

"About nine months ago." He didn't see any reason to mention the book proposal.

"You were not close?"

How often was it normal to see one's adult children? He shrugged. "Why all the questions? Have they caught the bastard who did this?"

"The Italian police will keep us fully informed," said the male officer.

"What would you like to happen to the body?" asked the female.

Russell Hughes stared at her, appalled.

"I mean, after the autopsy in Venice," she explained. "Would you like her body flown back here? You and your ex-wife are her official next of kin and we have not been able to reach Mrs. Hughes. Do you know where she is?"

"I haven't had any contact with her for thirteen years," he said.

The policewoman did a mental calculation. "Who had custody of the two girls when you divorced?"

"My wife. It's always the wife, isn't it?"

"And you haven't seen her since Kathy was—what?—fourteen?"

"That's right."

"But you had contact with Kathy? And her sister?"

"Of course," he said irritably. "Their mother just kept out of my way."

"Do you have contact details for Kathy's sister, Mr. Hughes?" asked the policewoman. "We're trying to get in touch with her."

"You want to tell her what happened to Kathy?"

"Not necessarily. We assumed you'd want to phone her yourself. But we'd like to ask her about Kathy's Venice trip. She might have said more to her sister."

"I don't think they saw that much of each other," he said. "But I'll go and get Tabby's details. My Filofax is in the study."

He took another swig of malt and left the room unsteadily.

The policeman rolled his eyes. "What kind of a father has to look up his daughter's address?" His own little girls were aged nine and seven.

"One who's just had a shock?" suggested his colleague.

The gondolier community of Venice is a close-knit one. There are just over four hundred of them. Two are women. One has published a right-wing book. Three have recorded albums. But usually they are not in the headlines. They are background figures, charging outrageous prices for less than an hour's ride—shorter than even a psychoanalyst's hour—but feeling exploited if a passerby takes their photograph without permission. And now Taddeo Columbini has his picture in every local paper, his wife has red-rimmed eyes, and his friends shake their heads.

Taddeo had been arrested though not charged, and released after twenty-four hours. But the word on the canal was that it was only a matter of time before he was charged and remanded for the murder of Kathy Hughes. A strand of her hair had been found twisted around a button on his shirt and his DNA had shown up on her clothes too. There was no other suspect.

But why would he kill her? That was what they were saying amongst themselves. It would have been like slaughtering the golden goose. She was giving him plenty by all accounts. And stealing a laptop? Without taking its cable, which would not be that easy to replace in Venice. It didn't add up.

And it was having a bad effect on trade. No female tourist would get into a gondola alone now, and though this had never been a large part of their custom, it was a slur on their reputation. Yet they did not spurn Taddeo, who was not working at the moment; they banded together to give him money and support. He was one of them, and when a gondolier was in trouble, it was them against the world.

They decided to mount an investigation of their own.

There were not many mourners at her funeral. The body had been flown back once the pathologists were through with it, and was about to be cremated in East Finchley. Her father and sister were the chief mourners and there was a handful of friends; Kathy Hughes had not been much liked. Of her mother there was no sign.

The service was impersonal and brief. Russell Hughes and his surviving daughter, Tabitha, sat two feet apart in a front pew. She gave a suppressed sob as the coffin slid away between the curtains to its fiery destination, but her father remained almost impassive. Ever since the police officers had first contacted him, he had moved like an automaton, numb to what was going on around him.

After the service, an awkward knot formed on the gravel drive outside where a light summer rain was falling; they decided against going to a pub and drifted apart again.

"Can I give you a lift anywhere?" the father asked the daughter formally.

She flashed a glare at him. "I came in my own car," she said, walking quickly to where she had parked. She hoped she would never see him again.

Two mourners at the back of the chapel came out and saw the parting of the ways. No one ever recognized them when they were off duty.

"That's one messed-up family," said the policewoman.

"I can't get over Tabitha not knowing her mother's address," replied her colleague.

They had followed up on the last known address for Caroline Fletcher, formerly Hughes, but it was five years old and she was no longer there. There just wasn't enough person-power in the force to follow the trail any farther, and she'd missed the funeral now. Perhaps Kathy's mother would never know she'd died.

The gondoliers mobilized to find out what would release one of their number from suspicion. Taddeo might cheat on his wife, might overcharge a customer, might lie if in a tight corner, but not one of his colleagues believed him capable of murder. He had an honest, open face and a generally sunny nature; had he not been Mr. August a few years ago in one of Piero Pazzi's calendars that sold so well to tourists, especially middle-aged women and gay men?

The gondoliers who moored up regularly near the Gritti Palace got more out of the doormen than the police had. The one who had been on duty the night of the killing was nephew to one of the gondoliers and willing to talk over a Cynar with his Uncle Giorgio and two others when his shift ended.

"I told the police all I knew," he said. "They told me the lock on her door wasn't broken and no one could have climbed in the window, so she must have opened the door to her killer."

"So he came in through the main door of the hotel?" said his uncle.

"Yes, I suppose he did. There are staff entrances but you need a card to get through those. As I told the police, I don't stop people and ask for their ID, do I?"

"Calm down, young Stefano!" said Giorgio. "No one's blaming you. No one expects you to know what the killer looks like. They don't all wear shades at night and have a bulge in their jackets."

"No," agreed Stefano, draining his drink. "And this one didn't have a gun—he strangled her."

All the gondoliers knew the gory details; Taddeo had told them everything. These three nodded and crossed themselves.

"But can you remember any strangers, any people you hadn't seen before?" one of them inquired.

"They asked me that. She was killed at about eleven o'clock, but her body wasn't found till the next morning when the maid brought her breakfast. She's still out sick, poor Eva—can you imagine? But the killer could have come in earlier and had a drink in the bar or just hidden somewhere in the hotel. It's very busy in high season and there are many places he could have hidden."

It was a long interview for Stefano so they bought him another drink.

"I didn't recognize everyone who came in," he continued. "But it's the same every shift. The hotel is so expensive people come just for a few nights; they change over all the time. As long as they walk confidently, I just open the doors."

They all acknowledged that the doorman probably took more notice of guests and visitors leaving than arriving. Those coming out often wanted a gondola or a water taxi, and the doorman had all the relevant information on hand.

Something about this, or perhaps it was the effect of a second Cynar downed rather quickly, gave Stefano an idea.

The hit man had been lying low since the murder. He had done all the usual things—dyed his hair, wore glasses, bought new clothes—but first he had checked out of the Gritti Palace. The police had of course recorded the names of all hotel guests, but it was beyond their powers to keep nearly two hundred wealthy Americans, English, and other Europeans from continuing their holidays or flying back home. And once the police were sure of Taddeo's guilt, they forgot about the list.

And even if they hadn't, the assassin had used a false name and fake passport. He was now in a much less grand hotel that was costing his employer a fraction of the price of the Gritti Palace. He didn't really mind though. The bed was comfortable enough and while it didn't have air-conditioning, no one minded if he leaned out of his window wearing no more than boxer shorts. But he'd been holed up here for nearly two weeks now and was getting bored.

After drinking half a bottle of vodka a night and smoking his way through many packs of cigarettes, he did not feel very good. And he didn't sleep well either; the woman with the ponytail floated just behind his eyes whenever he closed them. He hated killing women. He charged extra for that.

One night when he couldn't sleep, he opened up her computer. His English wasn't great and it didn't look that interesting. But he couldn't sell it; that would bring the police right down on him. He decided the bottom of the canal would be the best place for it; indeed, this is precisely what he'd been instructed to do with it. The little silver thing shaped like a bullet, on the other hand, he kept in his inside jacket pocket

272 // VENICE NOIR

and was reluctant to part with. You never knew when it might be helpful to have something you could use for blackmail.

Tabitha Hughes had been in a daze since her father had phoned her a fortnight earlier. It was true she had not seen much of Kathy since they had left home, and as far as she was concerned she had no mother. Tabitha had created a new family for herself out of workmates and lovers. She didn't like reminders of the past. But Kathy had been her only sibling and no one else had shared the same childhood.

She had no idea that Kathy had been in contact with their father.

After a few days off work, she had gone back to her job at a catering firm in Holborn. It mainly involved making fancy sandwiches for upmarket offices, which a fleet of young men took out on bicycles with big baskets, but they catered some special occasions as well, usually office parties but sometimes book launches or after-show parties, where the clients were usually more interested in the drink than the food.

Home late after one such party, she poured herself a glass of white wine and opened up her computer for the first time in weeks, intending to catch up with some friends on Facebook. The first thing she noticed was an e-mail from her dead sister.

Hey stranger,

I'm in Venice! Remember how we used to talk about coming here? Not the Danieli but this place, the Gritti Palace, is quite cool. He is paying for everything, one way or another. Read the attachment, at least the last story. It's all there. I've had enough. Blackmail has lost its novelty, I'm up for revenge now. You?

* * *

The hit man answered his door as carelessly as the woman had. Three shots with a silencer and he was dead. The new assassin searched the man's possessions, took the flash drive from his pocket, and slipped down the stairs as quietly as he had come in. No one would ever associate this crime with the other one: no connection, quite different MOs, and nothing as sophisticated as CCTV in the Hotel Roxy. He waited till he had crossed several little bridges and was in another sestiere before pulling out his phone.

Stefano realized that they needed to concentrate on someone leaving with a bag concealing the victim's laptop. He asked the person who had worked the shift after his and then reviewed the records for checkouts late at night, which were not that uncommon in the upmarket hotels.

So the gondoliers had a name, almost certainly a false one. And a photocopy of a forged passport. The face was not very distinctive, but hundreds of copies were made of the man's photo. Before their inquiries had gotten very far underway, however, there was the same face, with a neat bullet hole over one eye, in the papers. He was a bleached blonde now, but the killer was dead.

At that point Giorgio and Stefano went to the police. The gondoliers were the only ones who had made a connection between the man at the Hotel Roxy and the murder at the Gritti Palace.

And the second hit man had made a silly mistake. He had gone to a bar and drunk several cocktails, then flagged down a passing gondola. There was a poster on it saying, *Have you seen this man?* And a reward offered. The passenger had started to laugh hysterically and the gondolier became suspi-

274 // Venice Noir

cious. He had leaped on his passenger and held him down, calling for help from his fellow oarsmen.

Stefano and Giorgio then took the detectives to where they had the man bound in a safe house and there they found the flash drive.

Russell Hughes thought he had gotten away with it, as he had last time. The computer had been deep-sixed somewhere in the muddy waters of a Venetian canal. The strangler had been eliminated.

There had been sympathy at work; a terrible thing for a father to lose his daughter so. Not one of the employees knew she had been given a contract for a book. He had drawn it up himself after hours, using the office template, buying time; he had never intended to publish it.

Now it was a closed book. He roused himself to take a tie from his desk drawer and a brush to push through his unruly hair. They were having a launch party tonight for a celebrity memoir whose advance orders were looking so healthy it was clear the house was going to make serious money. There was already the sound of laughter and clinking glasses coming from the boardroom; he must get a move on or he would be late.

A young woman in a black dress and a white apron gave him a glass of champagne as he entered the room to subdued greetings. The celebrity author had not arrived—was waiting to make an entrance. Another young woman in the same uniform stepped forward to offer him a canapé. There was something familiar about her.

"Hello, Dad," she said.

"Tabitha!" He didn't have a chance to wonder why she was there; a commotion erupted in the doorway, which could only mean the Big Name had entered the building.

But no, there were policemen and they were coming toward him. Handcuffs appeared and his rights were read. The house photographer was flashing away—at this stage everyone thought it was a stunt.

Everyone except Russell and Tabitha Hughes. He was staring at her. She looked like her sister—and her mother too. She was smiling. But how had she known?

"'The Good Father,'" she whispered as they took him away.

He had a stroke in the elevator as they told him about the evidence from his younger daughter's computer and the connection established by the gondoliers between two seemingly unrelated deaths in Venice.

They didn't know about Caroline. He tried to tell them. But all that came out was, "Short stories are notoriously difficult to sell."

They were his last words.

ABOUT THE CONTRIBUTORS

BARBARA BARALDI has been called "the Queen of Italian gothic." Her first book, *The Girl with the Crystal Eyes*, appeared in Italy in 2006 and has been translated into English. She has since written a variety of acclaimed novels and books for young adults, including *Il Bacio del Demone* and *Scarlett*. She was featured in the BBC documentary *Italian Noir* as one the foremost contemporary Italian crime authors, and has won several awards. She has also worked as a photographer and a model and lives near Bologna.

TONY CARTANO was born in Bayonne, France, where his father was exiled to following the Spanish Civil War. After studying in London and Paris, he enjoyed a distinguished career in French publishing, running a series of major imprints. He has written a dozen novels, of which *Blackbird* and *After the Conquest* are available in English, as well a travel book about America. His most recent, *Les Gifles au Vinaigre*, was published in 2010. He lives in Paris, France.

FRANCESCO FERRACIN was born in Venice and studied philosophy and linguistics there and in Germany and Sweden. He writes for many magazines, including *Vogue Italia* and *Uoma Vogue*, among others. His crime novel *Una Vasca di Troppo* was first published in 2008. He is also a screenwriter with a handful of produced scripts, including a new film by Franco Battisto about Handel currently in production, featuring Willem Dafoe and Susan Sarandon. He lives in Berlin, Germany.

MICHAEL GREGORIO (the pen name of the Anglo-Italian husband-and-wife writing team, Daniela De Gregorio and Michael G. Jacob) writes historical thrillers. Their first novel, *Critique of Criminal Reason*, was praised by *Playboy* as one of the ten best books of the year. The novel features Prussian magistrate Hanno Stiffeniis, who also appears in three subsequent novels: *Days of Atonement*, *A Visible Darkness*, and, most recently, *Unholy Awakening*. They live in Spoleto. For more information, visit www.michaelgregorio.it

MIKE HODGES is best known as a filmmaker (*Get Carter, Pulp, The Terminal Man*, and, more recently, *Black Rainbow, Croupier*, and *I'll Sleep When I'm Dead*) but has also written and directed plays for BBC Radio and the theater. His first novel, *Watching the Wheels Come Off*, was published in 2010. The theme of all these works is a bleak and blackly humorous take on the world as he sees it. His lighter contributions to the cinema include *Flash Gordon* and *Morons from Outer Space*. He lives on a farm in England.

Jess Barber

MARY HOFFMAN has published over ninety books, mainly for teenagers and younger readers, but has recently been writing more for an adult audience. *David*, the story of the young man who posed for Michelangelo's statue, was published in 2011. She is also known for her popular Stravaganza series, set in Venice, which has now reached five volumes. Many of her books are set in Italy and her work in progress is currently titled *The Italian for Love*. She lives in Oxfordshire, England.

Clemence Meyer

MAXIM JAKUBOWSKI is an award-winning London-based British editor and writer. He has reviewed crime fiction for the *Guardian* and *Time Out* and ran London's Crime Scene Festival. He has lived in Italy and has been an advisor to the Courmayeur Noir in Fest film and literary festival for twenty years. His latest novel, *Ekaterina and the Night*, is partly set in Venice, and he edits the *Best British Mysteries* annual series. With Chiara Stangalino, he was the editor of *Rome Noir*.

Gareth Ransome

PETER JAMES is published in thirty-four languages. His latest Roy Grace thrillers, *Dead Like You* and *Dead Man's Grip*, went straight onto the UK best-seller lists at number one. Before becoming a full-time novelist, he was an established screenwriter and producer; among his film credits is *The Merchant of Venice* starring Al Pacino and Jeremy Irons. He is currently chair of the UK Crime Writers' Association. He lives in Notting Hill, London, and near Brighton in Sussex, England.

Marianne Taylor

MICHELLE LOVRIC was born in Australia. She is a novelist and anthologist with particular interests in art, medical history, and Venice, where she lives and sets her novels. Her highly acclaimed novels include *Carnevale*, *The Floating Book*, *The Remedy*, and, most recently, *The Book of Human Skin*. Her first children's novel, *The Undrowned Child*, was followed by *The Mourning Emporium*.

Kevin Mandel

EMILY ST. JOHN MANDEL was born in British Columbia, Canada. She studied dance at the School of Toronto Dance Theatre and lived briefly in Montreal before relocating to New York. She is the author of *Last Night in Montreal*, *The Singer's Gun*, and *The Lola Quartet*. She is currently a staff writer at *The Millions* (www.themillions.com) and her website is www.emilymandel.com. She is married and lives in Brooklyn, New York.

Francesca Mazzucato is a controversial presence in Italian letters, a prolific fiction writer, editor, translator, and blogger. She is the author of a dozen novels, including *La Sottomissione di Ludovica, Hot Line, Enigma Veneziana,* and *L'Anarchiste.* In 2011 she published an illustrated volume, *Storia dello Striptease.* Also a travel writer with books about various cities, she splits her time between the Ligurian coast and Bologna.

Giovanni De Sandre

Matteo Righetto was born in Padova in 1972. In 2008 he established and cofounded the Surgarpulp literary movement. His novel *Savana Padana* appeared in 2009, followed by another "folk noir" volume, *Bacchiglione Blues,* in 2011. Joe Lansdale has called him "one of the more knowledgeable noir practitioners, part of the new wave of sharp darkness." His website is www.matteorighetto.com. He lives in Padova.

Rosangela Betti

Isabella Santacroce has written nine books, including *Fluo, Destroy, Luminal, Lovers, Revolver,* and *Lulu Delacroix.* A highly visible figure in Italy (and once part of the New Cannibal movement of young writers), Santacroce is notorious for her public appearances and modeling. In 2011 she issued the first volume of her autobiography, *Io Non So Chi Sono,* in an edition of only ten copies.

Maria Tronca was born in Palermo, Sicily in 1962 and now lives in Milan where she runs a web and cell phone company. She lived for a number of years in Venice, where she jointly ran, with her partner, writer Massimiliano Sosella, a literary erotica imprint for the major Italian publisher Mondadori, which was very successful and included her 2005 book *L'Isola delle Femmine.* Her first noir novel, *Rosanero,* was published in 2010, and was followed in 2011 by *L'Amante delle Sedie Volanti.*

Also available from the Akashic Noir Series

ROME NOIR
edited by Chiara Stangalino & Maxim Jakubowski
280 pages, trade paperback original, $15.95

Brand-new stories by: Antonio Scurati, Carlo Lucarelli, Gianrico Carofiglio, Diego De Silva, Giuseppe Genna, Marcello Fois, Cristiana Danila Formetta, Enrico Franceschini, Boosta, and others.

From Stazione Termini, immortalized by Roberto Rossellini's films, to Pier Paolo Pasolini's desolate beach of Ostia, and encompassing famous landmarks and streets, this is the sinister side of the Dolce Vita come to life, a stunning gallery of dark characters, grotesques, and lost souls seeking revenge or redemption in the shadow of the Colosseum, the Spanish Steps, the Vatican, Trastevere, the quiet waters of the Tiber, and Piazza Navona. Rome will never be the same.

BOSTON NOIR
edited by Dennis Lehane
240 pages, trade paperback original, $15.95

Brand-new stories by: Dennis Lehane, Stewart O'Nan, Patricia Powell, John Dufresne, Lynne Heitman, Don Lee, Russ Aborn, J. Itabari Njeri, Jim Fusilli, Brendan DuBois, and Dana Cameron.

"In the best of the eleven stories in this outstanding entry in Akashic's noir series, characters, plot, and setting feed off each other like flames and an arsonist's accelerant . . . [T]his anthology shows that noir can thrive where Raymond Chandler has never set foot."
—*Publishers Weekly* (starred review)

PARIS NOIR
edited by Aurélien Masson
300 pages, trade paperback original, $15.95

Brand-new stories by: Didier Daeninckx, Jean-Bernard Pouy, Marc Villard, Chantal Pelletier, Patrick Pécherot, DOA, Hervé Prudon, Dominique Mainard, Salim Bachi, Jérôme Leroy, and others.

"Rarely has the City of Light seemed grittier than in this hard-boiled short story anthology, part of Akashic's Noir Series . . . The twelve freshly penned pulp fictions by some of France's most prominent practitioners play out in a kind of darker, parallel universe to the tourist mecca; visitors cross these pages at their peril . . ."
—*Publishers Weekly*

ISTANBUL NOIR
edited by Mustafa Ziyalan & Amy Spangler
300 pages, trade paperback original, $15.95

Brand-new stories by: Müge İplikçi, Behçet Çelik, İsmail Güzelsoy, Lydia Lunch, Hikmet Hükümenoğlu, Rıza Kıraç, Sadık Yemni, Barış Müstecaplıoğlu, Yasemin Aydınoğlu, Feryal Tilmaç, and others.

"The authors do an excellent job introducing readers to a city unknown to many American readers, exploring the many issues of religion and culture that face modern Istanbul. Landscape is essential to these stories, all of which convince the reader that they couldn't possibly have been set anywhere other than Istanbul." —*Booklist*

NEW JERSEY NOIR
edited by Joyce Carol Oates
288 pages, trade paperback original, $15.95

Brand-new stories by: Jonathan Safran Foer, Bradford Morrow, Bill Pronzini, S.J. Rozan, Edmund White, Robert Pinsky, and others.

"Oates's introduction to Akashic's noir volume dedicated to the Garden State, with its evocative definition of the genre, is alone worth the price of the book . . . Poems by C.K. Williams, Paul Muldoon, and others—plus photos by Gerald Slota—enhance this distinguished entry."—*Publishers Weekly*

BROOKLYN NOIR
edited by Tim McLoughlin
350 pages, trade paperback original, $15.95
*Winner of Shamus Award, Anthony Award, Robert L. Fish Memorial Award; finalist for Edgar Award, Pushcart Prize.

Brand-new stories by: Pete Hamill, Arthur Nersesian, Ellen Miller, Nelson George, Nicole Blackman, Sidney Offit, Ken Bruen, and others.

"*Brooklyn Noir* is such a stunningly perfect combination that you can't believe you haven't read an anthology like this before. But trust me— you haven't . . . The writing is flat-out superb, filled with lines that will sing in your head for a long time to come."
—Laura Lippman, winner of the Edgar, Agatha, and Shamus awards

Magical World

Stories, Reflections, Poems

Rabbi Sara Brandes

Neshama Press
www.neshamacenter.org/press
press@neshamacenter.org

For permissions, contact The Permissions Company:
47 Seneca Road
P. O. Box 604
Mount Pocono, PA 18344
570.839.7477

Dedication

This book is dedicated to my rabbis and teachers—my kind, soulful escorts who have guided me on my way. I strive to walk in your footsteps, to offer wisdom and heart to others as you have to me.

Special thanks to Moses Hacmon for use of the spectacular image on the cover, which Moses captured through a unique process of photography, in service of his conviction that water is the source and birthplace of life. Moses and his work are a testament to the magic and mystery in the world around us. To learn more, visit www.facesofwater.com.

Contents

A Note of Introduction

Hello Friend,

It is with great humility that I offer you my personal reflections, seeking and finding in this magical world of ours. Though the insights contained here are the result of years of study, this book is not intended to be a scholarly work. Rather, it is an account of my searching, and if my searching can accompany you along your way, then I walk with you in joy. With gratitude to my Creator and my teachers, I share my voice with you.

I am a mystic and a rabbi. Though I am certain that all paths lead to the One, my path is Judaism, and therefore this book draws on Jewish imagery, concepts, and texts. I have worked hard to make these concepts accessible to any reader because students of Torah and Judaism are not necessarily the intended audience for this work. Hebrew and Jewish terms are explained in footnotes on each page and defined in a glossary and the end of the book. If your heart, too, yearns for union with all of creation and the Creator who shaped us, then you are my sister and my friend. I hope that drinking from the wellspring of Jewish tradition can nourish you as it nourishes me.

The penultimate section of this work is a suggested spiritual practice based on the kabbalistic imaging of the Divine, brought to life in the Jewish calendar by the springtime ritual known as *sefirat ha'omer*. This section can be read as theology or enjoyed alone as a roadmap for contemplative spiritual practice.

In addition to poems and meditations, I share with you here the journey of my becoming, a work still in progress. I do so inspired by the most fundamental Jewish insight that guides our works of law and lore: all things have their story. Only by knowing the story of the thing can we hope to understand it. Law does not stand alone. Prayer does not stand alone. Truth does not stand alone. These things are embedded in story, and so I share mine with you. I hope one day, I can hear yours.

Blessings of Peace,
Rabbi Sara Brandes

Magical World
Stories, Reflections, Poems

"Bring your whole heart and your whole soul to Me.

For, these instructions that I am commanding you today, they are not too wondrous for you and they are not far away from you.

They are not in the heavens, that you might say 'Who will go up there to the heavens and bring them down to us, so that we might know them and do them?'

They are not across the sea from you, that you might say, 'Who can cross the sea for us and bring them to us, that we might know them and do them?'

No.

The matter is very close to you.

It is in your mouths and in your hearts."

—Deuteronomy 30:11-14

Womb

My earliest memory takes place in the sprawling backyard of my childhood home. There, I would explore, wild and free amidst the towering pine trees. There, I would flip and twirl, practicing my gymnastics, and there, I would play for hours with my imaginary friend. Her name was Juki. She lived in a world of imaginary friends, a world I was aware of, in touch with, and gained pleasure from encountering. We would have long, drawn-out conversations, sometimes in English and sometimes in her language, which I now do not recall. When I think back to that time in my life, I can feel myself sitting with Juki, though I can no longer see her, even in my memory.

A beautiful story is told in the Babylonian Talmud[1] about the experience of the infant in the womb. The Talmud recalls:

[1] "Talmud" generally refers to two edited complications of Jewish preserved tradition, lore, and law. The Babylonian Talmud, which contains sources written approximately 100 BCE–500 CE, was codified in Babylon; while the Jerusalem Talmud contains sources from a similar period but was codified in Israel in approximately the fourth century CE.

Rabbi Simlai taught: What does an embryo resemble
when it is in the uterus of its mother? ... A light
burns above its head and it looks and sees from one
end of the world to the other, as it is said, "then
[God's] lamp shined above my head, and by [God's]
light I walked through darkness." And do not be
surprised, for a person sleeping here might see a
dream in Spain. And there is no time in which one
enjoys greater happiness than in those days…[The
embryo] is also taught all the Torah from beginning
to end... As soon as it sees the light (of the birth
canal), an angel approaches, taps it on its mouth and
causes it to forget all the Torah completely.

—Babylonian Talmud, *Niddah* 30b

*So often, we imagine small children as blank canvases, but
the Talmud tells a different story. Our natural state is one of
light and knowledge, of a deep understanding that is drawn
from the source of understanding. But, once we are born, and
we begin to know ourselves, a veil of illusion falls. It
deprives us of the perspective that once was ours. As a child,
it seems I was able to lift that veil and to interact with the
world beyond it. In kindergarten, I must have forgotten how.*

The Real World

I want to live in the real world.
In a world where everything is real.

Real Spoon.
Real Chair.
Real Light.
Real Air.

We've gone too far, this race of ours.
        Toward faster and better and more.
We've raced past the real
        to the other than…

Where we touch,
        but not one another.
Where we look,
        but not at each other.
Where we are but virtually there.

I want to live in the world that is real.

Real spoon. Real chair.
Real friend, real care.
Real day, real night.
Real light. Real air.

God Wrestlers

The holiness of the Jewish people is that we are *Yisra-El*, the people who wrestle with God. Our historical memory extends back more than 5,000 years. Our memories recall our struggles—our cosmic dance with God.

We are a people defined by our memories. We recall a time when God guided the lives and destinies of our ancestors. We remember when God revealed Godself to us, striving to enter into relationship with us, and when we were blessed to have God dwell in our midst at all times, in the form of a cloud of smoke by day and a pillar of fire by night.[2] We remember when our people's hearts were moved to give of our most precious possessions to build a dwelling place for God. We recall when that portable dwelling place was given a permanent home in a holy land whose soil and seasons express God's will. We recall a time when we had a formulaic mode of worship, dictated to us by God, so that we could be in perpetual relationship with God.

---

[2] This was a feature of Biblical Israel's wandering in the desert. Divine presence was represented there as a cloud by day and a pillar of fire by night. See, for example, Numbers 9:15-23.

In our memories, we are lead by a king who is also a psalmist, who danced in ecstatic joy as he served his Creator. We remember our prophets, who knew God and God's will, who were able to discern God's presence in history, who guided our people in their grappling with God. And, we remember our banishment from God's land and God's house. It is these memories that help us to begin to imagine the world in which we now live, where God is so very hidden.

We remember the birth of the man about whom God said, "He will one day give meaning to the crowns atop the letters of the Torah."[3] [4] We remember a community engaged in God's law, that added layer upon layer of meaning to the Torah. These are our stories. These are our memories. They are holy because they are ours. They are holy because they contain God. Each ancestor helps us to imagine; each memory, to bring God into our lives.

As a living Jewish community, we add to these stories. Every time two students sit before the text, they carry on the great legacy of the Jewish people, those who wrestle with God. Every pair, for as long as we have been, evoke the

---

[3] Literally "teaching," Torah is a Hebrew term for the Old Testament or the Five books of Moses.

[4] Babylonian Talmud, *Menachot* 29b.

flame of God in their midst. She who contemplates the majesty of creation affirms its truth. He who meditates upon revelation causes it to be. In this way, our tradition evolves. The wisdom we evoke when we sit together to study is integrated into our people's long history. It too becomes part of our sacred memory. In this way, the Torah is revealed by each of us, within each of us.

Dazzling Darkness

Create, create, create again.
Bless, I bless, I bless again,
the unfolding of the here and now.

But, oh Great Dazzling Darkness,
Unconscious Mother,
this moment, it terrifies me,
I tremble within it.

Into it I dive, so that I might manifest again.

I listen as the soul cries out,
"Slow down, ye winds of change."

And it is uncovered.

Life, love, loss, purpose.
Buried in every moment.
In this moment.

Becoming

I have been so many people in this lifetime. When I was a child, my mother would awaken me each morning. Everyday, we engaged in the same ritual. She would sit softly on my bed and invite me back into this world. I would sense her presence and immediately open my eyes with a smile. Every morning she would say, "You are so happy when you wake up." I would smile in return. Presence, smile, affirmation, smile. Would I have awoken happy had she not labeled me so?

I remember as a child the World Wide Web icon on our version of America Online resting dormant for several months. The image, a beautiful swirling web of color, would one day connect computers everywhere, my father explained. I remember when that link came alive, and virtual relationships were born. I remember entering mysterious chat rooms as a young adolescent and knowing that I had entered a world of both truth and illusion. I remember knowing that there, I could be anybody, that all who I met there were only projections of themselves.

That was the world I grew up in, the virtual world.

Remember

I must remember and never forget,
The rolling laughter of a child at play.
Its gushing forth in wild abandon.
Unadulterated.

I must remember and never forget,
The tingle down the lover's spine.
More and more and more again.
So passionate.

We have forgotten so much.
We have forgotten it all.

Our day dreaming and night yearning;
Our imagine this and yes lets.
Our everything is possible.

I knew it once.
Now it is forgotten.

Remember.

"Blessed Art Thou"

A Hasidic parable tells the story of a spiritual seeker who goes to his rabbi. "Rabbi," he says. "I cannot pray. I go to the *shul*[5], and I begin to pray. I begin, 'Blessed art Thou,' I wonder, who is Thou? and I can go no further." To this, the rabbi responded, "My son, I'm so glad you've come to me, because I have the very same problem."[6]

For millennia, the angels cried "Blessed art Thou." But, then one day, one stopped to wonder—*"Thou, who is Thou?* More importantly, who am I?!" And in that moment, from the garden, he was thrown, and our world was born.

[5] A Yiddish word meaning school, but which is used to refer to a small or intimate synagogue.

[6] This story was relayed to me orally by my rabbi and teacher Rabbi Ed Feld, Rabbi-in-Residence at the Jewish Theological Seminary 2002–2008.

For "I" became "I am," which quickly turned into "I am not." From "I am not" can only grow "I am not you," and, thus, hatred was born.[7]

God created us, but we, blessed images of God, created hate.

Once hate was born, what was God to do but give us free will and create a realm in which we could remember to forget our hate and wipe its memory away?[8]

So, God committed the great loving sacrifice. God slowed and transformed and bestowed on us, creators of hate and other, the ability to create our own universes in which we could unlearn these things.

And here we are.

---

[7] See Genesis 3. This section is a retelling of the story of the fall from Eden, based on the thirteenth-century teachings of Rabbi Moses Maimonides in his *Guide for the Perplexed*, which teaches that the sin in the Garden of Eden is the act of turning aside from the Creator. Before the sin, Adam and Eve know only God, and God occupies all of their thoughts. The sin is the act of acknowledging privation, absent potential, a space that is not God.

[8] Judaism contains an ironic instruction to remember to forget hate incarnate, the symbol of which is the ancient tribe of Amalek, which attacked the Israelites from the rear, killing the weakest, the elderly, and the young as the Israelites wandered in the desert. We are commanded therefore to wipe away any memory of them. Paradoxically, in keeping the commandment, we perpetuate their memory. See Deuteronomy 25:17–19.

Here, in this realm, we are challenged to harness our fears, our biases, our commitments to "other" and make them manifest.

Here, we cause them to take on physical form so that we can wrestle with them, dance with them, sometimes, tragically, kill them, and, in the end, gloriously, embrace them.

These are our lives, our challenges, our woes, and our joys.

This is our family, our history, our context and landscape.

This is the world as we know it.

Training

Competitive gymnastics shaped my childhood. It changed me in three ways. There, I took hold of my body, I learned to fly, and I sealed my heart. From age eleven to fourteen, I spent 25 hours a week in the gym, allowing my coaches to push me beyond my limits. I stood on my hands for ten-minute stretches, did 1,000 sit-ups, and also had many light moments with my team.

My clearest memory from my time in the gym was the day that I learned how to stop crying. When I first began my period of rigorous training, I was physically weak and would cry during long warm-up runs. The tears were debilitating to me; I could not run, cry, and breathe all at the same time. They were also unacceptable to my coaches. I knew this, and I knew the tears had to stop.

One day, I discovered that if I counted my paces, I would not become overwhelmed by the prospect of the run and I could keep the tears at bay. Firm faced, I ran and counted, ran and counted. And I did it. No tears, but no feelings either. I turned it all off.

That day in the gym, I was liberated from one thing and enslaved by another. Now, my mind controlled my body. I was free of its cries of exhaustion or weakness. I came to learn that my body could do almost anything the mind willed, with time and practice. But, in setting my body free, my heart paid the price. It was sealed shut. My mind had no ear for its needs or its outbursts.

As it turns out, one cannot only seal the heart in certain circumstances, at least not as a child. For me, sealed is sealed, and sealed it was. I found that my stern-faced resoluteness would arise during painful fights with my father, or when shamed in public by my teacher. Challenged, there it was, my armored heart, feeling no longer. Life then became calmer, quieter—but so much duller, too. There were simply no more tears. All of the pain, the wonderful passions of childhood stood further off in the distance, no longer strumming the strings of my protected heart.

It has taken half a lifetime to shed the armor I dawned that day. To this day, I am not sure that I'm fully free of it.

One Day, the Cry

One day, the cry will come.
Long after all is gone.
Hard face, hard hands, hard heart.
       Life
       Love
       Fire forgotten.

One day, the cry will come.
When all has started to melt.
Whispers stirring softly,
Calling, calling again.

One day, the cry will come.
When the heart remembers to wonder.
When feeling returns to feeling,
To sensing what can be.

The return brings pain, so easily felt.
Pain brings again
          fire
      again
        wonder
      again
       self.

One day the cry will come,
And you will come again.

Love

When asked when my husband Hyim and first I met, I say "I have known him since before I was born." Our families are old friends. We have photographs together from when we were both toddlers. He was one of my first playmates, but during our childhoods, our families grew apart. We shared a common summer camp, where we both continued to return year after year, but where we always seemed to miss one another. Then, one winter night, I was working and he had come to visit. We shared a dance. We found ourselves trapped in a rainstorm together, and we experienced the spark of authentic connection.

The following summer, I was a counselor at the camp and he was not, but circumstances allowed him to come and visit on several occasions. We spent enough time together for me to convince him that he should accept a job there for the last weeks of the summer. He did. We flirted, courting as teenagers do.

The night that I consider our night of soul recall remains one of my most profound moments of spiritual encounter. Hyim and I had been spending an increasing amount of time together, but we were not yet romantically involved. The following is what I remember. At the time, the experience felt as though it transpired outside of the confines of time and space. It was magical and God was there.

I had fallen asleep. I awoke for no reason at 2:00 AM and was compelled to go and look for Hyim. I did not need to look. We met at the crossroad of the camp, each of us approaching simultaneously from opposite directions. He had been with some friends of ours, and they were going to bed.

We spent the night sharing our beliefs and our dreams. He was also looking for his soul mate. After hours of talking, we began to doze off, one at a time, each watching the other sleep. During one of my short naps, I had a vivid dream. I dreamt of a place I had never been. I was with Hyim, his brother, and several others whom I did not know. The sights, smells, and tastes of the dream were far more vivid than my usual dream state. I awoke and told Hyim the details, feeling that it was somehow significant. We talked until sunrise. The dream came to pass two weeks later, after we had professed our love. I had dreamt of the most important people in Hyim's life and of my acceptance by them.

I have only been blessed with two moments in my life when I have had the direct awareness of God's presence. At each one, and at no other time in my life, I have experienced a memory of something to come, a seeing enabled by the compression of time and space that characterizes the Divine realm.

During our first year in Israel, Hyim and I went on a weekend trip with our school community. The trip was to the north of Israel, visiting the ancient town of Tzippori, the city where many of the great early rabbis lived. On the trip, I experienced my second moment of soul-memory.

Our group was touring a series of caves that made up the system of aqueducts for the ancient Jewish community of the area. As we moved through the caves, I was overcome with the most overwhelming sense of déjà vu, such that I was forced to exclaim to my walking companion, "I know I have been here before." The feeling was overwhelming, silencing. I spent the morning in awe. I was touring a place where I know I have lived before. At the end of the morning, I approached Hyim. With a few words, we both understood that we were sharing the same memories. The experience was startling.

In that moment, my sense of time and my precise location in it broke open. Our knowing, our loving extended far beyond here and now, beyond any capacity for memory I possessed. I knew then that I would walk this lifetime, too, with this soul mate of mine.

Soul Mates

The Torah imagines the first human being as a dual-faced creature, made of the earth. Known as *Adam Hakadmon*, the creature is formed in the image of God and is both male and female. But, the creature is lonely and God observes, "It is not good that the human is alone."[9] So, God returns the earthling[10] to the earth, casting a deep sleep upon it and divides it in two, removing one of its sides, thereby creating two creatures. The new creature is called *isha*, woman, and the remaining creature is called *ish*, man.[11]

The notion, then, that we are but half of a whole, torn from our partner, destined to be reunited again, finds its

---

[9] Genesis 2:18.

[10] Based on Genesis 2:7, "And God formed *Adam* from the *adamah* (earth)." Translation of "Adam" offered by Everett Fox in *The Five Books of Moses*, The Schocken Bible, vol. 1 (New York: Schocken Press, 2000).

[11] Although lesser known in contemporary discourse, this interpretation of Genesis 2 is the accepted one among mainstream Jewish commentators on the Torah, most notably Rashi on Genesis 1:27. The word *selah*, generally translated as "rib," does not bear this meaning anywhere else in the Torah. Rather, it is used to mean "side," referring to the side of the Ark of the Covenant, several times in Exodus 25–37.

roots in the Torah. But, this is only half of the story. For, in this metaphor we are passive globs of earth, molded, shaped and separated. We are created so that we can be torn in two.

One can only understand the notion of soul mates in Judaism by considering both parts of the human. The original earthling is brought to life by *neshama,* Divine breath.[12] *Neshama* takes up residence within us, animating us as we grow and love, leaving us when we breathe our last. We humans are a mixture of earth and Divine breath. *Neshama* is of God; we only borrow it for a time. Through its eyes we see our world; and through its wisdom, we create our lives.

Which is it, then? Are we victims, torn from our partner, sent off on a life of searching, or are we Divine breath, co-creating our lives and our world?

We are both. Our truth depends upon our perspective. So often, we cannot help but gaze through our flesh and blood eyes, subject to a will far greater than our own. But, the soul too has eyes, and through these eyes, gazes only one Consciousness, shared by us and our Creator.

There is no more powerful force in the universe than love, ripping us open and tearing us apart. Like the blast that

---

[12] *Neshama* is one of several Hebrew words for soul. The etymology of the word stems from the Hebrew word meaning breath, yielding a conceptualization of the human soul as Divine breath.

bursts forth when an atom is split, our hearts too are part of the dance of separation and unification. They call us towards the other, moving us to become something other than who we presently are. We are pushed and pulled by the Universe, melting and emerging as we are drawn toward Oneness.

Soul mates come in myriad forms. They are vessels of love, packaged as a parent or a child, a lover or a friend. No matter the form, they enter our lives to help us grow.

Sinai

He stood at the foot of a mountain in the wilderness,
surrounded by nothing but mountains—dust and mountains.

She stood with her family, her parents and children,
her tribe, her community and her people.

He looked heavenward and his head began to spin.
Sights became sounds—lightening flashes and thunder.

Time stopped.
For a moment,
a moment that was at once fleeting and like an eternity—

She saw God.

In that moment, self, other, people, purpose—all became
clear.

There was order in the universe.
He was home.
This is Sinai.[13]

---

[13] Based on the accounting of revelation found in Exodus 19.

Halakhah: Walking the World

The Jewish narrative begins with the assertion that once we encountered God. Our experience of God was direct, it was personal, it inspired action. The revelation at Sinai is the point of departure for the collective journey of the Jewish people.

Likewise, the Jewish story has direction. We set out from Sinai millennia ago, and we began our journey toward "the promised land." We often think of these landmarks as historical moments. But their power for us exists not in their function as moments in history, but rather as claims of possibility. It is possible to organize one's life around two pillars, the flash moment of insight, in which we know deeply who we are and the potential arrival at our own promised land. This is the Jewish story.

Once we have experienced the flashing, fleeting moment in which we know deeply who we are and what it is we are meant to do with our lives, what then? How does one journey from Sinai? How does one build a life that honors the truth of that one, most precious moment?

Why is it so hard to construct a meaningful life? Why is the moment in which we know our deepest selves and what we are meant to do with our lives so fleeting? Why does it stand like a lone mountain in the wilderness, just as Mt. Sinai stands in the vast Egyptian desert? Why can't we preserve this clarity all of the time? Why is it so hard to remember?

I am sure that you can picture a person you know who does not forget, who seems to know at all times who they are and what they are meant to do with their lives. We call these people enlightened. They seem to stand always at the foot of their own proverbial mountains.

But, the Jewish narrative is honest. It speaks the truth that so many of us feel with great frustration. God is not ever-present for us. Revelation is a miracle. It does not happen daily. It is possible to find our way to Sinai again, but it must be a conscious process. It takes work.

The Torah's response comes in the form of a phrase that immediately follows its recounting of the story of revelation. It teaches, *"v'eile hamishpatim"*—these are the laws, the guidelines, the *halakhah*, that one can follow to walk the Jewish journey. Whereas a description of revelation occupies only a short chapter of the Torah, the legal sections that follow make up more than half of its teachings, which come to be known as *Halakhah*. *Halakhah* is a Hebrew word that is usually translated as "Jewish Law," but the word itself comes from the verb *lalechet,* meaning "to walk."

Halakhah is a path, or the way Jews walk through the world. It is a system of law made up of *mitzvot*, commandments, that legislate the smallest details of life.

Jewish tradition teaches that there are 613 commandments in the Torah pertaining to every detail of the life of a Jew. We have instructions for how one should get out of bed in the morning, how to eat, work, study, and treat one another; how one should go to the bathroom and make love. The rabbis of the Talmud offer an explanation for why we use this specific number, teaching:

> There are 613 commandments, 365 negative instructions, like the number of days in a year, and 248 positive instructions, like the number of bones in the body.[14]

On every day of the year, *halakhah* offers us the opportunity to bring meaning into our lives. 365 rules, 365 days. And, the system does more than say, "do this everyday." Each day has its own instruction, its own invitation, its own unique opportunity.

365 negative, 248 positive.

Consider your hands. What potential is contained in your hands? What unique potential—something that only

---

[14] Babylonian Talmud, *Makot* 23b.

your hands can do, not mine, just yours? What about your ears? your heart? What unique potential is contained in your mind or in your heart?

The rabbis teach that there are 248 parts of the body, and each, in its own way, contains the potential to make a difference, to connect you with your community and with your Creator. My hands were made to shape the potter's clay, my breast to nurse my child. What were your hands created to do?

Traditional Jewish living invites us to live consciously. It says that we are meant to walk the path from revelation to redemption. It calls this path *halakhah*, and it invites us to walk. It is a holy journey. Judaism offers sign posts, in the form of holy moments and holy days. It says, take pause in these moments, and in so doing, you will create space for the Divine.

Halakhah is a recipe for creating a meaningful life. By legislating interpersonal ethics, business ethics, ritual purity, and religious conduct, Jewish law teaches that each of these seemingly mundane moments of life, contains within them the possibility for meaning, of finding the way back to a moment of personal revelation, back to your own Sinai. The singular challenge of our lives is to honor the flash, Sinai moment; to construct a life in which we work, everyday, to be the person we were born to be, recognizing the Divine presence in our lives and in the world.

As we move through the world and through time, as we heed the call of our own inner voice, we are meant to look about and to see that God is everywhere. We use our hands, and our hearts, and all of the bones in our bodies to do the work of our lives. And in each step we take, each action we perform, we are meant to recognize the presence of the Divine walking with us. We are meant to come to realize that every moment of our lives brings us back to the mountain in the wilderness, where we once saw God. Every moment becomes a moment of revelation, such that we are eventually bathed in light.

~~

Bless us God, that we should be like one in the light of your presence. Help us to honor the purpose of our lives. Help us to sanctify the moments of our lives, so that our lives are filled with You, filled with meaning.

~~

Cracking

In college, I used to dance atop a bar at a place called BAR. I was alive, wild and free. I had endless energy. But, if I look deep into my memories of that time, I recognize a black terror that was there too. It was a nervous emptiness resting at the base of my stomach— the gray/black space between a candle's wick and its flame, the fuel that allows the candle to burn. Shortly after arriving in Israel, I was consumed by that blackness. That which had fueled me began to consume me. Everything burned. And yet, that fire distilled everything. I was twenty-one.

It was the year 2000. The hope of the Camp David peace accords soured, replaced by the violence of the Second Intifada. Just months earlier, I had traveled with friends to Egypt and Jordan, exploring the widening world. But, freedom and safety quickly evaporated, giving way to the explosions of suicide bombers on the streets of Jerusalem.

I spent that year in yeshiva, studying Torah by day, chain smoking at night. I covered my skin, donning the garb of a religious woman, experimenting with anonymity and invisibility. I cursed that girl I had been atop the bar, calling her dirty and bad. But, it was her wings that lifted me high as I searched.

I have known no greater pain than that time in Israel —and yet, I have never been closer to God. In his Guide for the Perplexed, *the great Jewish philosopher Maimonides presents an image of a human being's capacity for understanding. He says that most humans live in perpetual darkness, but that the blessed few experience fleeting flashes of light, which illumine our darkness and let us know that we are not alone. In Israel that year, I sat on my balcony, allowing those flashes to wash over me. They shook my world and cracked my heart open wide.*

Dreams

I dream of God.

Sometimes I wish God would reach down
    and in
    that we would not be alone.

I believe it possible that
    the God I know
    could penetrate this world.

Willing God.
Will gathered
Thrust beneath.
Here.
Where we stand trembling.

And if that God were to manifest below, the angels would
gather, in a chorus of song.
And the encounter would birth millennia of worship.

But were I to imagine the God I know.
And how that God
would enter my world.
Then all that is above
becomes that which is below.
Outside folds inward.

And the mountain dwells inside.
And the climb.
And the climber.

Heat and light.
Sense and sound.
A radiant center
Glowing.

A universe within.

Guide

After an ecstatic and terrifying year in Israel, I took refuge in my mother's house in Los Angeles. There, I met the teacher that would most change the course of my life. Her name is Diane, and she is a healer and energy worker. I have never felt as known and seen as I did by Diane even in the first few hours we spent together. As she laid her hands on my feet the first time we met, I was overcome by the most wonderful rush of love. The thought "I release my soul to you" spontaneously filled my mind, and I was gone.

Diane arrived at my mother's home in Los Angeles with a massage table, pillows and a stereo. She arranged for me, as she does for all of her clients, the most wonderful lush bed, which she then instructed me to climb into. She explained that 70 percent of what she would do would be massage, which I should relax and enjoy, and that she would also do 30 percent of her work without actually touching my body. A lover of massage, I nestled into the bed and gave little thought to the experience. While most of the three-hour session was pleasurable, there were also periods that were deeply painful. At times, I was filled with feelings of despair. At others, I felt totally free.

Midway through our session, Diane worked in the region of my chest and throat. As she did, I was overcome with a suffocating sadness. On the table, I nearly cried out from the pain. I was wading through pits of despair. I remember thinking vividly, 'Oh God, what could possibly be inside of me that is so black, so awful? I must truly be broken." After some time, the pain passed.

The hours that Diane worked on me were a very strange time. My eyes were closed, but I did not sleep. My mind was alive with thoughts, but they were largely random. I was curious. I did not know what to make of the experience. I only became aware of how far away I had drifted when Diane asked that I open my eyes and turn over. I had to find my body, find my limbs, in order to maneuver them. At that moment, I realized something significant was happening.

When she finished, she asked that I dress, so that we could talk. I remember much of our conversation verbatim. "Well, that was not what I expected," she began. She shared with me that her own energy work was evolving, that she had recently been taught (by her spirit guide) a new technique that had only been revealed to her with a few of her long-time clients. And yet, I, a young woman whom she had just met, cracked open before her.

Diane offered me the metaphor for the Divine that has guided my life since meeting her. She said, "You are

*cradled in the palm of the Divine Mother, Sara. She faces
you as you face her, her light shining down upon you
always." She is right. She could not have known that she was
borrowing an image from the Jewish morning prayer service
when speaking to me. In our meditation on peace, we affirm:*

> *Bless all of us, our Loving Parent, that we should
> be like one in the light of your face, because it was
> when we bathed in the light of your countenance,
> that you gave us our sacred living teachings* and
> *our love of kindness.*
>
> *- Ahavah Rabbah prayer from the
> Ashkenazi Jewish Morning Service*

*Diane emerged from our first session together
knowing my deepest history. She had met Hyim, although I
had not yet spoken of him and she had learned a great deal
about my Jewish passion. She had viewed me as an energy
being and had seen a number of my past lives. She saw
Tzippori. She described my existential reality. The pain I had
felt when she worked on my chest and throat was the
energetic manifestation of the emptiness I had been living in
Israel. She described my life experience. She put into words
the blessing I had always felt, that I could close my eyes and
know that God was there. We talked and talked. She helped
me to bless my union with Hyim. After she left, I laughed and
cried. I was forever changed.*

Why?

Why did God create the world?
       Why would God choose to slow down so,
            to transform
                 from no thing,
                     to light,
                        to form?
We are the reason.
       We are the telos of God's creation.
            Who are we? We are God's consciousness.
            We are they who stand in awe.

We are the sacrifice;
       The result of the contraction of God's great oneness.
            We are the manifestation of God as separate.

We were created so that we could be other from God;
       So that we could be aware of God.
            To be human is to stand in awe of God.[15]

---

[15] This poem is a meditation on the concept know as *tzimzum*. Drawn from Lurianic Kabbalah, the word *tzimtzum* literally means "contraction." If God is the totality of all that exists, including both creation and the canvas on which creation manifests, then as a prerequisite to creation, it is first necessary that the Creator contract, in order to create a void where creation can then pour forth. This contraction is known as tzimtzum.

Fate

My session with Diane began a new chapter in my life. I chose to remain in Los Angeles for the summer, to rest and to heal. During that summer, Hyim and I became engaged. I returned to Israel the following September, aglow with renewed love. For the first half of my second year in Israel, I focused on my learning, on my close friends and on Hyim.

The joy in my life kept me insulated from my fears of the violence around me. However, Diane had taught me to listen to my body. As the months passed, my dreams shifted, suddenly becoming filled with terrifying, consistent images. By March, I knew that if we did not leave Israel, we were putting our lives in danger. I persuaded Hyim to leave our graduate program with me and to accompany me back to America. My decision to leave Israel was a practical decision that was enabled by my newfound spiritual consciousness.

There was but one feeling that drove my choice to leave Israel then. It was this: the people here are determined to kill each other, and this is not my war. Three months after we left Israel, two close friends were killed. They were on a university campus, there to take a test Hyim was expected to take. Sitting together, enjoying lunch before their exam, their lives were ended by the blast of a bomb hidden earlier that day by a terrorist, who was also an employee of the university. I believe that if we had not left, Hyim or I too would have been killed.

I hate this truth, hate the terrorist's bomb and hate that my two friends died that day. I hate that I knew, although I know that I did, and that I could not know for them as well. When I question God, these are my questions.

Evil

There is evil about in the world today, unseen for some time. There is but one response to the darkness, whose root is found inside and out, that is engulfing so many.

Become a warrior of light.

Wield light.

Champion compassion.
Be a force for good in your world,
to offset all of the evil.

Commit yourself to creating space for the Divine in our world.

Affirm:

My hands are God's hands,
My eyes, God's eyes.
My feet, God's feet.
I walk, see, act as an agent of the Divine.[16]

Extend a hand in kindness. Replace judgment with love. See the unseen. Give ear to the silenced. Be God's hands in the world.

---

[16] After composing this meditation, I was surprised to find that a similar prayer, known as "Christ has no body but yours...," is attributed to St. Teresa of Avila.

Prayer at the Start of a Journey

Oh God, allow me to travel this journey on angel's wings.
Renew my humility everyday, and my confidence only when it
is depleted.

Allow me to shrink,
To refine every fiber of my being.
And then, oh God, allow me to expand.
Taking up my place in the world.

May I remain focused and driven.
May I remain humble and grounded.

Grant me strength.
Grand me discipline.
Grant me peace.

Calling

The first women to serve her community as a rabbi was the Maid of Ludomir, in the early nineteenth century. Her husband had been the formal rabbi of her small Ukrainian town, but after his death, she continued in his stead, teaching Torah and offering spiritual counsel. She would speak to her students from behind a door that was slightly ajar. She was a disembodied voice, allowing everyone to forget that she was a woman.

The Reform movement of Judaism began ordaining women as rabbis in 1972, and cantors a few years later. Once such cantor, Diane, joined the clergy at the Reform temple where my family spent the High Holy Days, and I saw her there when I was a child. The male rabbi, I liked very much, but I did not like Cantor Diane. I remember turning to my mother during one Yom Kippur, as she sang out in her exquisite soprano voice, and remarking, "It just does not sound right that it is not a man's voice." I was ten years old.

I cannot say that I was called to the rabbinate. To the contrary, it was something that I resisted at every turn. But by the time I left Israel in 2002, I was a passionate student of Torah, a teacher, and a spiritual seeker. I wanted to build and serve community, and in Judaism, the title you give to a person who does such things is rabbi.

I nearly dropped out of rabbinical school six times, once a semester for my first three years. "I would never be a man with a beard," I thought. And, I would never be as sure of myself as it seemed I would need to be to wield rabbinic voice. In rabbinical school, before I became a rabbi, I became a feminist, an activist, a yogi, an aspiring priestess, and a mother.

It was only in India that I would become a rabbi.

Voice

From the Jewish perspective, all people fall into one of two categories. Either you are a slave, or you are free, and the journey from slavery to freedom is one each of us must travel. Even in the 21st century, when modern societies agree that all human beings deserve the right to self-determination, slavery is still a struggle.[17] To be a slave, teaches Jewish tradition, is to be silenced, to be deprived of voice; to be free is to claim one's capacity to speak truth without apology.

The ancient Israelites spent generations without voice, suffering for 400 long years as slaves. For all of those years, they did not cry out to God, and God did not save them. Then, miraculously after 400 years, the Jewish people groaned. It was this groan that was first heard by the Divine, that initiated the process of redemption. It was a deep guttural noise, a stirring in the base of the belly that escaped before the mind could stop it.

[17] When discussing slavery as a metaphor, it must be acknowledged that actual slavery persists in nearly every country in the world. According to the International Labour Organization, "20.9 million adults and children are bought and sold worldwide into commercial sexual servitude, forced labor and bonded labor." ILO, *Global Estimate of Forced Labour: Results and Methodology* (2012), p. 13; cited by http://www.equalitynow.org/node/1010.

What gave the ancient Israelites the strength, the courage, to cry out after so many generations of silence? Some say it was the birth of Moses, the redeemer, that caused a cosmic shift— a lightening, such that breath could finally become prayer. Others say it was the unadulterated face of evil, a Pharaoh who tossed babies into the sea, pure darkness that set the light free. But, with the groan, the journey from slavery to freedom could begin.

To be free, the Jewish people would have to find their voice. It was a lesson learned in the desert, the *midbar* in Hebrew. The Hasidic masters pun this word, reading it instead as *"medaber"* the land of speech. Moses, the great prophet of the Jewish people, is the embodied symbol for the transformation of speech that must take place. When Moses is first called to his work as prophet, he initially refuses because he is *arel sfatayim;* literally, he is "of uncircumcised lips." Probably a euphemism for a lisp, what a powerful physical claim. "My mouth is incomplete," he proclaims. "It is covered by a barrier, a foreskin of sorts, that must be removed before I can speak freely." Over the course of his life, Moses does indeed liberate his voice, speaking boldly to the Jewish people and to God.

To speak freely takes the utmost courage. Most of us do not do it. We spend our lives encumbered by saying only "the right things." Our speech must be polite, social, light. It must conform to social norms. So many of us use our speech to mask our deeper selves—the selves that struggle, that feel pain, disappointment and loss. Listen to the speech of a small child, one who has only just learned to talk but has not yet learned the ways of social speech. Hear their freedom.

I have always loved the Zimbabwean Proverb, "If you can walk, you can dance, if you can talk, you can sing." According to the Hasidic masters, not only do the ancient Israelites master speech during their time in the desert, they learn to sing. Singing is freedom. Some of us know this, singing freely in the choir, at karaoke and with friends, and others only know the joy of singing with abandon in the car or in the shower. When you let yourself sing, really sing, it is pure joy.

The Jewish people learn this lesson when they face certain death. They are in the desert, slaves running toward freedom. They find the Egyptian army at their heel, a wall of water in front of them. They cry out to Moses and to God, and their prayers are answered; the Sea splits before them, the Promised Land on just the other side. It is here, filled with faith, that the people once silenced by slavery sing out.

"Who is like You oh God?!"[18] they cry, tasting freedom at last.

To sing is to transcend the ego. It is to let your voice pour forth, unencumbered by fear. In sharing your song, you contribute to the song of the world. A redeemed world then, as imagined by the Torah, is one in which every person, every aspect of creation, is free to sing out. In so doing, the voices of the many become the voice of the One. Differences melt away. All becomes one. This is redemption. This is freedom.

As the poet Naomi Shemer sings, inspired by the words of the great mystic Rabbi Nachman of Breslov:

> Know that each and every shepherd has his own melody.
>
> Know that each and every grass has its own song. And from the song of the grasses the tune of the shepherd is made...
>
> And from the song of the grasses the heart is filled and yearns.[19]

Sing your song. You are the only one who knows the tune.

---

[18] Exodus 15:11.

[19] Naomi Shemer, "Shir Ha'Eisavim," featured on *Al Hadvash ve'al Ha'oketz,* 1989. Translated from Hebrew by the author.

India

I found my voice as a rabbi at the Yoga Vida Gurukul Ashram in Nashik, India. It was a glorious combination of things that made it so. First, I was alone in the world—a girl, her convictions, and no one to support or challenge them. My roommates were Italian, German, and Croatian, and me, a nomad from the United States. But, we were all seeking souls, each who had found our way to this peaceful rural Indian village, on the pretense of becoming certified as yoga instructors.

Lena, the German, was most like my sister. Similar to me in age and appearance, at night, she would massage my scalp with coconut oil and speak of casual things. Then there was Vesna, strong, stern and serious, a Croatian who was like my mama and my mirror. We were so similar. She taught me ayurvedic medicine, that we were both Kafa-Pita, she and I— fire grounded by earth, earth elevated by fire. Years later, Vesna would become Aviva after rediscovering her Jewish roots and move to Israel for a time. My auntie was Donata, an elegant Italian who was herself a trained healer, who was light and fun, and who would travel the world with Vesna, sampling ashrams and courses on Eastern medicine.

Our days at the ashram were bookended by yoga, morning and evening practice. In the middle of the day, we would eat, rest, wander and study. At night, we gathered for kirtan, soulful singing, traditional Indian chanting.

Kirtan taught me to sing. Through song I found prayer—And through prayer, God. Sitting in a circle in a darkened room, we would chant for an hour each night, our words calling out to this Hindu deity or that. I had abstained for the first week, out of respect for Jewish tradition's most serious prohibition, not to worship idols. But, in time I found the simple clarity that has guided my religious life ever since. It is this:

> *There is only one God.*
> *All names for God can only refer to the One.*
> *All paths to God lead to the One,*
> *because…*
> *There Is Only One.*

With this I entered and chanted a song of love. One night, the most vivid and transcendent, I felt my energetic arms offer my energetic heart to the Shekhinah[20] and was

---

[20] Hebrew name for the in-dwelling presence of God, often associated with the feminine. In later kabbalistic literature, the term refers to one of the ten facets of the Divine. The source text for the name *Shekhinah* is in Exodus 25:8, "If you build Me a sanctuary I will dwell (*shakhanti*) within you."

forever changed. I surrendered myself to Her completely. She holds my heart in Hers, the Great Heart of the World. Together, they beat, seek, love and lose. Together they strive, yearn and forgive.

That night of kirtan was why I had traveled to India in the first place. How could I walk in the world as rabbi if my own Divine channel was not open? How could I be the vessel that holds space for the Divine for others, if God was not real for me? There, in that cool, candlelit room, it was.

It is.

One

Mystics throughout time, regardless of religious tradition, ascend to the highest heights and proclaim, "There is no place that is devoid of God."[21] This specific phrase is repeated again and again in the Jewish mystical text, the Zohar, and it echoes Isaiah's proclamation, preserved in the Bible: "The whole world is filled with God's glory" (Isaiah 6:3).

While conventional religious doctrine imagines us "down here" and God "up there," mysticism calls these distinctions false.

There is only here and now.

Here is God, evil, space, time.
Here is pain, struggle, blessing, bliss.

To be a monotheist is to know that all is God,
all comes from God.

There is nothing that is devoid of God.

---

[21] *"Leit atar panui minei,"* translated as "there is no place that is devoid of God," is a central proclamation of Jewish mysticism, found in several instances in the Zohar and other Jewish mystical texts.

Tradition

And then one day, I just ran out. I was only months into my five-year-long journey toward becoming a rabbi, and I could not take it anymore. My classmates and peers had gathered, along with our professors and the general community, in the chapel for the afternoon service.

I drifted in as I always did, chatting with friends. The service began. I opened my book. I commenced the ritualized whispering that observant Jews perform as we mutter our afternoon prayers. I whispered. They whispered. Nothing happened. Nothing at all.

It was the profound absence of energy that drove me from the room that day. There we were, some of the most learned Jewish minds in America, studying toward rabbinic ordination. There we were, engaging in the timeless ritual of Jewish prayer, and nothing at all was happening. In that moment, it felt as though I was the only one in the room who expected to talk to God, and expected God to respond.

The great Abraham Joshua Heschel too made his way to that synagogue every day, his located one floor down from where my friends and I had gathered. In the halls of the Jewish Theological Seminary, a quote of Heschel's (one of many) is passed among the students. Heschel said that he prayed three times every day so that every once in awhile, no more than perhaps five percent of the time, something would happen. And so, like him, we waited.

That spring day, I could wait no longer. I held in my hand ancient, holy words, words that were strung together to stir the soul and reach towards God. They had been penned by spiritual seekers who had come before me, preserving their respective moments of yearning or transcendence. I needed someone to teach me how to read those words, how to use them to reach for God. Instead, I found myself in a room of whispers.

In time, I brought my anguish to the beloved rabbi who escorted me through school. He heard my cries and bared his soul, which was indeed a ladder to the Divine. He blessed the day I fled from that room.

In running out into the open air during my first year of rabbinical school, I set myself apart. That day, I lost faith in tradition; or, more precisely, in doing something for only tradition's sake. I committed myself instead to studying our texts, to excavating our memories, so that I could bring them again to life.

My conviction was reinforced several years later, when I stood in the Pinkas Synagogue in Prague. Home to a vibrant Jewish community, the city of Prague bore the grotesque honor of being selected by Hitler as the museum that would preserve the history of the Jewish people, whom he had hoped to blot off the face of the earth. As such, its ancient synagogues survived the war intact. In memorial, years later the city selected the Pinkas synagogue to serve as a monument to the murdered. Its walls are covered floor to ceiling with the names of the Jews of Prague murdered by the Nazis. The Pinkas Synagogue is no longer a house of worship; it is a site for holy memory.

That day, as I fled from the synagogue, I vowed that I would not allow the siddur itself, our living collection of prayers and pleading, to become like the walls of that synagogue, a frozen monument to the past. Our prayers must pulse with life. They must live and breathe, celebrate and yearn. In fleeing from the room that day, I began my search for authentic Jewish prayer. It was a journey that would take me to great heights and great depths, to India and, also, back to Israel.

Part II: Holy Land

Arrival

My young family moved to Israel in 2014, after the strangest, most difficult summer. I, a mother of two, pride myself on being an honest and forthright parent. My children were seven and four at the time. We had spoken explicitly about life and death, sex and drugs, relationships and the messiness of things. And yet, as our move date drew closer, I found myself keeping the biggest secret of all. Israel is a dangerous place. There is war there.

I prayed that war would not return in our first months. I prayed (and still do) for my little ones, that they would apply their perseverance and resilience only to mastering Hebrew and making new friends, not to calming breaths and bomb shelters.

As for me, I found myself oddly suspended in time during our year of anticipation. I wanted to go the very moment we made the choice to leave Los Angeles, not a year later. That feeling didn't leave me, even during the Gaza war.[22] Still, we planned, wound down, embraced endings, and said so many heartfelt goodbyes.

---

[22] Operation Protective Edge in Gaza during July 2014.

I knew in my gut when we decided to move that an existential threat to the State of Israel was a key part of our decision. I did not have words for it in July 2013 or even in February 2014, when we made our choice. I could not tell if the threat was of an internal implosion or an external enemy; I just found myself saying, again and again, that if the modern State of Israel failed in my lifetime and I had not gone, had not done my part, I would never forgive myself.

Now, I know—the very factors that moved Herzl a century and a half ago and crystalized after the Holocaust remain. Jews must have a home of their own and an army that is unmatched. There is violence in this world, and cries of "never again" need teeth as much as they need voice.

The Torah makes no secret about life in the Land of Israel. Blessed, sacred, flowing with milk and honey, she is also a land that "devours her inhabitants."[23] In this move, I take my young, beautiful family into the eye of the storm and I pray for the Shekhinah's help and protection. But, as a Jew, if I am to merit a home of my own, it is my turn to do my part. I live my Zionism by walking the land, engaging in commerce, voting, and living. More important, I bring my nerves—not yet frayed—and my patience to a culture that has had its worn down. I bring the conviction that my home

---

[23] Numbers 13:32

will be a good and just one. And, I pray. I pray that in the coming years, I will do my tiny part to bring healing to the wounded Middle East and peace to our land.

In the Land

The first Chief Rabbi of Israel, Avraham Yitzchak Kook, was a great teacher of Jewish spirituality. In his view, the Jewish people had retreated into our heads, into the inner recesses of the intellect, during the seemingly endless exile. For him, the return to the Land of Israel was a return to the body, to embodied Jewish practice, which allowed for the expression of religious life through the hands that touch, the mouth that tastes, the feet that walk the sacred earth.

Rabbi Kook teaches that the initial cause of the ancient first exile in 586 BCE was an over-identification with the physical. The First Temple was destroyed because of idol worship, say the rabbis. Cultic Judaism, with its elaborate rituals of incense and slaughter, engaged the senses. But, the people became intoxicated by the body, reducing the totality of existence to the realm of the physical. As a punishment, they were exiled from the land and initiated into rabbinic Judaism, characterized by study and intellectual pursuit.

While there is great richness in the Jewish intellectual tradition, a full Jewish practice must reclaim its biblical roots, finding expression again in every dimension of life. This is the blessing and the challenge of the State of Israel, which today must wrestle with the toughest questions of governance and power. Israel is the Jewish State only when it brings the values and teachings of our tradition to bear on all aspects of life. The actualized, modern State of Israel heeds this call often but falls short sometimes. It is the price and challenge of statehood.

Bless us God, with the faith and courage to live justly,
even in the face of great fear and adversity.
May we daily prove worthy
of the blessing of a Jewish State.

Bread and Cheese

I moved back to the ancient homeland of the Jewish people to reclaim a certain basic knowledge, to correct a forgetting that happened long ago. Some time—way, way back—my ancestors set down their knowledge of how to provide for themselves in a direct and concrete way, just like I might set down my keys without noticing, only to realize moments later that they are missing. They left to build the future, but in so doing, they forgot their bodies and they forgot the earth.

Shortly after arriving in Israel, I found my way to a little place called "Kfar Kedem," where the world of ancient Israel, of the rabbis of old and of Jesus is brought again to life. On my first day there, I learned how to make cheese. We began by milking one of Kfar Kedem's goats. Then, after pasteurizing (boiling) the milk, the magic began. As it turns out, a branch of a fig tree, one of the seven delicious plant species native to the land of Israel, possess the right pH to transform milk into cheese. And so, my teacher walked to the tree, broke off a branch, stripped its outer bark and began to stir the milk. Within minutes, curds had separated from whey, ready to be strained through a cheesecloth, tied in the shape of a fig and hung to dry for 30 minutes. We enjoyed the fruits of our labor and of the land with our lunch. It was simple and it was miraculous.

Later that week, back in my kitchen, I tried the process on my own. I opted for using lemon juice instead of fig bark to curdle my milk, which gave my cheese a sweet tang. My whey, I mixed with three cups of whole wheat flour, salt, and yeast, and made the most delicious bread I have ever tasted. From goat to gourmet meal, I required just five ingredients—milk, lemon (or fig branch, or vinegar), wheat, salt, and yeast. The process took me twenty minutes (minus the waiting time for rising and straining). The simplicity is mind blowing. How could I not have known?

For me, the impact of reclaiming the most basic human knowledge, the knowledge that fed and sustained every generation from Cro-Magnon to pre-modern, is a cosmic shift. It actualizes the very purpose of religious living, to locate me in time and space, in a concrete and meaningful way. Am I really touching the earth where I stand if I don't internalize that my food grows from the same soil? Can I be fully alive if I cannot honor that the dairy that nourishes me is borrowed from a sweet mammal who has shared its mother's milk?

In Judaism, we are commanded not just to eat, but to be satisfied by our food.[24] Words cannot capture the depth of my satisfaction when it is my hands that transform nature into sustenance. When blessing bread we Jews utter a non-truth, saying, "Blessed are You, Holy One, Sovereign of the Universe, who brings forth bread from the earth." But, it is not bread that grows but only its components. It is my hands, agents of the Divine, that transform wheat into bread, so that I might feel nourished, and touched by God in the process.

---

[24] Deuteronomy 8:6-10, "Observe the commands of the Lord your God, walking in obedience to him and revering him. For the Lord your God is bringing you into a good land—a land with brooks, streams, and deep springs gushing out into the valleys and hills; a land with wheat and barley, vines and fig trees, pomegranates, olive oil and honey; a land where bread will not be scarce and you will lack nothing; a land where the rocks are iron and you can dig copper out of the hills. When you have eaten and are satisfied, praise the Lord your God for the good land he has given you."

My Brother, the Ass

I have a brother.
He is an ass of a man.
Always huffing, always kicking.
Never settled nor still.

I have a brother.
He is an ass of a man.
Violent and terrifying,
Angry and rage filled.

I have a brother.
He is an ass of a man.
But, he is my brother,
My own flesh and blood.

One Father,
One roof,
One history,
One name.

Though my brother torments me,
Our fate is one and the same.
One family, one home.
Our Father wanted it this way.[25]

---

[25] "Then the Angel of God said to [Hagar], behold, you are with child; When you will give birth to a son, call him Yishma-el because God has heard your pain. But, he will be a wild ass of a man, his hand upon everyone and their hand upon him. He will dwell in the face of his brothers." (Genesis 16:11-12)

The Union of Opposites

The magnet's pull to its inverse is immediate, faster sometimes than our minds can process. Before we've begun to notice, it has leapt from here to there, clinging to its brother, its sister, in union. In romance too, we feel the pull, the inverse calling out to us. We feel the longing and then the soothing peace, merging with another whose charge compliments our own.

In the click clinging of magnets, north and south uniting, we understand the opening metaphor of the Bible offered in Genesis 1. Ours is a world of dualities, once united and now divided, whose deep memories prompt us toward our eventual return. Chemistry and physics too tells a similar story. Ours is a charged world, filled with opposites.

It should not be so baffling then, and not so painful either, that this push and pull pervades every dimension of our world, even the human, even the moral. Despite all of the pain, the loss, the bloodshed, we seem to be unable to avoid the instinct to arrange ourselves into this group or that, only to face one another in conflict. Ours is a world of duality, for in the push and pull, we learn.

Why is this the case? This world of ours is a school room, a training house for souls, who must learn that all is love and all is One.

Jewish tradition teaches that the Torah contains 613 commandments, but the rabbis held in highest esteem throughout our 4,000-year history all select the same one as the most important. Hillel, Rabbi Akiva and Jesus after them agree, the Torah's most important message is found at its heart, in the very center of the book, Leviticus 19:18: "Love your neighbor as yourself." So simple, yet it is a message we have failed to learn for millennia. We must learn to love each other.

And so, the dance of opposites continues the push and pull of dark and light, of kindness and selfishness, of dominance and submission, of terror and love. On and on the wheel will turn until we learn this singular lesson.[26]

---

[26] I was first exposed to the metaphor of an existence on this plane as a school room in *Emmanuel's Book: A Manual for Living Comfortably in the Cosmos*, compiled by Pat Rodegast and Judith Stanton (New York: Bantam Books, 1987)

A Shared Existence

Kibbutzim are an experiment in communal living. My husband's grandmother Bobush, who moved at 18 years old from Prague to build the Land of Israel—who once lightheartedly quipped that there was no need for us to wait until marriage to provide her with a great-grandchild—relished sharing stories of the early days on the kibbutz. Then, all was open and free. Marriages were arranged so that young Israelis could spring forth, but did not limit the love that was shared by all. But her children, who fled that kibbutz, tell stories of endless gossip, rivalries, and the tyranny of life in a fishbowl.

Eighty five years later, I chose kibbutz life to be close to the land but also because of the very same struggle to achieve the right blend of openness and privacy. In the United States, I shared ad nauseam in the digital world, but only when all was shiny and bright. Now, I find myself living in a tiny bungalow, sharing a wall and a walking path, a synagogue and a mikveh, with several hundred other young people, and for me, it is paradise.

I was raised to be a good girl, polite and appropriate. I was raised to knock before entering, to respect fences with respect to neighbors, and to keep dirty laundry concealed. But here, as I hang my laundry on the line to dry (not family secrets, actual laundry), I feel the relief of lives gently bumping into one another, of a shared existence. Still, I also sense tensions beneath the surface of a community that has committed itself to realizing its potential as a collective. And, it is strange to be able to see directly into the windows of the family across the way as I do my dishes in the morning.

Although I had dreamed of making aliyah[27] to a kibbutz for years, it was the documentary "Happy"[28] that lit a fire under me. The film explores the assumptions, habits, and lifestyles of the world's most joyful and most miserable communities. It was the opening story in the film, of Manoj Singh and his family, residents of a shanti town in Kolkata, India, that moved me deeply. A rickshaw driver, he reflected, "In the summer, when my feet burn as I run my rickshaw, I am not so happy, but in the winter, when I am drenched by the monsoons, I know that in a few minutes I will dry, and I

[27] Literally "going up," this idiom is used to describe the decision to move to Israel.

[28] *Happy,* directed by Roko Belic (USA: Wadi Rum Films, 2011), film, Netflix, accessed March 2013.

am very happy. Here, [in our shanty town], we are very close with one another. We have everything we need. We are happy."

For me, our American dreams of personal picket fences separating nuclear family units—felt much more like a prison than a palace. The kibbutz environment, of little homes, surrounded by porches made for tea and visiting, redefines the privacy/openness questions entirely. Here, we are together. We just are. Privacy is negotiated from within the context of community; so far, it feels much better. I feel myself more human in this collective environment—calmer, freer, more social, more organic. True openness, the lowering of boundaries, the opening of the heart, is a tall order, the work of a lifetime. But, in the meantime, on Kibbutz Hannaton, I have discovered togetherness, and it has changed everything.

Paradise

I come from California, where it is warm and sunny,
       blue skies and perfect;
Where grass grows and rain falls,
       but not enough—
Where we fear drought as we enjoy our endless days of
       summer.

I have moved to Israel,
Where here too the sun shines from clear skies,
Where flowers bloom in December, and
Where children are raised to respect water and take short
showers.

In Israel, like in California,
One can visit the beach and ski on the same day if they wish;
Vast deserts separate lush lowlands,
Full of fruit blossoms of all kinds.

In reflecting on California, my rabbi once remarked,

"It is the Garden of Eden, just not for us."[29]

What is the difference then, between one promised land and the other?

There, fantasies reign and they become movies.
Here, faith reigns, and it becomes war.
Though much is secular here, this is a religious place.
Though spiritual hunger pierces there, meaninglessness wins out.

Here the moon is softer and bigger,
   and rainbows are brighter too.
But there, breath is more expansive,
   evaporating into the mist of the Pacific,
   no borders to encumber it.

Both California and Israel are contested lands,
   where native peoples weep for a life once lived.
Both rest on soil soaked with pain, bloodshed, and war.
Both are filled now with souls, seen and unseen,
   some who wish to turn back the clock,
   but most who would just live and let live.

---

[29] Rabbi Daniel Landes is the religious director (*Rosh Yeshiva*) of the Pardes Institute for Jewish Studies in Jerusalem.

My journey of 7,500 miles away from home and family
has everything to do with finding my place in the world.

Just as the green caterpillar is indistinguishable
        from the grasses where it lives,
And the Sunbird matches the Bird of Paradise flower,
So too do we each have a place where we belong,
that resembles us inside and out.

There is a place in the world from which our own dust was
gathered—
        that is of us, as we are of it.
There is a place in the world where our hearts are meant to
open,
        where we can find freedom in the here and now.

There is no perfect place, no perfect world.
There is no future time when everything will be different.

There is only me and who I was born to be.
And, in finding my way to that place—
I find I am in paradise.

Part III: Climb

Climb

Come and journey with me.
Let us climb the ladder together.
The limbs, like rungs.
Ascending toward the heavens.
Together, let us find God.

Why Practice?

It is not the natural state of a human being to see ourselves in our wholeness. We are masters when it comes to analyzing the various parts of us, chopping ourselves into bits and pieces. But we are a totality. At first glance, we lack the ability to perceive ourselves as such.

Spiritual practice combats this handicap. Through worship or mindfulness, we elevate the consciousness, briefly adopting the perspective of the soul. We look from above rather than from within, so that we can see. It is only from this vantage point that we can envision our days and our lives, that we can achieve our purpose.

Our experience as human beings is baffling. We open our eyes to each new day, experiencing the world through our bodies. Our eyes see. Our ears hear. Our hands touch. We are creatures of the physical world, and our senses confine us, largely to that world. And yet, deep in the recesses of our being, we know there is more to existence than the physical. We just know it.

Seemingly our prison, our body is also the key to our liberation. It is our greatest resource and tool. It is possible to relate to the body as a ladder to the soul, to the world of spirit that is concealed within the world of the physical. By climbing the rungs of the energetic self, each one grounded in a different part of the body, we come to know the soul.

Judaism, like many mystical traditions, is peppered with images of ladders. Peruvian shamans of the Amazon and Himalayan yogis report visions of the sacred ladder. Some suggest a connection to DNA, the very fabric of life, itself arranged as a spiraling ladder.[30] The sacred imagery of the Christian cross and the *Asherah* trees[31] of old are also ladders of sorts, with their feet planted in the earth and their heads extending toward the heavens. Even the Tree of Life at the center of the Bible's Garden of Eden, can likewise be viewed as a sacred ladder connecting heaven and earth.

---

[30] See Jeremy Narby, *The Cosmic Serpent: DNA and the Origins of Knowledge* (New York: Jeremy P. Tarcher/Putnam 1998; reprint 1999).

[31] Asherah trees and the *bamot* or high places where they were found in ancient Israel, are mentioned numerous times in the Hebrew Bible. From the biblical perspective, they are paradigmatic symbols of idolatry, and the ancient Israelites were instructed to tear them down. However, as sacred trees and embodiments of the Divine feminine, we witness their influence later religious traditions, including both Christianity and Kabbalah.

Ladder imagery reaches full expression in the Torah in the story of Jacob. A bold mystical traveler, Jacob's name is changed to God Wrestler (*Yisra-El*) when he has a mysterious, intimate encounter with the Divine and lives to tell about it. It is at the start of his journey, years earlier, when he is a young man, that he is graced with his vision of the ladder.

Jacob has run away from home, having stolen the coveted blessing of the firstborn son from his twin brother, Esau. Fearing for his life, Jacob's mother sends him away. Breathless, Jacob travels all day and finds himself by nightfall at the border of the ancient land of Canaan. There, Jacob takes a rock for a pillow and lays down to sleep for the night.

That night, Jacob dreams of a ladder on which angelic beings are ascending and descending. Although one might expect traffic on a heavenly ladder to flow in the opposite direction, the Torah is clear that the angels Jacob sees go up then down. Tradition explains that he is witnessing the changing of his guardian angels because the angels of the Holy Land do not leave those borders.[32] As Jacob flees, says the tradition, he is escorted by new angels whose place is out in the world.

----

[32] Rashi on Genesis 28:12.

Upon awaking from his miraculous dream, Jacob exclaims, "God was in this place and I, I did not know it. How awesome is this place!"[33] He takes the stone on which he rested his head, anoints it with oil, and there affirms his relationship with the Divine.

Although there is no explicit link in the Torah, the earliest Jewish mystical literature also imagines a ladder that connects heaven and earth. This ladder, however, is not located in some open field at the borders of the Holy Land, as Jacob experienced it; rather, it is found within each of us. It is the human body, attests *Shiur Komah*[34] and others, that is the ladder, the link between heaven and earth. The primeval body of the first human, *Adam Hakadmon*, soon became known as the Tree of Life, closing our loop, linking Genesis, Jacob, and the ascent each of us make as we journey our lives.

The map of the Divine, know in western mysticism as the Tree of Life, took shape over millennia, having been developed in several independent treatises, each with a philosophy and terminology of its own. First appearing in the third-century mystical treatise *Hechalot Rabbati*, its crown is

---

[33] Genesis 28:16–17.

[34] *Shiur Komah* is an early work of Jewish mysticism of unknown authorship, which scholars date to the Talmudic period.

found in the *Zohar*, the Book of Splendor, a thirteenth-century work of Jewish mysticism. There, we encounter the fully developed though cryptic map of the Divine, imagined as an interpenetrating web of ten cosmic facets, known as *sefirot.*[35]

According to the kabbalists, *Adam Hakadmon,* the Tree of Life, is also a map of the human energetic body, for the defining characteristic of human beings is that we are made in the image of God, as the Torah teaches, "Let us make the human in Our image, after our likeness."[36] While Jewish philosophers throughout the ages have debated the precise meaning of this bold claim, mystics take it literally. On the level of the soul, we look like God. In learning about God, we learn about ourselves. In exploring our own subtle bodies, we come to know our Creator.

---

[35]For more on the evolution of Jewish mystical thought, see Joseph Dan, *The Heart and the Fountain: An Anthology of Mystical Jewish Experiences* (New York: Oxford University Press, 2002), 20–21.

[36] Genesis 1:27.

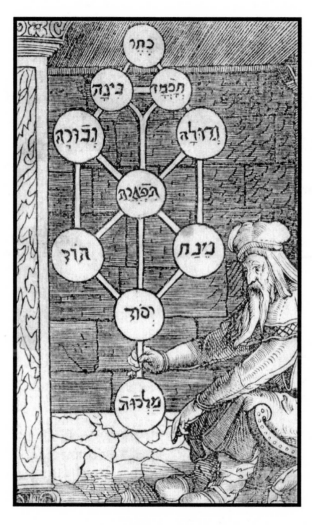

Kabbalistic image of the ten sefirot from
Portae Lucis
Latin translation of Gikatilla's Shaarei Ora,
Augsburg 1516

It was the sixteenth-century kabbalists of Tzfat who first invited us to explore the subtle body, the Tree of Life made up of the *sefirot,* as a spiritual practice. They found the context for such a journey embedded in the Jewish calendar, in an instruction whose name shares a root with the name for the Divine attributes (*sefirot).*

In a ritual known as *sefirat ha'omer*—the counting of the *omer*—Jews are commanded to count seven weeks, seven sevens, every spring. The point of departure for the journey is the Jewish festival of Freedom, Passover; its destination is Sinai, recalled on the holiday of Shavuot, which celebrates, among other things, the revelation of our holy book, the Torah. The two festivals are separated by seven weeks, which Jews number off, one day at a time. Freedom and revelation, separated by seven sevens. For the kabbalists, such holy commands are also an invitation to climb the ladder and cleave to the Divine.

What follows is a taste of the transformative, meditative journey offered by the kabbalists during the seven weeks in the spring, between the Jewish holidays of Passover and Shavuot, when Jews fulfill the commandment of *sefirat ha'omer*. Because the mystical counting of the *omer* is an interlocking system, each day we are meant to consider a different attribute, or *sefirah*, through the lens of the *sefirah* for that week. For example, the theme of the entirety of the

81

first week is love. However, for each day of the week, we will mix in a second posture and observe how the two work together.

The mystical journey of *sefirat ha'omer* is meant to be traveled slowly, as the concepts that follow are complex and need time to be digested. Devote one of each of the days of this week to the following postures. Embody the divine attribute that is also an aspect of your highest self. You might choose to make each *kavanah* or intention below the focus of your morning meditation, or you might choose to write it on a Post-it note and stick it on your refrigerator, computer screen, or bathroom mirror. For these 49 days, find a simple way to return your thoughts to the *kavanah,* the intention, for the day, again and again.

Week One: *Hesed*—Unconditional Love

Although *Hesed*, unconditional love, is not the first of the ten *sefirot*, the three that precede it—*Keter, Hokhmah,* and *Binah* —are deemed too remote, too esoteric, by the kabbalists to serve as an accessible ladder for us. They are beyond language, beyond conceptualization, and beyond our reach. Our journey, then, begins with *Hesed*, with unconditional love.

There is no greater mystical posture than love. In love, we melt. In our mundane lives, we are so protective of our separate selves, our personal identity and integrity, but in love, we yearn for union. Indeed, our bodies ache for it. "Penetrate me, and I will penetrate you. Become me, and I will become you," the body cries. We know love through our human relationships, but love is love, whether for another or for the Divine.

In this first week of your journey, consider: What would it be like to make unconditional love the foundation stone of your identity, your personality?

<u>Loving</u>

✦ **Day 1**: Loving is Divine. Connect to God by connecting with your loving self. (*Hesed*)

✦ **Day 2**: What limits must we impose, inspired by love? (*Gevurah*)

✦ **Day 3**: Who am I when I am loving? *(Tiferet)*

✦ **Day 4**: How does my loving help me to taste the eternal? *(Netzah)*

✦ **Day 5**: Love casts the world in radiance. Honor that all is beautiful with love. *(Hod)*

✦ **Day 6**: What does your loving self yearn for? *(Yesod)*

✦ **Day 7**: Acknowledge the ways that you are loved. *(Shekhinah)*

Week Two: *Gevurah*—Cosmic Boundaries

Jewish tradition teaches that it took the Creator many tries to form a world that could function. The first attempt was a world created entirely from God's capacity for loving-kindness. It was a world without limits. Nothing was ever refused in that world. Nothing was protected, and the world could not endure.

The Creator then brought into being a world governed only by judgment, and it too quickly descended into chaos. So harsh and unforgiving were its creatures that no relationship survived. It was a world of "falling short" and "not enough," and it too could not endure. According to the Midrash, it was only when God combined God's capacities for loving-kindness (*Hesed*) and judgment (*Gevurah*) that God could create a world that would thrive.[37]

The story of creation recalled in the first chapter of the Bible, the creation of the world in seven days, is a story of creation by *Gevurah*. Setting boundaries is the means by which the Creator creates, separating light from darkness, land from sea, day from night. So too do we create our lives

---

[37] See Rashi on Genesis 1:1

by erecting boundaries, sorting and labeling our passions, interests, needs and responsibilities. The ability to erect boundaries is a fundamental force in the universe, for better or worse. Sometimes, our separating brings understanding; At other times, it brings distance. Dedicate this week to cultivating balance in your ability to erect and honor boundaries.

<u>Defining the Parameters of Me</u>

✦   **Day 1**: How do you express love by setting limits? (*Hesed*)

✦   **Day 2**: Boundaries are Divine. Emulate God by setting a boundary for yourself. (*Gevurah*)

✦   **Day 3**: How do your boundaries define you? (*Tiferet*)

✦   **Day 4**: Filter your instinct for judgment through the lens of the Eternal. Practice releasing petty judgments. Honor cosmic boundaries. (*Netzah*)

✦   **Day 5**: What boundaries create beauty in your life? (*Hod*)

✦   **Day 6**: What boundary do you yearn to cross? (*Yesod*)

✦   *Day 7:* The Web of Life is woven with boundaries. Practice seeing boundaries as points of connection. (*Shekhinah*)

Week Three: *Tiferet*—Consciousness

The week of *Tiferet* invites the practitioner into the heart of selfhood, the "I," the ego. *Tiferet* means Divine Splendor, or the selfhood of the Divine. Kabbalists sometimes refer to this week's *sefirah* as "*Hakadosh Barukh Hu.*" When we say "God," we are referring to the face of God explored this week.

Bring this week's meditation to life by directing attention to your body. As you whisper the words, "I am, I am, I am...," notice where in your body your attention rests. For some, your "I am" will take you to your head, for others, to the heart, and for others still, to the gut. This week, as you traverse the terrain of "I am-ness," cultivate curiosity about your own sense of self. Which region most governs you? To where do you retreat when you are feeling weak, scared or wounded?

Where did your attention go when you whispered "I am?" Head? Heart? Gut? An essential step on the journey of the spirit is to feed the ego to the heart, to allow "I am-ness" to reside in an opened heart. It is the work of a lifetime. Make it your work this week. Recite daily, "I am" and feel your heart shine. Locate your selfhood within an open heart, and know, with faith, that the Holy One, *Hakadosh Barukh Hu*, faces you from *Tiferet*, an open heart shining back at you.

<u>Saying "I"</u>

✦ **Day 1**: How does unconditional love feed your awareness of who you are? (*Hesed*)

✦ **Day 2**: How do boundaries support your sense of you? (*Gevurah*)

✦ **Day 3**: What is the essence of you, the face you offer the world? (*Tiferet*)

✦ **Day 4**: What parts of you are eternal? (*Netzah*)

✦ **Day 5**: What parts of you are radiant? (*Hod*)

✦ **Day 6**: What fuels you? (*Yesod*)

✦ **Day 7**: Where is your place in the various Webs of Life (family, community, nation, nature)? (*Shekhinah*)

Week Four: *Netzah*—Toward Infinity

In its many teachings about the *sefirot*, the Zohar notes that it is hardest to attain understanding of this week's *sefirah*, *Netzah*, and its sister, *Hod*, which we will explore next week, because they are "concealed within the *Shekhinah*."[38] *Netzah* is the infinite in the Divine and in all of us. The forces of *Netzah* and *Hod* push and pull, in balance and tension within us, to generate the lower aspects of our ego. They are the two voices forever calling out to us as we journey the material world. *Netzah* cries: "What about me is timeless?" "How will I be remembered?" "Will I matter, always?"

We sacred beings, souls encased in bodies, are a paradox. We are, at once, fleeting and timeless. The shadow of *Netzah* is the call of the ego that dreads its own mortality. Its radiance is the persistent reminder that we are One with our Creator, timeless and immortal. *Netzah* is both the ego's shackles and the key that unlocks them.

---

[38] *Zohar* II 164b–165a, trans. by David Goldstein, in *The Wisdom of the Zohar,* edited by Isaiah Tishby (Washington DC: Littman Library of Jewish Civilization, 1994) 1:349–50. See also Footnote 446 there.

As you journey this week of *Netzah*, hear your ego's voice. See it for what it is, an ephemeral mask. Recall our work last week to dissolve the ego into the heart, to allow *Tiferet* to shine out through an open heart. This week, allow *Netzah's* call to soften your journey as all things change. Listen past the clamor of the ego, for the soft voice of your timeless soul.

Beyond Mortality

✦ **Day 1**: Your loving nature is timeless. Honor the part of you that is eternal. (*Hesed*)

✦ **Day 2**: Soften your judgment. All things change. (*Gevurah*)

✦ **Day 3**: Consciousness endures, even when the body returns to the earth. (*Tiferet*)

✦ **Day 4**: Timelessness is Divine. Know God in knowing the part of you that is timeless. (*Netzah*)

✦ **Day 5**: Your radiance is timeless. (*Hod*)

✦ **Day 6**: The fire that fuels you is timeless. (*Yesod*)

✦ **Day 7**: You are a timeless being, moving though an ephemeral world. (*Shekhinah*)

Week Five: *Hod*—Finding Humility

Humility is a mystery to so many of us, especially those who are deeply grounded in a Western ethos. We confuse humility and humiliation. In truth, Jewish mysticism reminds us, humility is the key to splendor (*Hod*). When we can settle into a posture of humility, we become grounded; we find calm and freedom. Your challenge this week is to embody humility.

To be humble is to know one's own worth with certainty, without question. As a result, a humble person does not impose the need to be praised on others, so self-contained is she in her knowledge of her own self-worth. A humble person walks with perfect faith in his path, such that he can sit tight with it, not thrashing around, switching from this choice to that, searching for his purpose. To be humble is to know that you are always, exactly where you belong.

Our capacity for prayer comes from this week's *sefirah*, from *Hod*. In humility, we incline the eyes heavenward, open the mouth in supplication. Through the lens of humility, we find the capacity to surrender to the challenges laid out before us.

"Please God, help me to see my purpose in every moment.
Help me to know that I am, always, exactly where I belong."

This week, with every breath, inhale humility.
Exhale gratitude.

<u>Finding Prayer</u>

✦   **Day 1**: Pray with humility to know unconditional love. (*Hesed*)

✦   **Day 2**: Pray with humility to honor cosmic boundaries. (*Gevurah*)

✦   **Day 3**: Pray with humility to know and honor your authentic voice. (*Tiferet)*

✦   **Day 4***:* Pray with humility to know your timeless nature. *(Netzah)*

✦   **Day 5***:* Humility is Divine. Know God in embodying humility. *(Hod)*

✦   **Day 6**: Pray with humility for balance in your sexual desires. *(Yesod)*

✦   **Day 7:** Pray with humility to feel as one with the Web of Life. *(Shekhinah)*

Week Six: *Yesod*—Yearning

We must call upon great spiritual resources to properly work
with the *sefirah Yesod*. *Yesod*, the sexual fire that animates
the world, is the most revered, most misunderstood, most
powerful force that drives liberal Western society. A survey
of the advertisements and billboards that pepper any major
Western city center demonstrates this point. Sexuality and
sexual yearning pulse through our culture, but they are laced
with shame. Painfully few of us allow our sexual fire to
energize us in the way it was intended to, alighting our lives
with passion.

Although much of Jewish ethical literature is
dedicated to subjugation of the evil inclination, called in
Hebrew the *yetzer hara*, (not exclusively but closely linked
to one's sexual drive), a surprising story is told about it in the
Babylonian Talmud. There, the rabbis wonder if the world
would not be better off if God had created human beings
without a *yetzer hara*, an evil inclination.

> Once, [The Jewish People] said "Let the evil
> inclination be handed over to us." They prayed and it
> was given to them. But, the Prophet [Elijah] warned
> them, "Understand that if you kill the evil inclination,
> the whole world will collapse." Nevertheless, they

imprisoned the evil inclination for three days, but when they looked for a fresh egg, none could be found in all the land of Israel. "What shall we do?" the people asked each other. "Shall we kill it? But, without the evil inclination, the world cannot survive."[39]

The sexual drive, though often a complicating factor in our lives, is the energy that drives the world in its entirety. Its nature is yearning, and, says the Jewish mystical tradition, it is a yearning shared by all of creation; a yearning whose source is found in the great yearning of the Creator to reunite with all of creation.

The Sufi mystic Rumi says it best in this stirring poem:

Surely there is a window from heart to heart:
they are not separate or far from each other.
Though two earthenware lamps are not joined,
their light mingles.

No lover seeks union without the beloved also seeking,
but the love of lovers makes the body thin as a bowstring,
while the love of loved ones makes them shapely and
pleasing.[40]

---

[39] Babylonian Talmud *Yoma* 69a–b; translation from Daniel B. Kohn, *Sex, Drugs, and Violence in the Jewish Tradition: Moral Perspectives* (Northvale, NJ: Jason Aronson, 2004) 156–57.

[40] Rumi, "Heaven and Earth Do Intelligent Work," in *Love's Ripening,* translated by Kabir Helminski and Ahmad Rezwani (Boston: Shambala, 2008), 71–73.

In Judaism, an often-used name for God is *Elohim Hayim*, the Living God or the God of Life. The very best way to know that God is near, to know that you are who you were born to be and where you were born to be, is to feel yourself vitally alive. A life without intimacy is a life not fully lived. A life without passion, including sexual passion, feels weighty and dim. When you greet the day with energy, when your veins pulse with life, passion and curiosity, you can know that you are in line with the God of Life, *Elohim Hayim.* It is this feeling that characterizes our *sefirah* for the week, *Yesod.*

<u>Igniting Passion</u>

✦ **Day 1**: What do you love? What do you yearn for? (*Hesed*)

✦ **Day 2**: What boundaries must you place on your passion? (*Gevurah*)

✦ **Day 3**: Who are you when you are alive with passion? (*Tiferet*)

✦ **Day 4**: What are those passions that do not change in you, even as the externals of your life shift? (*Netzah*)

✦ **Day 5**: Feel your own beauty. Know that you are worthy of another's desire. (*Hod*)

✦ **Day 6**: Passion is Divine. Know God in knowing passion. (*Yesod*)

✦ **Day 7**: See the world as the Divine interplay of seeking and finding, of yearning and uniting. (*Shekhinah*)

Week Seven: *Shekhinah*—The Web of Life

We have come far along our way by the time we have arrived at the week of *Malkhut* or *Shekhinah*. We have affirmed the unconditional love that pulses through us (*Hesed*); we have blessed the divine boundaries that help us to know all that is around us (*Gevurah*); we have embraced the "I-am-ness" with which we face the world, replacing the small-minded ego with an awareness of our pure consciousness (*Tiferet*). We have discovered the aspects of ourselves that are eternal (*Netzah*) and radiant (*Hod*). We have done the hard work of finding and disciplining our sexual fire (*Yesod*), allowing it to unite us with all of creation.

At long last, we arrive at the final step of our journey, the end that is also a beginning. Although we have borrowed the metaphor of a ladder, climbing toward the One, when we take up residence in *Shekhinah*, we realize that our ladder is in truth a looping spiral, returning us to where we began.

Known both as *Malkhut* and also as *Shekhinah*, the final *sefirah* is Divine Mother, the loving palm of God that protects and cradles us, and also the point of union between all that is above and all that is below. It is the navel of the world from which all begins and ends, the precise point of contact between us and our Creator.

Shekhinah is the dimension of the Divine that is made manifest in the world. Therefore, as we explore the dimension of God and of ourselves that is *Shekhinah*, we at once affirm: "The *Shekhinah* is in me. I am part of *Shekhinah*." With this, we echo the seemingly heretical claim uttered by mystics across spiritual traditions, throughout time. In embodying *Shekhinah*, we can't help but exclaim, "I am Thee."[41]

---

[41] For example: "I am thee and thou art me and all of one is the other," Ernest Hemingway in *For Whom the Bell Tolls*; "I am all orders of being / the circling galaxy / the evolutionary intelligence / the lift and the falling away. / What is and what isn't. / You who know Jelaluddin, You / the one in all, say who / I am. Say I am You." Rumi in "Say I Am You."

Divine Affirmation

✦ **Day 1**: I love with Unconditional Love. (*Hesed*)

✦ **Day 2**: I am in balance with Cosmic Boundaries. (*Gevurah*)

✦ **Day 3**: In knowing myself, I know God. (*Tiferet*)

✦ **Day 4**: I am one with the Eternal. (*Netzah*)

✦ **Day 5**: I am one with Divine Perfection. (*Hod*)

✦ **Day 6**: I am fueled by the Life-force of the Universe. (*Yesod*)

✦ **Day 7**: I am one with God. (*Shekhinah*)

Time Travel

I recently traveled back in time. Drawn through a portal buried in my heart, I found myself transported back to one of my earliest memories. I saw myself there on my swing set, gliding back and forth on a warm, sunny day. I was full of joy, surrounded by the green grass and lush trees of my childhood home. I felt that warmth again. And then, there she was, large and radiant, just above my head.

I had recalled this moment with my waking mind many times before, that non-special day on the swings at home. I remembered it as a day with my beloved imaginary friend. We swung, Juki and I, back and forth, to and fro, laughing and talking together.

But now, facing her again, having traveled back through time and space, it was not Juki that drew my eye, that caught my breath. She was there, of course, that little mirror projection of me, two girls at play, but she was not alone. The essence of Juki was the angel above us, around us, winged and bright, feeding our hearts, which were one.

Who was she, so glorious, so light? She was Mother, Guardian, Emissary, Shekhinah. She had been there all along, her light burning bright from this side of the world to the other. There She was, shining down on me, protecting me, guiding me along my way.

And yet, I had spent so many years not knowing she was there, so alone, feeling as though I was without a guardian, without a guide. It was a veil of illusion, a necessary forgetting that is a prerequisite for this place, for the living and learning I have come here to do. I imagine it was this very angel who tapped my lip that day I was born, causing me to forget it all.[42]

---

[42] A reference to *Niddah* 30b, quoted on pages 2 - 3 of this book.

Magical World

There is a particular man in the Torah known only as "the man." Our ancestor Joseph encountered him when he was a child. Among Jacob's eleven sons, Joseph is most loved, rendering the others as less than. Jacob sent Joseph out into the fields, a lamb into the lion's den. But, the wilderness was vast and Joseph's brothers were nowhere in sight. Just then, Joseph came upon the man. "Are you lost?" he asks. "I am looking for my brothers," Joseph replies. "Yes, I have seen them. They have gone toward Dothan," says the man. With these words, Joseph sets off toward his brothers, who at that moment are plotting to kill him.

Were it not for the man, Joseph would not have found his brothers that day, would not have been thrown into a pit to die, then sold into slavery, imprisoned in an Egyptian jail, called before the Pharaoh, then elevated to his second in command. Were it not for that man, the Jewish people might never have chosen to stay in the land of Egypt, where they would eventually become enslaved, only to be rescued by God and enter the covenant that would make them the Jewish people. In the Torah, the man is the symbol for the angel in disguise, sent to guide us on our way.[43]

Somewhere along the way, the world became magical for me. I find souls like "the man" everywhere. I use the word "coincidence" now so often that it has lost its meaning entirely. Like Joseph in the Bible, I find my landscape decorated with angels in disguise, here to guide me on my way.

For years, I struggled with "this world" and "that world," perfect and imperfect, heaven and earth. Now, I cannot imagine a world more perfect than this one, where time is slowed to the speed of matter, were we can touch and feel, laugh and cry; where we struggle then learn, strive then celebrate.

Jewish tradition has always imagined angels to be both perfect and, also, jealous of us humans. I would be jealous too if I could not touch my lover, did not experience yearning before satisfaction. It is only by virtue of our separation that we can relish union. And, it is magical.

---

[43] See Rashi on Genesis 37:15.

~~~

Barukh Ata Adonai, Eloheinu Melekh ha'olam,
shehechianu, v'kiamanu, v'higianu lazman hazeh.

Thank You, my Master and Creator,
for giving me life, for sustaining me,
and for bringing me to this precious moment.

~~~

Glossary of Terms

Adam Hakadmon: Literally "the early human," this term refers to the first human being, whose creation is described in the opening chapters of the Hebrew Bible. A being who is at once physical and spiritual, the term *adam hakadmon* can also refer to the energetic map of the human body, a reflection of the image of the Divine.

Amalek: The Jewish symbol for hate or evil incarnate, the ancient tribe of Amalek attacked the Israelites from the rear as they journeyed from Egypt to the Promised Land, killing the weakest, the elderly, and the young.

Arel Sfatayim: Literally "of uncircumcised lips," this is the term Moses uses to describe his speech impediment in the book of Exodus. Likely referring to a stutter or lisp, when viewed in light of the Hebrew Bible's instruction to circumcise the penis and the heart, this description can be understood as metaphorically referring to an imperfection in speech that can be transcended.

Asherah **Trees:** Canaanite religious symbols, Asherah trees and the *bamot,* or high places where they were found in ancient Israel, are mentioned numerous times in the Hebrew Bible. From the biblical perspective, they are paradigmatic symbols of idolatry, and the ancient Israelites were instructed to tear them down. However, as sacred trees and embodiments of the Divine feminine, they influence later religious traditions, including both Christianity and Kabbalah.

Elohim Hayim: Literally "Living God" or "God of Life," this is an oft-used name for God in Jewish tradition.

First Temple: Located in Jerusalem, the Temple or the *beit hamikdash,* was the central place of worship for the Jewish people from 960 - 586 BCE. The First Temple was destroyed by the Babylonians in 586 BCE and rebuilt approximately seventy years later (known then as the Second Temple). It was destroyed in 70 CE by the Romans.

Hakadosh Barukh Hu: Literally "the Holy One, Blessed be He," this phrase is a commonly used Hebrew name for God. In a kabbalistic sense, the name refers to the male aspect of the Divine in general, and to the attribute known as *Tiferet* in particular.

Halakhah: *Halakhah* is a term that refers to Jewish Law, but the word itself comes from the verb *lalechet,* meaning "to walk." *Halakhah* is a path, or the way Jews walk through the world. It is a system of law made up of instructions that legislate the smallest details of life.

Hasidism: A Jewish spiritual revolution that spread across Europe beginning in the 18th century and continues to this day. Hasidism was initiated by the mystic known as the *Baal Shem Tov,* and is characterized by its organization of regionally-based communities led by charismatic spiritual leaders or Rebbes.

Hechalot Rabbati: *A* third-century mystical treatise, which is a part of the genre of literature known as the *Hechalot* literature, as its central focus is the exploration of Divine palaces (*hechalot*).

Hillel: A great early rabbi, the sage Hillel lived in the first century BCE and was the head of the rabbinic school known as *Beit Hillel*, or the House of Hillel.

Kabbalah/Kabbalist: A Kabbalist is a devotee of the Jewish mystical literature generally referred to as *Kabbalah*. The word *kabbalah* is derived from the Hebrew root *k.b.l.* meaning receive. *Kabbalah* then is an esoteric or received tradition, passed from teacher to student, largely in secret. In contemporary times, the study of *kabbalah* has become widespread, engaged by Jews and non-Jews alike.

Kavanah: Derived from the word *kivun* or direction, *kavanah* is the intention or mental direction of one's thoughts as s/he is engaged in an act of meditation or worship.

Kibbutz: The collaborative social movement established in Israel in the early 20th century. *Kibbutzim* (pl.) were initially founded as zionist, socialist, agrarian communities, but have evolved substantially in recent years. In 2010, there were 270 active kibbutzim in Israel.

Leit atar panui minei: Translated as "there is no place that [God] is not," this is a central proclamation of Jewish mysticism, found in several instances in the Zohar and other Jewish mystical texts.

Mitzvot: Literally "commandments," *mitzvot* are the collection of instructions given to the Jewish people in the Torah. The word can also be used colloquially to refer to a good deed.

Mikveh: A body of living waters used in Jewish ritual for spiritual purification. The waters of a *mikveh* are considered "living," as they are gathered in a precise and intentional manner from a natural water source, such as an ocean, lake or the rain.

Mt. Sinai: The mountain in the Sinai desert where the Jewish people gathered to receive its sacred teachings, as described in the Hebrew Bible.

Neshama: *Neshama* is one of several Hebrew words for soul. The etymology of the word stems from the Hebrew word meaning breath (*neshima*). We can imagine then the human soul as the breath of God, giving us life until we breathe our last, when it returns to God.

Rabbi Akiva: A great early rabbi, *Akiva ben Joseph* lived in the second century CE. He is said to have taught tens of thousands of students, before being murdered at the hands of the Romans in 137 CE.

Sefirot: Plural for *sefira, sefirot* are the attributes or facets that make up the kabbalistic map of the Divine.

Sefirat Ha'omer: Literally "the Counting of the *Omer,*" *Sefirat Ha'omer* is a springtime ritual when Jews ritually count the seven weeks that separate the festivals of Passover and Shavuot. Kabbalists saw spiritual significance in these seven sevens (seven weeks), and linked the practice to an exploration of the *sefirot* (defined above).

Seven Species: A term that refers to the local produce of the ancient land of Israel, including pomegranates, figs, date honey, wine, olives, wheat and barley.

Shekinah: Hebrew name for the in-dwelling presence of God, often associated with the Divine feminine. In later kabbalistic literature, the term refers to one of the ten facets of the Divine.

Shul: A Yiddish word meaning school, but which is used to refer to a small or intimate synagogue.

Siddur: The Jewish prayer book.

Talmud: Two edited compliations of preserved Jewish tradition, lore, and law. The Babylonian Talmud, which contains sources written approximately 100 BCE–500 CE, was codified in Babylon; while the Jerusalem Talmud contains sources from a similar period but was codified in Israel in approximately the fourth century CE.

Torah: Literally "teaching," Torah is a Hebrew term for the Old Testament or the Five books of Moses.

Yeshiva: A religious academy where sacred Jewish literature is studied.

Zohar: The Book of Splendor, a work of Jewish mysticism traditionally attributed to the second century rabbi, Shimon bar Yochai. However, scholarly consensus is that it was written by Moses de Leon in thirteenth-century Spain.

CPSIA information can be obtained at www.ICGtesting.com
Printed in the USA
BVOW05s1406300815

415149BV00001B/20/P